DOCTOR WHO

THE SUNS OF CARESH

PAUL SAINT

Published by BBC Worldwide Ltd,
Woodlands, 80 Wood Lane
London W12 0TT

First published 2002
Copyright © Paul Saint 2002
The moral right of the author has been asserted

Original series broadcast on the BBC
Format copyright © 1963
Doctor Who and TARDIS are trademarks of the BBC

ISBN 0 563 53858 9
Imaging by Black Sheep, copyright © BBC 2002

Printed and bound in Great Britain by
Mackays of Chatham
Cover printed by Belmont Press Ltd, Northampton

Prologue

Dassar Island, Caresh

Lord Roche had the uneasy feeling that there was someone else in the Citadel. An unseen intruder who watched him while he worked, who sometimes appeared at the edge of his vision but vanished the instant he turned. Twice he thought he heard footsteps in the entrance tunnel, and once while he was in the side room he thought he heard the bell chime in the main chamber indicating the arrival of a visitor. He was actually expecting a visitor – a native woman from Dassar College – but it was too early for her, and in any case the chamber was empty.

'You've been working too hard,' he told himself at last. 'You need a break.' He returned to the side room and lay on the couch. It was halfdawn according to the chronometer, the time when the more distant sun had risen and the nearer sun was still below the horizon. He did not expect the native woman until fulldawn, which was over an hour away.

His mind was too active for sleep so he decided to update his personal log instead. In response to a spoken command the couch tilted a few degrees forward and a monitor screen attached to a metal arm positioned itself at a comfortable distance from his face. 'Yesterday,' he began, 'checked mechanism in eastern turret of Citadel. Inspection hatch was frozen. Used heat gun to get it open. Mechanism in working order. Torch rolled off gantry, shattered on rocks two hundred feet below.'

He paused for a moment, then continued. 'Sea ice spreading at expected rate. Reports of Leshe swarms sighted outside polar lands. Effect on general morale… uncertain.' He paused again. 'Neutron star is now twenty days away at thirty billion miles. Despite satisfaction with plan of action, have decided to consider

1

data from independent source – there remains the possibility that I've overlooked something. For this reason I am expecting a report from…' He halted, frowning, as he realised he'd forgotten the name of the woman from Dassar College. She would be arriving at the Citadel shortly; it would look bad if he didn't know what to call her.

After a few moments' thought it occurred to him that he could simply address her by her title. She was a sun watcher, and that was what he would call her. Satisfied with this, he made to continue the entry but before he could do so the bell chimed in the main chamber; this time there was no mistaking it. He pushed the monitor aside and rose from the couch. He stepped through the archway into the chamber.

There was nobody there.

'This is starting to get quite annoying,' he said.

Perhaps the native woman was hesitating in the entrance tunnel, afraid to approach. He hoped not; he couldn't abide the diffident sort, found them near impossible to work with. Yet who else could it be? It was still not fulldawn but it had to be her, or someone of her clan – nobody else knew the entry code to the Citadel. In as gentle a voice as he could muster, he called, 'Sun Watcher? Is that you?'

It was not the sun watcher who replied. The voice was masculine, ponderous and harsh, and needlessly loud. Strangely, it did not reverberate at all. It said, 'Must not continue.'

Roche turned, unable to locate the source of the voice. Then he saw it: a patch of brightness, roughly human in outline, standing beside the horseshoe-shaped control table that dominated the main chamber. The brightness flickered. It was as if the image of a man on a badly tuned television set had stepped out into the real world.

The image flickered, then spoke again. 'Your activities here must not continue, Time Lord.'

Roche frowned and peered closely. The image wrapped, shimmered, jerked to one side, then briefly stabilised. It was giving him a headache. 'Who are you? *What* are you?'

'I am Magus Amathon of the Curia of Nineteen.'

'Curia?' Roche looked blank. Then realisation dawned. 'You're a Vortex Dweller!' This was not good news, not good at all.

But if Roche was taken aback, so too was Amathon. 'You know of us?' he said.

'I know a little of your Realm,' Roche replied.

'How much do you know of us?'

Roche hesitated. Clearly Amathon's people valued their privacy. Perhaps he should not have spoken. But he had spoken; it was too late to deny all knowledge. A degree of diplomacy was called for, then. 'The Realm of the Vortex Dwellers is an intricate mathematical construct mapped onto a region of space-time,' he said, speaking in what he hoped were flattering terms. 'It is otherwise independent of and intangible to the universe at large. It's an island of stability in the maelstrom that is the vortex.'

'You know more than you should, Time Lord.'

That rankled. 'What do you expect? I've spent a lot of time navigating this part of the cosmos. I was bound to notice it sooner or later.'

'You know more than you should, but not all of it is right.' The Vortex Dweller was still having trouble maintaining itself. Its image flickered, briefly disappearing from view; much of what it was saying was lost in white noise. When it stabilised again Roche made out the words 'Not intangible.'

'If you think I've overlooked something, by all means tell me what it is. I'm a reasonable man. I'm sure we can work something out.'

'There is nothing to work out. Your activities harm the Realm. If continued they will destroy it. You must cease.'

'Cease? Just like that? Do you have any idea what's at stake here? You seriously expect me to abandon my work on your say so?'

'I speak with the authority of the Curia,' Amathon declared.

'I'm sorry, Amathon, but that really doesn't impress me. I will listen to reason but I will not be commanded. Or threatened. As things stand, I do not believe my activities threaten your Realm in any way whatsoever.'

'You question our mathematics?'

'I question your *motives*,' Roche retorted, all thoughts of diplomacy forgotten now. 'You underestimate *my* mathematical skills. It is my informed opinion that the Realm is in no danger from my actions.' Then he lost his temper. 'What I'm doing is hardly frivolous, Amathon! The survival of a civilisation depends on what I do. I don't know what it is you really want, but I have no intention of changing my plans. Understand this, Vortex Dweller: *I will not abandon my people.*'

'That is your final decision?' Amathon said calmly.

'Yes.'

'We will convince you otherwise.'

Roche's eyes narrowed. 'Are you threatening me?'

'Yes.'

'With what, I wonder?' But Amathon had vanished, and Roche was alone in the main chamber.

No, not alone. Roche was aware of the native woman standing by the entrance tunnel. He had no idea how long she had been there, no idea how much she had seen or heard. Did it matter?

Lord Roche turned to her. She seemed familiar, but he could not say for sure whether he had met her before. She was typical Dassari stock: a little over five feet tall, thin hair, large irises. Her fur-lined coat was open to reveal the two-piece blue uniform of Dassar College, where she had been schooled in astronomy, botany, oceanography and pure mathematics. 'Sun Watcher,' he said, bowing slightly. 'I trust you have come directly from the college observatory.'

'I have, my lord.' She met his eyes and there was no timidity in her voice. That was something, he supposed. She showed no curiosity about his exchange with Amathon.

'Make your report then, please.'

'The neutron star was sighted three nights ago, an hour after the beginning of fulldark. It was at the limit of visibility in the constellation called the Semaphore Tower, twelve arcseconds south of the star we call the Flag. Two nights ago the sky

4

remained overcast and no observations were possible. This night past, the neutron star was marginally brighter and had changed its position by two arcseconds to the north and one to the east.'

Roche grimaced and clenched his fists; this was not what he'd hoped for. Then he relaxed and nodded. 'Very good, Sun Watcher,' he said. 'We'll begin work immediately, I think.' He indicated the horseshoe-shaped control table. 'I take it you're familiar with the layout of… Hello, what have we here?'

Something was shimmering in the air by the far wall of the chamber. Was Amathon returning to discuss matters sensibly? No, that wasn't a single shimmer – it was *two* shimmers. They were becoming more substantial now, taking the form of vertical columns, like transparent fleshy tubes just wide enough to accommodate a man.

The fleshy tubes throbbed. Something leathery and heavy tumbled down first one tube and then the other.

The tubes withdrew. Roche found himself looking at a pair of egg sacs. They were waist-high, and dark brown in colour. Something inside them was moving. An unpleasant suspicion crossed Roche's mind and he began to back away, but before he could tear his gaze from it the first egg hatched. An intensely bright light erupted from the rents in the sac, dazzling him. He heard the sun watcher scream, but when he turned to look for her he could see nothing but afterimages. He groped for the control table and reached it just as a wave of oven-hot musky air enveloped him: the first creature had emerged from its egg. It flopped to the ground and emitted a cry like the tearing of sheet metal.

Then the second egg began to hatch.

Israel, 1972
At midnight on the night before the dig, Professor Ezekiel Child switched off the desk lamp and rose to look out of the Portakabin window. The moon, nearly full, hung over its shimmering reflection in the Dead Sea, bathing the desert landscape in its pale light.

A few more hours, he thought, *and it will all be over. One way or another.*

A long time ago, something unprecedented had happened here. A huge burning object had appeared in the night sky. It had fallen to the earth, and had partly buried itself in the western shore of the Dead Sea.

There had been witnesses who kept written records of what they saw. In other circumstances they might have investigated further, but it was not to be; they were preoccupied with more pressing matters and the incident was duly forgotten. Then the years passed, and the shifting sands buried the object completely.

But it would not remain buried for much longer.

Professor Child took off his glasses and rubbed his eyes. He tried to imagine the landscape as it had been on that night. Pretty much the same as it was now, perhaps, but without the two Land Rovers, the stacked crates of equipment, and the scattering of tents and Portakabins that made up the camp. He wished Maria was with him, but she was a thousand miles away, both literally and figuratively. He'd found himself thinking about her a lot lately; when he had first conceived of this expedition several years before it had not occurred to him that, when it finally happened, she would not be there to share the discovery with him.

Perhaps it was a night like this, Child thought, replacing his glasses. *Silent, still, suspended.* He looked beyond the camp at Masada; the hill fortress was just visible if you pressed your face against the window.

Behind him, the door opened. Child turned. A female figure stood framed in the doorway, a silhouette against the moonlit landscape.

'Working late, Ezekiel?' she said. She entered the Portakabin and closed the door behind her.

'Maria,' said Child, and at once he knew he was dreaming. It didn't matter. To see her again, even in a dream…

'You came after all,' he said, a slight quaver in his voice.

'I've never once forgotten your birthday, you know that.'

'My birthday's not till tomorrow.'

'It *is* tomorrow. Happy forty-sixth Ezekiel.'

He made to approach her, then hesitated. *If I cannot remember what it feels like to hold her, to kiss her, if I cannot remember that...* Suddenly it became important to maintain the dream at all costs. In all their years apart he had never once dreamt of her. She had to be here for a reason; his subconscious was trying to tell him something.

And of course he wanted to prolong her visit for as long as possible.

'Are we just going to stand here in the dark?' she asked sharply.

'Forgive me,' said Child, reaching for the desk lamp. He half expected to find his own sleeping form slumped across the desk.

In the light he could see that she had aged (surely that was unusual in a dream?) but was little the worse for it. She was beautiful. Her red hair was long and luxurious, her face gentle and intelligent. She wore a long dress, which made it seem as if she had called in on her way home from an evening out.

'When did you grow a beard then?' she asked, a hint of amusement in her voice.

'Soon after you left, as a matter of fact.'

'I like it. It suits you. Are you going to show me what you've been working on?'

'Yes, of course.' Child invited her to sit, then took a ring binder down from a shelf. 'I'm looking for a meteorite.'

Maria raised her eyebrows. 'A meteorite? I assumed this was an archaeological expedition.'

'It's multidisciplinary. A lot of expeditions are these days for economic reasons, but *this* one is multidisciplinary by its very nature. We've already carried out magnetic and resistivity surveys; early indications suggest that *something* is buried here. If it's what I think it is... Well, see what you think.'

He opened the binder and placed it on the desk in front of her. Inside a plastic pouch were five scraps of parchment of great age.

Maria picked up a large magnifying glass and examined them. 'The Dead Sea Scrolls,' she said.

7

Child nodded. He thought, *My God, I wish you were really here.*

Maria looked up, puzzled. 'But I've never seen these fragments before.'

'They are not generally available. As a matter of fact... Well, you wouldn't believe what I had to do to get hold of them. But then, I've got a lot riding on this.'

'You *are* full of surprises, Ezekiel.'

'So what do you make of them?'

Maria, studying the fragments, did not answer. Child sat on the edge of the desk, glancing at her from time to time, careful not to distract her. There was no hurrying her when she was engaged in a translation; Child's only worry was that he would wake up before she finished.

But as yet the dream showed no sign of ending. It even occurred to Child to wonder if it was a dream after all. He was aware that one of the tests for dreaming was to read something, look away from it and then try to read it again – if it didn't change, you could be sure you were awake. But each time he glanced at Maria she was unchanged – the first sign of a crow's foot in the corner of her right eye, the pout of concentration, the slight inclination of her head...

Why is she so much more real in a dream than she is in my waking memories? The thought pained him with an intensity that emotions rarely assume outside dreams. *Do you remember the old farmhouse in the Loire valley, that afternoon when we walked beside the river and we talked about the future? Do you remember that evening, when the wind was howling and the rain was pattering against the window, and we sat inside by the open fire drinking port? Do you remember what you promised me?*

Maria cleared her throat. 'Well,' she began.

'Well?' echoed Child.

She rested the magnifying glass on the desk. 'It seems to me that if these fragments are all part of one bigger fragment, then what they have to say is very interesting. Very interesting indeed.'

'And how would you interpret them?'

'I'd say they were a description of a meteorite. The noise it made, where it landed, its approximate size…'

'How big, would you say?'

'Oh, roughly the size of this Portakabin.'

Child nodded. 'Pretty much my interpretation. Have you any idea how much a piece of rock that size would *weigh*?'

'I'm not a geologist, Ezekiel.'

'All right. Putting it another way, how much damage do you think a piece of rock weighing several thousand tons would do if it fell out of the sky?'

Maria shrugged. 'Substantial, I suppose.'

'Substantial is the word. The fall of a meteorite this big would *substantially* increase the size of the Dead Sea.'

'Unless it was hollow. Or its fall was somehow… slowed?'

Child's heart raced. 'A crash-landing.'

'You think it was some sort of spaceship?'

'Yes I do.'

Maria nodded slowly, 'It's a nice idea. And not wholly unreasonable. But…' She held Child's gaze for a few moments. 'But as I said, it assumes we're looking at a single fragment of Dead Sea Scroll.'

'We are, surely?'

'I don't think we are, Ezekiel. Look, the style of the script is quite different between these two fragments. And the edge here suggests an upward tear, which is inconsistent with this one, even though the shape appears to match…'

Maria went on, her words beginning to blur one into the other. Child listened in dismay, then watched as she closed the binder, rose from the desk and headed for the door. Then, belatedly realising he was never going to see her again, he called after her:

'Why should I believe you? You're not even here. It's just a dream.'

Maria stopped in the doorway. She turned. 'It's *never* "just a dream", Ezekiel.'

* * *

By late morning, there was no doubt in anybody's mind that there was something unusual beneath the desert floor. Things were beginning to fall into place; clearly, the object was roughly where Child had expected to find it, and the results of the magnetic and resistivity surveys suggested it was about the right size.

But was it a crashed spaceship? In the cold light of day Child had to admit it was pretty unlikely. Realistically, it was probably a large meteorite – and he could think of several natural explanations for the absence of a crater. Then again, it didn't really matter. Whatever it was, it had fallen out of the sky and its fall had been recorded by the Brotherhood at Qumran.

Child's professional reputation had taken a battering in the last few years. Almost as much as his personal life had. He had staked a lot on this expedition and taken some considerable risks. It was finally showing signs of paying off. Alien spaceship or meteorite, the buried object was undoubtedly of great archaeological significance.

Yet he couldn't quite shake off the doubts the dream had raised. It had been so vivid; even after he had awoken to find himself slumped across his desk with a crick in his neck, Maria's presence seemed to linger, along with her words.

After lunch, when the excavation had begun in earnest, Child's assistant director McAllen drew his attention to a speck of black low in the sky to the north. 'Are you expecting visitors, Professor?' he asked.

Child frowned. 'No,' he said absently. He watched the speck for half a minute. It did not move but it appeared to grow. 'Whatever it is, it seems to be coming this way.'

Suddenly suspicious, he climbed out of the trench and hurried to his Portakabin, where he quickly located a pair of binoculars. By the time he looked again, it was clear that the object was what he thought it was: a helicopter. Most of the team had stopped work to watch, and it was possible to hear the distant thwocking of rotor blades.

'What do you make of it?' he asked, handing the binoculars to McAllen.

The assistant director watched for a minute. 'It's a Huey,' he said at last. 'I think it's military.'

'Military? What would they want with us?' But even as Child spoke the answer came to him. *They know what I'm onto. I'm on the brink of uncovering something that they'd rather remained hidden. They are going to try to stop me.*

The Huey was so close now that the sound of the blades was deafening. It kicked up a cloud of sand and dust, temporarily blinding Child. By the time his vision was clear again the helicopter had landed and two people had emerged. They were not what he had expected at all.

One was a man with white hair and the face of an athlete. The other was a very pretty, very petite young woman with blonde hair. Neither of them wore uniforms; indeed, the man was dressed like a Carnaby Street dandy, and the woman wore a long flowing dress.

'Are you here to stop the dig?' Child asked the white-haired man, who introduced himself as the Doctor.

'It's too late for that,' the Doctor told him. 'The most we can hope to do now is contain it.'

'Contain what? Is there some sort of danger?' McAllen asked.

The Doctor smiled down at the assistant director. 'Nothing you would understand.'

Child bristled at the Doctor's manner; he was more affronted for McAllen than McAllen was for himself. 'Now look here, by whose authority…'

The woman, Jo, smiled disarmingly. 'I'm sure he didn't mean to be rude, but we have to get these people away from here.'

'Is it some sort of bomb?' asked McAllen.

'No,' said the Doctor.

'Yes,' said Jo at the same time.

The Doctor gave her a look, then said, 'Not a bomb, precisely. But an explosive device of sorts.'

Child was sure the Doctor was improvising. 'The thing's been buried for nearly two thousand years,' he protested. 'How can it possibly be dangerous now?'

11

'The "thing" has been *dormant* for nearly two thousand years. And you, sir, have just disturbed it.'

'How can you possibly know that?'

'Because it's my job to know. Now if you'd kindly get these people out of my way I can get on with the business of disarming it.'

'You mean to dig it up?'

'I mean to dig down to it,' the Doctor said. 'On my own.' He took a spade from an unprotesting expedition member and strode over to the marked area. 'Here, I believe?'

'Now listen to me, Doctor,' Child protested. 'I've staked a lot on this expedition, and now you're trying to turn it into a treasure hunt! Do you hear me? I will not have you taking the credit for my discovery.'

The Doctor gave him an exasperated look. Eventually he said, 'Very well, but on your own head be it. Grab yourself a spade and get over here.' To Jo he added, 'In the meantime, make sure nobody else comes within a hundred yards of this spot.'

Afterwards, Child was unable to pinpoint the moment at which the antagonism between himself and the Doctor subsided and they found themselves working as a team. They began at opposite ends of the place where the object appeared to be buried.

'I think I've found something,' Child declared.

The Doctor hurried over. 'Let's be careful not to disturb it any more than it has been already.'

'I'll get a trowel and some brushes.'

A little later they had uncovered a short, stubby wing.

'A fin,' suggested Child. 'To give the vessel stability when it enters the atmosphere.'

The Doctor nodded slowly. 'Originally heat-resistant, but the effects of corrosion might have removed all trace of that.'

'Yet part of it is still active, you say?'

The Doctor nodded again. 'I was able to track it down all the way from London,' he said.

'You must show me your equipment some time.'

'Now,' said the Doctor, 'I'm going to have to ask you to stand back. If this is what I think it is there will be a small service hatch just aft of the fin. The hatch is spring-loaded, and it's my guess that the latch is gone and it's only held shut by the weight of the sand. Assuming the spring hasn't rusted through, of course.'

'You make a lot of assumptions.'

The Doctor grinned. 'I make a surprising number of correct assumptions.'

Child stood back and the Doctor continued working with the trowel. Confidently at first, but Child could tell from his posture that he was beginning to have his doubts.

Suddenly the Doctor dropped the trowel. 'Oh no,' he muttered. 'No, it can't be.'

'What's the matter, Doctor?' asked Child, alarmed.

The Doctor turned. There was a strange look on his face, a look almost of… embarrassment?

'It seems I was wrong,' the Doctor said. 'This is not what I was expecting. Not what I was expecting at all.'

Chapter One
The Woman Who Lost the Sea

The first thing she remembered was the building. It was two storeys high, and made entirely of metal and glass. It stood apart from the row of stone buildings that lined one side of the road.

The building was howling.

The encounter could not have taken more than a dozen heartbeats, all told, but in her dreamlike state she imagined herself standing entranced as she attempted to understand what the howling meant.

Then, abruptly, she knew exactly what it meant. The building was telling her to *get out of the way*.

It had not occurred to her that the building was moving. It had not occurred to her that something so big *could* move, let alone move so fast. She snapped out of her trancelike state and attempted to dodge to one side. But she weighed much less than she should, and her sense of balance was out of kilter. She stumbled.

The building screeched and swerved. It almost missed her.

She awoke, afraid and in pain.

She was in a blue room without doors or windows. She was lying on a bed, staring up at the ceiling. A lamp bathed the room in a harsh glare. From outside the room she could hear a babble of voices: snatches of conversation, an angry shout, a sharp cry of pain. Somewhere a door flapped, rubber squeaked on ceramic, a light metal object fell clattering to the floor. A pungent chemical smell suffused the thin air.

She closed her eyes. She tried to imagine sunlight, and the sea.

Someone had come into the blue room. She kept her eyes shut, feigning sleep. The thought that one of those *people* might be in the room with her was almost too much to bear; she could not bring herself to look at it. She could hear its breathing as it leant over her, so close that its impossibly long hair might brush against her skin...

And then she could see herself. For a fleeting moment it was as if she were the one leaning over the sleep-feigning body on the bed.

When she was sure the intruder was no longer leaning over her, she opened her eyes. She found herself alone in the room once more. Next time she would open her eyes sooner, and find out how the intruder passed into and out of a doorless room. But that could wait.

In the meantime she would work on her injuries. The howling building had hit her right shoulder, and she had struck her head as she fell. These were the most serious hurts. She concentrated on them and slipped into a deep, controlled sleep.

She dreamt of sunlight, and the sea, and the time before the coming of the permanent ice. She was walking along the rim of the crater-lake above her home on Dassar Island, close to the causeway that gave access to the Citadel on the central peak. From this vantage point high above sea level she could see fourteen of the fifty-two islands that made up the Southern Archipelago. To the west, Shess Island was a volcanic triangle framed by the blood-red halo of Ember, the lesser sun, as it sank below the horizon. Beacon, the greater sun, hung overhead, casting its reflection in the strait between the islands of Dair and Orm.

Wherever you were in the Archipelago, you could always find your way home. Even on the largest islands, the sea was rarely more than two days' walk away. Once you found the sea, you could navigate by the suns and the stars, or even the magnetic core of Caresh itself if you knew how.

16

But first you had to find the sea.

She awoke. She remembered her name: Troy Game.

Her head and shoulder still hurt. Sleep speeded recovery, but it was not enough on its own; she needed sunlight. According to her body clock both suns should be up now; even if her time sense was out of kilter, at least one sun must have risen since her arrival in the blue room.

She sat up, bemused. She was being deliberately deprived of sunlight. But by whom? Even on Fell Island such barbaric practices were outlawed.

So where on Caresh was she?

There were voices beyond the blue wall, footsteps approaching. Troy Game could hear individual words but they were not spoken in the language of Dassar or its neighbouring islands. In order to understand she had to reach out with her own mind to locate that of one of the speakers. The words took form: 'Patient confidentiality, you know I have no choice…' said one, while another, possibly in an unrelated conversation, said, '…don't you understand, without it it's not *informed* consent…' Then Troy Game's mind recoiled in shock and the words became incoherent once more.

She had picked up too much. She had felt the speaker's compassion and exasperation, and other emotions she had not had time to register, and which had not been apparent in the meaning of the words. It should not have happened; language-telepathy did not work like that.

More footsteps, coming closer. Troy Game climbed over the rail that ran along the side of the bed and stepped onto the tiled floor. She was light-headed, and felt as if she had lost a lot of weight although it did not show. The wall in front of her, she realised, was not a wall at all but a curtain.

And in that moment of realisation the curtain was thrust aside. Troy Game froze.

There were two of the *people* in front of her. One of them, fully a head taller than her, was evidently a woman. Her femaleness was

17

exaggerated, obvious even under her clothing; Troy Game would have supposed that the woman had recently given birth, had it not been for the fact that the birthing season was half a year away. The man – again, his maleness was overemphasised – was taller still. He turned his gaze on her, his pupils and irises like tiny islands lost in the whites of his eyes, and turned up the corners of his mouth in a gesture that Troy Game supposed was meant to be reassuring.

She might have been able to cope with their alienness – the eyes, the ears, the teeth and the skin – if it had not been for their hair. It was so *long*. It put her in mind of crawling things, of the tangleweed that grew inside the underwater vents off Shess Island. The woman with the blonde hair that reached to her *shoulders* was approaching her, uttering intermittently coherent words like 'concussion' and 'need to examine'.

Troy Game fled. She vaulted across the bed, pulled another curtain aside and ran out into a corridor of curtained-off rooms. The *people* were everywhere. A man, barely taller than she was, his matted hair divided by a furrow of naked skin, stepped out of a doorway in front of her. She considered disabling him but he hurried out of her way as soon as he saw her. She ran on, risking a quick look behind her, but no pursuit was evident. Up ahead a glass door, and beyond it, sunlight! Handle one side, hinge the other; a moment later she had it open and was through it. She ran across a forecourt, past rank after rank of glass-and-metal structures that looked like smaller versions of the howling building. She kept on running until she was short of breath, then slowed to a walk.

Her terror began to subside. She had escaped the blue room and she had found the sunlight. Now she had only to find the sea.

The Hunter Fury's directive was a simple one: pursue, catch and kill the prey. The prey was swift, but the Hunter Fury was swifter. The prey's mindscent was distinctive and strong. It should have been a short chase with an abrupt conclusion.

But the prey was devious. Its mindscent should have been emanating only from its mind. Instead, its mindscent was everywhere; the mind itself could not be distinguished from the background noise.

The Hunter Fury could not understand how this had happened. But then, understanding was not part of its make-up, at least not at this stage of its development. Still a creature of instinct, it gave vent to its rage by lashing out at the first mind within its reach. But unauthorised kills did not go unpunished. Working alone, it was conditioned to punish itself. In time it might learn to overcome this conditioning, but that development was a long way off.

When the Hunter Fury had recovered from the pain it had inflicted upon itself, it remembered its directive. The hunt, it seemed, was going to be a lot harder than expected, but the directive was unchanged: pursue, catch and kill.

Finding the source of the scent would not be easy when the scent was everywhere. But there would be giveaway irregularities or the prey would slip up, however devious it thought itself. It was only a matter of time.

There was something decidedly odd about the sun. Troy Game wasn't even sure *which* sun it was.

She had found a place where there were few of the *people*. A quiet area between one of the roads and a crumbling stone wall. Parkland. There were paths and benches, and short grass. There were also trees and bushes, quite unlike any she had ever seen before, but at least they were recognisable *as* trees and bushes – and on an island where everything was strange that counted for a lot.

There was an unoccupied bench in a sunlit part of the park. She sat down, feeling the rays on her face and her hands and forearms. Her shoulder still ached where the howling building had struck it, but she was reluctant to remove any of her clothes in case she had to leave in a hurry. The injured part would have to stay covered for the time being.

The sunlight was efficacious, but the sun itself remained a mystery. It was too bright and too warm to be Ember. Beacon was only that bright at the time of year when Caresh was between suns – and when Beacon was the dominant sun, of course, but that had not happened for a very long time.

The implications were just beginning to dawn on Troy Game when the disturbing presence of one of the *people* intruded on her thoughts. A female, slightly older in appearance than Troy Game herself, her hair yellow and very long, was walking past her bench. But this time the hair was not the cause of Troy Game's disquiet – indeed, the revulsion hair had previously aroused in her was already beginning to subside. Rather, it was the woman's smell – her personal, hormonal smell – and the swelling around her belly, for all the world as if she was in an advanced state of pregnancy. Which, at this time of year, should have been quite impossible, unless...

Just how *long* had she been in that blue room? Long enough to completely lose track of the seasons? Or was there another explanation entirely? What if the sun was neither Ember *nor* Beacon? The idea was absurd, but how could a sun watcher not know which sun she was looking at? What if...?

She shook herself. There was no benefit in following that train of thought, at least not yet, not until the more rational explanations had been ruled out. Clearly she was on a hitherto unknown island much closer to the equator than the Southern Archipelago, hence Ember was higher in the sky with less atmosphere for its rays to pass through. That was why it looked brighter and felt so much warmer. The island's inhabitants, though strange to her, evidently did not think of themselves as strange. Come to that, there was no indication that they found *her* strange. Granted, there were aspects of the island and its *people* that made no sense at all, but she had only been here for a few hours. No doubt there were things on Dassar Island that they would have had difficulty understanding.

Reassured by this thought, Troy Game turned her mind to more practical matters. She was hungry, and she needed to find the sea. But the sea was a long way off, further than she had ever known it. Although its scent was carried in the breeze it was almost lost among the other scents, some of them unidentifiable and some of them far from pleasant. Evidently this was a bigger island than most, and she would have to get moving at once. There was no time for a full healing sleep, and no telling how long the search for the sea might take.

Roads were the single worst aspect of the island so far. The glass-and-metal structures – the vehicles – were everywhere. Evidently the *people* had a heightened ability to judge their speeds and distances; Troy Game was not so gifted. But by observing the behaviour of the *people* themselves, she was able to deduce some of the rules of the road. Her understanding was by no means complete, for there were far too many inconsistencies, but it was apparent that there were places where vehicles did not go at all or where they went only at certain times, as dictated by coloured lights on poles or painted markings on the ground. But she was confident that there would be no repeat of the incident with the howling building; with luck, she would not be on the island long enough to need to learn much more than that.

After a while that thought began to seem hopelessly optimistic. She believed she had been following the scent of the sea, but now it seemed more distant than ever or else the masking smells had become more overpowering. Her increasingly haphazard wanderings had taken her into a town or a city where stone-and-glass buildings towered over her on either side of the thoroughfare. Some of the buildings were four storeys high, which was all the more remarkable given that they were built for *people* much taller than she was. Troy Game had seen architectural marvels in the Archipelago but they had been palaces and fortresses; here, they were the dwellings and trading places of the general populace. Many of the ground-level storeys were glass-fronted and displayed wares: mannequins, mostly female, in various states of dress, some of them missing heads or limbs, all of them frighteningly realistic; stacked boxes with moving pictures on their fronts, each showing the same view of a group of muscular animals running on a grass plain with riders on their backs; three women, sitting in chairs facing a wall-length mirror while three other women cut at their hair with shears...

Nauseated, Troy Game backed away quickly. She nearly collided with a man sitting on an unpowered vehicle. It had only two wheels, one in front and one behind, yet he seemed to have no difficulty balancing. Further on, a man was shouting at nobody while he pressed a small box against one side of his face, and an old woman on a nearby bench set fire to a white tube she was holding in her mouth.

Troy Game felt the stirrings of panic. She fought for control. *I need to understand*, she told herself. *I need this to make sense to me. I need to* believe *it makes sense.*

She was lost and hungry, and still no closer to finding the sea. There was so much she was going to have to learn after all. She needed to know where to get food, whether they used money, how to earn it if they did, how to avoid offending them, what to do if she failed to avoid offending them, and so on. She would have to watch them closely (but discreetly – she had already learnt not to stare); she would have to listen to what they said and, although it didn't feel right, she would have to look directly into their minds to pick up the sort of information they weren't likely to volunteer.

And, sooner or later, she was going to have to *talk* to one of them. Face him, keep her attention on his tiny eyes, try not to think about his hair and ask for directions to the sea.

Troy Game bit her lower lip. Sooner or later she would have to. But not *yet*...

Ambassador Theon's transfiguration had been triggered too early, Secretary Carst had betrayed his own people to the Whitespace Hordes, and Laurenia had been stripped of her psi powers.

22

Captain Lefanu was her only hope of rescue, but he was last seen making an unplanned (not to mention unpowered) landing on the doomed volcanic moon of Hastor.

Book Two of James Warren's *Creation's Echo* trilogy had ended on one hell of a cliffhanger.

Book Three was supposed to have come out over a year ago, but it had been delayed, and delayed again. Today, though, the waiting was over. Not for Simon Haldane, alas – his four-day shift in the St Ivel factory had just ended at six o'clock, half an hour after the shops shut – but at least he could look at it in the window of Hammicks. Tomorrow he would buy it – they opened on Sundays now – and he'd have the next four days free to immerse himself in it.

Chichester was fairly quiet at this time in the evening, it being too late for shopping and too early for many people to be out on the town. Simon headed purposefully towards the bookshop, passing two or three couples out walking, a scattering of window-shoppers like himself and a scruffy bearded fellow on a flight of steps who asked for spare change. Simon hurried past him, eyes averted. He did not like ignoring the homeless, it made him feel bad, but what could he do? He could give away his hard-earned cash and that would at best give partial and temporary relief to a few; in the long term, it solved nothing.

As he turned into North Street he decided he would get himself a curry from the Indian restaurant and take it back to his flat. Some of his colleagues had invited him to join them in the pub and go for a meal afterwards, but he had politely declined. Their conversation could not compete with a good book, and he had one he wanted to finish before he started the new James Warren.

His heart leapt: there it was, on prominent display in the window in its own cardboard rack, with four pounds off the recommend-ed retail price. *Creation's Echo Book Three: The Cartographer's Song*. It was, at a guess, six hundred pages long, with a cover illustration rich in yellow, orange and black. It showed Captain Lefanu in space armour minus the helmet, gun in hand, face to face with a monstrous creature – undoubtedly a

Threxel – while in the background his battered landing craft rested at an awkward angle against a volcanic outcrop.

It wasn't great literature, Simon was the first to admit that. It wasn't even great SF. He'd read the greats, the likes of Ursula LeGuin, Greg Egan, Gene Wolfe and David Langford, and he admired them. But after a twelve-hour stint in a factory you didn't read books just to admire them. He didn't care that the *Creation's Echo* books had been slated in *SFX*, or that *Interzone* had pretty much ignored them; when it came to sheer *immersibility* they were unbeatable. With James Warren, you were *there*…

Simon was suddenly aware of somebody behind him, standing much too close. Leaning over him, breathing on him, mouth almost brushing against his scalp for God's sake. Warily, he looked up from the display rack and his heart clenched in shock, for there in the window he could see its reflection. It was… not human. It was more like the anthropomorphic jackal of Egyptian legend, but with a thick, forked tongue that glistened.

For a moment he stood staring at the reflection, frozen in shock. But a part of his mind remained calm, rational; the reality that cast the reflection could not be as terrible *as* the reflection, because the reality would not be augmented by the distorting properties of the glass or his own imagination. He would turn and confront the prankster in the mask. He did not relish confrontation, but he was more than capable of rising to the occasion when the situation demanded it.

He turned. A figure stood looking at him but it was not the figure he had expected to see, not the figure in the reflection. It was less tall than he was, and too far away to account for the intrusive presence. It was human, and female; despite the boyish figure and a haircut even more severe than his own this was evidently a young woman. Astonished, he found himself saying, 'Did you *see* that?'

'What am I supposed to have seen?' asked the woman. She spoke with the precision of someone whose first language is not English.

'Someone who was... I mean, something...' Simon trailed off and shook his head, bemused. He had absolutely no idea what he had meant by the question, no idea what he had been about to say. It was as if he'd forgotten something that had seemed terribly important but evidently wasn't important enough to remain in his mind. 'I... I must have been mistaken,' he said at length, effectively ending the exchange.

But the woman was still looking right at him, her eyes wide as if she found him fascinating. It had been quite some time since a woman had found him fascinating. The idea that it might be happening again appealed to Simon, even though she was not what he would have thought of as his type.

She was not exactly *not* his type either.

'Is there anything I can do for you?' he asked, aware that her attention was making him blush.

'What island is this?'

'What *island*?' The question took him aback somewhat. Not just the words, but the way she said them. She spoke as if she had been travelling from one Greek island to another, taken a wrong turning, and had somehow ended up in West Sussex. As a matter of fact she might well be Greek. She had olive skin and her hair – what there was of it – was black. She was smaller than Simon, who was himself below average height, and she was dressed in a loose-fitting blue-cloth tunic, trousers made from the same material and a pair of boots probably made of leather.

'This isn't an island that you're on,' Simon explained. 'Well it is, but we tend to think of it as mainland.'

'I am lost,' said the woman. And she was too; Simon could hear it in the depths of her voice. She was alone, and vulnerable, and her home was immensely far away; if it *was* Greece, it might have been the Greece of the distant past or a future that was no longer destined to happen. Unobtrusively she had moved towards him, and now he could see her eyes up close. The blue irises almost filled the space between the lids; only in the corners did the whites show. She might have been drugged but Simon did not think she was; this was the real her he was seeing. Somewhat otherwòrldly and, in her own way, attractive.

And she wanted his help.

Simon was suddenly conscious of his own heartbeat. The possibilities were… interesting. And not a little humbling. The woman was homeless; not in the usual sense, perhaps, but the fact remained that she was. Those innocent otherworldly eyes of hers were decidedly appealing, but would they appeal in a few days' time when she was no longer clean and presentable? When that happened, he could imagine her sitting on some steps asking for spare change while someone just like himself walked on by with his eyes averted. Or else (and this seemed more likely) she would find help from someone tonight, but it would come at a price.

Not with me, he thought, making a vow of it. *If anything does happen between us, it will be because she wants it to.*

He asked her, 'Are you hungry?'

She said, 'Yes.'

He said, 'Would you like me to take you somewhere for a meal?'

They sat opposite each other at a table for two in the window of a food place. He asked her her name. She told him, and he tried to repeat it back to her: he said, 'Troy Game.' She put a hand over her mouth to stifle her laughter at his pronunciation; it was the first time she had laughed since her arrival on this place they called Mainland. He knew she was laughing at him but he was not offended. He tried a few more times until he got it more or less right. She then tried to pronounce his name: 'Sai-mahn Ahl-dine.' More laughter.

He asked her where she was from. She told him Dassar Island in the Southern Archipelago. He did not know it. She asked him if he knew of Shess Island. He did not. He took a thin tube from out of his tunic and asked her to show him. She did not understand so he demonstrated by pressing one end of the tube against one of the folded sheets of paper that had been placed on the table. She exclaimed in recognition – it was a kind of stylus, but with its own ink supply. She was not skilled at drawing but she made a brave attempt at portraying the islands of the Southern Archipelago, with parts of the Western Archipelago thrown in for good measure. But he still did not know what she was talking about. Reluctantly she dropped the subject. When she had first seen him she had hoped against hope that he was one of her countrymen. His small stature, his short hair, his sense of loneliness, of having been to immensely distant places... But then he had turned to face her and she had seen his eyes.

The food arrived, a thick disc of bread topped with cheese and unidentified vegetables and pieces of fish. She watched her benefactor handle the unfamiliar cutlery and attempted to emulate him, not entirely successfully. The food was... edible; not unpleasant exactly, but she was unaccustomed to the smells and flavours and not sure she would be able to keep it down. She did like the sparkling mineral water, though; she had never tasted anything like it before. When the meal was over there was an interchange of paper and metal discs – evidently the local currency. Simon was apparently content to pay for her food, and Troy Game wondered if anything was expected of her in return. She risked another look into his mind. Most of what she read there was very confusing indeed, yet she was left with the distinct impression that her company was payment enough.

Afterwards he asked her if there was anything else she wanted. She told him she needed to find the sea. The statement seemed to puzzle him and for one terrifying moment she thought he was going to tell her that he did not understand, that there was no sea, or that there was no way of getting to it from this place.

What he actually said was, 'I've got a car. I'll drive you there.'

Later, as he drove his battered Metro along the road to the Witterings, Simon found himself glancing uncertainly at his passenger. Who was she, really, and where did she come from? And what was his own role where she was concerned?

Troy Game was foreign. That much was obvious, but worth

stating because, by doing so, he made a point of avoiding the use of that other word: alien. He would not use that word in connection with her. She was different and, whatever his faults, Simon was not one to fear or reject the different without due cause. She sat somewhat rigidly in the passenger seat watching the evening landscape with evident apprehension, even though Simon was a careful driver and was not going particularly fast. It was as if she had never been in a car before. He had had to belt her in; she had not known where to put her arms or how to engage the clasp.

Of course it occurred to him that the whole thing was a wind-up, something cooked up by his work colleagues. They knew about his penchant for science fiction, even if they did not understand it. They thought he believed in flying saucers, alien abductions, Elvis living on the moon and so on, however many times he told them he did not. Science fiction was not about believing; it was about suspending disbelief, considering credible alternatives, and looking back at the real world with fresh eyes and a degree of objectivity. It was a means of enriching reality, not a replacement for it.

They knew he was waiting for the new James Warren book, and they could probably have guessed that he'd look in the bookshop window on his way home. So they could have primed a young woman – a would-be actress from the local art college, maybe – to accost him, trick him into believing she was from outer space and see how far she could go with the charade.

It was not beyond the bounds of possibility. She'd cut her hair very short, but maybe that was how she normally wore it. She had no ear lobes, which was unusual, but that in itself would be added reason for casting her for this role. Her eyes, though... he supposed she could have used belladonna to get that effect, but would anyone really go to those lengths just for a practical joke? Would a young woman spend an entire evening with a man she'd never met, who had not had a girlfriend for longer than he cared to think about, who might (for all she knew) react very badly when he discovered the deception, who was, right now, driving her several miles out of town?

He glanced in the rear-view mirror. Nobody was following along the country road. She had not specified a destination, and there was more than one beach he could have chosen. Given these factors, it seemed increasingly likely that Troy Game was pretty much what she claimed to be.

But what was that? When it came down to it, she hadn't exactly claimed anything specific. She certainly hadn't claimed to be from another world. She behaved as if the idea hadn't even crossed her mind, as if - and this was the frightening bit - as if everything would suddenly fall into place for her if the idea *did* cross her mind. If it was all an act she was damned convincing.

If it was not an act… He swallowed. This was not a book he could close whenever he felt like it. Then again, perhaps that was just what he needed. Whatever the explanation for her sudden appearance and interest in him - and he hoped he would *get* an explanation - Troy Game was pleasant enough company, and attractive in her own way. She was - for the time being at least - depending on him. Once she had done whatever it was she needed to do at the Witterings she would no doubt need somewhere to stay. She could stay in his spare room if that was what she preferred, at least to begin with. After that…

Well, they would take it from there. In time, things might develop or they might not, but if this *was* a first-contact situation it was vital that he maintain standards. It was fortunate that he was on twelve-hour shifts at the factory because it meant he had the next four days free. He could use the time to give her a crash course in late twentieth-century etiquette, culture and technology so that she could get about without drawing attention to herself. Oh, and first thing tomorrow he would buy her a pair of sunglasses.

The glass-and-metal vehicle came to a halt among a row of similar vehicles on a patch of ground bordering onto a sandy beach. Troy

Game could see the sea once more; at last, normality was returning.

Sai-mahn showed her how to release her seat belt, then leant across her to open her door. She climbed out of the vehicle and walked onto the beach. She felt the sand scrunch beneath her feet. There were other people walking along the shore, mostly in male and female couples. The sun was lower in the sky now but the air remained warm. There was still no sign of the other sun, not even a glow on the horizon presaging its rising.

For several minutes she stood watching the slow roll and crash of the breakers. This close to the equator the sea was completely free of ice. There was something slightly peculiar about its smell, but that too was probably an aspect of the latitude.

She had found the sea. It was almost impossible for her to contain her joy: *she had found the sea.* She turned to Sai-mahn, who was standing beside her.

'Thank you,' she said, with absolute sincerity. Then she began to undress.

'Er, Troy Game, don't you think you should wait for your meal to go down if you're… oh!'

She was aware of onlookers watching her. There was amusement, which she could not understand, and something like disapproval but nobody made any attempt to restrain her or follow her as she stepped into the shallows. She felt the wet sand beneath her bare feet, the warm breeze on her skin, the sun's soothing rays on her bruised shoulder. She relished the feeling then waded further in. The water covered her thighs, her hips, her stomach, her small breasts, her shoulders. A wave lifted her so that her feet no longer touched the sand. She swam.

Homewards.

Alone on the shore Simon watched as she dived under the surface. A minute passed, two minutes. He found himself muttering, 'Great! My first date since 1997, and she goes and drowns herself before the evening's over.' It was a flippant remark, of course, but when another minute passed, and another, it seemed increasingly likely that this was exactly what had happened.

Sick with worry, Simon considered a possibility that should have occurred to him before. Troy Game was not from the future, or from another planet or dimension. Neither was she an actress from the art college. She was in fact an inmate from Graylingwell, the mental hospital outside Chichester. Lonely and delusional, she had wandered into town and latched onto the first passer-by who, by an incredible stroke of bad luck, just happened to be him. If it had been anybody else they would have recognised the situation for what it was. They would have phoned the hospital or the emergency services or whatever.

But not him. Ignoring the woman's real needs, he had chosen instead to see things in science-fictional terms. He had involved her in his childish fantasy and, in doing so, he had assisted her suicide.

Yet she'd been so convincing…

He imagined how that would sound at an inquiry. But what could he do? If he ran away now he could pretend it had never happened; she was just someone he had met briefly and who had made her own choice. But that would not be right at all; evading responsibility for his actions would compound his guilt. In any case it wasn't practical. Even on a beach in 1999, a woman who strips naked – completely naked – in public draws attention to herself. Especially if she then proceeds to drown herself.

Only one thing for it, then: go in after her. He was almost certainly too late to save her, even if he found her immediately which was not likely, given the distance she had already swum. But he had to try. Had to be *seen* to try…

In the event, there was no need. Halfway to the horizon a black dot appeared. She had surfaced. She was alive. The feeling of relief was exhilarating. Simon called out to her, waving frantically, then without looking to see if she waved in reply he hurried back to his car and returned with a large blanket that he kept in the boot.

He stood on the beach, looking out to sea, awaiting her return.

* * *

31

The sea felt wrong on her skin. Its unfamiliar salts stung her eyes so that she had to close them. She could sense the magnetic field of the planet, but it was distant and it did not flow in the way she had expected, even allowing for her closeness to the equator. A single thought entered her mind that was at once wholly irrational yet undeniably true.

The sea was rejecting her.

The realisation was as painful as the loss of a limb or a loved one. In a very real sense she had lost the sea. She would not find her way home this way, and that, as far as she could tell, did not leave her any options at all. Her grief was so great that, had the cause of it been anything other than what it was, she would have drowned herself at once; in the circumstances that would not have been seemly. Instead she found her way to the surface and, for lack of any other direction, headed slowly back to the shore.

But the worst shock had yet to come. As she approached the beach she suddenly saw that the other sun had finally risen. What was left of it. Its disc was no longer a full circle. It did not shine as Beacon and Ember shone; rather it glowed, pale as corpse light. The light of a dead sun.

Sai-mahn was waiting for her. She emerged from the water in which she no longer belonged. She let him drape the blanket around her and guide her to his glass-and-metal vehicle. At some point he must have gathered up her clothes; they lay in a neat pile in its back. He took his position behind the control wheel in the seat beside her. 'Is there anything I can, er, do for you?' he asked.

Troy Game sat rigid in her seat, stared straight ahead through the vehicle's glass front, at the sea, at the dead sun. Her body shuddered with sobbing. Everything had changed, everything was lost. 'Take me home,' she said. She used the phrase in its ritual rather than its literal sense, but he did not seem to understand. Instead, he put the restraining belt around her (she did not resist) and started the vehicle's engine.

'I'll see what I can do,' he said.

Chapter Two
The Lady with the Labrador

She was tall, of stately bearing, her straight brown hair showing flecks of grey. She wore a long white toga, a pair of sandals and a copper bracelet on each wrist. In her right hand she held the harness of her dog Jess, and with her left she took a small device resembling a Braille compass from out of a large pocket. She walked confidently along the rocky shore, the Labrador guiding her around the rock pools. The lowering sun was warm on the exposed skin of her hands and her face. The smell of cinnamon wafted in on the onshore breeze; she sniffed the air and smiled.

This world was unmistakably Dagusa.

The compasslike device emitted a short beep, and the Lady Solenti gave a nod of satisfaction. 'That's him,' she said aloud. 'He's arrived at last.'

'You can smell him?' thought Jess. 'I'm impressed.'

'Don't be ridiculous,' said Solenti. 'His ship's landed about a mile up the coast, and half a mile inland. Somewhere among the ruins of the Old Suburb, I would estimate.'

'Assuming it *is* his ship. If you can't smell him you can't be sure it is him.'

'It's a pretty fair assumption, Jess. Nobody else would travel in anything quite so archaic and untrustworthy. And that, I believe, has something to do with why he's here.'

They walked briskly along the shore, the waves crashing to their left, the cries of seabirds echoing off the cliffs to their right.

'It must be nearly a century since my last visit,' said Solenti. 'Two billion years in the future I came to watch the sun leave the main sequence. The sea had long since evaporated and the remaining population had retreated to the south pole.'

'Was that the occasion when you lost your sight?'

'No!' said Solenti sharply. More gently, she added, 'No Jess, that happened much later. Another time, another sun, and I had grown complacent.' After a short silence she said, 'No matter. We're not chasing novae this time, we're looking for a man.'

'The owner of the archaic ship?'

'Yes.'

'Why?'

'Because I need him to do something for me. Something quite outside my own area of expertise.'

'Not something I would understand, then?'

'I wouldn't think so for a moment.'

Jess digested this. Clearly Solenti was not going to volunteer information. 'Does he owe you any favours?' she asked at length, trying a different tack.

'Him?' Solenti laughed. 'Owe *me* a favour? Oh no! No, quite the contrary. Nevertheless I think he will do what I ask.'

'Why?'

'Because he shares a particularly, ah, *manipulable* vice with you. If there is such a word.'

'You mean curiosity, I suppose.'

'I most certainly do.'

'Lady, forgive my presumption, but I can't help noticing certain *misgivings* in your tone.'

Solenti frowned. 'Misgivings? Me? Of course I have misgivings! Anyone would.'

'You think he will fail?'

'Far from it, Jess. I'm afraid he'll succeed *too* well.'

'Lady?'

'He's a loose cannon, Jess, a wild card. You ask him to carry out a simple investigation, and he ends up uncovering conspiracies and corruption at the highest level.'

'You have something to hide?'

Solenti adopted a mock-severe tone. 'What do *you* think?'

* * *

On Erekan the flowers thrived on cold; they bedecked a mighty meandering glacier that straddled a continent and crossed the planet's equator forty-four times.

Gau-Usu was a rocky world where the day was five weeks long. It was blessed with a ring system that arced across the sky like a permanent monochrome rainbow.

Cern was a savannah world, the moon of a swollen salmon-pink gas giant that hung perpetually in the same part of the sky, its disc crossed with dark bands that ran parallel to its equator.

They had landed on each of these worlds, stayed a while and left. Each visit had been quite without incident, each world quite without apparent mystery or immediate danger. They had not been shot at, captured or separated from the TARDIS. Most importantly, as far as Jo Grant was concerned, the Doctor had not darted off in pursuit of something he insisted would 'only take a minute' to investigate; she knew where *that* always led.

It couldn't last.

After Cern they had landed among a cluster of ruined villas and overgrown gardens and dust-choked fountains. Weeds sprang up through cracks in the roads. Jo was unable to shake off the impression that this appearance of abandonment and neglect was somehow *managed*. The TARDIS itself – a tall blue police box as seen from the outside – was placed incongruously against an ivy-covered wrought-iron gate in a garden wall.

'Well, Jo,' said the Doctor, 'the Time Lords have certainly kept up their side of the bargain.' He gave the police box an affectionate pat. 'She's running rather smoothly now, don't you think? Quite the precision instrument.'

'We're still no closer to finding Metebelis Three though, are we?'

'On the contrary. I've been giving the TARDIS navigation computer a much-needed recalibration.' The Doctor took in his surroundings and began walking along the main road in the direction of the late afternoon sun. Jo followed. They walked through a landscape that reminded her of a recent visit to Greece although it was a lot less hilly: rocky land, trees that might have been olives and white stone buildings in the distance. The climate was distinctly Mediterranean too.

'Why does the navigation computer need recalibrating?' she asked.

'Things change, Jo. The universe expands, old stars die, new stars are formed. Besides which, the old girl needs her memory jogged once in a while.'

'I see,' said Jo doubtfully.

'Do you?' The Doctor gave Jo his full attention. 'Consider the last few worlds we've visited. What in particular struck you about them?'

Jo considered. 'Each one was unique in some way?'

The Doctor smiled. 'Good. Very good indeed as a matter of fact.'

'Landmarks! That's what they were – some sort of galactic trig point.'

'Top of the class, Jo.'

'So how does that help us? I mean, if you found *them* so easily what's to stop us going straight to Metebelis Three?'

'It's a question of scale, Jo. These worlds are all within a few dozen light years of Earth.'

'Practically on our doorstep then,' said Jo, refusing to engage her imagination just for the moment. On Gau-Usu the Doctor had pointed out Earth's sun to her and she had watched it twinkle, a not especially bright star in that planet's night sky.

'Quite so,' the Doctor continued, oblivious to her flippant tone. 'It means the margin of error isn't very significant. The TARDIS can usually locate a planet herself so long as it's within a few million miles of the destination coordinates.'

'Is Metebelis Three much further away then?'

'Metebelis Three is in a different galaxy altogether. The same degree of inaccuracy can give rise to a much greater error. You end up missing not only the planet but its entire stellar neighbourhood.'

'So that's why we ended up on Inter Minor!'

'Ye-es.' The Doctor rubbed the back of his neck. 'Fortunately I can calculate the exact fraction of error by comparing the coordinates in the navigation database with the actual coordinates of the landmark worlds. One more should just about do it.'

'Are we on a landmark world now?'

'That is precisely what I intend to find out.'

At length the road took them close to the edge of a cliff before turning sharply to the right. Beyond it, Jo could hear the crash of waves on a beach. One particularly large wave struck a particularly large rock, and a gust of wind whipped sea spray against her face. The smell of the spray made her think of hot cross buns.

'Dagusa,' said the Doctor with satisfaction. 'The only planet in the galaxy with a sea that smells of cinnamon. That's the confirmation I was looking for; now, all I need to do…'

'Doctor, look!'

The Doctor broke off and looked where Jo was pointing. He rubbed his chin and frowned. There was movement below; a figure was walking along the beach with what appeared to be a large dog. From this distance it was hard to say for sure that the figure was a woman, but…

'Jo,' said the Doctor, his tone unexpectedly grave. 'Do you think you can find your way back to the TARDIS from here?'

'Yes of course, Doctor. But what…'

'Listen to me carefully. When you get there, go inside and lock the doors. Here's the key. Don't open them up until you see me on the scanner. And Jo.'

'Yes?'

'Make sure I'm completely on my own.'

Jo was dumbfounded. Why on Earth should a woman out walking her dog cause the Doctor so much concern? 'Well all right,' she said doubtfully. 'But don't you think you're overreacting a bit?'

'I can assure you I'm not.'

'What are you going to do?'

'I'm going to talk to her, of course.'

Unable to resist, Jo said, 'Well, isn't that a bit dangerous? I mean, if she's so much of a…'

'Jo, for once in your life do you think you could just do as I say?' He held her gaze for a few moments, then smiled to take the sting out of his words. 'This will only take a minute. I won't be in any danger, but I'm rather anxious that she doesn't meet you. That could put me at a considerable disadvantage.'

And then he was off, scrabbling down a barely visible path that led to the bottom of the cliff.

Jess was unharnessed. She ran back and forth along the sandy part of the beach barking at the waves, her paws splashing in the cinnamon-scented water.

The Lady Solenti sat cross-legged on a shelf of rock, facing out to sea, Jess's harness beside her. The sun was low but she could still feel its warmth on her face. She heard footsteps, the shifting of loose stones under a single pair of booted feet, and a figure interposed itself between her and the sun.

'Alone, Doctor?' Solenti ventured. 'Don't tell me you're travelling alone.'

The Doctor's voice, when he finally spoke, was unfamiliar. Somewhat deeper than she'd expected, courteous, and inclined towards emphasis through understatement. 'Lady Solenti,' he acknowledged. 'I can't say I'm altogether surprised to see you here.'

'It is quite beautiful, is it not, Doctor?' The Doctor did not reply but she imagined him nodding agreement. 'I have always loved the sea. The sound of the waves: eternal, unchanging, yet never quite repeating. And never quite the same on any two worlds.'

'I take it this meeting is not entirely coincidental?' said the Doctor.

Solenti shook her head.

'What, no pretence?' She imagined him raising one eyebrow. 'You surprise me.'

'In which case you must be confusing me with somebody else. I don't pretend, Doctor. You should know me better than that.'

'No,' he conceded. 'Your skills of manipulation go quite beyond the need for anything so obvious. So, perhaps you'd be so good as to tell me what you want?'

'We need your help.'

He might have raised his eyebrow again at that 'we'. Or it might be that eyebrow-raising was not one of his character traits at all. 'And I just happened to be in the area.'

'Something like that.'

'Another errand for the Time Lords? Is that it?'

'Not at all, Doctor. "We", in this particular context, does not mean "the Time Lords". It means two individuals who happen to *be* Time Lords. And I emphasise it is a *request* for help.'

'Two Time Lords? Might I ask where the other is?'

'I'll come to that.'

'Forgive my scepticism, Lady Solenti, but…'

'Come now, Doctor. You saw me from the cliff top, did you not?'

'I saw a figure in the distance.'

'But you had a pretty good idea who you were dealing with. You know of my affinity for the sea, and besides I had Jess with me. There was nothing to prevent you from going on your way, but no; your curiosity was piqued. You wanted to know if it really was me and, if so, why was I on Dagusa at the same time as you? So you came down to find out. Now tell me honestly, is that the *modus operandi* of the Time Lords?'

'No,' the Doctor admitted. 'If it was official business I would have absolutely no say in the matter.'

'Precisely. Shall we walk?'

Solenti rose, picked up Jess's harness and took the Doctor's arm. He was wearing a velvet jacket, not at all what she had expected. They walked, back in the direction she had come from, Jess following close behind. Solenti had become quite practised in what she thought of as nonvisual body language: a rigidness in the Doctor's poise, and a reluctance to face her when speaking, suggested that his dislike of her had not diminished over the years. Which was frustrating because really they were so alike in so many ways, if only he could swallow his pride and admit to it! But it wasn't going to happen, not in the foreseeable future at any rate, and Solenti was glad she didn't have to rely on his goodwill where this particular request was concerned.

Dagusa had a nine-hour day and a pronounced axial tilt; its arctic circle was only two thousand miles from the equator. At midnight in midsummer, at those latitudes, the sun did not quite set; rather it would scud along the horizon, slowly sinking until the lower half of its disc was hidden, after which it would resume its equally gradual ascent.

From the beach where the Doctor walked with Solenti, the place where the sun half-set was a sea horizon framed between two headlands. He was rather regretful that Jo had missed it. Assuming she had obeyed his instructions, of course.

Solenti was making small-talk. This consisted of scientific observations about Dagusa's sea, sun and climate interspersed with gossip about people back home, none of whom would ever amount to anything. It was probably her way of sounding him out – mention a few mutual acquaintances, observe how he reacts, that sort of thing. Either that or she liked the sound of her own voice. Nevertheless, the Doctor was wary. Solenti's methods seemed inept and transparent but they tended to work. She had found him easily enough, for instance. Getting the right planet wasn't especially clever – she knew his exile had been recently lifted, and Dagusa was an obvious choice for someone whose navigational skills were a bit rusty. But getting the right beach at the right time of the right year – now that *was* impressive.

'So why me?' he asked. His affected weariness did not quite disguise his curiousity.

'You always work best in an unofficial capacity,' Solenti said, as if it was self-evident. 'You're also the acknowledged expert in all matters pertaining to the planet Earth. I understand you were exiled there recently.'

'You *have* done your homework.' There was bitter irony in the Doctor's voice; his exile was common knowledge.

'I also understand that you left some business unfinished, did you not?'

'Unfinished business? Well, now that you come to mention it, there was that mysterious consignment of nonregulation paperclips that arrived at UNIT HQ last April. We never did get to the bottom of that.'

'Your sarcasm does you no credit, Doctor.'

'No? Well in that case perhaps you'd be so good as to remind me what it was.'

They had arrived at a wooden structure, an eight-sided raised platform with a thatched roof supported by eight poles. A gazebo, here in the middle of an otherwise deserted stretch of rocky coast. The oddest thing about it was the fact that it did not appear in the least incongruous.

'Your TARDIS?' asked the Doctor.

'The atrium,' said Solenti, nodding. 'It's a development you possibly missed out on while you were… out in the field, shall we say. It's an extension to the chameleon circuit. At higher settings it provides a powerful psychological defence, considerably harder to penetrate than mere camouflage. At its minimum setting it's simply useful.'

Access to the platform was provided by a set of three wooden steps. There was a large, awkwardly placed rock pool right in front of the steps, and the Doctor was obliged to walk around it. He turned to guide Solenti around it too, but she was evidently aware of it.

There was a round table with four chairs on the platform. On the table was a set of four cups and saucers, a large teapot and a tea strainer, milk jug and sugar bowl. Solenti had expected the Doctor to be accompanied, then. He felt a certain childish glee at confounding her expectations.

'Practical and convenient,' he mused as he took a seat.

'Quite. Shall I pour?' She located the cups with a downward-palm manoeuvre, then poured in the correct amounts of milk and tea. Accuracy born of practice. The tea was hot and infused to perfection. Which was odd, given that Solenti could not have made it within the last half-hour. Either she had a servant on board her TARDIS or else some property of the atrium circuit kept tea fresh.

'During your exile you detected a temporal anomaly,' Solenti began without further preamble. 'Given the circumstances, that in itself was impressive; you had only partial use of your TARDIS, and the equipment at your disposal was barely adequate for an investigation into anything of that nature. Nevertheless, you detected it. Furthermore, you tracked it down to one of the desert regions of the planet.'

The Doctor nodded slowly. 'A temporal fracture,' he said. 'It originated in Israel, a thousand miles from the UNIT headquarters where I was working at the time. It was difficult to read its signature accurately, but it was more or less consistent with leakage from a decaying hypercore that had not been properly shut down.'

'A crashed starship?' suggested Solenti.

'Crashed and buried. That was my guess.' The Doctor thought for a moment, then continued. 'We flew out to Israel, and…'

'"We"?'

'My, er, team. Colonel Amichai, the head of UNIT in Tel Aviv, had a helicopter ready and waiting for us. A Huey. I remember asking him if that was the best he could do.' The Doctor adopted a rueful tone. 'Perhaps I was a little ungrateful.'

'What about the anomaly?' prompted Solenti.

'The only time you can detect a time fracture is when it begins and when it ends. It's the gradient you detect, not the absolute level. It was starting to even out just as we arrived at Masada, which was its point of origin – we'd managed to triangulate its exact location. When we got there we found a team of archaeologists slap bang on top of it.'

'They had disturbed it?'

'So it seemed. But the director of the dig – Professor Ezekiel Child, that was his name – said they had barely begun the excavation.'

'What did you do then?'

'We dug it up, of course. Or rather, that's what we thought we were doing.'

'What you *thought* you were doing? What do you mean?'

'We found a buried Spitfire,' the Doctor said, his tone oddly sheepish. 'It presumably crashed during the Arab–Israeli conflict of 1948.'

'Was its hypercore leaking?'

The Doctor sucked air through his teeth. 'A Spitfire is not a starship,' he explained, somewhat impatiently. 'It is a purely mechanical device built for travel within the atmosphere.'

Solenti frowned. She was silent for a minute before saying, 'Forgive me, Doctor, but I do not quite see how that accounts for the time anomaly.'

'It *doesn't* account for the time anomaly. Or much else for that matter.' Rueful again, the Doctor added, 'It quite ended the professor's career, poor chap.'

'Perhaps the starship was buried deeper?'

'We dug deeper. Very much deeper, as a matter of fact. But we found absolutely nothing.'

'Perhaps this "Spitfire" was merely the plasmic shell of a…'

'Believe me, that was the first thing I thought of. I had it airlifted to the headquarters at Tel Aviv – at great expense, I might add. They identified the remains of the crew using dental records, and concluded that the aircraft was no more and no less than it appeared to be.'

'You know less than I thought, then,' Solenti said, more to herself than to the Doctor. 'I have a particular interest in this time anomaly,' she explained before he had a chance to reply. 'You see, after a cursory survey the Time Lords declared it a navigational hazard. This was around the same time that my partner went missing.'

'Your partner?'

'Lord Roche.'

'Hmm. Lord Roche.'

'You know him?'

'Only by reputation. You think he was caught up in the time anomaly?'

Solenti nodded. 'You will help?'

'I will consider it,' the Doctor said warily, knowing full well what she meant by 'help'. Solenti was not one to do anything herself if she could possibly delegate it, nor was she inclined to back up whoever did her dirty work for her if they got into any trouble. She was complacent, passive, manipulative, egotistical and needlessly secretive. And the Doctor knew perfectly well that he should have nothing to do with her. Really, the moment he saw her from the clifftop he should have gone back to the TARDIS with Jo and left Dagusa. But...

But he hadn't.

'That's all I ask – that you consider it,' Solenti said innocently.

'I need to know all the facts. For a start, exactly why was he on Earth in the first place? How precisely am I supposed to find him? And how can I be sure that I won't find myself caught up in the anomaly?'

'To the first,' said Solenti, 'I simply do not know.'

'But you know more than you are saying.'

'Of course I know more than I am saying, but in this instance I am telling you as much as you need to know. Really Doctor, Earth might be your favourite planet but I doubt that Roche would put it in his top hundred.'

'Am I missing something here?' The Doctor was exasperated. 'You are *asking* me to undertake this mission as a *favour* and you won't even give me all the facts!'

'I wouldn't call it a favour exactly. You aren't curious about the cause of the anomaly? The unfinished business?'

'Well yes, of course I...'

'In answer to your second question, this is how you find him.'

From her toga pocket Solenti had taken a black box, a device consisting of three slider controls, half a dozen buttons and, at one end, a two-inch-by-one-inch screen. 'The controls are quite intuitive,' she said, placing it on the table in front of him. 'It's a tracking device. There are two modes of use: short-range and long-range. Short-range is anything up to fifty miles, accurate to within a yard. For long-range mode it interfaces with the console of your TARDIS. I understand you travel in a Type Fifty, is that right?'

'Type Forty.'

'Good heavens! However do you manage... No matter, the device is backward-compatible. On its present setting it will direct your TARDIS to arrive at the location of the fracture two days before it begins. That should give you ample time to find Lord Roche, if that's where he is.'

Solenti picked up Jess's harness and called to her. The dog, who was some distance away, trotted towards the gazebo.

'Two days.' The Doctor considered. 'I don't like it. What if I'm delayed in Israel? My younger self is due to arrive at the dig, in case you'd forgotten.'

Solenti was rising from the table as if the meeting was over. 'What of it?' she said.

'Don't you see I run the risk of meeting myself? An occurrence like that could be the very cause of the fracture.'

'Doctor, when the Time Lords declared the anomaly a navigational hazard your name was not mentioned. Not once. Now, if there was the slightest chance that it even *looked* as if it carried your signature, don't you think someone would at least have *tried* to pin the blame on you?'

The Doctor had to concede that this was sound reasoning.

'I can tell you about one other finding from the survey,' Solenti said, sounding as if it was something she had just remembered. 'The anomaly persists for twenty-seven years. In the local year 1999 it ends as quickly as it began.'

The Doctor's interest was piqued. 'Does it end at the same location?'

'Oh yes,' Solenti confirmed. 'The anomaly occurs entirely on the planet Earth.'

The Doctor's hearts sank. 'I was rather hoping you could tell me if it was the same *part* of Earth.'

Solenti shrugged. 'As I said, the survey was somewhat cursory. Do you have any more questions?'

'I certainly do,' said the Doctor. 'But I shouldn't think for a moment that they'd elicit useful answers.'

'In that case, it only remains for me to wish you good luck.' With that, Solenti walked down the steps. This time she did not avoid the rock pool; instead she walked straight into it. Although it only appeared to be a couple of feet deep, she continued to descend as if the gazebo's steps went on into the ground. Soon she was completely submerged. A moment later there was a flash of yellow as Jess leapt in after her; there was no splash. There was a repeated whirring sound, suggestive of a cooling fan, and the rock pool itself vanished. Where it had been only the rocky ground remained, without so much as a hint of indentation.

The Doctor found himself standing on the rocky beach. The gazebo had gone but there had been no sense of falling. He did not remember picking up Solenti's tracking device, but he held it in his hand nonetheless. He smiled grimly. Once again Solenti's manner had annoyed him intensely, and once again she had got her way. Tempting as it was to toss the tracking device into the nearest rock pool and forget all about the anomaly, it was simply not in his nature.

'Curiosity,' he muttered. 'One of these days it's going to cost me dearly.'

Chapter Three
The Mark of the Fury

Alone in her college room, Helen Ayre was attempting to work on her dissertation. She was finding it difficult to concentrate. At the back of her mind she was waiting for the sound of footsteps in the corridor outside, the knock on the door and James Preedy's grinning face appearing in the opening, ready to utter some inane chat-up line or suggestive invitation. He didn't always wait for her to say 'Come in' when he knocked, so she was careful to lock her door whenever she was getting ready for bed.

She liked to think she took his antics in her stride; certainly his behaviour did not normally affect her concentration. But this evening was different. This evening an irrational part of her knew it was not going to happen. This evening she *wanted* it to happen, not because of any secret longing for James (though she admitted to a certain sneaking fondness for him, immature as he was) but because, if he *did* make one of his appearances, it would assure her that she was mistaken and he was still alive.

She had not seen him die. She had not even seen his body. Not exactly. She had seen *something*, and she had understood at once what it meant. But she also understood that her interpretation of events had no place in the real world. It followed, then, that she had to be wrong. If James Preedy called on her tonight it would confirm that she was wrong, and that the world made sense after all.

Helen's heart leapt as she heard the distant but distinctive clack of the Yale latch in the fire door at the bottom of the stairwell. A moment later the door slammed shut again. There were heavy footsteps on the stairs. It was usually about this time of the evening that James Preedy paid her a visit; if the world had not changed after all she saw no reason why this particular evening would be exceptional. If, for instance, the events of the day had been part of an elaborate and extremely strange practical joke he would be round, surely, to see her reaction. It was inconceivable that he would be able to leave it for a day, even though the 'joke' would have benefited from the delay.

She'd thought about going to the police. But James Preedy was an adult, and he'd been missing for considerably less than forty-eight hours. They would not be interested. If she told them about the… the *thing* she'd seen outside Room 18 they would tell her to stop wasting their time.

The fire door on her own floor opened and shut. Helen sat rigid as the slow footsteps approached. There was a gentle knock at the door. She was about to say 'Come in', but the words caught in her throat. It took her several seconds to regain control of her voice, but before that happened there was another gentle knock and hope died in her.

The caller was not James Preedy. He would not have knocked a second time.

She opened the door. A tall dark-haired man stood in the entrance. He was in his late twenties to early thirties, dressed in light trousers and a short-sleeved shirt. He carried a laptop computer in a leather case. From his bearing and his manner of dress she supposed he normally wore a suit, but in this heatwave that would have been impractical. Nevertheless he had the appearance of a plain-clothes detective.

'Ms Helen Ayre?' the man asked. When she nodded he continued, 'My name is Michael Sheridan.' He brandished an open wallet; Helen stared at it without seeing it. He closed the wallet and put it away. 'I'm investigating the disappearance of one James Preedy. Do you know him?'

She nodded again.

'In that case, I wonder if you would mind answering a few questions?'

* * *

48

Helen had a part-time job as a cleaner at the Regis Seaview Hotel in Bognor Regis, as did James Preedy. The pay was not great, but it more or less covered the cost of her board and lodgings. It had been partly thanks to James's recommendation that she had got the job, which was one of the reasons why she tended to be tolerant of him. He was a surprisingly diligent worker and they had quickly fallen into a routine. She would begin cleaning rooms on the ground floor and James would start on the second floor. They would meet somewhere on the first floor.

Today had been different.

It had been an eventful morning. In addition to several minor incidents, including a laundry mix-up, a double booking and a jammed window – no trivial matter in this heatwave – there had been one major incident. The accounts given by the kitchen staff were contradictory, but apparently a guest (or possibly the friend of a guest) had argued (or possibly fought) with his much younger girlfriend (or possibly his daughter). Eventually she stormed out, and he proceeded to have a heart attack. Or perhaps it was an epileptic fit. Whatever it was, the manager had to call an ambulance and the man was taken away. All this happened shortly before Helen and James arrived for work. James expressed his regret at missing out on the excitement, then went off to start work on the second floor. And that was the last time Helen saw him alive.

There were four rooms on the ground floor and six on the second, so it was quite usual for Helen to start working on the first floor before James did. It was only after she had finished cleaning the en suite in Room 6, which had been left in a disgusting state, that she noticed James's absence. She was not unduly worried; quite the contrary, in fact, as she wasn't in the mood to counter his usual repertoire of suggestive comments. She didn't even mind getting through more of the first floor rooms than he did. James was no slacker; the chances were he was dealing with something even more horrific than the toilet in Room 6.

When she had finished cleaning Room 8 – working in numerical order, as she tended to do whenever she could – and there was still no sign of James she began to feel just a little concerned. Either he *was* slacking today or there was something wrong. And now that she thought about it, the floor above was unusually quiet. Ordinarily James banged doors, operated a Hoover, burst into song once in a while, much of which could be heard on the floor below.

Not today, though. And that was unusual enough to warrant investigating. Helen put down her cleaning things and set off for the second floor.

At the end of the corridor furthest from the stairs, outside Room 18, stood James's Hoover. There was something lying on the floor beside it. It looked like a body – James's body – but as Helen got closer to it she saw that it was not. Could not be. Because it wasn't made of flesh and blood.

It was made of grey stone.

A cold nothingness spread through her body. As she got closer still she saw that it was a statue. A granite statue of James lying prostrate on the floor, his head twisted to one side and his mouth contorted in terror or agony.

She crouched beside the statue. It wore stone trainers, slightly rucked stone jeans with a rip beside the left knee and a stained T-shirt, the folds and bunchings of the stone cloth perfectly rendered. A discoloration on the upper right arm exactly matched a dirty mark Helen had noticed earlier on James's right sleeve. She imagined that if she turned the statue onto its back she would be able to read the lettering on the front of the T-shirt.

Helen had seen James drinking in the union bar with John Redmond, a sculptor from the sister college in Chichester. Could he be responsible for this? She doubted it. For all his talk of the importance of abstract art and the inspiration of Henry Moore, it was obvious to everyone that John Redmond was incapable of sculpting realistic human figures. Unless he had been hiding his talent under a bushel it was inconceivable that he had made this fantastically detailed statue of James; even if he was capable of doing so, what earthly reason did he have for leaving it here for her to stumble over?

There was one other explanation which was even more far-fetched, but which fitted the facts better. Helen had studied Greek mythology in her first year. She remembered writing an essay on the symbolism of the story of Perseus and Andromeda. But what if it hadn't been symbolic at all? What if…

A moment later fear engulfed her, and she was running along the corridor and down the stairs, taking them three at a time. She collided with an elderly guest and jostled a member of the kitchen staff who was carrying plates, but she kept on running, desperate to be as far away from the hotel as possible. Even as she ran, it occurred to her that her fears might seem very silly once she was out of the building and out of a job. But looking silly was something she could live with.

Michael Sheridan sat at Helen's desk typing up her account on his laptop. He had a very fast typing speed. Helen sat on the end of her bed, leaning forward with one hand gripped in the other, staring at the opposite wall. She had finished her story now but she continued to stare. Eventually Sheridan broke the silence.

'You think your friend was turned to stone?'

Helen started. She looked at Sheridan for the first time since he had sat down. She had never been interviewed by a policeman before but she was pretty certain they didn't ask questions like that. In fact, now that suspicion had finally dawned…

'I've been a bloody idiot!'

'Not at all,' said Sheridan soothingly. 'There is nothing irrational about a fear of the unknown…'

'I didn't mean that and you know it. Who are you really? And who are you working for?'

'Ah, perhaps I didn't make myself clear. I work for *Open Minds*. It's an independently published magazine dealing with matters outside the ordinary.'

'Oh God.' She held her head in her hands. 'I thought you were a… Look, I really don't need this right now.'

Sheridan nodded slowly, sympathetically. 'That's perfectly understandable under the circumstances. This is clearly not a good time for you. Perhaps it would be better if I let you have some time on your own.'

'I'd rather you hadn't come in the first place. I mean, what is it with you people? Why does every socially inadequate creep think they're Fox bloody Mulder?'

'Very well. I'm sorry to have intruded.' Sheridan closed his laptop and got up to go. He hesitated at the door. 'Only…' Then he shook his head vehemently. 'No.'

The words were out before Helen had a chance to stop herself. 'Only what?'

Sheridan turned. 'Only, I'd feel I was leaving you in rather an awkward situation. It's a question of habeas corpus. You see, the police would treat this matter as a suspicious death if there was a dead body. But of course there is nothing of the sort. At least, nothing they would recognise *as* a dead body. All they can do is register him as a missing person. And even if the explanation is not what you and I think it is, you can probably imagine what chance they'd have of finding him.'

'So what are you saying?'

'I'm saying, maybe I can help.'

The sky over Chichester was a deep blue, punctuated by the three bright stars that made up the Summer Triangle: Vega, Deneb and Altair. On a night like this in 1983 Sheridan had lain on the grass on Portsdown Hill with his girlfriend, looking up at the stars. It had been the fifth of August, her thirteenth birthday; he was a few months older than her. That very morning he had learnt that astronomers had discovered a solar system forming around Vega – that was the blue one, directly overhead and twenty-six light years away. The knowledge had changed him; it made him realise that the universe was a richer place than he'd been led to believe.

It was a realisation that had long-term consequences, of which his role as freelance investigative journalist was the most recent.

It seemed to be working out. Tonight, he had overcome the hostility of a sceptical student. He had obtained good copy from her under what she clearly thought were false pretences (although he had not actually lied to her and he *had* shown her his ID), yet in the end he had convinced her that he was the one who was helping her. She'd even thanked him before he left.

Sheridan had not deceived her, not really. But, if he had, it was surely justified. Something very strange and very serious was going on; it needed investigating and if that meant using underhand tactics, then so be it. As an active player it was something he had to do.

She'd remembered more. She knew they had taken him – the guest who had collapsed – to St Richard's Hospital in Chichester rather than the nearer hospital in Bognor Regis itself, though she did not know why. And one of the kitchen staff had mentioned his name, she was sure of it now. Sorrand, or was it Sarrand? Definitely Sarrand. Phil Sarrand.

The plump, grey-haired receptionist at St Richard's Hospital looked at him over her glasses. She smiled pleasantly and asked if she could help him. She had a lilting, sing-song voice, a Welsh accent.

'I've come to visit a friend who was taken ill this morning,' he told her. 'I believe he was brought to this hospital.'

She asked him the name of the patient and he told her. She repeated it as she typed it into her PC. After a few moments she frowned at the screen. 'This morning, you say?'

Sheridan nodded. 'Early this morning.'

'Well, I can't find anyone of that name, I'm afraid. Are you sure it was Phil Sarrand?'

'Quite sure.'

'Let me look again. Phil Sarrand, Phil Sarrand…'

She repeated the name a few more times as she continued her search. Sheridan waited patiently. She told him the server had gone down earlier that day and they probably hadn't updated the links to the hospital database yet. He shook his head in sympathy and told her to tell him about it. Then she said the man's name once more and this time it didn't sound like Phil Sarrand.

Realisation finally struck Sheridan. 'Bitch!' he spat.

The receptionist looked at him sharply. Flustered, he tried to assure her he did not mean her. He apologised anyway, and made a hasty departure.

The student had not remembered the man's name, she had made it up. It was a name that, if you kept repeating it in a lilting voice, started to sound more like *fool's errand*.

The little room was full of ghosts. The patient lay on the bed with his eyes closed, listening. The ghost voices were on the very threshold of hearing (or whatever sense it was that corresponded to hearing): there was Judith Winters, with her memories of her schooldays in Shoreditch in the 1960s and the encounter that had permanently unhinged her; there was Ian Whittaker, the bit-part actor whose nervous breakdown coincided with the realisation that he was never going to be a household name; there was Jo Stevenson, the young woman who starved herself in her anxiety to hold back the changes that her body was undergoing. There were others.

The difference in character between past ghosts and future ghosts was as distinct as the difference between the sound of an approaching police siren and a receding one. There was the ghost of himself from a few days hence, and another who only believed that that was who he was. There were the doctors, the orderlies, the nurses, the two visitors (one of whom he felt he should know). And there was something else…

The thing he feared above all else. It was imperative that he be gone from this room when *that* arrived.

Thinking was unsafe; thinking would bring the thing here. He had to suppress his thoughts and rely as much as possible on instinct. He opened his eyes and the ghost voices receded. Above him was a white ceiling, a single light fitting hanging down. He sat up. The room held no surprises: a door, a basin, a chair and the bed he was sitting on. Daylight, the light from a single afternoon sun, streaming in through the window casting the shadows of bars on the far wall. The bars distressed him, not because they confined him but because they were so wholly ineffectual a defence against the thing that was out there.

He climbed off the bed, went over to the window. He closed it, despite the heat. Outside in the hospital grounds there were trees, paths, patients walking or standing or sitting on benches. The ground was cracked in places and winged ants were streaming out and taking to the air, flying awkwardly at first. They flew at his window, impacting against the glass. He watched them, imagined them larger, the size of large dogs, so large he could make out their insect faces. They resembled locusts as much as they resembled ants. He imagined them crawling, hopping and occasionally flying over a plain of ice that stretched to the far horizon in every direction, endless hordes of them making for the two low suns, moving with a collective sense of urgency, turning on any of their brethren who showed any sign of weakness or injury.

'Leshe,' he said aloud. Then, as if afraid of what might have heard him, he withdrew from the window and stood rigid with his back against the wall. Hoping the universe would not look in and see him. Hiding in a smaller universe that consisted of this room, the sunlight, the sound of plumbing and the movement of people in adjoining rooms, and the heartbeats that echoed from within his own chest.

He remained like this until the fear passed.

Chapter Four
Dream of Caresh

She was having the dream again, the dream she'd had in the blue room without doors or windows when she'd arrived two weeks ago, but each time she dreamt it the dream went a little further. Sometimes the details changed; this time the crater-lake on Dassar Island was frozen over, but that had only happened recently, and she did not want to trust her weight to it, so she made her way around the lake's edge to the causeway.

There was a figure on the causeway, heading towards the crater rim. She could not make out any of the figure's features, for it was some distance away and dressed from head to foot in robes that covered the body. Curious, she quickened her step but the causeway was slippery and it was hard for her to keep her balance. The time before last she had awoken at this point; last time she had reached the figure and he had pushed back his cowl and she was afforded a fleeting glimpse of his face; not quite long enough to be sure that he really was a 'he'.

This time she saw his face clearly. She memorised it as best she could, even though her visual memory was not very reliable. He spoke to her. 'You must be Troy Game,' he said. 'Your presence here is unexpected. Do you know who I am?'

She was about to answer when she awoke. She lay in her benefactor's bed – or rather on it, for she had pushed the duvet off during the night. Mornings here came sooner than she was used to and light from the single sun was already shining in through the window and onto her skin. She welcomed it, for it served her body's needs as well as Ember or Beacon. On this particular morning, however, she would have preferred to have slept longer, for she had been on the verge of addressing the man by name. If she had done so, she would be able to remember it now.

She rose from the bed. She reached for the door handle, then remembered just in time to take the dressing gown from the door hook and put it on.

Simon Haldane knew he was going to be late for work. It could not be helped.

He had cleared a space on the breakfast table for his sketch pad. Already he had nearly filled the pad: there was a map of the Archipelago, a landscape drawing of the volcanic island of Dassar, four frozen seascapes, the two suns at different times of year, diagrams of the Careshi solar system showing the planet's figure-eight orbit, a quartet of fur-clad fishermen in a skiff navigating the channels between ice sheets. This morning he sketched in the robed figure from Troy Game's dream as she described it to him. The face was round, slightly sad-looking, aged about sixty. The nose was small, the mouth wide, the whites of the eyes all but crowded out by the brown irises. The hair was very short.

Across the breakfast table Troy Game regarded Simon with her big blue eyes as he drew. He looked up at her briefly, then returned his attention to his drawing. It was dangerously easy to misinterpret her eyes. You could think she was bovine, slow-witted, when she was anything but. Or you could think she was looking at you with adoration when she was not. At least, Simon had come to assume she was not. In the two weeks since she had moved in with him there had been no indication of any intended intimacy on her part. Apparently oblivious to his tentative hints, she seemed perfectly happy with the current sleeping arrangements – she slept in his bed, he slept in the spare room, and so matters remained.

It was not as straightforward as that, however, for she was not averse to physical contact. She would take his hand or arm whenever they crossed a road, press herself against him if she was afraid, even hug him with a childlike spontaneity if something made her especially happy. But it was never the kind of touch that led to anything. She had no hang-ups about nakedness and that could be very disconcerting, given her sexual disinterest. It was a cultural thing, Simon told himself; she was, after all, literally from another world.

'How's this look so far?' he asked, holding up the sketch pad for her to see.

Troy Game was peeling an orange, her third that morning. She put it down and gave the portrait her full attention. 'That is much as I remember, Sai-mahn,' she said. She clenched her eyes shut in concentration then added, 'The eyebrows were slightly more prominent. And he had...' She opened her eyes, leant across the table and touched Simon's ear lobes with both hands. He felt a tingle of pleasure at the touch. 'He had these.'

'Ear lobes,' Simon said. Troy Game giggled girlishly and he asked, 'Don't you have a word for that?'

'Why should we?'

'Fair point.'

Simon added the ear lobes to the sketch. Troy Game nodded in approval. He gave the drawing a satisfied look and said to himself, 'I really should have done an art degree. I could have got a job doing photofits for the police.' To Troy Game he added, 'That might be significant. The ear lobes, I mean.'

'In what way?'

'Well, it suggests he's not originally from Caresh.'

Troy Game nodded, and began peeling her orange again. 'I understand it would be easy enough for him to cut his hair' – she said that with a shudder – 'whereas he would need surgery to remove his – those bits. But if he is one of your people, how do you explain the eyes?'

'There are ways,' Simon said, 'but I'm not suggesting he is from Earth.' He drew the pushed-back hood and began shading it. It looked wrong, so he erased it and began again. 'You don't have space flight at all on Caresh, and we no longer have it on Earth.

Not to speak of. It makes sense that he's from another world entirely. Neither Earth nor Caresh.'

'You are thinking he brought me here? Then where is he now?'

'I don't know. It's such a pity you can't remember his name. It would be so much easier if I could search for it on the Web. He brought you here, he must have. Maybe he crash-landed. That could account for your memory loss, you know, and it would mean he's still here.'

'So all you need to do is find out which spacecraft crash-landed near here in the last few weeks.' There was a twinkle in Troy Game's eyes as she said this.

Simon raised both hands in a gesture of surrender. 'I know, I know,' he said, nodding. 'I'm making one hell of a lot of assumptions, aren't I?'

Troy Game smiled. 'He does have *ear lobes*, remember.'

'Remind me to include "ear lobes" next time I do a Web search. You know, I never believed in flying saucers until I met you. Now I have to accept that at least one of them exists. The trouble is, there are too many people with the opposite problem. They want to believe so badly that they delude themselves into seeing something that isn't there. Consequently there are thousands upon thousands of reported sightings that are nothing more than lies or misidentifications. There's just no way of sorting the wheat from the chaff.'

Troy Game frowned at him, her brows furrowed. 'No way?' she asked. Simon got the feeling that she knew he was hiding something. He was quiet for a long while.

'I sort-of know someone who might be able to help,' he admitted at last. 'His name's Michael Sheridan. I've never actually met him, and I wasn't going to mention him but his name keeps coming up in the search results.'

Troy Game said nothing, but she did not take her eyes off him.

'Look,' Simon went on, 'he might be worth contacting but only if nothing else turns up – and I mean *nothing* else. Honestly, if I thought he was likely to do more good than harm I'd be onto him like a shot, but as it is I think he's best avoided. Really.'

Still the look. But then her expression changed. 'I remember something else from the dream,' she said. 'A marking or symbol. I saw it on a door.'

'Can you describe it to me?'

'Better than that.' She gave him a broad smile which showed her too-many teeth. 'I can draw it for you.'

She reached across the table and took the sketch pad and paper. She closed her eyes. In a corner next to the portrait – what Simon thought of as a photofit – she blindly drew the number '18'. She definitely drew it rather than wrote it; she drew the figures slowly and deliberately, and needlessly large.

She opened her eyes and looked at what she had produced. 'That was it!' she declared with evident delight.

'Eighteen,' said Simon, just a little annoyed that she had effectively defaced his photofit. 'Eighteen what? Eighteen light years? Eighteen potatoes? Eighteen Mornington Crescent?'

The smile faded. 'It seemed important, Sai-mahn.'

Simon looked at the clock, then at Troy Game's face. He had explained digits to her; he thought she understood them. But she evidently had trouble remembering them and besides, if her number system wasn't base ten she'd have no way of knowing what digits meant in combination. 'OK,' he said gently. 'Let's give it some thought and we'll talk about it tonight, see if we can come up with any ideas as to what it might mean. Right now I've really got to get to work. I'm late enough as it is.'

He could pinpoint the exact moment when it had become real for him. It was a Monday morning, two days after she had moved in with him. He'd risen early so that he could surf the Internet before the lines were busy. He did searches for every unfamiliar word Troy Game had used: the name of her planet, the name of its suns, the islands, her own name, people she had mentioned. He tried a variety of spellings to allow for dialect: Caresh, Karesh, Cairsh, Quirsh and so on. But the searches yielded nothing relevant.

Next he tried one of the astronomy websites. From this he learnt that double stars were commonplace throughout the galaxy. He found a program called Solar System Simulator, written in C by an amateur astronomer. He downloaded it.

It was surprisingly easy to use. He took two sunlike stars and placed them three hundred million miles apart. He highlighted one and simultaneously increased its luminosity while reducing its mass. He named that one Beacon, the other Ember. The two suns took about two months to revolve around their common centre of mass. Simon adjusted the view to compensate for this motion so that they appeared fixed on the screen, with Beacon to the left and Ember to the right.

He added a blue dot and gave it a mass one and a half times that of the Earth. He called it Caresh. He placed it close to Beacon and speeded up time. Caresh moved around Beacon in a perfect circle. He increased its distance from Beacon. Caresh continued to orbit Beacon. He moved it still further out, and it began to circle Ember instead – now the nearer of the two suns. He moved the dot back towards Beacon.

After several attempts he achieved the effect he was looking for. Caresh circled Beacon; when it reached the midway point between the two suns it went into orbit around Ember. It approached the midway point again and continued its orbit around Ember, but next time it reached the midway point it went back to circling Beacon. The pattern was apparently random: Beacon, Ember, Beacon, Beacon, Beacon, Ember, Ember, Beacon, Ember, Ember, Ember, Beacon, Ember… He speeded up time again. Caresh continued to switch from one sun to the other. On average there were as many warm years as cold years, but that still allowed for considerable variation. Too many warm years did not pose too much of a problem; apparently the planet had natural mechanisms which reflected excess heat away. A succession of cold years was another matter, however. Vegetation might darken to absorb heat, but if it wasn't getting the heat in the first place…

Troy Game had entered the room. He could hear her bare feet

on the parquet floor. Without turning he said, 'Your planet has a chaotic orbit. That would account for your ice ages.'

She stood behind him, leaning against the back of his chair. Simon could feel her breath against his face. It would have been so easy to turn and kiss her.

'We know it is Caresh that moves, not the suns,' Troy Game said. 'But we tend to think of it in terms of which sun is dominant.'

'It's all true then,' Simon said. It had not occurred to him before. 'You really are from another planet.'

He'd imagined situations like this many times but had never expected it to happen to him. Science fiction was fiction, after all, and anyone who felt they had to believe what they were reading had missed the point. But now it was really happening. It was happening to *him*.

He stood up and turned and took Troy Game in his arms. It was not until he had turned that he realised she was completely naked. He hugged her anyway and she hugged him back, seemingly unwilling to let him go. Her skin was very pleasant to the touch. Her bristly hair tickled the side of his face. He moved his mouth towards hers.

Her eyes widened in fear. 'Look!' she cried, breaking away from him.

On the computer screen Caresh had gone into a fixed orbit around Ember. A permanent ice age.

'It's… it's not real,' Simon explained desperately. 'It's just a limitation of the software, the way C handles integers. You've got to believe me… that's not an indication of the fate of the real Caresh.'

But the spell was broken. He wanted to reach for her, take her in his arms once more, feel her body against his. But he knew it was not going to happen.

There was an old record player in Sai-mahn's flat. Troy Game preferred it to the CD player. She liked the look and feel of the black vinyl discs, and the way you could touch the turntable to slow it down while the records were playing so that the music slowed and the voices became deeper. Certainly there wasn't any other reason to play them. Troy Game found it remarkable that a society that held music in such high regard could be so hopelessly incapable of producing any works worthy of the name. That was perhaps something of a generalisation – Sai-mahn had introduced her to the works of a composer called Bach who showed some promise – but for the most part the music of Earth could be fairly summed up in one word: cacophonous.

Nevertheless, for one studying the culture, there were interesting aspects to it. For instance, whereas the vocal range of individual singers tended to be very limited the difference between the sexes was shown, once again, to be pronounced. For the most part there was no mistaking the gender of a singer, not even when a man sang in a high voice or a woman sang in a low voice.

Earth lacked music but it had one thing Caresh did not have: television! Troy Game found it endlessly fascinating. It was like having a hundred theatres performing continuously, and you were allowed to switch between them as and when you wished without being glared at by the actors. True, it was often difficult to work out what was going on – Careshi language-telepathy did not work with recorded speech, for there was no mind to read – but that, if anything, was part of the fascination. There were the adverts that came on so often that she had taken to imitating some of the catchphrases, not understanding what they meant unless Sai-mahn explained them to her. He also had to explain the bizarre practice whereby huge gatherings of people simultaneously began hitting their hands together – that indicated 'approval', apparently. Then there were the shows which featured fat people who shouted and sometimes fought, but the fights were too ineffectual to be taken seriously.

The real violence occurred on the news programmes. They could be recognised by the earnest style of presentation. Troy Game found them so frightening that Sai-mahn had to explain to her that the incidents were not happening locally; eventually he had shown her their relative positions on a globe. That was the first time she fully appreciated that Earth was a world in its own right, comparable in scale to Caresh itself.

One of the things Troy Game was puzzled by was the number of pregnancies on television dramas. She had even come to recognise the English word for the condition. But Sai-mahn was at a loss when she asked him what she thought was a perfectly straightforward question: when is fertile time on Earth? Clearly it couldn't be when Earth was between suns, because it only had one sun – the seasons were due to the planet's axial tilt rather than its distance from the sources of heat. But Sai-mahn didn't seem to understand the question. He talked about cycles, hormones, even something called the rhythm method. Troy Game was left with the impression that it was something immensely complicated that had to be calculated for each individual. Which was possibly true. It reminded her not to make too many assumptions, and to resist being lulled into thinking Earth and Caresh were more alike than was in fact the case.

Sai-mahn had named his flat Cloud Base. Technically it could be described as a penthouse, but such a description would be misleadingly grand. Rather, it was a half-storey that occupied part of the roof above a shop, with glass doors opening onto a patio that occupied the rest of the roof. Troy Game liked the patio. It allowed her to enjoy the sun while making a minimal concession to the peculiar local clothing conventions. She liked the potted plants, at least the ones which had survived the heatwave and Sai-mahn's neglect; she had even managed to bring some back from the brink by the simple expedient of watering them. She also liked looking over the barrier at the main street three storeys below, where people went about their business – shopping, for the most part – unaware of her watching them.

Today, she decided, she would go shopping too.

She put on appropriate clothes and a pair of sunglasses. After checking she had her key and some money, she stepped into the lift that was shared between Cloud Base and the electrical shop on the ground floor. She went out of the door onto the side road that led to South Street. She felt rather pleased about this; two weeks on Earth and she was already passing herself off as a native.

Someone was covering for Simon Haldane. Someone had risked disciplinary action, possibly even dismissal, by clocking on for him. It was a heart-stopping realisation, and Simon did not know whether to be alarmed or relieved. He had done it for other people in the past but nobody had ever done it for him. It had never been necessary.

Simon did shift work: four twelve-hour days daytime, four days off, four twelve-hour days night-time, four days off. The hours were unsociable, but the pay was good. It was hard work, but he was up to it. At least he normally was.

They knew about Troy Game at work. He had not planned on telling anyone, but someone had seen them together in the pizza restaurant on the night they met. The news had spread throughout the factory. He now had to endure an endless barrage of innuendo and ribbing, most of which was good-natured, but nevertheless it irked him because it was so wide off the mark. What really galled him was that Amelia Stewart, the leggy blonde from Accounts, had started giving him the come-on. She had shown absolutely no interest in him when she thought he was available; he had no doubt that she would lose interest just as quickly if and when Troy Game disappeared from his life.

Now that was something he was going to have to consider, seriously and soon.

It seemed to him that there were two real possibilities. Either he would find some way of getting her home or he would not. If he somehow succeeded, she would be out of his life, out of his *solar system*. If he failed... Well, what reason would she have for staying with him then? He had no doubt that she liked him, and that she was grateful to him for taking her in when she had been on the point of despair, but that was not a basis for spending the rest of her life with him. There was also the small matter of the authorities. Did she count as an illegal immigrant? Could she apply for citizenship?

At least repatriation was not a realistic option.

Simon spent the morning on the production line known as J4. Pots of custard came through on the conveyor belt; he had to put the chocolate-chip cookie into each pot before the chocolate mousse and cream were added. It was demanding, but it was also mechanical, repetitive work; it had already been automated on some of the newer machines. He could almost do it in his sleep.

Almost.

There was, of course, a third possible outcome. It was such a seductive possibility that Simon felt he should dismiss it as fantasy. But it kept coming back to him as he worked. Assuming for the moment that he *did* somehow find a way of helping Troy Game return to her home, what if she then asked him to go with her? He had nothing to keep him here after all. The culture would be different, of course. He would put on weight – gravity, that little detail so often neglected in science fiction stories, would change him from a nine-stone weakling (in appearance if not in fact) to one of a more respectable twelve stones. His diet would be mostly fish. He would need to get his hair cut regularly, perhaps have his ear lobes surgically removed. The cold would be a problem, of course, but there was no reason why he shouldn't adapt to that too…

The machine stopped. It was not his fault – one of the new starters had failed to ensure that the custard reservoir was being replenished. He clicked his teeth together three times in impatience – a habit he realised he had picked up from Troy Game. Eventually the machine was restarted.

He had to pursue every possibility, however remote. It was unfair on Troy Game not to.

Two years ago a colleague had offered him a stack of *Open Minds* magazines. They had belonged to her seventeen-year-old son who had just died in a motorcycle accident. Simon had accepted the magazines with good grace; he even found time to read some of the articles. They were the usual nonsense: UFO sightings, miracle cures, hauntings, conspiracy theories and so on. Some of the alleged sightings had occurred in and around the Chichester area, and Simon noticed that these were generally covered by Michael Sheridan.

One wet Wednesday afternoon Simon had written a very polite e-mail to Sheridan commenting on his articles. He pointed out five basic scientific errors, four misattributed quotations and seven instances of specious reasoning. Sheridan had sent back an equally polite reply a few days later, thanking Simon for his interest but arguing that the supposed errors were probably due to differences in perception, and that in any case strict accuracy was less important than raising awareness of the issues in question, as he was sure Simon would agree. Simon emphatically did not agree, and his next e-mail was a little less polite than before; Sheridan's reply to *that* was even less polite, and so it had gone on until the exchange had become abusive and Simon closed the correspondence.

Re-establishing contact with Sheridan – and asking him for help – was not an attractive proposition. The chances of him knowing anything useful were remote and in any case, if his track record as a journalist was anything to go by, he was hardly reliable. But at least he was active in the field.

There were other considerations. Troy Game was a real alien. Introducing her to Sheridan would be like handing over the Holy Grail.

What if Sheridan fancied Troy Game? What if she fancied *him*?

The machine stopped again and this time it *was* Simon's fault. It was his responsibility to maintain a steady supply of chocolate-chip cookies. It seemed pretty trivial in comparison with the survival of an alien civilisation on the brink of an ice age, but it was here and now, and it was his problem. He resolved to keep his mind on the task at hand; all matters relating to Caresh would have to wait till the morning break.

This was undoubtedly easier said than done.

The morning break came. Come what may, Simon would call Michael Sheridan. But before he could get to the phone he was stopped by his line manager.

'Simon, I'd like to have a word with you. Do you mind?'

His heart sank. So this was it. His poor performance and lack of punctuality had been noted. This would be his first verbal warning, the first blemish on his record. 'Sure,' he said, trying to sound offhand about it.

The line manager took him aside so that none of Simon's colleagues would hear the conversation. 'You know it's Philip Morcroft's last day today, don't you?'

'Er, yes I did.'

'Now I know you don't tend to socialise with your colleagues outside work, but Philip Morcroft has been here a long time, and you may remember he was very supportive to you when you first started. Some of the team are having a farewell drink with him in the Globe this evening. It would mean a lot to him if you could join them.'

Simon gaped back at him, overcome by this unexpected reprieve. 'Yes, that would be fine,' he said. 'I mean, I'd like that very much.'

The line manager grinned. 'You're sure your good lady will let you out?' He laughed aloud and patted Simon on the shoulder before walking off. Simon gathered his wits and went to make his phone call.

It was a Saturday morning, and Michael Sheridan was pushing a trolley around a supermarket when his mobile rang.

'Michael Sheridan?' said the caller uncertainly.

'That's me.'

'This is Simon Haldane. I don't know if you remember me. We, er, corresponded a couple of years ago.'

'Si-mon! Of course I remember you. You're the brainy one. You live in Chichester, right?'

'That's right.'

'Pity you're so entrenched in the sceptics' camp – we could do with people like you. There's some seriously weird stuff going on in your area, you know that? I was over your way a couple of weeks back, investigating a bona fide case of human petrification. Anyway, I'm forgetting my manners. What can I do for you?'

There was a very long silence. Sheridan was about to ask Simon if he was still there when he finally replied. 'Two weeks ago, you say?'

'Yes, that's when I was down your way.'

'Let me get this straight. You were investigating this case of petrification two weeks ago? *Exactly* two weeks ago?'

Belatedly Sheridan noticed the urgency in Simon's voice, almost as if he believed him. This was not a normal reaction from anyone outside his circle. 'Yes, I suppose it was. Am I to take it you know something?'

'Look, this is really important. What did the… victim look like? I mean, did he have short hair? How tall was he?'

'How tall?' Sheridan laughed. 'It's hard to say. He was lying down. They found him outside a hotel room.'

'A hotel room?' Simon sounded genuinely afraid. 'Look, was the hotel room number eighteen by any chance?'

Sheridan frowned. He had the disconcerting impression that he was about to deliver some appalling news. 'It was,' he said. 'Yes, I'm pretty sure it was.'

Time stood still; the end of the supermarket aisle seemed to recede to some distant place. The 'statue incident' was not general knowledge; the local paper had dismissed it as a practical joke and refused to cover it, and the *Open Minds* article had yet to see print. Truth to tell, the latest issue was well overdue. Yet Simon Haldane knew something…

Sheridan's investigation had ground to a halt shortly after he realised he'd been duped by the student. Now he was being handed a fresh lead. How lucky was that?

'Listen Simon,' he said. 'We have got to talk.'

* * *

The streets no longer seemed alien. Even the *people*, with their absurdly long hair, no longer made her feel uneasy. The traffic could still be a problem – her underdeveloped spatial sense would never allow her to judge speeds accurately and there were few pedestrian crossings – but when there were no vehicles in sight she could cross roads safely.

She found a light blue summer dress she liked in a shop on North Street. While she was trying it on she sensed the concerns of a woman in the adjacent changing room. The woman was afraid someone would see her over the top of the door. Troy Game stifled laughter; as if anyone *cared*! But the nakedness taboo was taken very seriously, and she had to play along if she was to fit in. The trouble was it was so arbitrary, and so confusing! Indoors at Cloud Base it didn't seem to apply at all, but on the patio Sai-mahn had insisted she at least wear a two-piece thing he called a bikini. He had bought it for her and she could sense that he had been embarrassed buying it. It had not been her size and she had had to make some adjustments just to get it to stay on. It was not acceptable wear in the street, and it was sometimes optional on a beach depending on some sort of prevailing consensus.

Where was the logic?

The summer dress cost £18.00. Now that the double symbol '18' had been explained to her she was seeing it everywhere. It was a number, just like any other. It so happened that those particular symbols were easier to remember than the others. Apart from '7' – that was an easy one too.

Troy Game joined the queue to pay for the dress. While she was searching through her purse for a pair of orange notes a yellow-and-black insect flew into the shop. Its buzzing alerted her; she looked up and saw that it was harassing the customer at the front of the queue. The woman's hands were occupied with her purchase and she tried to repel the creature with wholly ineffectual movements of her elbows. Troy Game could feel the woman's discomfort, and then her fear. It was a quiet fear, but a deep one, wholly out of proportion to the harm the creature could do; its sting was unpleasant, but very rarely fatal.

She remembered that fear. She was sure she had felt it herself, recently. The creature – a *wasp*, that was what Sai-mahn had called it – was flying towards her face. It had a face too. She imagined it much larger, its body more elongated, its broad crystalline wings refracting the light from Beacon and Ember in a myriad of fluttering rainbows...

She was overwhelmed by panic. Her legs buckled under her and she found herself gasping for breath in the suddenly too thin atmosphere. For one terrifying moment the mindvoices around her fell silent. People were staring at her and she had absolutely no sense of what they were thinking!

A shop assistant – a woman with pieces of metal in her ear lobes – was helping her up and into a chair. She had a concerned expression on her face but just then the mindvoices returned and Troy Game sensed her thoughts. They were impatient and critical and Troy Game instantly disliked her. Whatever the reason for the panic, it was gone as quickly as it had arrived. Without another word Troy Game rose from the chair, dropped the dress and walked out into the sunlight.

For one tantalising moment she had *remembered*. When the mindvoices went quiet everything had come back to her. But it was big and it was overwhelming and there was much she had not understood even at the time. Now it was gone again. But she remembered remembering.

She hurried back to the flat. If she was going to recover any of it she would have to follow her instincts and act quickly. Inside the flat she switched on the computer and started the astronomy program. Sai-mahn had shown her how to do this, but even so it was all she could do to remember which icons to click on and how to respond to prompts written in a language she could not read.

It took several attempts but she eventually had the little model of the Careshi system up and running. After maybe fifty warm years, and as many cold years, the little planet settled into a stable orbit around Ember, just as it had done when Sai-mahn had first shown it to her. That had given her quite a turn, she recalled. Even stranger was Sai-mahn's reaction when she had pointed it out to him; she sensed anger, disappointment and sorrow in him. Perhaps he thought she was criticising him, and was taking it badly. But he did not say anything, and she thought it wise not to refer to it again.

Viewed sideways on, the path described by Caresh resembled a figure 8. Troy Game wondered if that had anything to do with the symbol in her dream. But if so, what was the significance of the '1'? Why not just '8' rather than '18'?

She racked her brains, sure the answer was there if only she knew where to look. She had to find the answer because the real Caresh was in danger. Not from entering a permanent orbit around Ember, perhaps; Sai-mahn had explained to her that if something like that could ever happen it would have done so by now. On the other hand, the orbit didn't have to be permanent. Just prolonged.

Not entirely convinced that she was on the right track, she ran the simulation over and over again, searching for the clue that would make sense of the other clues.

She did not find it. Instead she remembered the name of the man in the dream.

Simon was finding it extremely hard to concentrate on his work, and it was starting to show. But who could blame him? How many of his co-workers knew what it was like to be harbouring an alien?

This really wasn't like the *Creation's Echo* trilogy – it was not a book he could simply close. (How long ago that seemed now! He had not found the time to buy *The Cartographer's Song*, let alone read it.) Some time tonight he would have to go home to… to what? Had Troy Game really turned a man to stone? Even assuming Michael Sheridan's account was exaggerated to the point of being fanciful (and Simon was less inclined to be dismissive these days) it did sound as if a murder was involved.

What did he really know about Troy Game? The answer to that was simple: he knew as much as she wanted him to know. Clearly she had telepathic powers of some kind, otherwise she would be unable to speak to him in English or understand what he was saying to her. But what else did she pick up? And how much of her personality was real, how much a mere reflection of his expectations?

No, he told himself, Troy Game could be taken pretty much at face value. That was an assumption he would have to work to, and on balance it seemed like a safe one. No dog had ever explained that wagging its tail meant it was happy; some things you could simply *tell*.

Simon was quite pleased with his reasoning. The problem was, that wasn't the end of it. For even if Troy Game was not responsible for the corpse-statue, she was almost certainly linked to the event. Sheridan had only told him a few of the details of his investigation over the phone, but it seemed highly probable that both Troy Game and the man from her dream had been in the hotel on that Saturday morning two weeks ago.

What if the… monster that turned people to stone was looking for him and Troy Game? Would Cloud Base offer any protection? Could the creature climb walls or slither up the lift shaft? Could the police help? 'Excuse me officer, my alien girlfriend is being stalked by a monster from Greek mythology.'

Somehow he got through the rest of the day.

After work they gathered in the Globe. They gave Philip Morcroft a leaving present everyone had contributed to. He in his turn bought a round of drinks for all of them.

Simon had asked for a lager. He was given a pint of Grolsch and had drunk half of it without realising what he was doing. He rarely drank alcohol, but these were unusual circumstances.

'I've just got to make a phone call,' he said, getting up suddenly.

One of his workmates said, 'Use mine,' and handed him a mobile. 'Letting your good lady know where you are?'

'Yeah. Cheers.'

He moved off into a relatively secluded corner and rang his own number. He clicked his teeth together three times as he waited for Troy Game to answer. Eventually she did.

He spoke slowly and precisely, aware that he would probably sound condescending to anyone overhearing him. 'Troy Game, it is me, Simon. Can you understand me?'

'Sai-mahn!' She sounded excited. 'Il athran muolas pasha! Athran ushanti logosa baltusan!'

'Oh God,' said Simon. He had been afraid that this might happen. Clicking his teeth, he went on, 'Look, er, this is difficult. Your language-telepathy – its range is more limited than I thought.'

'Erris athran Roche! Dassar synapa logosa erum yast!'

'I'm sorry, Troy Game. I can't understand what you're saying. Look, I'll try not to be too late and I'll… I'll talk to you when I get back.'

Simon broke the connection. There was no point in explaining, no point in saying anything else. And no point in listening. Suddenly it was just… heartbreaking. They had been together for two weeks, and now they could not communicate at all.

'Perhaps I should go back to the flat,' he mused. He looked around the pub. Nearly everybody was a colleague. He had held onto his position by being competent; now that he had let that lapse he was going to have to fit in somehow, to socialise. He dismissed the thought of leaving. 'I can't, not this early.' He put on a smile, and handed back the phone.

'You get through to the *Enterprise*?' someone said. There was laughter, and it was directed at him, but it was good-natured. They *so* didn't understand that *Star Trek* was not where it was at. He downed his Grolsch, saluted and in a mock-military voice said, 'All systems normal'. More good-natured laughter. Someone bought him another drink.

'So what's she like?' the someone asked him. 'Is she a Klingon?'

He shook his head and sipped his drink. It was not a Grolsch this time, but a short which tasted like liquorice. He liked it. 'Place of origin: Dassar Island on the planet Caresh. Distinguishing features: no ear lobes. Hardly any whites to the eyes. Hair never grows longer than three millimetres. Special abilities: can hang from a pole by her toes, and hold her breath while swimming under water for up to eight minutes.' What was he saying? Had he really got this drunk this quickly?

It hardly mattered. He was not the centre of attention any more; he never was for long. Someone warned him to be sure she didn't implant any eggs in him, but most had tired of the subject already. Soon he was aware that only one person was listening to what he was saying.

Amelia Stewart. The leggy blonde from Accounts.

'So what's she like, then, this Troy Game? Is she any good in bed?'

He did not remember mentioning her name. 'It's not like that,' he said, shaking his head. 'She… she doesn't do sex. Not with me. I don't think it's even crossed her mind. You know, I really don't know why I'm telling you this.'

'Don't you think it's time you started asserting yourself? You're not a child, you've got your own flat, your own car. You should be asking yourself what you want, not letting people dictate to you.'

He shook his head, his thoughts nowhere near as fuddled as they had been a moment before. 'Perhaps I should begin with people like you,' he told her.

'You're saying what you're thinking.' She nodded approvingly. 'That's good. I like that.'

He imagined a menu of appropriate responses, like in *The Terminator*. 'Perhaps I don't care whether you like it or not.' 'Perhaps you should mind your own business.' 'Perhaps…' No, there were too many 'perhapses', and they sounded passive. Besides, he wasn't so sure he needed to be confrontational after all. In her own brash manner she was trying to be friendly. So he offered to buy her a drink. She accepted. He went to the bar. It took him a long time to get served. When eventually he was served, Amelia had joined him at the bar. He was back on the Grolsch because he didn't know what the drink with the liquorice taste was called. He had bought her a rum and coke. She downed it in the time it took him to drink half his Grolsch. She put her empty glass on the bar. She took his half-full glass from him and put it down on the bar next to her own glass. She took him by the hand and led him into the secluded corner where he had made his phone call earlier. She was taller than him. She put her hands behind his head and drew him towards her and started kissing him. He put his arms around her and returned the kiss. Her clothes were stiff, her skin was smooth, her mouth tasted of rum. It occurred to him that she was more drunk than he was. Maybe she always behaved like this and he had missed out because he never went to the pub after work. At least he had the excuse that he was in fear of his life. If only he hadn't made that call to Michael Sheridan!

'I have a boyfriend,' Amelia confessed when they stopped to breathe.

'I don't doubt it.'

'He doesn't own me, though.' They kissed again.

Back at Cloud Base Troy Game would be on her own, countless light years from home and in danger from a creature that turned flesh to stone. What could she do? She could call the police. He had taught her which button on the phone she should press three times in an emergency; it did not matter that the operator would not understand her because they could trace the calls these days. When the police arrived she would be able to make herself understood. There was nothing he could do for her that a policeman could not do at least as well.

No, that was not true. He could *be* with her.

Reluctantly he disengaged himself from Amelia. 'I'm sorry,' he said, 'but I have to go.'

She lowered her eyes. 'You love her very much, don't you?'

He thought this over. 'Perhaps I do,' he said at length. 'Perhaps I do.'

It was still light when he got back home. He fumbled with the door key and eventually got into the lobby. He pressed the button to call the lift.

Nothing had really changed, he reflected. The only difference was that he now *knew* something strange had happened at a hotel in Bognor Regis. There was circumstantial evidence to suggest it might have some bearing on Troy Game, but that was all. The creature, if that was what it was, had had two weeks to track down its prey, if that was what it intended.

The lift arrived. He pulled open the outer door, slid back the lattice gate. It was dark inside; the bulb had gone and nobody had replaced it. He staggered in, closed the doors and felt for the button for the top floor.

He did not *feel* as if Troy Game was dead. Whatever happened tonight, he did not envisage finding her petrified body lying on the floor of the flat. That did not mean it would not happen, but…

The lift stopped. He stepped out into the hall of Cloud Base. There was no sign of any disturbance, nothing was out of place. And yet…

I think she's in terrible danger.

He could hear her. She was in the bathroom, in the shower. She was singing a song from her homeworld. She had by far and away the most beautiful singing voice he had ever heard. It had occurred to him many times that she could make a career as a singer. It might yet come to that.

He leant against the wall waiting for the shower to stop. When it did he called to her to say he was home.

'Sai-mahn!' she called back. There was excitement in her voice, just as there had been on the phone. He could hear her padding across the bathroom floor. The door opened. She stood there, naked and dripping, looking at him with those big, adoring eyes. 'I remember!' she said. 'I know who it was who brought me here. I need your help, Sai-mahn. My world is in danger and we must find him.'

Simon heard her say, 'I need you.'

It's time you started asserting yourself, Amelia had told him.

So he did.

Chapter Five
Going Ballistic

The Doctor brought his fist down on the console panel. 'Of all the inefficient, counterintuitive, inflexible *rubbish*…'

'Cup of tea?' asked Jo sweetly as she carried a silver tray into the control room. She set it down on an upturned packing case that the Doctor had 'borrowed' from one of the storerooms back at UNIT HQ and was now using as a table.

'Not now, Jo,' said the Doctor absently. He removed Solenti's device from the slot in the console panel, turned it over, examined it, pressed and held a little red button on the back, released it, then slid the device back into the slot. 'I just had one.'

'Doctor, that was ten hours ago.'

'Quite.' He pressed a button on the console panel. The little screen on the device lit up and a somewhat larger screen on the console panel did the same. Each displayed a schematic: a representation showing the device and the six-sided console with a thick line connecting the two. The Doctor pressed another button. The thick line pulsed and a horizontal bar graph at the bottom of each screen slowly progressed from zero to 99 per cent. Then it stopped. The Doctor stared at it as if he could force it to finish its task by sheer effort of will. 'Really Jo,' he said without turning, 'welcome as your ministrations are…' Then he did turn, his eyes wide with disbelief. 'Ten hours?'

Jo nodded. 'I know you Time Lords don't need as much sleep as us mere mortals, but you should at least take a break.'

She had hung around for the first hour or so, but it soon became clear that there was nothing she could do to help. She didn't want to go outside in case the Doctor accidentally dematerialised the

TARDIS without her; besides, the Doctor didn't want her to run the risk of encountering Solenti. There was after all a real possibility that the Time Lady would pop back to Dagusa just so that her guide dog could get Jo's scent.

'Would that really put you at such a disadvantage?' Jo had asked.

'She's a very capable manipulator. Let's just say the less she knows about who *I* know, the happier I will be.'

'Is everyone from your planet so... so *devious*?'

The Doctor's eyes had sparkled then. 'It would be a very dull world if everyone was as guileless as me, wouldn't it?'

Jo had laughed at that, then told him to give her a call if he made any progress, or if anything came up that she could help with. But it didn't happen. She was only mildly surprised to find him still at the task several hours later. His single-mindedness was legendary.

'You can control the TARDIS yourself now,' Jo said as they sat on two smaller packing cases drinking tea. 'Why don't you just set a direct course for Israel instead of wasting time with that thing?'

'I must admit it is tempting,' the Doctor said. 'But the margin of error is critical, and I can't be sure I can work to the same sort of accuracy. Not yet. The tracking device gives us a clear two days before our original selves turn up; running into *us* is the last thing I want.'

Jo frowned. 'But we met ourselves once before. *Twice* before, in fact. That didn't have any repercussions. Did it?'

'To be perfectly honest with you Jo, that was probably more due to luck than judgement.' He finished his tea then sprang to his feet. 'There's only one thing for it,' he declared. 'I'm going to have to take the navigation system off-line.'

Jo looked at him in surprise. 'But you've only just finished calibrating it.'

'With a bit of luck it will stay calibrated. Unfortunately I've no choice.' He moved a set of three console levers to their off position, inserted the device into its slot for the final time and flipped a switch on the panel beside it. The now-familiar schematic reappeared on the two screens. 'You see, Solenti's device is a cut-down navigation system in its own right, capable of directing the TARDIS to its destination. What it's *not* capable of doing is synchronising with the Earth's speed of rotation, or making sure we're the right way up when we arrive. In theory it's supposed to work in harmony with the TARDIS's own navigation system. In practice the wretched thing has more unnecessary features than the old girl can cope with – and you can't switch them off individually.'

'Let me get this straight. If you disconnect your own navigation system Solenti's device will get us to Israel, but the landing might be a bit... bumpy?'

'Not necessarily, Jo. We can calculate the Earth's speed of rotation at Masada's latitude easily enough – then it's just a matter of programming the device to move the TARDIS due east at the same speed when we begin to materialise.'

'But without its navigation system, how will the TARDIS know which way is east?'

'She has a built-in magnetic compass. It's simple and reliable, and it works even if she materialises on her side or upside down. And that, unfortunately, is a distinct possibility right now.' Oblivious to Jo's alarmed expression, he abruptly declared, 'Still, that can't be helped.'

The twilit Dagusan ruins echoed the moans of a gigantic living engine. A startled squirrel-like creature perched on the ivy-covered gate fled as the nearby blue box faded out of existence.

Inside the TARDIS, the Doctor nodded in satisfaction. 'We're on our way,' he said. 'For once I'm not so much concerned about *where* we arrive as *how* we arrive.'

'Don't you have any safety belts in the TARDIS?' asked Jo, only half jokingly, but the Doctor did not seem to hear. Given the unusual circumstances she reviewed her surroundings with a renewed curiosity tinged with apprehension; she had never *quite* gotten used to the TARDIS, had never quite decided how she regarded it.

Take the control room, for instance, the place where it all happened. It was white, polygonal and *large* – about the size of the dining room in a medium-sized restaurant. There were sunken circles in the walls, arranged in honeycomb-fashion, inordinately large double doors that led outside and a single door that led deeper into the Ship's interior. Then there was the imposing six-sided console in the centre of the room, with its ergonomically sloping panels and central glass column, the movements of which indicated take-off, flight and landing.

This was the first room you entered when you came in through the police-box doors. It was the room that made you realise at once that the TARDIS was bigger inside than out. Jo wondered if it had to be that way. Couldn't the first room be a police-box-sized anteroom, with a disguised door on the far side that gave access to the control room? No doubt the Time Lords could work out such an arrangement, but would they necessarily want to? Besides, it wouldn't be much use if the Doctor ever got his chameleon circuit working again and the exterior changed to something more appropriate than a police box.

Jo sometimes thought of the control room as the gondola of a very large airship, but more often she didn't think of the TARDIS as a vehicle at all. The occasional difficult take-off and rough landing notwithstanding, she was more inclined to think of it as a futuristic castle with a magic gateway that opened onto different lands, some in the past, some in the future and some on other planets. Sometimes it landed in UNIT HQ, often when she least expected to see home again; once it landed on a planet covered entirely by an ocean that was nowhere more than knee-deep; on another occasion it materialised inside a small cave, blocking off the exit so they had no choice but to depart without ever seeing what the world outside looked like. This had frustrated the Doctor no end.

'We're coming in to land,' the Doctor announced. He switched on the scanner, the wall-mounted monitor that showed what was going on outside. At that moment it showed nothing but the swirl of the vortex, but the glass column in the console was beginning to rise and fall in a determined manner. It was an unusually short journey, Jo thought. Evidently Solenti's device was intent on taking the TARDIS directly to its destination; not like the TARDIS's own navigation system, which was more like a curious dog sniffing interesting bushes and lamp posts that lay along its route.

'Hold on tight,' instructed the Doctor. Jo gripped the sides of the console. The Doctor, she noted, was not obeying his own instruction. He watched the scanner intently, hands poised above the console in the manner of a concert pianist about to deliver the climactic crescendo. Jo assumed – hoped, rather – that he was preparing himself to operate the controls to right the Ship, should that become necessary.

The TARDIS began its familiar landing noise, something between the roar of an animal and the sound of a very large slab being dragged over concrete. An image began to appear on the scanner.

It was a tree. The tree was upright. That was encouraging; it suggested the TARDIS was upright too.

What was mildly puzzling was that the tree did not look at all like the sort of tree one might expect to find near the shores of the Dead Sea. What was even more puzzling was that the tree appeared to be moving towards them. It was hard to say exactly how fast it was moving, but Jo thought it unreasonably fast. It whipped past them, so close that if the outside of the TARDIS had been as large as the control room they would have collided.

'Something is seriously wrong,' said the Doctor. His hands still hovered over the console, but the situation that had arisen was not the one he had been preparing himself for. Jo still gripped the sides of the console. She looked at the Doctor, then back at the scanner. 'Doctor, look!' she cried.

The view on the scanner was rushing forwards at the speed of an express train. There were more trees – even over the roar of the TARDIS's engine Jo could hear branches whipping and snapping against the police-box exterior. The Ship smashed through a wooden fence, its straight path following the country road beyond for about a hundred yards. A Land Rover appeared around a corner in the road; the driver swerved just in time to avoid them. The TARDIS smashed through another fence on the other side of the road where there were more trees.

'Good grief!' said the Doctor. His hands came down decisively on the scanner controls. He switched its view to look back the way they had come. They saw that the Land Rover had gone into a ditch, but then it was gone from view. There was a swathe of destruction behind them, a ragged, police-box-shaped tunnel through a forest. And then there was no tunnel; the TARDIS was seemingly passing through trunk and branch without doing any damage. The Doctor frowned in puzzlement, then noticed that the glass column was still rising and falling, the engines still roaring.

'Of course!' he said. 'The TARDIS is repeatedly going through a complete materialisation cycle as it tries to get some purchase on the ground. We're only substantial for half the cycle. Though quite why she's moving in the first place is another...'

'Doctor, can't you stop it?'

'I'm not sure how, Jo.'

'Well, wouldn't it be better if we could see where we're going rather than where we've been?'

The Doctor saw the wisdom in this and complied with Jo's suggestion. He was evidently at a loss; he was also more than a little angry. 'When I get my hands on Solenti, I'll...'

The TARDIS burst out of the forest and onto another road. This one ran due east for nearly two miles. They effortlessly over-took a motorcyclist who was going flat out – in the left lane, Jo noticed. Further up the road, half a dozen cars had to swerve to dodge the oncoming police box. Jo only just had time to hope that the motorcyclist had avoided these vehicles when they came to a bend in the road. The TARDIS smashed through a chevron sign and resumed its cross-country careering. A mile further on it passed through the back gardens of several houses, churning up flower beds and collecting half a dozen washing lines which it promptly discarded when it reached the dematerialisation part of its cycle and became intangible once more.

Jo stared at the scanner in morbid fascination while the Doctor tried everything he could think of to halt their incontinent progress. He was on the floor now, having opened an inspection hatch in the central pedestal that supported the console. 'Jo,' he called up, 'would you pass me the surge gauge.'

Jo selected the tool from a tray by touch alone and handed it to the Doctor, never taking her eyes off the scanner. The Doctor took it, made an adjustment and said, 'There, that should do it! Any change?'

'None at all,' said Jo bluntly. She was watching a pair of golfers running for their lives across a putting green. 'Doctor, I think we're in England. I saw a sign earlier that said Funtington, and I think I can see the spire of a cathedral.'

'Pass me the differential regulator,' said the Doctor crossly, adding, 'It hadn't completely escaped my attention that we have not landed in Israel.'

'I'm sorry Doctor,' said Jo, feeling for the differential regulator. They were approaching a built-up area; if the Doctor didn't hurry up things could get very serious very soon. 'It's just that, well, I thought with England being further north than Israel, and the TARDIS speed being set for Israel's latitude… Oh no. I do not believe it. This cannot be happening.'

Two men were carrying a large sheet of plate glass across a quiet road when they saw the TARDIS heading for them. Unable to decide between them whether to hurry forward or go back, they dithered in the middle of the road as the blue box hurtled towards the glass…

The Doctor was on his feet. 'Jo, why didn't you say this before?'

… and the blue box became transparent and insubstantial as it passed through the glass without doing any damage at all.

'I only just thought of it,' said Jo.

'No wonder none of my adjustments made any difference – the

85

TARDIS is taking its instructions directly from Solenti's device.' He looked at the scanner. They were in the built-up area now and were sweeping, ghostlike, through an unoccupied office block. Jo saw rows of desks and chairs and what appeared to be a television set on each of the desks, though it was hard to be sure as she was afforded the most fleeting of glimpses. They sped across a road in the direction of a stone wall. In a moment the TARDIS would be tangible again and would pass destructively through whatever was on the other side of the wall.

There was no time to calculate the Earth's rotational speed at this latitude. All the Doctor could do was whip Solenti's device from out of its slot and hope for the best…

The Northgate car park was less than a quarter full, it being quite early on a Sunday morning. There were only a few people about: a pair of stage-builders making their way to the adjoining Chichester Festival Theatre, a man checking the pay and display board to make sure they didn't charge for parking on a Sunday, a woman with a dog taking a short cut and a driver who was just leaving.

They were the only ones to see the solid blue box as it appeared to emerge from the stone wall on the west side of the car park. It hit the side of a parked Volvo, sending it spinning and smashing into two other cars, its alarm whining uselessly. It cut an estate car in two and demolished a sports car. It passed across several unoccupied spaces, felled a pay and display machine and stoved in the rears of three more cars. None of the collisions appeared to deflect it from its perfectly straight course. It continued across an open space, destroyed a Mini, then headed for a chain-link fence that separated the car park from some tennis courts. It hit the fence and stopped.

The witnesses looked on in amazement, except for the departing driver who departed with increased alacrity. The woman with the dog called the emergency services on her mobile phone; she was unsure which service to ask for, but supposed it was probably a police matter. The stage-builders and the man who had just parked viewed the damage with detached curiosity – after all, the incident (for want of a better word) had not harmed *their* vehicles.

By the time their attention turned to the strange blue box they had been joined by two other witnesses. Nobody had noticed their arrival, but then it was a big car park. The white-haired man was talking to his pretty female companion; in a voice loud enough to be overheard he told her it must have been a freak tornado which had swept up the box, he had seen something similar once in the Bahamas. Satisfied with the explanation, and satisfied that the box wasn't going to do anything else unexpected, the witnesses duly dispersed.

But all this happened a little later.

When the Doctor removed Solenti's device from the console the TARDIS's navigation system came back on-line. It matched speeds with the Earth's rotation almost as quickly as it did this – perhaps a little more quickly than its occupants would have preferred.

Jo picked herself off the floor, galvanised by the Doctor's sense of urgency: 'Come on Jo. We've done a considerable amount of damage. If we're seen emerging from the TARDIS we're going to be held responsible.'

He stepped over the broken crockery – the tea set had slipped off its packing-case table – and pulled the lever on the console that opened the main doors. The doors swung open inwards, revealing the chain-link fence stretched across the entrance. Undaunted – and apparently unsurprised – the Doctor thrust Solenti's device into one capacious pocket and pulled a pair of wire-cutters from another. He cut a slit in the fence and squeezed through, Jo following close behind. With some difficulty he managed to close and lock the door behind him. A short distance away an open gate gave them access back through the fence and into the car park where the onlookers were starting to gather.

* * *

'Well, at least we know where we are,' said the Doctor once they were alone again. 'That rather splendid building is the Chichester Festival Theatre. You know, I keep meaning to come here for the opening night of Peter Shaffer's *The Royal Hunt of the Sun* but I always seem to overshoot one way or another.'

'That's all very interesting, Doctor, but aren't we supposed to be in Israel?'

The Doctor rubbed his chin thoughtfully. He had a sheepish expression which changed rapidly as he remembered that on this one occasion the mislocation was not his fault. 'Quite,' he said. 'I'm not entirely sure that we're even in the right time zone. I wonder, could it be that the fracture has moved?'

Jo looked around the car park. The cars certainly appeared to be different from the ones she was accustomed to seeing in 1972. Vaguely futuristic, she supposed, with the letters and numbers of their registration plates in an unfamiliar order. The weather was hotter than she had ever known it, which was unexpected – wasn't Earth supposed to be entering a new ice age? Nevertheless, it seemed pretty likely that this was the future, and the near future at that. Possibly near enough that Jo could reasonably expect to live to see it in the ordinary way, assuming she eventually returned to her own time. Could it be that there was an older Jo Grant wandering about somewhere? Would she even be called Jo Grant, or had her name changed to something else – Jo Yates, perhaps? Would she even recognise herself if she bumped into her? The thought was intriguing. Maybe her future self remembered visiting Chichester and was hanging around in the hope that just such a meeting would occur, perhaps *had* occurred...

'What do we do now?' she asked.

'Well, we could go after Solenti and tell her her tracking device didn't work. Or we could try again.'

'Try again?' Jo looked uneasy. 'Let me get this straight – that would mean taking the TARDIS navigation system off-line again?'

'Precisely, Jo. I don't mind telling you, I don't like the idea any more than you do.'

'So what does that leave us?'

'Well, as we are here, I don't suppose it would do any harm if we had a quick look around, don't you think?'

'OK.'

As they talked they were making their way towards one of the car park's exits. This was partly the result of collective curiosity, partly a desire not to be in the vicinity if and when the authorities arrived to investigate the freak occurrences that had scarred the landscape in a perfectly straight, fifteen-mile-long dashed line.

They left the car park and crossed a dual carriageway, arriving in the main part of Chichester. Chichester in the future, Jo reminded herself. There was nothing overwhelmingly futuristic about the place, but there were little details that drew her up short. The fashions, obviously; fashions went in cycles, but Jo's travels usually took her so far into the past or future that the differences were generally lost against the changed background. The cars, too; they didn't hover and, if anything, they were more *sensible* than ones from her own time. As she took in her surroundings Jo accidentally jostled a couple walking hand in hand; it was only after she had exchanged apologies with them that she realised they were both men.

'Doctor,' Jo asked in a hushed voice.'What year is this?'

The Doctor frowned. 'Jo, you may recall we had to leave the TARDIS rather hurriedly. I did not have time to check the yearometer.'

'But you do have the equipment that brought us here.'

Realising what Jo meant, the Doctor took the tracking device out of his pocket. He made some adjustments to it and read the display.'Ah yes. According to this we are a little more than halfway through the local year 1999.'

'1999,' Jo echoed, awed. 'What does "a little more than halfway" mean?'

'The second or third week of July I would think. Really, Jo, you can't expect the Time Lords to program in the English names of the months. It's very odd, though.'

'What is?'

'Well, I've been in 1999 before. I'm sure it wasn't as hot as this.'

'Perhaps you were in another part of the country,' Jo suggested.

'Perhaps.' The Doctor sounded doubtful. 'On the other hand, I suppose a time fracture could have an effect on the weather. You know, Jo, I think we're looking at this back to front.'

'How do you mean?'

'Well, according to Solenti, the time anomaly is supposed to have a duration of twenty-seven years, running between 1972 and 1999. Her device was supposed to deliver us to the location of the anomaly's beginning two days before it happened.'

'But it failed,' said Jo.

'I'm not altogether sure that it did.'

'But it must have done! The anomaly began in Israel in 1972.'

'That's what we've been assuming up till now. But supposing that was when it *ended*. Suppose it *began* in Chichester in 1999?'

Realisation dawned. 'You mean it's running *backwards*?'

'Precisely, Jo. A contratemporal fracture, brought about by an event which has not happened *yet*. It carries Roche's mental signature, which suggests it's the result of something he's destined to do.'

'Is that possible?'

'Not normally, no. But that's what makes it an anomaly. It would certainly explain why we didn't find anything before – if the starship crashed anywhere, it would have been near here rather than in Israel.' The Doctor made some further adjustments to the tracking device. 'Or will be here,' he added under his breath. Then something on the device's screen caught his eye. 'Now wait a minute. That's odd. That's very odd indeed.' He hit the side of the device with the palm of his hand and frowned, a look of disbelief on his face. 'Good grief!' he muttered. 'She really has landed us in it.'

'What do you mean?'

'Well, for a start it's come up with three traces instead of one.'

'Three?'

The Doctor nodded. 'There's a prominent white dot, and two much fainter green ones. I'm fairly certain the prominent one marks the centre of the fracture. I don't suppose the other two traces could be reflections – they're too far apart and they display different characteristics. So what on Earth are they?'

'They can't *all* be the source, can they?'

'Of course not,' the Doctor said. 'At least I don't think so. Well, the nearer of the two faint traces is precisely two point eight one yards away…'

Jo looked around in surprise. 'Where?'

'Dagusan yards,' the Doctor explained. 'Two point eight one Dagusan yards is roughly a mile in terrestrial units – a mile to the north, I think. The prominent trace is thirty-three point seven… No, wait, thirty-three point *eight* yards away. Now that's very strange. Very strange indeed.'

'Is it moving?'

'Of course it's not moving!' He frowned. 'No, that doesn't make sense. It can't be *moving*.' Then he exploded. 'Why does the wretched woman always do this? Why does she always insist on being so secretive! She must have known this was on the cards. She's all the worst qualities of the Time Lords embodied in one person.' He zoomed in so that only the main trace appeared on the display. Its motion was unmistakable. 'Thirty-three point *nine*? *Nine*? That's not even remotely…' A thought struck him. 'I wonder if there's a playback on this. Ah, here it is.' There were several minutes' worth of data stored in the device's memory. The Doctor rewound and watched the prominent trace move about in apparently random directions.

'It's moving,' he declared, as if he'd never been in any doubt about it.

'What about the other signals?' Jo asked. 'Are they moving too?'

'They don't appear to be at the moment. Let's have a look, shall we.' He zoomed out again and made some other adjustments. 'That's odd. They really are very elusive. They show up during a live scan but they don't show up on the playback at all. It's as if the device can't remember detecting them.' He frowned at the device some more. 'It could be vortex leakage, I suppose. But why? What would cause that?'

'Could one of them be Lord Roche and the other be his TARDIS?' Jo suggested brightly.

'It's possible,' the Doctor said doubtfully.

'You said "for a start".'

'Did I? Oh yes. That's the worst of it.' He gave her a grim smile. 'It would seem we have rather less than two days to locate the cause of the fracture.'

'How much less?'

'To be fair we can't really blame Solenti for *that*, tempting as it is – the tracking device wasn't designed to be used *within* the anomaly. It is a navigational hazard after all.'

'Doctor, how much time do we have?'

'Just a few hours, Jo. Just a few hours to track down the source of the time fracture. And two other widely separated source signals. The event that precipitates the temporal fracture will occur some time between three and four o'clock this afternoon.'

The hordes of the Leshe gradually dispersed. The two suns low on the horizon faded away and the single sun reappeared high in the sky. The icy plain became the hospital grounds once more.

He had tried to hypnotise an orderly. That was a bad mistake. He was insufficiently familiar with the human mind and he had failed; worse than that, he had exercised his mental activity beyond the safety threshold. Something became aware of him then, a creature far deadlier than the Leshe. It knew he was close at hand; it had almost picked out his mindscent from the background noise. He had been able to shut down his mind and withdraw into the past, but it had been a close thing and there was a limit to the number of times he could evade it that way.

The creature was learning.

Only a few hours to go. After that, he would be vulnerable. He had one other technique at his disposal, but it would be difficult and dangerous to use it and the collateral damage was likely to be high.

The ghosts from the future whispered, their faint, indistinct outlines now visible, their voices increasingly clear as their time drew near. He watched them and listened to their words without understanding, but his instinct told him there was information here that he would need later. If only he could think freely! But instinct was all he was allowed, for instinct did not show up against the background hum of the time fracture.

In a few hours there would be no more background hum to hide in. Mental silence would no longer protect him, and there would be no question of withdrawing into the past.

Through the barred window he could see the outline of two ghosts from the future walking in the hospital grounds. He recognised them both, for he had seen them already among the ghosts in his room, but the one with the fainter outline was the more familiar of the two.

There were two possible futures. In the first, the more established ghost would come alone, and in the second both ghosts would pay him a visit. Instinct told him that the ghost with the fainter outline was the important one. It was imperative, then, that the second future should come to pass.

Chapter Six
The Resentful Angel

The doorbell sounded in Cloud Base. It had been doing that for at least a quarter of an hour. Someone was pressing the bell push, waiting maybe half a minute, then pressing it again.

Simon Haldane lay on the hall floor outside the bathroom. There was a swelling under his right eye and one of his ribs was cracked. He stared into space, unable to will himself to move, and unwilling to think.

Last night.

He'd made mistakes before - everybody did - but the consequences were never as bad as he'd feared. Or sometimes things turned out for the best, like the time he'd lost his job only to find himself in a better one before he'd even spent his redundancy money. Or if things did go wrong it usually turned out it wasn't really his fault.

He could not blame anybody else for what had happened last night. Not even Amelia. Not for what he had tried to do. He had tried to... tried to...

He hadn't done it. She had fought him off easily. He had been drunk and he had misread the signs. If he had been sober he would not have behaved that way. If his line manager had not asked him to go to the pub after work he would have *been* sober.

Troy Game was gone. She had taken some clothes and she had fled. He supposed she had dressed in the lift on the way down. He had made her understand that nakedness was not acceptable in public; if only she had understood what effect it had on *him*.

It did not occur to him that Troy Game might not have taken her key with her, and that it might be her who was ringing the bell to be let back in. If it had occurred to him he would have dismissed the thought as being too unlikely to be worth considering. And in any case the bell had stopped ringing.

Michael Sheridan rang the doorbell one last time. He stepped backwards into the narrow side road and looked up at the window high above the door. There was no sign of any movement.

He had worked out that the door provided access to a lobby and a lift that was shared between Cloud Base and the shop. So it was possible to get to the lobby via the shop, but that meant going through the door marked 'Staff Only'. He didn't like going through doors marked 'Staff Only'; the staff didn't like it and it made him uncomfortable.

Simon had told him he was on a shift system, working from six till six on this particular Sunday. But Sheridan had phoned his place of work a short while ago. Simon was not at work and he had not phoned in sick.

Simon had also referred to a woman who was sharing the flat with him. Sheridan had hoped to interview her while Simon was at work. Of course, she could be the very reason why Simon was not at work right now, but it seemed unlikely. Sheridan had been ringing the bell for about twenty minutes; surely one of them would have come to the window to tell him to go away.

Uncomfortable or not, then, it was going to have to be the 'Staff Only' door.

But just as Sheridan was coming out of the side road and onto South Street, his mobile phone rang. For a moment he thought it might be Simon calling to tell him to stop ringing his doorbell. In fact, it was the editor of *Open Minds* magazine.

'Where are you right now?' the voice on the phone demanded.

'Chichester.'

'Excellent. Brilliant. Great. Super. You anywhere near somewhere called… er, Northgate?'

'Five, ten minutes' walk away. Why?'

'Smashing. I want you to get over there right now. Make sure you have your camera with you.'

'Er, OK. What exactly am I supposed to be looking for?'

'Something big. It's really, really fortunate that you happen to be on the spot. Something very strange is going on. Something fell out of the sky, did millions of pounds' worth of damage and left a huge crater in the middle of the car park. Roads closed for miles around.'

'I'm glad I parked in the Friary car park,' muttered Sheridan. 'What was it, a meteorite?'

'No.'

'Flying saucer?'

'No, not exactly.'

'What, then?'

The editor mumbled something and Sheridan had to ask him to repeat it, which he did.

'A Portaloo,' Sheridan echoed in a reasonable tone. 'OK. Was it dropped from a plane or something?'

'I don't think so. I heard it from someone in the Met Office whose cousin works as an emergency operator, which was an outstanding piece of luck. My guess is it was probably picked up by a freak tornado or something.'

'But this Portaloo hit with enough force to form a crater?'

'Apparently.'

'Was anyone *using* it at the time?'

The editor's eyes narrowed – that was obvious even over the phone. 'What do you mean?'

Remembering belatedly that the editor had lost his sense of humour during a bungled abduction attempt, Sheridan said, 'I mean, was someone storing plutonium in it or something?'

'Michael, it's an *investigation*. That means *finding out*.'

'OK, I'm on my way,' said Sheridan, an uncharacteristic note of scepticism in his voice.

I've been stupid, thought Troy Game bitterly. *The clues were there and I failed to see them!*

She had asked Sai-mahn when fertile time occurred on Earth. The reason he had not been able to answer her was because the concept simply did not apply. For his people, sex was not a seasonal thing at all. *That* was the reason why women could be in different stages of pregnancy at the same time. It was the reason why men looked at her the way they sometimes did. If fertile time had been closer she would have been able to recognise their emotions for what they were.

She should have guessed. There were many examples of it on Caresh – the wolves of Cram Island, for instance, and some of the hardier species of ruminant. But it wasn't something one associated with *people*, with *sentience*. She was stranded on a planet of animals!

No wonder they were incapable of creating music.

Sai-mahn had tried to have sex with her. She was so shocked and surprised when she realised what he was doing that she had forcibly rejected his advances, injuring him in the process. She had no idea what laws and taboos she had broken by doing that. Perhaps he would report her to the authorities. Maybe not out of spite, but out of duty – after all, as far as he was concerned, she might do it to someone else…

She had to get away from this place. Caresh was in great danger, and she was in danger if she stayed here. But how? She had spent the last two weeks trying to find some way of getting home, and that had been with Sai-mahn helping her. He had fed her, clothed her, sheltered her and surfed the Internet for her. Not only had she lost all that, she had also fled Cloud Base with very little money.

But she had something she didn't have before: a name.

She had a plan. She would find some way of getting money, and then she would go into a cybercafé and pay an animal – preferably a female animal – to search for the name.

She hoped she would be able to find a cybercafé that opened on a Sunday. If not, she would have to spend another night in the park and try again tomorrow. But she needed to get the money first, and she had an idea how she could do that.

* * *

Jo sat on a bench outside W.H. Smith, a map of Chichester spread out on her lap, a protractor, ruler and pencil in her hands. The Doctor had given her the distance and bearing of the nearer of the fainter traces – thankfully translated into familiar units – before going off after the bright trace himself.

He had not been at all happy with her idea of splitting up. 'Have you any idea of the potential dangers of a time fracture?' he had asked her. But before he could begin reciting them, Jo had smiled sweetly and tapped her watch. There wasn't time to argue.

As she was drawing a line from her present location to that of the trace she was distracted by a sudden burst of electronic music. A slim, bearded man in jeans and a yellow T-shirt was coming out of Smith's holding a newspaper in one hand and a tiny black box, roughly the size of Solenti's tracking device, in the other. The newspaper was the *Independent on Sunday*, Jo noted; it was unfamiliar to her, so presumably it had begun its run after her time. It was the little black box that was emitting the tune, and when the man held it to his ear and spoke into it Jo realised it was some kind of walkie-talkie. From the look of him the man wasn't in any of the armed forces, and nobody paid him any special attention, so Jo assumed the things were commonplace in this time.

I could have done with one of those, she thought. Keeping the Doctor informed of her progress was not going to be easy given the time restrictions. And time was ticking away. With nothing in her purse apart from some thirty-years-out-of-date shekels from the TARDIS's money dispenser, she had gone to a second-hand jeweller. She was offered a hundred pounds for a gold bracelet the Doctor had bought her in a market on Erekan – a reasonable price, she thought, until she was charged nearly five pounds just for a map of Chichester!

Jo turned her attention back to the map. The trace, it seemed, was emanating from a hospital on the outskirts of town. Had the hospital been built on the site of a crashed starship with a leaking hyperwhatsit? No, the Doctor had been sure it was the bright trace – the one he was investigating – that marked the centre of the fracture. Of course it was perfectly possible that he was wrong, and the starship had not crashed *yet*. What if it crashed on the hospital while she was in it? That was a little worrying. Maybe she should have let the Doctor lecture her about the potential dangers of time fractures after all. But it was too late now.

Retracing her steps, she found the traffic on the dual carriageway busier than before. But a little further on she found the entrance to a subway. There was a busker at the bottom of the steps, a small, boyish-looking woman wearing dungarees and a crumpled T-shirt, a severe haircut and a pair of dark glasses that hid her eyes. She was, quite simply, the most wonderful singer Jo had ever heard. She sang unaccompanied. Her range was phenomenal. The song was bittersweet, passionate, intense, and not a little resentful. The words were not English, but they conveyed a depth of emotion nonetheless, and Jo imagined herself standing on a twilit beach at the end of time, alone, watching the waves break gently on the shore while overhead the stars died. Evidently she was not the only one affected for people were slowing down, even stopping, in the subway tunnel to listen, putting coins and notes into the woman's collection box.

Jo had heard a wide variety of music during her travels with the Doctor. She had attended the first-ever performance of Stravinsky's *The Rite of Spring*, which had proved too shocking for its contemporary audience. She had heard the hatching song of the so-called choristers of Azathonal, a species which sang during the larval stage of their phenomenally complicated life cycle; afterwards the creatures attained sentience but with it lost the ability to sing ever again. This was different, though; one did not expect to stumble across something so… so *angelic* in such an unexotic setting.

The singer's glance fell upon Jo and for one brief moment she faltered in her singing. But she quickly recovered, and Jo could not say for sure that she had been the cause of the hesitation. Reluctantly, she pushed on through the small crowd and emerged on the other side of the dual carriageway.

She resisted the temptation to take a slight detour through the Northgate car park to check on the TARDIS. Instead she made for a country road called College Lane where a meandering, tree-lined pavement took her past St Richard's Hospital and Bishop Otter College. The sight of a hospital surprised her; she had not expected to come across it so soon. She checked her map – no, this was not her destination. The trace originated from another hospital a little further out of town.

Why two hospitals so close together? Jo wondered. St Richard's appeared to be a general hospital, so perhaps the other one was for private patients.

She folded away her map and continued walking. She was conscious of a slight breeze trying feebly to push her back the way she had come. The odd thing about the breeze was that it did nothing to alleviate the oppressive heat, and it did not appear to cause any movement among the leaves on the trees.

If he could find Troy Game he might be able to explain his actions to her, and if she understood she might find it in her heart to forgive him and then things might go back to the way they had been before…

No, damn it, he would find her because he *owed* it to her to find her. He had taken her on because of what she was, and he had made a promise to himself that he would not take advantage of his position. He had not kept that promise. She might not want to see him again, but she would still want to get back to Caresh and, for all that he had not been much help so far, he at least knew what it was she was trying to achieve; he at least believed her. He had to let her know that he was still available if she wanted him. Once he had done that, it would be up to her.

First of all, though, he had to get cleaned up, and dressed. This proved to be more difficult than he had expected. Whenever Captain Lefanu cracked a rib, chances were he'd forgotten about it after a couple of chapters; Simon was not so lucky. The pain was sudden and intense whenever he leant forward or twisted round.

Sneezing was especially painful, and Simon was prone to hay fever. Even putting on a shirt was an ordeal; reaching down to put on socks and shoes was agony.

The swelling under his eye was tender but it did not look too hideous. He gritted his teeth, turned away from the bathroom mirror and entered the lift, ready to face the world.

He pressed the ground floor button and the lift lurched into motion, taking him away from Cloud Base for the last time.

With each step the 'breeze', for want of a better word, was getting stronger. Jo was beginning to feel as if she was walking through treacle, a sensation she was familiar with only from dreams. According to her watch it was only about ten minutes since she had set off from the bench outside W.H. Smith, yet her personal time-sense was insisting that she was already too late for the afternoon deadline.

The pavement ended and continued on the other side of the road. There was only one car in sight, at the limit of vision, yet when Jo stepped out onto the roadway she was greeted by the blaring reprimand of its horn. The driver had to swerve to miss her. She hurried to the safety of the other side.

The pavement on this side was not lined with trees. The effect was to make the landscape even more unchanging, so that her walk seemed even more interminable, if that were possible.

She pressed on.

A single step lasted for half a minute, a minute, two minutes. An old lady with a poodle was coming towards her; if Jo looked out of the corner of her eye they appeared to be walking at a normal speed, but if she looked directly at them they appeared to be as stationary as mannequins. Jo tried closing her eyes as she walked, but her attention was still on her footsteps and so it didn't help. She looked at her watch again. The second hand was sweeping around at its normal speed, yet it was still less than twelve minutes since her journey had begun.

She kept her attention on the second hand and continued

walking. It did not take much of a conceptual leap to guess that it was some aspect of the time fracture that was pushing her back. By looking at her watch she was effectively fighting time with time.

Even so, it was with glacial slowness that she reached her destination, and discovered that it was a hospital for the mentally ill.

There was nothing to stop her entering the grounds. Nothing physical, at least; she had expected a high perimeter wall and electronically operated gates. Nevertheless, a geological age passed as she followed the service road between two tree-planted lawns. There were patients walking among the trees and some of them watched her as she unfolded her map once more. One of them, a young woman with straggly brown hair and an awkward gait that made her seem much older than her years, approached Jo.'It comes out of that wall sometimes,' she said, pointing at one of the outbuildings and sounding as if she was speaking from a very long way away.'Everybody's seen it but only I can remember what I've seen.You'll see it too but you won't remember it either. Memory has its blind spot just as the eye does.'

The 'breeze' was turning into a hurricane; Jo imagined she could hear it screaming in her ears. Heading for the outbuilding the patient had indicated, Jo found herself passing a barred window on the ground floor. The patient inside the room was moving towards the window; Jo glimpsed him out of the corner of her eye but, before she had a chance to turn, her attention was arrested by a shimmering in front of her.

A distortion was forming in the air in front of a blank section of wall at the side of the outbuilding. A creature emerged. It stood upright like a man, had the poise of a man, but it was a snake. A man-sized snake, hooded, its head reminiscent of a jackal. It reared and Jo stood transfixed, but the creature did not appear to be showing any interest in her.

Was this the origin of the trace?

There was a knock at the barred window. Jo turned, instantly forgetting about the jackal-snake. A sad, round-faced man of about sixty was beckoning to her. His lips were forming silent words. Jo moved towards him. His eyes were all iris; they held hers. Everything about the last half-hour had been dreamlike to an extreme, but this man's face was like the face of the one who awakens you from a fevered sleep. Uncertainly, Jo said, 'Lord Roche?'

Instantly the spell was shattered. Jo felt as if she had shouted an obscenity during a church service. She was once more aware of the jackal-snake (how could she have forgotten about *that*?); it was bearing down on her, and the man who might have been Roche was looking both angry and terrified. He shook his head and waved one hand urgently, then turned the movement into a pushing gesture. Jo found herself thrust backwards with overwhelming force, for all the world as if she'd been spat out of a huge mouth.

She seemed to stumble backwards for a very long time. A myriad of images flashed past her, some of them glimpses of the route she had taken but seen in reverse and speeded up, some of them confusing views of unfamiliar and half-familiar scenes: a vast, ice-covered plain; a mountain peak, seen from a few feet above; a burning forest; a corridor resembling a cathedral nave that stretched to infinity; a herd of albino giraffes galloping across a beach; a huge iceberg covered with domed buildings; a globular star cluster; a fleet of veined, translucent airships; a mercury lake. Jo squeezed her eyes shut, aware that her time-sense had gone again. Then something hit the back of her knees, her legs buckled under her and she fell backwards. She did not fall far; there was something solid beneath her.

A bench.

She opened her eyes. Somehow she knew what she was going to see: a slim, bearded man in jeans and yellow T-shirt coming out of W.H. Smith carrying a newspaper. And there he was. He stood in the doorway for a moment, blinking in the sunlight and looking up the street. Jo knew his portable telephone was about to start ringing any second... now!

The phone rang.

Jo looked down at the map on her lap. She had marked the bearing of the trace but she had not yet drawn the line through it.

So what had she been doing for the last half-hour? Had the walk to the hospital really happened, or had she momentarily dozed off on the bench and dreamt the whole thing? If it hadn't really happened, how had she known about the phone?

It might have been a lucky guess but Jo didn't think so. She rose from the bench and set off once more. She had never been to College Lane before today; if she recognised its tree-lined meandering pavement, and the view of the hospital and the college across the field beyond the stone wall by the roadside, then she would know she had not imagined the earlier walk.

Yet something was nagging at the back of her mind. It was some minutes before she managed to work out what it was.

When the bearded man had come out of W.H. Smith originally he had been carrying the *Independent on Sunday*. This time the paper he had bought was the *Sunday Telegraph*.

The crater in the Northgate Car Park was conspicuous by its absence. Nor had Sheridan seen a single roadblock. But the report had been right about the Portaloo. Well, nearly right. It had apparently been blown to one side of the car park where it stood pressed against the chain-link fence, seemingly undamaged by its ordeal.

But it was not actually a Portaloo.

It was a police call box. Sheridan had seen one very like it outside the underground station at Earls Court. Could it be the same one, carried from there to here by a tornado? No – quite apart from anything else, the one at Earls Court had a CCTV camera on top whereas this one had a rather old-fashioned lamp.

He pushed the police box to see if it would rock. It was quite solid, and either very heavy or else fixed to the ground. It seemed to vibrate, hum even, in the manner of a transformer. Each of the three visible sides consisted of a pair of frosted-glass windows at the top with three pairs of sunken panels below them. There was no sign of any door; that, by process of elimination, must be in the fourth side, the one pressed against the fence.

Sheridan went through the gateway in the fence. This was indeed the side with the doors. There was a lock halfway down the door on the right and a notice indicating the purpose of the box in one of the panels in the door on the left. Everything about it made perfect sense apart from its positioning. Frowning, Sheridan touched the lock through the links in the fence. Even if he had the key he would not be able to open the doors. Unless they opened inwards, of course, but that would substantially reduce the box's capacity.

In summary, then, it was a box that could not be accessed. Yet somebody had tried. Somebody had cut a vertical slit in the chain-link fence. At least, that was how it first appeared. But Sheridan saw beyond first appearances. He was sufficiently experienced with chain-link fences to know that there was something distinctly suspect about the cut. In 1988 he had broken into a secret government installation – OK, so it had turned out to be a prosthetic limbs factory, and he'd nearly got himself arrested – but the point was, he had made a very similar cut to get through the establishment's perimeter fence.

This cut appeared to be recent. And, unless he was very much mistaken, it had been made by somebody on the police-box side of the fence. Quite how they'd done it he didn't know, but the fact remained that they had.

'Perhaps the cut was made *before* the police box was put here?' he wondered aloud. 'But why? Someone desperate for a game of tennis had found the gate locked? No, I'm missing something very obvious here.'

The police box, he noticed, was blue. It took a few seconds for this to register, but when it did he slapped his forehead in belated realisation. 'Of course!' he exclaimed. 'How could I have been so stupid?'

There was an entry for Blue Box in *The A to Z of Alien Encounters*, a book he had studied for so long he could quote long passages from it. The entry was almost as long as the previous one, for Blue Book.

He opened the laptop-computer case and took a Sony Mavica digital camera from one of the compartments.

Jo had not imagined the singer in the subway. She was there now, and once again she was pulling a crowd. The song she was singing was not quite the one Jo remembered, and Jo wondered if she was slightly ahead of schedule this time round. Or perhaps the singer was making it up as she went along, responding to her surroundings and maybe even the reactions of her audience. Jo could well believe it. Somehow the thought that the same song would never be sung twice gave the singing an added poignancy.

This time Jo took the ramp into the subway rather than the stairs. While she was still some distance away the singer glanced at her and, as had happened the previous time, she momentarily faltered. This was too much of a coincidence, Jo decided. Clearly the whole experience was some kind of side effect of the time fracture; somehow she had been caught up in its backward flow. Unnerving as it was, Jo realised it could have been far worse. She had only been thrown back half an hour, not the full twenty-seven years!

This explanation was not wholly satisfying, however. After all, nobody else had been affected. But what if someone was somehow *using* the fracture? The man she had seen at the window – well, if he was Lord Roche, as Jo supposed, then he was one of the Time Lords. For all she knew he might have some sort of control over the fracture. Enough control to allow him to reverse time for one person. But why would he want to do that? It didn't make sense! It was more likely that Jo's experience was a side effect of whatever it was he was doing.

Abruptly the woman stopped singing. Jo halted a few paces away from her, aware that the singer was looking directly at her.

There were murmurs among the impromptu audience, their disappointment turning to curiosity as it became apparent that Jo was somehow responsible for the cessation of their entertainment. But Jo was too intent on the woman's words.

'You've seen him.' It sounded like an accusation.

'What are you talking about?'

'Roche. You've seen Roche.'

The image appeared in Jo's mind once more. 'How on Earth can you know that?'

'You must take me to him. You must.' The woman grabbed Jo by the shoulders. 'Please! It's very important.'

The subway was beginning to empty. Some people were hanging around, either waiting for the singing to start again or else interested in the latest development, but Jo was too taken aback to pay them any heed. 'You saw him in my mind?' she asked, disbelieving what she was asking as much as she disbelieved what the woman was claiming.

'Yes, I saw him in your mind,' the woman confirmed, tightening her grip on Jo's shoulders. 'I can do that, or else I can remember, but I can't do both. All I know is, I'm trapped here, and if I don't get back to my world soon, I won't have a world to go back to. Do you understand?' The woman tightened her grip still further, then abruptly relaxed her grip and Jo wriggled free. 'I have to see Roche. He's my only hope.'

'All right,' Jo said at last, thinking furiously. If the woman was mad, then the mental hospital was probably the best place for her. But Jo didn't think she was mad. There was no reason why Roche shouldn't have a travelling companion, just as the Doctor had one in Jo – and she and the Doctor were always getting separated. But the thought that the stranger had seen Roche in her mind made Jo feel distinctly uncomfortable. Yet she could hardly ignore the woman's plea for help. She knew only too well what it was like to be many light years from Earth, with little prospect of ever getting home.

'Very well,' Jo said. 'I'll try and take you to where I think he is.

But it might not be easy for us to get there, and he might not be there even if we do.'

'I'm prepared to take that chance,' the woman said, in the voice of one who had all but abandoned hope.

'Please. I've got to find her. She's about so high, Greek in appearance, very short hair and dark glasses.' Simon looked expectantly at the faces of the elderly couple seated on the bench. They shook their heads. He moved on.

If only he had a picture. He had taken photographs of her but the film was still in the camera back at the flat. Perhaps if he bought a sketch pad from a newsagent he might be able to draw her.

Somebody was selling the *Big Issue*. Why hadn't he thought of that before? Troy Game was, well, homeless now. He approached the seller, feeling in his pocket for a pound coin. 'Er, I'm looking for a friend,' he said once he'd paid for a copy. 'A young woman. She's about my age and build. Greek in appearance. Very short hair, sunglasses.'

The *Big Issue* seller was shaking his head sympathetically. 'I'm afraid not, mate.'

'Please, think!' Simon pressed. 'She's about so high, blue eyes, she may not be wearing her sunglasses, and...'

A gruff voice behind him said '... and she sings like an angel. That the one?'

Simon turned. He almost wept. The man who had spoken was a scruffy fellow with a beard. Simon recognised him; he remembered walking past him, ignoring his request for spare change, on the evening he had first met Troy Game. 'You've seen her?'

'Less than half an hour ago. She was pulling a crowd in the subway. I tell you, she could pull ships to their doom. I've never heard anything like her. I mean, *never.*'

'Thanks. Thanks very much. Look, I'm really... Thanks.' Simon hesitated, unsure whether to offer the man some money. But he hadn't asked for any, and it didn't seem right, so he turned and ran for the subway as fast as his injury would allow.

But when he got there she was gone.

With the precious few hours ticking away the Doctor was sorely tempted to 'borrow' a vehicle in order to track down the moving trace. Under some circumstances he would not have hesitated. According to Solenti, though, the time fracture was merely a hazard to navigation. Urgent, but not necessarily important enough to warrant such a measure.

Besides, he knew Jo would not approve.

The people in the car hire company had seemed pleasant enough until he admitted he had neither British currency nor a driving licence to hand. He had wasted several minutes trying to reason with them but it was fruitless. The only way to get a vehicle in time to deal with the time fracture was to play by their rules.

It came as something of a surprise to the Doctor that someone was showing an inordinate amount of interest in *his* vehicle. A tall, smartly dressed man with a leather case at his side was photographing the front of the TARDIS where it pressed against the fence. Evidently the camera was of the digital variety, because as the Doctor passed through the gateway in the fence the man was removing a floppy disc and replacing it with another one.

'Unusual sight, wouldn't you say?' said the photographer.

'On the contrary,' the Doctor replied. 'Now, if you wouldn't mind getting out of my way…'

But the photographer had discreetly positioned himself in front of the cut in the fence. 'Does it belong to you by any chance? My name's Sheridan, Michael Sheridan. And you are?'

'If you must know, I am known as the Doctor. Now, much as I'd like to stop and chat I really am in rather a hurry, so…' As he was speaking Sheridan took a photograph of him. 'Do you mind sir!' the Doctor finished angrily.

'Am I to take it you're responsible for the damage to the fence?' Sheridan said, unperturbed by his anger.

'Look, I really don't have time for this. Will you kindly step aside!'

'It's a strange kind of vandalism. But then, it's a strange place to put a call box, wouldn't you agree?'

'Stand aside sir!'

'I'd be happy to – if you wouldn't mind answering a few questions first. For instance, what is your interest in this call box?'

The Doctor sighed. Ordinarily he had no qualms about employing physical force when circumstances demanded it, but he was uneasy about initiating it. Still, he'd tried being polite. A minimum of force would suffice, he reasoned – Sheridan did not look like a fighter, and besides he was probably too concerned about his equipment to offer any real resistance.

A moment later Sheridan was sprawled across the tennis court, looking as if he'd been hit in the stomach with a battering ram. The Doctor unlocked the TARDIS door and squeezed his way through the gap in the fence. A moment later he was inside the white control room. He pushed the red lever on the console and the doors swung closed.

The scanner was still switched on. Outside, Sheridan had recovered his composure. Despite his anger and humiliation he was trying to sound like the voice of reason. 'That wasn't very sensible, was it? You're going to have to come out sooner or later, you know.'

Ignoring him, the Doctor strode purposefully through the interior door, along the corridor and through the fourth door on the left. Into a room the size of a hangar for light aircraft, filled entirely with filing cabinets. He knew exactly which one to make for, and which drawer held what – a testament to a fit of obsessive organisation that had seized him some twenty years earlier and which had lasted as many days. Money suitable for this time and place in the second drawer down, driving licence in the one below that.

He found the money. The licence was… missing.

He *knew for a fact* that he had put the licence in that drawer.

He had taken it out once since then, but he distinctly remembered replacing it.

At least he'd intended to replace it…

He slammed the drawer shut in disgust. What now?

Forge a licence? No, that would be too time consuming. Use his UNIT pass? Unlikely to impress a car hire firm; besides, he didn't know which jacket it was in.

On the other hand he could just move the TARDIS.

He bit his lower lip thoughtfully. There were all sorts of reasons why he was inclined to avoid doing that; a possible repeat of the events of the morning was one that immediately sprang to mind. But there weren't very many options left. He could cycle, he supposed, but three of his four bicycles had been taken to bits for cleaning and repairs, and he'd never gotten around to reassembling them. As for the fourth – well, it was decidedly uncomfortable and it had looked ridiculous enough in the 1890s, let alone the 1990s.

Like it or not, he was going to have to move the TARDIS.

On the scanner in the control room Sheridan was still ranting. He was holding his mobile phone in a significant manner as he said, 'Has it occurred to you that the police might be interested in what you're doing with their equipment, Doctor?'

The Doctor checked Solenti's device again but, as he'd expected, none of the traces showed; their signals were unable to pass through the TARDIS's shell. No matter; he had only been inside the TARDIS for a few minutes. He used the playback feature to show him the position of the prominent trace just before he'd come through the doors.

The trace had not moved much since he'd last looked. It was now about forty Dagusan yards due west of his current location. Call it fifteen miles. As before, the other two traces did not appear during playback.

Much against his better judgement he slid the device back into its slot on the console, ready to whip it out again if it showed the slightest sign of taking control of the TARDIS. All three traces appeared at once, their signals no longer blocked by the TARDIS's shell.

'I've warned you, Doctor,' Sheridan was shouting. 'I have no other recourse than to phone the police, and I am going to do it right now.'

The Doctor was fairly sure that one of the secondary traces – the one Jo had gone to investigate – had moved since he last looked. The other appeared to be stationary.

'I'll give you a count of three.'

He removed the device from the slot once more. He would stick with his original plan and head for the location of the main trace.

'Look, I only want to ask you a few questions. You're going to have to come out sooner or later. Don't make it harder on yourself.'

That meant risking a short trip in the TARDIS. It *was* a risk; the old girl was not fully run in yet, and the time fracture was a hazard to navigation. Still, his destination was only fifteen miles away. Nothing could go wrong in that distance, could it?

'Right, that's long enough. I'm dialling them right now. I'm pressing the "yes" button. I can hear the phone ringing right now. I can't understand why you prefer to face them rather than answer my questions, but if that's the way you... Oh, hello, my name's Michael Sheridan, I wonder if I could talk to someone responsible for police call boxes in the Chichester area. Yes, Chichester. In West Sussex. That's right. Yes I'm quite sure I mean Chichester, I'm here right now. Yes, of course I am. I used to live near here, and besides, I saw a sign on the way in. No, I don't mind holding.'

The Doctor entered the coordinates via the console's keyboard. He flipped a switch and the dematerialisation process began.

On the scanner Sheridan stared, slack jawed, oblivious to all but the unexpected behaviour of the police box. Recovering his wits he pocketed his phone and, taking out his camera, took a rapid sequence of shots.

The Doctor noticed him at last. 'Oh dear,' he said ruefully, 'I'm afraid it just won't do, old chap.'

Before the TARDIS had fully dematerialised the Doctor flipped a big silver switch on the underside of the console.

Sheridan regarded the space on the other side of the fence with some satisfaction. Blue Box was real; not only had he seen it with his own eyes, he had photographic evidence. If only he'd had a camcorder! But no matter; once his editor had seen what he'd got hold of, he'd probably be *given* a camcorder. If the *Open Minds* budget didn't stretch to that now, it soon would; sales of the magazine would surely be boosted by the new material, and they might be able to lure back some of their former advertisers.

Blue Box had been solid, then transparent, then it was gone. Curiously, it was while it was transparent that Sheridan felt a sudden thrust in his trouser pockets; his keys and his steel comb were yanked towards Blue Box as if by some mysterious force.

He sat on a bench, rested the computer on his lap and switched it on. He took the floppy disc from the camera as he waited for the computer to boot up.

A message appeared on the computer's screen. It said, 'INVALID MEDIA TYPE'.

He frowned at the message, puzzled at first and then worried. He found a spare boot disc in the case and slipped it into the drive.

The message 'INVALID MEDIA TYPE' appeared once more.

It took him an unreasonably long time to come to the conclusion that all his discs had been wiped, including the computer's hard drive.

Blue Box had a way of covering its tracks.

Chapter Seven
Zeke Child

To: "Ben Keller" <benkeller@erewhon.co.uk>
To: "Patric Keller <patkeller@erewhon.co.uk>
Subject: Westbourne Lake, Mysterious Emptying Of
Priority: High

Hi Guys

Just back from Noel's party. Complete disaster. Only unattached female was Freeman's sister, and she left before 10 p.m. Didn't bother hanging around after that.

Discovered something truly amazing on way home. Stopped by nature reserve in Westbourne Forest to relieve myself. Water level in Westbourne Lake visibly lower than on way in. Thought it was trick of the moonlight at first, but I climbed over the fence to get a proper look. Level's down by at least a metre! Rumbling noise under nearest bank, like water flowing in underground tunnel. Made my way to the bank to investigate. Not easy, only had bicycle lamp and moonlight to see by. Glad I did though.

Found a pair of stone doors in a stone frame set into the bank. Not concrete, actual stone. Still mostly submerged, but top few inches fully out of the water now. Thought they were some kind of sluice gate, but if so, they weren't fitted recently. Those doors are ancient! Managed to clear some of the dead leaves and stuff off them to get a proper look. They've got raised figures on them showing winged snakes and wolves, and hieroglyphics.

Westbourne Lake is ancient – dates back to Saxon times. If it does have a drainage system it wasn't built during the *last few centuries. Don't think anybody living knows the gates exist at all.*

So why has the level never dropped before? I reckon the doors were held shut by water pressure, and they stayed watertight only so long as they remained firmly shut. But the heatwave caused the lake's level to go down, reducing pressure on them. Earth movements over the years (centuries?) together with vibrations from passing lorries made them a less tight fit. So now the lake is emptying like a bath when the plug isn't in properly.

Didn't hang around long because there wasn't much more to see, but I reckon the water is going to continue emptying out during the night. Suggest we check it out tomorrow before anyone else finds out about it. So be ready for 8 a.m. tomorrow at the latest.

Have the following equipment ready:
Torch with fresh batteries
Cycling helmet
Rope
Bull Whip :-)
Crowbar
Lighter
Camera
Water Bottle
Mobile Phone
Towel
Boots
Waterproofs
Mars bars, crisps etc.
Please acknowledge ASAP.
Zeke

Ben, the younger of the Keller twins, was more than a little annoyed when Zeke finally turned up. 'Where the hell have you been? You told *us* to be ready for eight!' he said.

'Sorry,' said Zeke. 'I was more tired than I realised.'

'Everyone will know about it by now.'

'Not necessarily. The lake's mostly screened from the road by trees and it's a long way from the main footpaths. It might be days before anybody else notices the drop in level.'

'Days? It's a bloody nature reserve! These places are maintained, you know.'

'Today's Sunday,' Zeke said in what he hoped was a reasonable voice.

'All right, all right,' said Patric. 'Let's not waste what time we have left. I suggest we redistribute the gear so nobody is overburdened.'

Even after doing this Zeke's backpack seemed inordinately heavy – and that was without the boots and waterproofs which they had deemed unnecessary. But the twins' backpacks were just as heavy so he made no complaint as they set out on their mountain bikes.

Eventually they arrived at the place where Zeke had stopped the previous night. To his relief there was nobody else about. They dismounted and leant their bikes against the wooden fence. There was a broken gap in the fence that Zeke was sure had not been there last night. They looked in at the nature reserve for a good half-minute without speaking.

Patric was first to break the silence. He said, 'Well, what happened to it then?'

'Where did all that water go?' asked Ben.

Zeke exhaled explosively in a manner that resembled relieved laughter. 'I didn't dream it, then. My God, it really happened!' He led the way through the gap in the fence.

Westbourne Lake was not a particularly big lake. Nevertheless, its transformation was remarkable, not to say shocking. It was less than a quarter full. Dead fish floated on the much lowered surface. A supermarket trolley and an old bedstead stuck out of the mud.

'Let's find those doors,' said Patric.

As Zeke had expected the water was level with the threshold of the doors. The doors themselves were about four foot in height and tilted by about thirty degrees from the vertical. The carvings seemed less spectral in daylight, but no less mysterious.

Just above the bank stood a large oak tree with a stout branch that jutted out over the lake. Zeke considered it. 'As we don't know if the tunnel slopes, we could tie a rope to that branch and trail as much of it as possible through the doorway.'

'Sounds sensible enough,' said Patric. 'Only I don't think the rope's as long as you think.'

'One of us should stay outside to keep watch and be on hand in case anyone needs rescuing.'

'You're very safety conscious, aren't you?' Ben said.

Zeke shrugged. 'I want to see my twentieth birthday. I want to go to university, get married some day...'

Ben imitated the shrug. 'Accidents happen.'

'Doesn't mean you have to go looking for them.'

'Well, I'm not staying outside. Where's the need? We've got a phone.'

'What happens if the branch breaks? I doubt it can take the weight of all three of us.'

'Let's just get the doors open first,' said Patric.

They let Zeke attempt the doors first. It seemed only fair; he had discovered them after all. He tied the rope to the overhead branch and used it to keep his balance as he clambered down the bank. He stepped onto a protruding sill at the bottom of the door frame.

'There's no handle of any sort,' he told them. 'The carvings don't move. The gap's too small to get my fingers in. Can one of you hand me the... oh!'

One of the doors suddenly sprang outwards, missing his head by an inch. If he hadn't been holding the rope he would have lost his balance. The other door remained resolutely shut.

He shone his bicycle lamp into the opening. There was a large space inside; the beam only just showed on the far wall. There was a stone structure in the middle of the cavern which put him in mind of some kind of altar. The stone floor sloped downwards. It was only damp, he noted; the lake water had passed through the cavern but had not gathered in it.

'You better see this,' he told the Keller twins.

They climbed down the bank and joined him. There was only just room on the sill for the three of them, only room for two to look in at a time.

'What do you make of it?' Zeke asked.

'Wow,' said Ben. 'I mean, really wow.'

'A secret place of worship for some nature cult?'

'Could be. It's just so amazing!'

Patric swept his torch around the cavern, his expression thoughtful. 'It must go right under the road,' he said. 'Funny nobody's ever noticed it before. But do you know what strikes me as especially odd?'

'What's that?'

'The way the ceiling appears to be higher than the height of the bank.'

'Yes, I must admit that struck me as odd too,' admitted Zeke.

The second walk to the hospital was as difficult as the first, but for entirely different reasons. There was no physical resistance this time, but there was Troy Game. Jo did not know how to take her. She did not want to talk about her homeworld, she did not wish to speculate about how she came to be on Earth and she was not interested in Jo's assurance that her friend the Doctor would put everything right.

But despite Troy Game's unwillingness to engage in conversation, Jo persisted in questioning her about her telepathic ability. She had to, for her own peace of mind.

Eventually Troy Game opened up on this subject, albeit briefly and grudgingly. After clicking her teeth together three times she told Jo, 'I don't know how I've got it. I did not have it before I came here, and it's not as strong as it was when I first arrived. I'm sensitive to certain emotions and impressions, and once in a while I pick up on an image, but very rarely do I get actual words. As to whether I can read *your* thoughts, I don't know and frankly I have no desire to find out. I am not interested in what anyone from this place is thinking about.'

There was no mistaking Troy Game's tone, and there was no more conversation until they reached the hospital grounds. Jo recognised the woman with the straggly brown hair, who in turn seemed to recognise Jo. 'You again,' she said, but would say no more.

Jo made for the outbuilding. There was something caught on a drainpipe, something clothlike and very wispy that resembled a large piece of cobweb. Like dust caught in a shaft of sunlight it was invisible from some angles, but from others...

It was like the Turin Shroud. Or a skin cast by a snake. The skin of a jackal-snake. The more Jo stared at it, the more solid it seemed.

Against all her training, experience and instinct, Jo reached for it. Her hand appeared to pass through it. Then abruptly the skin-thing collapsed in a shower of dust.

To the Doctor's relief the TARDIS materialised without incident. It had arrived in a forest. A beech tree dominated the view on the scanner. He patted the console approvingly then pulled the lever to open the doors.

A sign nailed to a tree read 'Nature Reserve. Keep Out'. Three mountain bikes leant against a wooden fence, close to a broken gap. The Doctor regarded the gap for half a minute, then consulted Solenti's device. The source of the time fracture was less than ten yards - Earth yards - away and behind him. He turned and strode through the undergrowth towards it.

There was a crater of sorts, with wet muddy banks and brown water in the bottom. Was this where the starship had crashed? The Doctor dismissed the idea. Impact craters were generally simple circles or ellipses, whereas this was approximately kidney-shaped. It was clearly a lake, minus most of its water.

So where had the water gone? It did not appear to have evaporated naturally over the course of the unusually hot summer. He supposed it *could* have happened explosively, the result of the sudden immersion of a glowing-hot mass of metal. But if a spaceship *had* crash-landed in the lake, where was it now, and why was there no indication of a splash?

No, this lake had the appearance of being partially drained.

A little further around the lake three figures were scrambling down the bank. The Doctor only noticed them because of their movement; they had not seen him through the trees. He moved a little closer so that he could make out their features. He was not quite sure what he had expected – aliens, perhaps, trying to recover their ship – but they seemed like ordinary enough youths, no doubt the owners of the bikes. He was about to call to them when something about the appearance of one of them made him hesitate.

Two were obviously twins. Medium height, very thin, faces heavily freckled. They wore cycling helmets, but the Doctor guessed from their complexions that they had red hair.

It was the third one who caught his attention. He was somewhat smaller than the twins and had a distinctly Semitic look. He wore glasses. He looked as if he was attempting to grow a beard, but without much success; the effect was at best patchy.

The Doctor had met him before, he was sure of it. The youth would not remember the meeting, because from his point of view it had not happened yet, would not happen until he was at least twenty years older. But for the life of him the Doctor could not remember when they had met. It must have been in the 2020s, but he had not visited that era at all since his exile had been lifted.

While he was considering this the three youths disappeared into the bank.

Lord Roche had had no visitors, carried no identification and had said very little that made any sense since he'd been transferred from the other Chichester hospital. To the staff he was an enigma.

When Jo Grant and Troy Game turned up to see him they were pressed for information by Dr Calder, who happened to be on duty at the time. Jo was forced to concoct a cover story to explain how she knew him. According to her he was a government scientist and she was his assistant; he had been overworking and had gone missing while she was on holiday. As Jo continued with her account she was sure she sounded as if she was making it up as she went along, which indeed she was. Eventually, she ended by saying, 'So I wondered if he might have turned up here.'

'I have a picture of him,' Troy Game said unexpectedly.

Jo supposed she had a photograph. What Troy Game actually took from her pocket was a folded-up page torn from a sketch pad. It was a very good likeness of the patient she had seen through the barred window. For some reason Jo could not fathom there was a large number '18' pencilled above the picture.

Dr Calder frowned. He started to say, 'I really don't think…' when Troy Game took him by the arm and drew him aside, out of Jo's hearing. They conferred in low voices, Troy Game standing with her back to Jo. Then Troy Game removed her sunglasses. Dr Calder's eyes widened as they met hers, and for a shocked second Jo thought she was trying to hypnotise him. But no; she was simply showing him her eyes.

Then Dr Calder gave a decisive nod. Troy Game turned to Jo with a triumphant expression, then put her sunglasses back on even though the light was not bright in the reception area. Jo had a fleeting glimpse of the woman's eyes: they were almost all iris, just like the eyes of Lord Roche. Whatever the significance of this might be, it seemed to impress Dr Calder. Despite Jo's blatantly unconvincing cover story they were allowed to visit the patient.

'I would very much like to talk to you both afterwards,' Dr Calder told them.

They were greeted by a cheerful young man who introduced himself as Donald MacRae. Jo was not sure what his role was supposed to be; he was certainly not dressed for the part. He wore a pair of purple trousers with scuffed knees and a blue T-shirt.

122

There was a picture on the front of the T-shirt of a cartoon dog resembling Snoopy flying a small aeroplane that looked for all the world like a motorcycle sidecar with stubby wings.

'I help out sometimes,' he explained, aware that Jo was looking at his unconventional clothes. 'Cleaning, carrying, that sort of thing. I'm standing in for the orderly at the moment – he's got gastro-enteritis. I'm told I have a calming influence on the patients.' He grinned. 'Well, some of them anyway.'

He led them to the secure ward. 'I should warn you he was pretty violent when he arrived a couple of weeks ago, but he's calmed down a lot since then. I don't think he'll give you any trouble.' He took them through a set of double doors. 'He's in the third room on the left.' He indicated a bell push to one side of the doors. 'Just ring the bell when you want me to let you out.' Then he shut the double doors behind them.

The door to Roche's room was closed. Before Jo had a chance to knock Troy Game turned the handle and walked straight in. She had a look of anticipation on her face, as if her quest was finally coming to an end.

The look quickly gave way to one of disappointment. Roche, dressed in a hospital gown, was lying on his bed, his large irises visible through half-open lids as he peered up at the ceiling. He was completely unresponsive, wholly oblivious to the presence of his visitors.

'Hallo!' Ben called out. The word reverberated around the large stone cavern. When the echo had died away there was complete silence, broken only by the distant sound of water drops.

Zeke, who had been standing in the doorway, followed the twins into the cavern. The floor appeared to be made of marble. It sloped downwards and was still wet and slippery which made walking difficult.

'I think we ought to…' he started to say, but got no further. The door had just slammed shut behind him.

There was a sickened silence. The three of them froze in the near darkness, their torches pointing uselessly at the sloping floor. Then Ben, speaking with a nervous giggle, said, 'I honestly didn't expect that.'

'I *told* you someone should have stayed outside!' Zeke said angrily.

'I thought you *were* staying outside,' Ben pointed out.

'You have the phone?' Patric asked his brother.

'Yes.' Ben put down his pack and took the phone from one of its pockets. 'Oh God. I can't get a signal. Oh God, oh please God…'

'The walls must be acting as some sort of Faraday cage,' Zeke mused. 'Signals can't get in and we can't get out.'

'We could try pushing the door,' Patric said. He made his way up the floor to the large slab of the door. Somehow it seemed much bigger on this side. He pressed one hand against it and it flew open.

'Well, that's a relief,' he said.

Roche shuddered. The convulsion passed from one end of his body to the other.

'Did you see that?' Troy Game asked.

'No,' said Jo. She was standing by the window, sure she'd seen something moving about outside. Something other than one of the patients.

They had been here for nearly half an hour and nothing was happening. Jo was at a loss. Having found Roche, she had no idea what to do next. She wasn't quite sure what she'd imagined, but she'd expected to find something tangible, a problem she could identify and perhaps solve. As it turned out, Roche didn't appear to be trapped in anything; he merely seemed wholly apathetic. Perhaps it amounted to the same thing, if that was how the anomaly affected people, but if that was the case what was she supposed to do about it? Somehow bring him out of his apathy, or carry him bodily from the hospital?

The most realistic option was to go back to the TARDIS, tell the Doctor where Roche was, and describe the condition he was in. But she didn't want to do that yet. It felt somehow… useless. Besides, Troy Game was determined to get some sort of response out of him. She'd had no luck up till now, but if there was any chance of her succeeding surely it would be best that Jo be on hand?

But time was ticking away. The end of the anomaly – or the beginning, whichever way you looked at it – was less than two hours away. For that matter the hospital visit could not go on indefinitely.

As if reading her mind – a disturbingly real possibility, of course – Troy Game said, 'You need not stay, Jo Grant.'

Jo moved away from the window. Swallowing her ire she said, 'You know, I'm sure we could sort everything out a lot more quickly if we worked together.'

'There is nothing else to sort out. I need him to return to my planet.'

'He's in no fit state to do anything! Can't you see that?'

'Then I shall wait until he is in a fit state. I will give him whatever assistance I can.' Jo was about to reply to this but Troy Game continued, 'Jo Grant, you brought me to him as I asked. I am grateful to you for that but I no longer need you.'

Her tone annoyed Jo intensely. 'I'm staying here,' she declared angrily.

Troy Game turned her attention back to Roche. She stroked his forehead and began to croon to him. Jo endured this for a minute or two. Then she said, 'I'm going to get a cup of coffee.'

'Bring me one,' said Troy Game. 'Decaffeinated. No milk. Five sugars. And see if they have any oranges.'

'Switch your torches off,' Zeke said. 'Let's get used to the light from the doorway.'

The twins complied. Gradually their eyes adjusted. In time, most of the cavern was dimly visible.

It was the structure in the middle of the room that most attracted their attention. It would have looked like a natural rock formation if it hadn't been so geometric.

'Like a giant hexagonal mushroom,' Zeke mused. 'Sloping sides smooth as marble. But it doesn't make any sense. Stone can't form like this naturally, surely? Yet I can't believe…'

'Don't tell me,' said Ben. 'You're going to be a geologist as well as an archaeologist.'

'It's not all smooth,' said Patric. 'This side's as rough as granite. And rippled. You might care to look at this too.'

He was indicating an oval depression in the floor, on the side of the formation furthest from the door. It was about five feet across at its widest and eight inches deep, with a flat floor. Like the surrounding floor it sloped downwards at about ten degrees from the horizontal. Muddy water had collected in its lower part.

'Vot do you make of zat, Dok-tor Kind?' asked Ben in a mock-German accent.

'Ritual paddling pool?' Zeke replied. 'Presumably the floor was level when the place was built – the ground must have shifted. Or maybe the altar was used for sacrifices and the blood was collected in the pool.'

'It's too far away from the altar for that,' said Patric.

'True,' conceded Zeke. 'I was half serious about the paddling pool, though. Ritual washing of the feet before approaching the altar, maybe.'

'I don't think the altar was for sacrifices. You'd have to stretch too far over the sloping part to reach the victim.'

'Are you two going to spend the day speculating?' Ben asked impatiently. 'Because I intend to explore the place properly. Look, there's a door in the far wall.'

The door was in the lowest part of the cavern, and it was open. There was a great deal of mud on the surrounding walls, the floor and even the strangely high ceiling.

The twins slid-walked down to the doorway. They stopped on either side of it and shone their torches in through the opening. 'Come and look at this, Zeke!' Ben called.

Zeke glanced back at the main entrance. If he'd had his way they'd have brought more rope. They were going deeper into this strange place with very little thought about getting out again. They'd already ignored one warning; what if the door swung closed again and didn't open this time? What if it *rained*?

But it hadn't rained for weeks, hadn't even been cloudy. And the main door evidently didn't have a latch. Going through one more doorway was hardly reckless behaviour, Zeke decided. He gave the altar a mock-affectionate pat then hurried after the Keller twins.

The Doctor stood at the top of the bank, above the doors. He checked the tracking device. The primary trace had disappeared the instant the youths went through the doors, but the two secondary traces remained more or less in their original positions.

The lake had drained through the open door in the bank. It had happened very recently – hours ago at the most. There was an oak tree growing at the top of the bank. It was well over a hundred years old by the Doctor's estimate. Its roots had grown around the doorway, suggesting the doors had been there at least as long as the tree, possibly much longer.

The doors had remained watertight until a few hours before the start of the time fracture. Was that coincidence?

The Doctor took hold of the rope hanging from the branch and began to climb down the bank.

The creature stirred. Somewhere a door had opened, letting in the scent of the vortex.

For 927 years the creature had been cut off from the vortex. It should have died long ago. Its sibling *had* died long ago. But this particular creature was driven by a determination to survive that was not common to its species. Without the vortex to feed on, it was forced to find other forms of nourishment.

Its environment was alive, in a sense. It had fed on parts of its environment, then slept, then moved onto other parts.

Even so, it should not have survived this long. It had exhausted its environment long ago and it had exceeded its allotted lifespan several times over. But it had been given instructions, and it had not yet carried them out. It would not rest until it had done so.

The instructions were to kill someone; it understood that much. What the creature had difficulty remembering was *whom* it had to kill. It had been so long ago, after all. But it was sure it would know when it had the right victim.

First, though, it must find the door to the vortex so that it could feed properly. Then it would be ready for anything.

'Someone is walking on my grave.'

Troy Game started. She looked around to see if Jo Grant had heard, but she had not yet returned with the coffee.

'What did you say?' Troy Game demanded.

'Intrusion. Violation. Someone is inside my tomb.' He spoke very strangely; he reminded her of the record player in Sai-mahn's flat when she put a finger on the turntable to slow it down. But that was not all. Roche had not been speaking English. She had understood him without engaging her language-telepathy. He had been speaking Dassari!

'Lord Roche!' She stood by the side of the bed, looking down at him. 'Listen to me. You must take me back. My world is in danger. I don't know why you brought me to this terrible place, but you are the only one who…'

But Roche was no longer on the bed. Troy Game was momentarily aware of a white blur. She turned, and Roche was standing behind her. He towered over her. He was much bigger than she remembered from the dream. 'You ask a lot of me,' he said in his time-distorted voice. 'It shall be considered. But first there is something I wish of you.' Gently he reached forward and removed her sunglasses, and his Careshi-like eyes bored into her own.

The Doctor stepped through the open door in the bank and drew in his breath sharply.

He was standing on the sloping floor of the control room of a TARDIS. A petrified TARDIS.

For one heart-stopping moment he thought it was his own, but it clearly was not. It almost certainly belonged to Lord Roche. It had materialised in the side of the bank many, many years ago and had remained there ever since. Nobody had known about it until today, when the waters of the lake had finally found a way in.

'It's just as well it didn't land in the sea,' the Doctor muttered. He checked the tracking device. Now that he was inside the stone TARDIS the primary trace appeared once more. It was still moving. He did not expect the other two traces to appear – they were both outside – but to his surprise one of them did show up on the little screen. It was somewhat fainter than before, but it was the same distinctive green. It was some distance from the primary trace but it was drawing closer.

The Doctor regarded his stone surroundings, a nasty suspicion dawning. 'Furies,' he said with a shudder.

Furies were creatures of the vortex. When they manifested themselves in the space-time universe they resembled rearing snakes with jackal-like heads. When they hunted they primarily sought out their victims by mindscent, and when they attacked they turned flesh to stone. They had other peculiarities too; they were not invisible, but only their intended victims and Time Lords remembered seeing them. Nobody else did; even electronic devices failed to record them.

He pressed the playback on Solenti's tracking device; this time the faint green trace *did* show up in the recording. That could mean one of two things. Either the trace was not due to the presence of a Fury in the stone TARDIS after all.

Or else the Fury was hunting without discrimination. In which case everyone was its potential victim.

There was a corridor on the other side of the door. It ran more or less at right angles to the floor's inclination, stretching out of the range of the torch beams in both directions. It was muddier than the cavern, but it was easier to balance with a wall to lean on. As Zeke did this his curiosity was aroused by a circular depression under the mud. There was another one next to it. And another. Now that he thought about it, he'd seen something similar in the cavern – a honeycomb arrangement of roundels.

'Which way?' Patric asked.

'We could split up,' suggested Ben.

'No!' said Zeke. 'It's too dangerous.' It occurred to him, too late, that Ben was provoking him.

Ben shrugged. 'We'd cover more ground that way.'

'Let's be sensible about this,' Zeke said. 'There probably isn't much more ground to cover. I don't know how big this temple complex is, if that's what it is, but it can't be all that big and most of it is probably submerged anyway.'

But Ben was not one to back down. 'I'm going to see where this corridor leads.'

He headed off. Zeke made to follow but Patric held him back. In a low voice he said, 'There's no stopping him when he's in this mood. Let him get it out of his system now rather than later.'

Zeke switched off his torch and Patric followed suit. For several minutes they stood in total darkness. As before the silence was complete apart from the distant sound of heavy water drops.

'Eerie, isn't it?' Zeke said.

'Like we've left the world altogether.'

They heard a distant shriek, the sound of someone losing their balance.

'Ben!' called Zeke.

'He's arsing around,' said Patric. 'Ignore him.'

'We don't know that.' Zeke switched on his torch, adding, 'Next time I discover an underground temple complex, he's not invited, right?' He headed along the corridor, Patric following close behind.

They passed three or four doors, but there was no sign that they had been opened so they paid them no attention. They came to a T-junction. The new corridor continued to descend to the left, but to the right it soon rose above the level the water had reached so after a few feet it was clean granite. In the torchlight the roundels were clearly visible in the walls.

'Which way, do you suppose?' Patric asked.

'He's more likely to have slipped in the lower part. Unless he got complacent. Or he's messing about.'

'Or that's him up there.' Patric's torch was more powerful than Zeke's; as he shone it up the corridor a figure was visible at the limits of their vision. He shouted, 'Ben, stop being a jerk and get down here.'

The figure did not move. Zeke said, 'Why doesn't he answer?'

'He has no concept of mileage. Just as it never enters his mind that a practical joke can be too obvious to be worth doing.'

'He could be unconscious,' Zeke pointed out.

'While he's standing up? Yeah, right.' But Patric followed as Zeke made his way up the sloping corridor.

Ben was making no attempt to hide from the pair, yet he persisted in not responding and after a while they stopped calling to him.

'Perhaps he's waiting to show us another way out,' said Zeke. 'We must be nearly at ground level by now.'

Patric suddenly stopped. 'No,' he said calmly. 'That's not Ben.'

'What do you mean it's not Ben?' Zeke said. 'You can see it's him.' The figure was less than a dozen paces away.

'Ben's dead,' said Patric, with such matter-of-fact certainty that Zeke shuddered.

'I thought you didn't believe in that psychic-link-between-twins bullshit.'

'I don't. This is something else. Something more… obvious. It's obvious Ben is dead.' Then Patric's voice cracked. 'Tell me that it's *not* obvious, Zeke! Tell me it's not obvious!'

They had arrived at the figure. It was not Ben. Rather, it was a lifelike, full-sized granite statue of Ben, complete with granite torch, granite cycling helmet and granite backpack. The expression on the stone face was one of abject terror.

* * *

'Too close! Too soon!' said Roche. He thrust Troy Game aside and in one blurred movement he had crossed the room and was pressing himself against the wall, as if he were hiding from something that was looking in through the window.

Troy Game felt as if they'd been interrupted in the middle of an interesting and important conversation, although she had no recollection of what they'd been discussing. 'Too soon for what?' she asked.

'Too soon for me!' Without appearing to have moved, Roche had her pressed against the opposite wall, his forearm across her throat. His eyes shone with rage.

Troy Game punched him twice below the ribs. This had no discernible effect. He grabbed her wrist and pressed his body against her other arm. She tried to bring one foot down on his shin but he evaded her. He outclassed her as much as she had outclassed Sai-mahn.

Jo Grant entered the room with the coffee. Troy Game managed to croak out a cry for help. Roche glanced at the tray and, perhaps recognising the threat of hot liquids, turned and kicked it out of Jo Grant's hands. Before Troy Game had a chance to take advantage of the distraction Roche was on her again. Jo Grant made a creditable attempt to break his grip, but it was to no avail so she hurried from the room to get help.

Roche did not press his attack; he seemed content merely to restrain Troy Game. She let herself relax, conserving her energy. Then Donald MacRae burst into the room. His efforts to break Roche's grip were as futile as those of Jo Grant. But Dr Calder followed him in. He was carrying a needle-tube – Troy Game had seen their like on Sai-mahn's television and had deduced that they were used for dispensing drugs. He used it on Roche. The pressure on her throat increased; her eyes widened in terror. Then she felt him slump.

'Just like before,' said Dr Calder to himself. 'It makes no sense.'

'Are you all right?' asked Jo Grant, genuinely concerned.

Troy Game rubbed her throat. She recovered her sunglasses and put them back on, although by now everybody had seen her huge irises. 'There's been a change of plan,' she said. 'I'm going to have to move quickly.' She walked out of Roche's room, then stopped in the corridor. She had found something in her pocket which had not been there before.

'What do you mean?' Jo Grant asked, following her out.

Troy Game ignored her. She looked back into Roche's room.

Donald MacRae and Dr Calder had placed Roche on his bed, exactly as he had been when she first saw him except that his eyes were now closed. But the two men were not facing him when he raised his head off the pillow, opened both eyes, winked at Troy Game then returned to his 'unconscious' state.

Dr Calder saw her standing in the doorway. 'Ah, I'm sorry about that,' he said. 'Perhaps I could get you another coffee. Then perhaps you wouldn't mind answering a few…'

'I have to leave,' Troy Game said. 'Immediately.' And she did.

Once she was out of the hospital Troy Game took the object out of her pocket. It was a key with a metal disc attached. The number '18' was engraved on the disc, along with some other writing.

'Jo Grant,' she said, 'what is this?'

'It looks like the key to a hotel room.'

'A hotel! Yes, that's it. Can you read English?'

'Yes, of course I can.'

Troy Game gave a satisfied nod. 'Then you are still needed,' she said.

Zeke was not sure how long the two of them stood staring at the petrified remains of their friend and brother. Eventually he said, 'What do we do now?'

'We get out of this place,' said Patric. 'While we can.'

'Aren't we going to look for…'

'What do you think *that* is?' Patric was nearly screaming. 'For God's sake, do you have an explanation other than the one you know to be true? I mean, do you? *Do you?*'

'Just now you said it wasn't your brother. Now you're saying we shouldn't even bother looking for Ben because of *that*.'

'I'm saying that thing *was* Ben but it's not *now*.' A solitary sob intruded into Patric's voice as he added, 'My brother's dead now, he's dead!'

There was a sound of movement from further up the corridor. Patric flashed his torch in that direction.

'Oh my God,' said Zeke.

'Run,' said Patric, sounding frighteningly calm now.

'It's not even human. It's not human, Patric! It's killed your brother, now it's coming to kill us.'

'I said run!'

They ran down the corridor. They reached the T-junction, where the side corridor led back to the big cavern and thence to the exit.

Patric had allowed for the muddy floor. Zeke had not. He lost his footing and slid past the junction. He regained his balance quickly enough but by now the creature was gaining on him. There was no way he could turn back and make it to the side corridor before it did. He kept running, going deeper into the temple complex.

The corridor opened onto a gallery. A broad flight of steps descended steeply into the huge room below. He dropped his torch as he lost his footing once more and fell down the steps, landing in the pool of cold dirty lake water that had gathered in the room.

At the shallow end of the room he could stand up with his head above the water. He marvelled at his good fortune. There was no sign of pursuit; the only sound was the reverberating noise of condensation from the ceiling dripping into the pool below.

He almost screamed when something butted against him. He pushed it aside, but touching it gave rise to curiosity. He felt for it in the dark, then made out its shape with his hands.

It was about the size of a man. Its arms were very thin in proportion to its build, its ears more like those of a dog. Its texture was leathery. It was a waterlogged mummy; it had been dead for a very long time.

But there was a living thing just like it roaming the corridors above him.

'We need a car,' said Troy Game. 'Do you have one?'

'Not here,' Jo said.

'Then steal one. You must drive us to the hotel.'

'Now just a minute!' said Jo. 'I am not stealing a car, and I am not taking orders from you. If you want my help you can start explaining what you're up to, and you can also start showing a bit of common courtesy. Besides which, you've probably made enough money from busking to be able to afford a taxi to anywhere in the country.'

Troy Game looked like a schoolchild riding out a teacher's reprimand. Not rebelling, just not understanding. When Jo had finished she asked, 'Where can you buy a tak-see?'

'You don't buy one, you hire it.' Jo had an idea. 'Give me the hotel key,' she said. She took it, read the writing on the disc and pocketed it without telling Troy Game what it said. Then she took a notebook out of her handbag and began writing. 'I'll phone for a taxi in a minute, but from now on we're doing things my way.'

Zeke pressed himself into the angle between the wall at the shallow end of the room and the stone stairs. He stilled his breathing and prayed that his heart would beat less noisily. All to no avail; the footsteps on the gallery above drew nearer. They were descending the stairs. They stopped at the water level.

There was no possibility that they were Patric's footsteps. He had not stayed for his twin; he would certainly not risk his life to come looking for Zeke.

A torch shone on his face. A cultured male voice said, 'Ezekiel Child, I presume?'

Zeke looked up in astonishment. 'Yes, th-that's right,' he stammered. 'Who are you?'

'I'm the Doctor. I've come to get you out of here. I don't mind telling you, you're in considerable danger.'

'I never would have guessed. Is it safe to move from here?'

'It is at the moment. The poor thing's confused, blundering about in all directions. But it's only a matter of time before it wanders back this way.'

Zeke abandoned his backpack. With the Doctor's help he climbed onto the stairs. He was soaked, he was filthy and he was frightened half to death. But the Doctor was an unexpectedly reassuring presence, as if he had some inkling as to what the hell was going on. He also had a spare torch.

'What *is* that thing?' Zeke asked as they made their cautious way up the corridor. 'I've never seen anything like it, not even in a nightmare.'

'That's a particularly apt description in the circumstances, Ezekiel. Like a nightmare, the creature doesn't normally register in your waking memory.'

'Doesn't normally register? I don't think I'll ever forget it!'

'That pretty much confirms my theory that the creature is hunting indiscriminately. You're very lucky it didn't find you.'

'How did *you* find me?'

'A simple tracking device,' the Doctor replied. 'It took me long enough to realise, but you're the Ezekiel Child I met in Israel in 1972.'

Zeke shook his head. 'No way, Doctor. I was born 1980.'

'Yes, well I'm afraid that's going to take some explaining. Assuming we get out of here alive.'

'Why do I suddenly find you not so reassuring after all?'

They had come to the junction. The Doctor shone his torch along the corridor. There was no movement but there was a stationary figure in the distance. Zeke's heart sank; this was too horrifyingly familiar. Unfortunately there was no choice but to continue in that direction.

'I'm afraid your friend didn't make it,' the Doctor said, confirming Zeke's fears. 'I realise it's not the best time to tell you this, but it really is terribly important, believe me. In 1972 I tracked down the source of a time fracture to the shores of the

Dead Sea, where you – your older self – were leading an archaeological expedition. I naturally assumed that the signal was coming from whatever it was you were trying to dig up. It didn't occur to me that it was in fact coming from the person doing the digging. In other words, you.'

'Doctor!' Zeke said, waving a hand in a warding off gesture. 'I really, really don't need this right now.'

They were passing the stone form of Patric Keller. Succumbing to his morbid curiosity Zeke shone his borrowed torch on the face of the statue. Patric had died with a detached, disbelieving expression. In its own way it was as horrifying as his brother's look of terror. Zeke fought back the urge to vomit.

'Don't you see, man, I *have* to tell you now. *You* are the time fracture. Whatever the event was that caused you to be there at that time, it's due to happen imminently. I've got to get you away from here before… Good grief!'

Further along the corridor was the unmistakable form of the creature.

Zeke halted. The Doctor grabbed him by the arm. 'Come on! It's just beyond the door to the control room. We can still get out – *have* to get out while we can.'

'Shouldn't we try to get away from it?'

'That's the worst thing we could do. It's not hunting us right now; what it's doing is far more dangerous. It's found a stream of vortex energy flowing in from the main entrance. It's feeding on it.'

'If it's all the same to you, Doctor, I'd rather take my chances and find another way out.'

'There *is* no other way out, believe me.' The Doctor tightened his grip and propelled Zeke towards the control-room door.

When the taxi arrived Jo made Troy Game sit in the back. She handed the sheet of written instructions to the driver. 'Don't read this aloud, please,' she said.

The taxi driver glanced at the note and nodded. They drove off.

Troy Game did not realise they were not going straight to her intended destination until the taxi pulled in at the Northgate car park.

'What are we doing here, Jo Grant?' she demanded.

'Things are getting complicated. I have to let the Doctor know what's going on.'

'But we need to get to the hotel!'

'All in good time.'

'We don't *have* time,' Troy Game insisted.

'Did you have a particular *part* of the car park in mind?' the taxi driver asked.

'Over by the tennis courts,' said Jo. 'Next to the police...' She trailed off.

'Just here?'

'Yes,' Jo said, much less confident than she had been a moment before. 'Right here.'

The taxi stopped. Jo motioned Troy Game to stay where she was, then got out.

There was the chain-link fence with the slit in it, just as it had been earlier that day. But the TARDIS was gone. There was no note, and no other indication that it had ever been there.

It was by no means the first time something like this had happened. On one occasion the Ship had been carried off by natives, another time she had seen it tumbling down a mountainside on Peladon. Then there was the incident in the grounds of the Imperial Palace of Cythera when it disappeared before her very eyes following the outbreak of a moderate hailstorm. The Doctor later explained that the TARDIS had simply activated its Hostile Action Displacement System, or HADS, and relocated itself, but it had been a nerve-racking few minutes before they eventually found it beneath a raised walkway. Afterwards the Doctor had sheepishly admitted that the sensitivity setting for the HADS had been set a little too high.

No doubt the TARDIS would turn up again, safe and sound, just as it had on those other occasions. Or perhaps this was the occasion when it would not. Given the manner of their arrival, and the unknown dangers of the time fracture, there were just too many worrying possibilities. And one possibility was that she was stuck here for good.

All in all it hadn't been a very successful day.

On the other hand, it hadn't been a complete failure. She had found Roche, after all. It was true that he was still not at liberty, but then again, without the TARDIS to take him to, it might not have been in his best interests to remove him from the hospital.

There was more to it than that, though. It wasn't just the hotel key that had passed between Roche and Troy Game. He was clearly up to something. He had attacked Troy Game but it was obvious that he had had no intention of hurting her. Why?

Perhaps it was to ensure that he stayed in the hospital; if he put on a show of being violent, the staff would not let his visitors take him away. But why did he want to stay? Was it dangerous for him to leave?

He had hypnotised Troy Game; Jo was sure of it. How else could he have impressed upon her that sudden sense of urgency? Unable to leave the hospital himself, he had to get someone else to do whatever it was that needed doing. And that had to be something to do with the time fracture. It would explain the urgency – from what the Doctor had told her, it didn't have long to run.

The biggest problem, Jo decided, was that she had no idea what a time fracture actually *was*. Aside from her own unnerving experience, all she knew was that it presented the Time Lords with a hazard to navigation and that Lord Roche was somehow trapped in it. Since Roche was the only Time Lord around right now, it would probably be in her best interest to go along with his plans, whatever they were. She might be glad of his help before too long.

She got into the taxi and they set off once more. She looked back once in the faint hope that the TARDIS might have returned, but it had not. Soon they were out of the car park and on their way to the Regis Seaview Hotel.

* * *

The creature was feeding. It writhed as it tore and rendered at something unseen. The more it ate the more frenzied it became.

'Can it see us?' Zeke whispered.

'It knows we're here,' the Doctor said. 'But it's too preoccupied to do anything about us. We have to get out of here before it… Good grief!'

He broke off and made a dash for the control-room door, Zeke following close behind. The creature's frenzied feeding was accelerating; its movements were a blur, it buzzed like a giant fly. Then it began to scream.

They were through the door and into the control room just as the creature exploded. A rain of fleshy gobbets smacked against the walls and ceiling of the corridor. The ground began to rumble.

'It's overfed,' the Doctor said in alarm. 'It must have been trapped here for years. Come on, we haven't much time!'

He scrambled up the sloping floor. He was past the petrified console and almost at the main door when he realised Zeke Child was no longer following him.

Zeke was hanging back at the lower door, peering through it into the corridor.

'Come on!' the Doctor bellowed.

'I want to see the corpse of the thing that killed my friends.'

'There isn't time!'

'What's the hurry, Doctor? It can't harm us now.'

'Listen to me, Ezekiel. We're inside a pocket universe which is about to undergo catastrophic collapse. If we don't leave now we're going to be caught inside it.'

The ground stopped rumbling. There was a sound like the snapping of a colossal stalactite, which echoed and re-echoed far into the distance. And from the distance there came the unmistakable sound of walls tumbling and ceilings collapsing. The sound grew steadily nearer.

At last Zeke recognised the danger he was in. He hurried up the slippery floor, nearly lost his footing in the sunken feature he had dubbed the paddling pool, recovered and made for the main door.

The Doctor was already at the opening. He grabbed the rope that hung from the oak tree and pulled himself out into the sunlight. He found a secure position on the threshold and readied himself for Zeke's emergence.

The control-room ceiling was falling. Zeke took the door at a run. He launched himself into space, heedless of where or how he landed.

From his ledge the Doctor watched as the blue-green rush of temporal energy erupted from the doorway and caught the youth squarely in mid-air. He hung there for an impossibly long time. Even in the sunlight the energy was almost unbearably bright. Then the torrent died down and Zeke Child fell. He landed face down in the muddy water at the bottom of the lake.

The branch of the oak tree had been struck a glancing blow by the torrent. It was visibly shorter than before, and its leaves had reverted to flowering buds.

Hurriedly the Doctor descended the bank and waded out to Zeke's prone body. He lifted him out of the water, slung him over one shoulder and, with considerable difficulty, climbed back up the bank.

Zeke had been rendered unconscious, either by the fall or by the rush of energy. He had not broken any bones and he had not taken any water into his lungs. In appearance he was still nineteen; unlike the branch of the oak tree his age was unchanged.

But he had not come out of it unscathed. The temporal energy forced out of the collapsing TARDIS had profoundly affected him. So long as he was unconscious the effects would lie dormant, but sooner or later he would have to wake up.

When that happened, his nightmare would finally begin.

Chapter Eight
Room 18

The ghosts had fallen silent in the hospital room. From Lord Roche's point of view the time fracture was over and done with, its protection gone.

It would no longer be possible for him to retreat into the past.

It would no longer be enough for him to keep his mental activity to a minimum.

Everything depended on the Careshi woman carrying out her orders.

She was taking too long. It was possible that she had not received the full instructions. He had been distracted by the presence of the Fury outside the window; this had forced him to break off communication immediately, not knowing if he had given her enough information. Despite this the Fury had come perilously close to finding him.

He could not stay in this room; it was only a matter of time before the Hunter Fury passed this way again. He had to keep moving, had to keep ahead of it. If the Careshi woman was merely delayed then he would probably not have to evade it for long. But if she had somehow been prevented from completing her task, or if she did not know all of what was required of her... That was a frightening thought. Terrans were generally less suggestible than Careshi, and consequently much less susceptible to hypnotism; there was no prospect of sending someone else.

Still, he wasn't dead yet. There was always the possibility that something would turn up. Maybe he could catch up with the Careshi woman and so get the opportunity to reinforce the instructions.

First he had to escape from the hospital. He was not happy about what this entailed, for he was not a callous man, but the situation gave him no alternative. He had another talent which, unlike his hypnotic skills, worked on Terrans just as well as it worked on Careshi. It was an altogether more brutal talent which often caused lasting harm to the subject. In these circumstances, however, the long-term effects were unlikely to be an issue.

Muddy water dripped from Zeke Child's clothes and onto the white floor of the TARDIS as the Doctor carried his unconscious body through the corridors to the sickbay. The brown marks lingered for a few moments alongside the Doctor's bootprints, then they all slowly faded away as the TARDIS's cleaning system absorbed all but the biggest dirt particles.

The Doctor placed the youth on one of the room's three couches and pulled down an overhead medical scanner. A cursory check confirmed that there was nothing seriously wrong with him aside from a few bruises and a moderate concussion; he would regain consciousness within a few hours at the very most.

So much for the physical diagnosis.

Zeke's conscious mind had been thrown into reverse. The instant he awoke his body would follow the direction of his conscious mind, and he would vanish from sight as he began his backward life. Each morning he would awaken to yesterday; in 1998 he would be twenty years old, twenty-one in 1997 and so on until the fracture finally lost its momentum in 1972. That would be his forty-sixth birthday. After that, his life would go back into forward gear.

Zeke's situation was by no means unique. Known as Jeapes' Syndrome, it was a common enough hazard whenever people began experimenting with time travel; a miscalculation could easily result in the reversal of the experimenter's lifeline, which usually lasted for several days. When this happened the mind and the universe had ways of dealing with it; memories and events would alter to accommodate the anomaly, so that as often as not the victim wasn't even aware that he had the syndrome until it was over.

A reversal of twenty-seven years was comparatively rare, however. When something of that magnitude occurred it put a lot of strain on the local region of space-time, which occasionally resulted in a fracture. This greatly increased the build-up of entropy, which in turn took a substantial toll on the lifespan of the universe. There were usually other side effects as well, often more serious than mere navigational hazards.

The Doctor looked down at the youth. He was unhappy about leaving him in his filthy state, but to remove his clothes or clean him up would be to risk awakening him. The best he could do for the time being was to administer a mild sedative. He did so, muttering, 'Sleep on, old friend. The longer you sleep, the longer I have to come up with a solution.'

But for the life of him he could not think what that might be.

Bognor Regis was a typical seaside town which somehow contrived to be small and yet sprawling. Jo had never visited the place before, but she found it to be pretty much as she had expected, or would have expected if she'd given it any thought. In the town and on the seafront it had amusement arcades, souvenir shops, fish and chip restaurants, something called a kebab house and a kiosk that sold fresh shellfish. There was a pier, a street sign giving directions to a Butlin's holiday camp and several parks, including the grandly named Rock Gardens, a crazy golf course and a recreation area with a curious arrangement of curved surfaces – this, according to the sign, was a skateboard park. If it hadn't been for the skateboard park, a single tower block and the miniature radio telescopes on the fronts of some houses, Jo might have thought she'd gone back to the early fifties rather than forward to the late nineties.

The taxi deposited Jo and Troy Game outside a large hotel which fronted onto the High Street, set back some distance from the sea. Its windows were boarded up and its wooden balcony had not been painted since... well, probably since Jo's own time. This was not the Regis Seaview Hotel, however; that was the hotel next door and it was in a much better state. The R, S and H on the signboard were embellished with the same elaborate curls as the ones on the key ring for Room 18. It had a fairly well-kept front garden, a recently painted white facade and a short flight of steps leading up to a pair of glass doors which slid open automatically as they approached.

They were already very late. A lorry had spilled its load on the A259, the only road into Bognor, and that had resulted in huge tailbacks. Jo had endured an hour and a half in a baking taxi while Troy Game, sitting in the back, had alternated between clicking her teeth in impatience and asking questions that must have sounded idiotic to the driver.

The fracture event had occurred during that wait. The Doctor had not specified the exact time when it was supposed to happen, but Jo knew. She had picked up a degree of sensitivity in the course of her travels, and she had sensed the cessation of the time fracture. Like a ticking clock, it was something you didn't notice until it stopped.

And that was all it did. Jo had expected some sort of climax, but it wasn't forthcoming. It was as if she'd failed to defuse a time bomb before the countdown reached zero and yet it still hadn't exploded. It left her with an odd feeling of disappointment. But Troy Game was as anxious as ever to get to Room 18, regardless of whether or not they'd missed the deadline.

Behind the reception desk the manager of the hotel was on the phone. He was a portly man with a thick beard and thinning hair, and looked to be in his late forties. He acknowledged the presence of the two women with a nod, mouthed the words, 'Be right with you', and turned his attention to the register on the desk in front of him. He did not appear to notice when Troy Game's impatience got the better of her and Jo had to grab her by the arm, hissing at her to wait, before she could make for the stairs.

On the wall behind him there were pigeonholes for each of the rooms, arranged in four rows of five. Each one had a number and a hook, apart from the last two which were marked 'Staff'. There were keys on some of the hooks, and letters in some of the pigeonholes. There was no mail for Room 18.

The manager finished the phone call. He told Jo they had one room available, Room 5 on the first floor. It was a double, and it was only available for one night because of a last-minute cancellation – that was what the phone call had been about, in fact. It had an en suite but it did not face the sea.

'That will be all right for us,' Jo said.

The manager gave her a look, then he gave Troy Game a look. 'Do you have any luggage?'

'No!' Troy Game said sharply.

'We're, er, travelling light,' said Jo.

He raised one eyebrow and smiled strangely at Jo as he gave her the room key. 'Well, I hope you both enjoy your stay here,' he said pleasantly. 'If there's anything you want don't hesitate to give me a call. Oh, and there's a "Do Not Disturb" notice on the back of the door. Should you need it, that is.'

'Animal,' muttered Troy Game. The manager gave her a puzzled look as if she'd spoken in another language. Jo tightened her grip on Troy Game's arm and drew her towards the stairs.

'What was that all about?' Jo hissed when she was sure they were out of earshot.

'I did not like his thoughts.'

'What do you mean? I thought you said you didn't care what…' Then Jo brightened. 'Oh, I see! You mean he fancied one of us! Is that all? Well I can't say he's exactly my type either, and he's old enough to be my…' Jo broke off as she realised what she was saying; the man was *not* old enough to be her father. He had been born around the same time she had, maybe even later. For all she knew he could be married to her future self, though *that*, it had to be said, was extremely unlikely.

It was more than unlikely if she didn't find a way of getting back to her home time. With the Doctor gone and Lord Roche securely locked away, the prospects of that happening were not looking too good. But at least she had somewhere to stay for the night. Tomorrow she would see if she could get in touch with any of her friends and colleagues from UNIT. She smiled as she imagined their surprise at seeing her turn up for work nearly thirty years late and not looking any older.

Assuming there was anyone there to remember her.

The woman on reception was finishing a phone call when a tall figure swept past her desk uttering the words, 'I'm off now, Rosemary. See you tomorrow.'

Her reply caught in her throat; for one fleeting instant she'd had the impression that the man was not Donald the orderly, but the mystery patient wearing Donald's clothes. A moment later she realised she was obviously mistaken. He was out of earshot by the time she replied, so he probably thought she was being moody or unfriendly. But Donald was never one to bear a grudge. Tomorrow she would apologise for ignoring him, and he would assure her there was nothing to apologise for. He was like that.

Lord Roche quickly located the orderly's car. Donald kept a photograph of his girlfriend in his wallet, a tall woman with long black hair and a warm smile; the picture showed her emerging from the passenger door of a silver car. There was only one silver car in the car park, a Peugeot. It took Roche a moment to work out the gears, the clutch and the ignition for it was a long time since he had driven anything like this. The car moved somewhat jerkily at first, but once out of the car park he felt he was getting the hang of it.

He looked at himself in the rear-view mirror. Donald's face looked back at him, and returned his satisfied wink. The arrangement was mutual; if the hospital staff looked in his room they would see an unconscious body on the bed whom they would identify as their mystery patient.

Roche and Donald had not changed physically but they had exchanged mindscent, and that determined what onlookers expected to see. It was not a complete exchange – it was certainly not enough to fool the Sentry Fury – but it would confuse and delay the Hunter Fury.

About a mile from the hospital Roche was briefly caught in a slow-moving traffic queue where a short stretch of dual carriageway approached a major roundabout. He took the opportunity to check the glove compartment and found a local map wedged in beneath a large pair of binoculars. A quick scan of the map confirmed he was heading in approximately the right direction for the hotel where his TARDIS was located. Then the traffic started moving again.

Before he reached the roundabout he happened to notice a figure on the far pavement near the subway entrance. The figure caught his attention because he was moving about in a state of near panic, accosting passers-by, presumably questioning them and getting a negative response, and moving onto the next passer-by.

The man was small in stature and his hair was very short. It was hard to get a really good look at him, given the distance and the traffic. Nevertheless, it seemed to Roche that he had the appearance of an Islander from the Southern Archipelago of Caresh. Roche had not given much thought to the possibility that there might be more than one Careshi on Earth. Then again, thought had been a luxury he could ill afford over the past couple of weeks.

Roche knew he should be putting as much distance between himself and the hospital as he could. But if the Careshi woman *had* failed to receive his instructions fully, then here was an opportunity for a second attempt.

He used the roundabout to double back along the dual carriageway. The Islander – if that was what he was – was still on the pavement, though he had run out of passers-by. Roche pulled up alongside him and lowered the passenger window.

'Excuse me,' he said, 'I wonder if you can help me?'

The man turned. With some difficulty he bent to look in through the window. Roche saw then that he had ear lobes and small irises. He was not from Caresh after all. Roche would have driven on if it had not been for an unexpected development: the man appeared to know him.

'You!' he said. 'I can't believe it. I *drew* you for my friend Troy Game. I thought you were just someone she'd dreamt… I never imagined you dressed like that.' The man stopped, shook his head, then added, 'I'm sorry, I'm probably not making any sense. I just didn't expect to meet you.'

'Troy Game?' Roche asked. Yes of course, that was the sun watcher's name! If only he'd remembered it in the hospital he might have done a better job of hypnotising her. Then again, he'd been too disoriented to realise who she was at the time, let alone wonder how she came to be on Earth. He hadn't intended to take her away from Caresh in the first place, but he had been temporarily blinded when the Furies attacked; she must have found her way on board his TARDIS in the confusion. 'You mean Troy Game of Dassar Island?'

The man's face broke into a smile. 'Yes! Yes I do! That's the island she said she was from.' Then he looked downcast. 'I was supposed to be helping her. But I let her down, let her down badly and now I've lost her.'

Roche was barely listening. He was being very slow on the uptake, he realised; something that should have been obvious from the beginning of the conversation had only just occurred to him. He looked in the rear-view mirror and his suspicion was confirmed: he saw his own reflection.

Either Donald had regained consciousness, or else the Hunter Fury had found him and killed him. Whichever it was, it had happened far sooner than Roche had hoped. There was nothing else for it but to effect another swap.

'Get in,' he said decisively, opening the passenger door. 'I'll take you to Troy Game.'

The man inhaled sharply as he climbed awkwardly into the car, as if the movement caused him pain. 'You know where she is?'

Roche nodded and pulled out into the flow of traffic.

'That's great! How is she?'

'She is fine. She was asking for you.'

'Really? Oh that's wonderful, I can hardly believe it. After all that's happened. When I first realised who she was – *what* she was – the prospect of...'

Roche motioned him to silence. 'In other circumstances it would fascinate me to know how you fit into all this. As it is, I am afraid there simply isn't time and there's far too much at stake.' Without stopping the car he reached across and put his hands on the little man's neck, pressing his thumbs into the carotid arteries.

A few minutes later Roche found a quiet side road where he pushed his unconscious passenger out of the car. He checked his image in the rear-view mirror and saw that the second swap had taken. The overall effect was less than convincing – his build was very different to that of his unwilling subject – but build was not a primary factor as far as the Furies were concerned.

As he drove away Roche allowed himself to consider the fate of the man he had left on the pavement. It might be hours before the Hunter Fury tracked him down, assuming the swap persisted that long. Maybe the whole messy business would be concluded by then, in which case the man would not even have to die.

That was Roche's sincere hope. But he doubted things would turn out that way.

In his own TARDIS control room the Doctor peered at the tracking device, which was once more connected to the console. He had hoped to return the TARDIS to the car park as soon as he'd investigated the source of the moving signal, but that had taken much longer than expected and the outcome was not what he had hoped it would be. By now, Jo was probably wondering where he had got to.

Unfortunately, Jo would have to wait; the Doctor had more

pressing concerns right now. He wasn't happy about having sent her after a Fury, for all that she was not its intended target, but it appeared to be moving away now. It was heading in the general direction of a south coast town called Bognor Regis, presumably to join its fellow Fury there. That was good; as long as Jo remained in Chichester she was safe.

Things were beginning to make sense at last. The stone TARDIS almost certainly belonged to Lord Roche; the time fracture had resulted from its collapse, so it followed that Roche would have had some sort of an affinity with the anomaly. More surprisingly, the tracking device showed identical characteristics for both the ancient Fury inside the stone TARDIS and the relatively young one in Bognor Regis, suggesting they were one and the same creature. But what was the connection between Roche and the Furies? Was he their intended victim and, if so, why? What had he done to upset them?

Further investigation was required. The Doctor set a course for Bognor Regis, being careful not to land too close to the Fury. He had seen what they were capable of; against them, even the TARDIS did not guarantee protection.

The late afternoon sun shone in through the dormer window over the stairs. Somehow its light failed to reach the far end of the second-floor corridor. An occasional table was set against the wall between two rooms on the left and on it stood a tall vase containing bulrushes. A reproduction of Constable's *The Haywain* hung on the wall between two rooms on the right. Each odd-numbered door faced an even-numbered one, except for Room 17 which faced a broom cupboard and Room 18 which was on its own at the furthest end of the corridor. There was a sign saying 'Do Not Disturb' hanging from Room 18's door handle.

The carpet in the corridor was light blue with a dark blue geometric pattern. It was springy underfoot; Jo noticed this only when she stepped on a patch that was decidedly not springy, as if something very heavy had been left on it.

'Room 18,' Troy Game said, speaking in an almost reverential tone. 'This must have been where I first arrived. I had no context, so none of it made any sense to me.'

Jo knew what she meant; she remembered her own first experience of finding herself on another world, and how her mind had fought to translate the things she saw into familiar terms. She had likened the planet to North Wales, which had worked well enough at the time despite the two moons and absence of vegetation.

'You have the key,' Troy Game said. 'Please unlock the door.'

Jo took the key from her handbag, then hesitated. She felt strangely uneasy about entering the room, which was absurd considering the places she'd been in. 'I probably ought to knock first,' she explained. 'Just in case there's anybody in. But the sign does say…'

Troy Game was doing the teeth-clicking thing again; she was getting impatient. Jo went to put the key in the lock and once more she hesitated. There was nothing physically stopping her, just an overwhelming feeling of intrusion, a sense that breaching the sanctity of Room 18 was simply something that one did not do.

Then she had an idea. She pointed at the sign hanging from the door handle. 'Can you read that?' she asked.

'No.'

'In that case would you mind removing it?'

Troy Game obeyed. She looked blankly at the sign, unsure what to do with it, and eventually decided to hang it from the handle of the broom cupboard.

And the door to Room 18 was just like any other door. Jo slipped the key into the lock and turned it. Then she turned the handle and pushed. The door opened and Jo stepped over the threshold, closely followed by Troy Game.

When Dr Calder went to check on the mystery patient later that afternoon he found the room empty except for a life-sized statue of Donald MacRae lying on the bed. That same afternoon Simon Haldane briefly regained consciousness only to discover that most of his right side had been turned to stone. This imperfect assassination attempt would later be diagnosed as a freak medical condition, though Simon would not live long enough to care.

Lord Roche parked the late Donald MacRae's Peugeot in a small car park behind a shop, next to a sign warning that unauthorised vehicles would be clamped. He chose this particular location because it gave him a reasonably clear view of the front of the Regis Seaview Hotel without being dangerously close to it. With the aid of the binoculars he would be able to see Troy Game entering the building, assuming she had not already done so. All he had to do was stay awake, be alert. Unfortunately that was proving more difficult than he had anticipated. Dr Calder's sedative was beginning to take effect.

The thought of giving in to sleep was so, so tempting. But he had to stay awake. He had already left a trail of death behind him; he owed it to the innocent victims to finish what he had started.

After Simon Haldane he had swapped with an old man on a park bench, the driver of a sports car who had stopped at some traffic lights, a shopkeeper, a young mother with a child in a pushchair, a traffic warden, a tramp, a lone cyclist, the vendor of a hamburger stand on the road to Bognor, an elderly priest, an attendant at a petrol station. He'd taken a zigzag course to throw off the Hunter Fury. It had bought him some time but except for the most recent swap, which had lasted more than thirty minutes, he was getting diminishing returns.

If Troy Game had already gone into the hotel she was taking a very long time to carry out her task. Roche was tempted to go in himself and find out, but the risk was tremendous; even if his latest borrowed identity didn't evaporate at the most inconvenient moment, it was unlikely that the Sentry Fury would be fooled by the swap. It would sniff out his underlying mindscent wherever he was in the building, and it would hunt him down.

Better to stay where he was: at a safe distance from the hotel, but close enough for his TARDIS not to remain in the vortex for a second longer than necessary. For the Furies were creatures of the vortex, and they could outrace a TARDIS in their own element. On Earth, or anywhere else in the space-time continuum, they were comparatively sluggish. Not as sluggish as he had hoped – eleven dead swap-partners were testimony to that – but it was as well to be aware of any possible advantages.

Someone was approaching the hotel now: a short woman with short hair. Peering through the binoculars Roche strained to see if it was Troy Game, but he was finding it hard to maintain his concentration. He just wanted to sleep. But sleep would have to wait...

It was not her. Roche lowered the binoculars and rubbed his eyes. It was too hot in the orderly's car, even with the windows open. He checked the mirror – his reflection was still that of the petrol station attendant – then pocketed the car keys and stepped out onto the pavement. He swayed; he leant on the car roof for support. He needed fresh air, he needed to stay alert. His TARDIS would seek him out just as soon as the Careshi woman operated the controls according to his instructions. If he kept his wits about him he could be aboard before the Sentry Fury even knew the Ship had left the hotel.

And then he could sleep, for a while at least.

Sleep. He had to sleep. Soon.

The Doctor's TARDIS landed without incident in a field behind a pub in Nyetimber, about three miles away from Bognor Regis. That was somewhat further than the Doctor had intended, but he did not wish to push his luck by moving the Ship again. Nevertheless, time was pressing; sooner or later Zeke Child would wake up.

There was nowhere in Nyetimber to hire a car as far as the Doctor could tell. There was not even a taxi rank. But there was a bus stop. The next bus to Bognor Regis was due in about a quarter of an hour.

While he waited the Doctor found himself dwelling on uncomfortable possibilities. Dealing with Furies was never pleasant, even if you were not their intended victim. They were quite capable of mistaking bystanders for their quarry, especially if both happened to be Time Lords. They were easily riled, and inclined to lash out. They were notoriously difficult to banish or kill, and there was no shaking them off once they'd got your mindscent.

Nevertheless, he had to find out what they were up to. The Fury in Bognor Regis was destined to end up in the stone TARDIS; if he could discover how that came about, he might be able to prevent it from happening. In which case the stone TARDIS would never have collapsed. Result: no time fracture.

Only it was rarely that simple.

The Doctor checked his watch. Surely the bus should be here by now? But he had only been waiting for five minutes. It was many years since he had last waited for a bus; he had forgotten quite how soul-destroying it could be.

There were two single beds in Room 18, neither of which appeared to have been slept in. There was a television and facilities for making tea, and a rail with coat hangers in lieu of a wardrobe, and drawers in diverse places, and an armchair and a fridge and a pair of curtains which concealed a very large window but failed to block out the sunlight.

There was a door into a dark room. Jo found and pulled the light cord. A fan began to whirr as the light flickered on. This was the en suite bathroom, or rather shower room, for it was too small to contain a bath. It had a basin, a toilet and a frosted-glass shower cubicle. Next to the cubicle was a heated towel rail on which hung a large white bath towel.

As the light came on Jo got the impression that something was scurrying into the shadows, but she could not for the life of her remember what she thought she had seen and, besides, there weren't any shadows to speak of for it to scurry into.

Nevertheless, the impression persisted; when she looked in the mirror over the basin she imagined the thing pressing itself against the adjoining wall in the reflected shower room so that she would not be able to see it from the real room.

Troy Game's reflection followed Jo's into the room. She pushed past Jo and made straight for the shower cubicle. She pulled the door open, hesitated, then exhaled sharply and stepped boldly inside.

'Troy Game, this is no time to be taking a…' Jo began. She did not finish the sentence.

There was a white glow coming from within the cubicle, a white tinged with blue. The colour reminded Jo of the glacier on Erekan. The space inside the cubicle was much greater than the external dimensions should have allowed. As Jo's eyes adjusted to the light she was able to make out familiar forms within the impossible space: the walls decorated with sunken circles, the mushroom-shaped table with levers, dials and switches. There was a low hum that seemed to her to indicate a quiescent readiness; she wondered she had not noticed that before.

In short, she was looking into the control room of a TARDIS. It was pretty much what she had been expecting to find ever since they had left the hospital; it was very much what she had been hoping for since the Doctor's TARDIS had disappeared from the car park. Even so, its presence came as something of a surprise.

Troy Game was inside the control room. She walked towards the central console. She stopped beside it, reached for one of the controls, then hesitated, her hand poised above a lever. She turned towards the entrance, looked at Jo, then pressed her hands to her temples. 'I can't… remember. The instructions were not complete. Please help me Jo Grant.'

Jo made to enter the TARDIS, then stopped short. Something about it was not quite right. It was not its outward appearance that concerned her; Jo was well aware that TARDISes were usually equipped with a chameleon circuit that allowed them to blend in with their surroundings. The one in Lord Roche's TARDIS was evidently working normally; a shower cubicle was the obvious choice in an en suite shower room.

The trouble was, it fitted in *too* well. Because without it the room made no sense; without Roche's TARDIS, the shower room had no shower.

Troy Game's expression changed from one of confusion to one of terror. She was looking at Jo – no, she was looking at something *behind* Jo. Afraid to turn, Jo made for the entrance of Lord Roche's TARDIS, but in her panic Troy Game had hit a red button on one of the console panels. The door of the shower cubicle swung closed.

At last Jo turned to look behind her. Standing in the doorway between the en suite and the bedroom was the man, the creature, the human-wolf-serpent. She had seen it before, several times; each time she had forgotten about it the instant she looked away. She remembered it now; she remembered reaching out with her right hand to touch the skin it had shed in the hospital grounds. She remembered the skin crumbling under her touch. She turned back to the shower cubicle and reached for the door handle.

From the other side of the frosted glass a blinding, blue-white pillar of light momentarily engulfed the room. Then it was gone, together with the shower cubicle. Jo was left staring at the tiled floor space of the showerless shower room.

The human-wolf-serpent thing was in the room with her. She had turned away from it but this time its presence remained in her memory. She turned back to face it. It was a huge rearing snake with the head of a jackal and thin arms that ended in clawed hands which reached for her. She tried to scream but terror constricted her throat. Instead, it was the creature that screamed, or rather shrieked, and Jo thought of the mandrake, the plant whose root drove people mad. She squeezed her eyes shut. Curiously, the effect was as if she had blocked her ears. There was a muffled silence, and a sudden sense of claustrophobia. She backed into something hard. Groping behind her, her fingers felt not tile, but wood, and a metal handle. A door! Then something brushed against her face; she fought it off, but it kept coming back at her. She found the handle again, turned it and stumbled through the opening door.

She fell onto her back on thick carpet. She opened her eyes.

An elderly couple were coming out of Room 17. They gave Jo a strange look, and she realised they had caught her stumbling out of the broom cupboard while fighting with an overall.

The late afternoon sun was shining through the dormer window over the stairs. There were three doors on either side of the corridor: Rooms 13 to 17, and the door to a broom cupboard which had a 'Do Not Disturb' notice hanging from its handle. The corridor ended in a blank wall.

There was no Room 18. There had never been a Room 18.

Behind the reception desk the hook for key 18 disappeared; the writing on the pigeonhole label changed to 'Staff'.

Unnoticed by the manager's wife as she laid the tables in the dining room, the small table with the reservation number '18' vanished.

All references to guests in Room 18 quietly erased themselves from the hotel register; other entries shunted up the pages to close the gaps.

The key to Room 18 remained in Jo's handbag, as she discovered when she looked for the key to Room 5. There was no particular reason for this; it was simply a glitch in the atrium circuit of Lord Roche's TARDIS.

Room 5 had a double bed instead of two singles, and the window was north-facing with a view of the tower block, but in most respects it was similar to Room 18. The en suite had a toilet, a basin and a frosted-glass shower cubicle. If the presence of the shower cubicle raised any hopes in Jo's heart they were short-lived; this one was no more and no less than it appeared to be.

Jo was quite sure Troy Game had not operated Lord Roche's TARDIS. She had hit the door control by accident. What happened after that… well, Jo had a pretty good idea.

Roche had known about the wolf-serpent creatures. There were at least two of them; one was looking for him and the other was guarding his TARDIS. That was why he had hypnotised Troy Game; knowing he himself could not get past the creature on guard, he had instead instructed her to enter his TARDIS and operate it. Perhaps he had been telling her how to pilot it to the hospital.

But he was interrupted and she had received incomplete instructions. She had gained access to his TARDIS but – as she had said herself – she did not know what to do next.

Nonetheless, the shower cubicle had vanished. It had done so the instant Jo touched it with the hand that had touched the discarded skin. Had Roche's TARDIS detected the cells from the wolf-serpent?

Jo held her hand under the basin's cold water tap for half a minute. Then she hurried out of the hotel. If Lord Roche's TARDIS thought it was under attack – if it had activated its HADS – it should not be too far away. She had to get to it before the creature did.

She walked briskly along the esplanade, heading east. It was as good a direction as any other; perhaps the TARDIS had gone the other way, or headed inland, or even materialised in the sea. She gave her attention to each parked car, pillar box, phone box or seaside kiosk that she passed. She took a left turn at Clarence Road, doubled back along Belmont Street. She looked in the windows of shops and houses and restaurants and down alleyways. Nothing hummed, nothing looked like an incongruously placed shower cubicle. It had probably changed by now, but to what? She kept walking. That little windmill in the crazy golf putting green – had it been there before? Or that caravan without a car? Or…

It was hopeless and she knew it. She imagined the Doctor's gentle admonishment: *To lose one TARDIS might be considered a misfortune, to lose two seems like carelessness…* She had even lost Troy Game. There was the faint possibility that the alien woman would emerge from the TARDIS while it remained on Earth; maybe Jo would run into her again, or maybe Troy Game would make her way back to the hotel.

Unfortunately, the hotel was no longer an attractive option. Room 18 had disappeared but Jo doubted that the creature inside was far away. She had had one lucky escape from it; if she returned to her room it would have little difficulty finding her again.

She found herself in a quiet street behind some shops. Her attention was drawn towards a strange object lying in the road. It was a beautifully crafted life-sized statue of a seagull, each individual feather intricately carved. Yet the sculptor's efforts had been wasted for the statue had been dropped and one of the outstretched wings had broken off. The wing lay nearby, but its edges had crumbled and it was obvious even from a cursory glance that it was damaged beyond repair.

Chapter Nine
A Typical Arcalian Affectation

The Sentry Fury was disoriented. It had been maintaining its vigil, quietly guarding the quarry's vehicle, when everything changed without warning.

Despite the continued absence of the quarry, the vehicle had disappeared. This was not a wholly unexpected development, but when the Sentry Fury attempted to follow the vehicle into the vortex it was unable to do so. The reason for this was straightforward enough: the vehicle had not *entered* the vortex. It had been relocated by some other means.

The Fury had given free reign to its wrath, but then it too had been relocated. One moment it was inside the building that housed the quarry's vehicle, the next...

The next it was outside, wandering aimlessly over stones and sand. It felt sunlight on its scales and the presence of a thicker layer of atmosphere on its lower body. It was aware of its sibling, the Hunter Fury, still some distance away but drawing closer.

The hunter had been unable to catch the quarry. There had been several occasions when it thought it had fulfilled its task, but each occasion proved to be a false alarm.

They would find the quarry's vehicle once more. It might take some time, but they could work at their leisure whereas the quarry would be constantly on the lookout for its assassins. The quarry would not be allowed to rest.

Troy Game's second trip was not as bad as the first.

As before, Roche's TARDIS attempted to close down parts of her mind and open up others. But this time she resisted. The

TARDIS seemed to respect her wishes; it did not persist.

The sight of the creature in the shower-room doorway had scared her badly. She had reacted partly in response to Lord Roche's incomplete instructions and partly in sheer panic. She had pressed a button and the doors had closed, locking Jo Grant out and leaving her to the creature's mercy.

That was a terrible thing to have happened. It was true that Jo Grant was a mere animal, but she had shown Troy Game considerable decency and concern. It was not right she should have died like that.

Almost at once the TARDIS had shifted. It reminded her of the lift in Cloud Base. She remembered imagining the cable breaking while she was in it; that was how it had felt. But the feeling did not last long.

She supposed at first that the TARDIS had fallen through the floor into the room below. If that was the case, the creature was probably still out there.

She went over to the big white doors to listen. There was quiet, then the sound of a passing car, just audible over the hum of the control room. More quiet, more cars.

Her curiosity was aroused. By pressing the red button on the console she had closed the doors, so presumably they would open if she pressed it again. That was an option she would try, but *not yet*.

There was a sunken oval in the floor to the side of the central console furthest from the main doors. It was dimly familiar, one of the things she thought she remembered from the first trip but which had made no sense to her at the time. The sunken surface appeared to contain a patch of short, slightly discoloured grass but when she knelt down to touch it the texture was that of thick glass. Evidently it was a television, albeit one with a large, oval, horizontal screen.

Was it possible that it was showing a view of the ground outside the TARDIS? That, and the sound of cars, suggested she was no longer inside the hotel. Perhaps if she opened the doors just long enough to look out, then quickly pressed the button again to close the doors…

She pressed the button once. The door swung open. She was looking out at a run-down park which was partly screened off from a curved stretch of main road by a row of bushes. The place seemed familiar; she was fairly sure they had passed this way in the taxi. She could smell the sea.

She made to press the button again but changed her mind. There was no sign of the thing that had killed Jo Grant. Cautiously she walked out through the large white double doors and onto grass that had the same discoloured look as the grass in the oval television. She turned to look back. It seemed that she had emerged from a small building with boarded-up windows. A sign indicated that ice cream could normally be bought from the building. She could not read the words on the sign but she recognised the pictures of ice cream cones. A pleasant but overrated delicacy on this strange world.

She had entered a shower cubicle and come out of an ice cream cubicle. That was just how it was; after a while it stopped being strange.

She squeezed through a gap in the bushes and stood on the pavement trying to decide what to do next. The traffic had just become busy, so she ruled out the idea of crossing the road. Then there was a lull in the traffic which lasted for a good half-minute until a double-decker bus rumbled into view. Troy Game remembered her first encounter with a bus, when her lack of context compelled her to think of it as a metal-and-glass building.

A man appeared on the other side of the road, running. It was a staggering sort of run. Troy Game watched him with some curiosity, sure that there was something oddly familiar about him. Not his face or his build or his gait, but something else… that was it, his clothes! The purple trousers, the T-shirt, the creature on the T-shirt that she knew was meant to be a dog. An anthropomorphic dog, Sai-mahn had told her, a word which didn't translate but which meant an animal portrayed as another kind of animal.

They were the clothes Donald MacRae had worn at the hospital. But the man was not Donald MacRae.

He was heading towards her. He had a dazed look about him. He stepped off the kerb, into the road. The bus was bearing down on him but like all the inhabitants of the planet he had an impressive ability to judge speeds and distances; the bus would not hit him. But what was she thinking of? He was not from here; how could she *possibly* have failed to recognise him? He was…

'Roche!'

Roche hurried through the blurring landscape. He was desperately tired and his TARDIS had moved. It should have materialised beside him; it had not done so. But he could sense its presence. It had not entered the vortex so he had a head start on the Furies. He had to hurry or he would lose his advantage.

Just a little further now. He would find it, and then he could sleep. After that he would do what he had to do.

He was partway across a road when he saw the figure. It stood between him and his TARDIS. It spoke, its voice a long slow howl. It spoke his name.

A single thought went through his mind: Sentry Fury

He halted in fright, then made to retreat.

The metal-and-glass building did not have time to howl. Roche, turning, had stepped back into its path. There was a sound midway between a thud and a crunch and he was thrown limply into the road just a few feet away from where Troy Game stood.

The bus driver braked hard. Passengers were thrown forward out of their seats, some sustaining minor injuries on the backs of the seats in front of them. But it was to no avail. The bus shuddered from the impact.

One of the passengers recovered more quickly than the others. He was a man with thick white hair and he was moving down the aisle telling people to let him through, he was a doctor. He was absurdly overdressed for the prevailing temperature – as well as a frilled shirt he was even wearing a velvet jacket – but he seemed unaffected by the heat.

Once off the bus the Doctor hurried over to the man in the road. He was lying on his back, one badly crushed arm awkwardly positioned beneath him. He was still conscious; he was trying to speak. The Doctor knelt and leant close to listen. That was when he caught the smell of his breath, and saw the eyes up close. The irises were huge.

There were no witnesses apart from the people on the bus itself and a distraught young woman with very short hair and sunglasses who was standing over the injured man. Without realising it, the Doctor found he was addressing his remarks to the woman. 'A typical Arcalian affectation,' he said, referring to the man's irises. 'I'm not altogether surprised. The other matter, though, is rather more serious.'

He glanced up to see that the bus driver had parked the bus on the wrong side of the road to ensure that one lane remained clear, and a couple of helpful passengers had volunteered to alert the traffic. To the young woman he said, 'Keep any onlookers well back, would you – I'm particularly anxious that as few people see this as possible. I take it he warned you what to expect – in the event of an accident or whatever?'

He did not wait for her to answer. The man was still trying to form words. The smell from his mouth was more distinct now: bittersweet and metallic. Then he stopped trying to speak. A most inappropriate smile spread across his face, as if he'd just thought of a terribly funny prank. Somewhat disturbed by this, the Doctor took off his jacket and laid it over the man, covering his face and as much of his upper body as he could. To the young woman he said, 'Have you been travelling with him for long?'

She jerked her head back as if he'd touched a nerve. 'I would not have put it like that,' she said coldly.

The Doctor clicked his tongue, too preoccupied to consider what she meant. 'The problem now is to get him to safety.

Unfortunately my TARDIS is somewhat further away than I would have preferred, otherwise I wouldn't be relying on public transport.'

His attention was drawn back to Roche, who had started to convulse. He made to calm him, knowing full well that there was nothing he could do. Still, it was an opportunity to search his pockets for any clues; there was always the chance that he had written his itinerary in a notebook. 'I'm convinced now that the chain of events leading up to the time fracture results from something Roche *intends* to do but hasn't done *yet*, so even now it's not too late to avert it.' He stopped and looked up at her. 'You know, I don't believe you've been listening to a single word I've said, have you?'

The woman's attention was elsewhere; she was looking towards the town, in the direction the Doctor was not facing. A smile was spreading across her face. Not a disconcerting smile; it was simply the expression of unexpected delight. She opened her mouth, displaying an unusual number of teeth, and called out, 'Jo Grant! I am so happy that you are alive!'

Startled, the Doctor turned back to look. Sure enough, his assistant was hurrying along the road towards him. At the same time he was conscious of the distant wailing of a siren. Someone on the bus had called an ambulance.

'Curse those infernal mobile phones!' the Doctor muttered.

Jo wanted to tell the Doctor how worried she'd been, how she thought she'd never find him again, how she thought she'd be stranded in the future, and how she'd met Troy Game and how they'd found Lord Roche but the poor man was in no fit state and his TARDIS was a shower cubicle in a hotel room, only it turned out it wasn't a real hotel room after all, and how they'd escaped from a hideous creature in the hotel room that was not a hotel room if you saw what she meant.

But there was no point because he didn't have time to listen. He had an injured man and an ambulance crew to deal with, not to mention the prospect of pursuit by the Furies. The injured man appeared to be Lord Roche, which meant he must have escaped from the hospital soon after she and Troy Game had left him. The Doctor told Jo that somehow he had to get Roche to the TARDIS, but that was not going to be easy because he had landed it in Nyetimber which was three miles away, and he had no transport.

But Roche probably did have transport. It was unlikely that an escaped mental patient could have got this far in a taxi; besides, the Doctor had found a car key and a wallet with a driving licence in it in the man's pockets. So all Jo had to do was take these, find the car, pick up the Doctor and Roche, and drive them to Nyetimber. He had no idea where Roche had left his car, but she had her friend Troy Game to help her search.

Her friend. Yes, that particular development had come as something of a surprise to Jo. Troy Game had been overjoyed to see that she was alive and well after her encounter with the creature in the hotel room; indeed, she had been so overcome with emotion that she had greeted her with an impulsive and wholly uninhibited hug.

She took Jo's arm as they crossed the main road. Jo knew the reason for this – Careshi were not good at coping with traffic – but Troy Game did not let go when they reached the opposite kerb and headed towards the town. Her personality appeared to have changed completely. It was certainly preferable to her cold, unfriendly self but it was also just a little bit embarrassing.

Jo disengaged her arm in order to open her handbag and take out the wallet and car key. Inside the wallet she found the photograph of Donald MacRae's girlfriend with the silver car in the background.

She and Troy Game walked some distance before they came across any silver cars. Then they found three, all parked quite closely together. One was in the street, the other two inside a private car park behind a shop. Jo remembered the Volvo in the Northgate car park, and the whining it had made when the TARDIS had struck it. What if the first car she tried had an alarm?

That might take some explaining. On the other hand, she *was* in a hurry. She was going to have to take a risk.

She picked the one parked in the street. She was about to insert the key into the lock when Troy Game prevented her from doing so. She said, 'Excuse me, Jo Grant,' and gently but firmly took the key from her hand. She indicated two buttons on the key fob. She pointed the fob at the car and pressed one of the buttons. Nothing happened. She walked into the small car park and pointed it at one of the silver cars parked there. When she pressed the button this time the car's lights flashed on and the door locks chunked open.

Troy Game flashed Jo her many teeth in a cheerful smile. 'I believe that's the one we want.'

What happened next rather depended on how long Lord Roche took to recover. If he took too long, the Doctor would be unable to prevent the ambulance crew from taking him away to hospital and that could result in untold complications, what with vortex creatures roaming the countryside. If he recovered quickly, the ambulance crew would see that he was uninjured and so they would take no action. But if he recovered *too* quickly – before Jo returned with the car – it would be very difficult to prevent him from returning to his own TARDIS and leaving before the Doctor could question him. The Doctor did not know where Roche's TARDIS was, but he had an inkling that it was close by.

Beneath the Doctor's jacket Lord Roche had stopped convulsing. The worst of his ordeal was over. By now his appearance would have changed. He would probably be disoriented, prone to sudden lapses of memory and susceptible to suggestion. The Doctor certainly hoped so; it would make his task a lot easier. On the other hand he might be stroppy, contrary and paranoid. It was difficult to tell in advance.

The fact was, the Doctor was no expert where regeneration was concerned. He had only vague memories of his own regenerations, and the few he had witnessed before he had left his own world had been planned months or years in advance. Emergency regenerations featured often enough in entertainment broadcasts – they made for good drama – but they bore as much relation to reality as did death scenes in operas and soap operas.

When the ambulance arrived the Doctor rose from his pretend-examination of Lord Roche. 'Thank you for coming so quickly,' he said, addressing the driver. 'However, I'm afraid you've had something of a wasted journey. You see, thanks to this man's quick reactions' – he indicated the bus driver – 'a potentially serious accident has been averted.'

The bus driver looked bemused. 'Quick reactions? But I hit him! There's a big enough dent in the front of the bus.'

'If he's not hurt, why is he lying on the ground?' the woman in the passenger seat of the ambulance demanded as she climbed out of the vehicle. 'And why have you covered his face?'

'Sunstroke,' said the Doctor airily. 'Allow me to introduce myself. I am Doctor John Smith, and…'

'If it's all the same to you, "Doctor", it might be as well if I examine him myself.' The woman knelt on the road and part-lifted the jacket. 'He seems to be… Oh! You didn't mention he was your brother.'

'I am quite capable of making a medical diagnosis,' the Doctor began, then did a double take. '*What* did you just say?' He lifted the jacket himself and looked under it. 'Good grief!' he said, his tone a strange mixture of anger and amusement. Then he took the jacket away. There were one or two gasps from the people who had come off the bus to see what was going on.

The man in the road was unconscious, but showed no sign of any injury. His appearance had completely changed, which was as the Doctor had expected even if it was a surprise to the passengers who had caught a glimpse of him before the accident. What was altogether *un*expected was the form his new appearance had taken. The new Roche had a lean, humorous, young-old face and a shock of exuberant white hair.

For a moment the Doctor was speechless. 'The sly old fox!' he blurted out once he'd regained the use of his voice. 'Well, I suppose it *is* the sincerest form of flattery, but I… Confound the fellow, how dare he?'

'That's never the man I hit,' the bus driver said.

The Doctor rallied. 'I keep telling you, old chap, thanks to your quick reactions…'

Lord Roche's eyes blinked open. He sat up, dazed but making an effort to take in his surroundings. 'Did I pass out?' he asked. 'It's a dreadful nuisance but I simply can't cope with this heat. Good heavens, I hope I haven't caused any inconvenience.' He stood up. He was unsteady on his feet, but clearly not injured.

The Doctor drew the astonished ambulance crew to one side. In a low voice he told them, 'As you can see my, er, brother is perfectly all right. But he's been under a great deal of strain recently. I think it would be best if I got him home. What he needs right now is familiar surroundings and a nice cup of tea. Or maybe a long cold drink in the circumstances. Non-alcoholic of course.'

The ambulance driver said, 'Are you twins?'

'No we are not!' replied the Doctor indignantly.

'Yes we are,' said Roche at the same time.

The driver and the paramedic glared at the Doctor. The Doctor glared at the regenerated Lord Roche. 'What I mean is, when I say we're not twins, we are of course… triplets. It's a point of semantics we've never agreed on.'

'Triplets,' echoed the woman.

'But there's only two of you,' said the man.

'Only two *present*,' the woman pointed out reasonably.

The Doctor raised his hands in exasperation. 'I really don't have time for this ridiculous conversation, and I don't suppose you do either for that matter.'

The driver was about to comment when he was interrupted by an elderly lady calling timidly from the door to the bus. 'Excuse me, my husband seems to be hurt.'

Now that the Doctor thought about it, he had seen an old man hit his head when the driver braked. In other circumstances he would have attended to him himself. 'Let's hope his injury looks far worse than it is,' he muttered to himself as the ambulance crew went to investigate. To Roche he added, 'I don't know what you're playing at, but whatever it is it's not going to fool anyone. The voice is a complete travesty. And as for the nose, you haven't got that right at all!'

He would have said more, but at that moment Jo pulled up in the silver Peugeot. The short-haired woman with the sunglasses was sitting in the passenger seat so the Doctor bundled Roche into the back and climbed in beside him.

There was a serene look on Roche's face until Jo pulled away. Then he glanced back at the ice cream kiosk and began to panic. 'No, not this way, not this way!' He attempted to open his door but the Doctor restrained him. There was a brief struggle; Roche started to say, 'You don't understand. I need to stop the… need to…' then slumped in his seat, unconscious.

'Turn left here,' the Doctor barked. 'Straight across at this roundabout. And Jo, do you think you could possibly drive a bit faster?'

'I'm already breaking the speed limit, Doctor,' Jo replied. Half a minute later she stopped at a red light and refused to drive on despite the Doctor's exhortation to do so. They were not at a junction, Jo noticed; these traffic lights were meant for pedestrians. While she waited for the lights to change she took the opportunity to look in the rear-view mirror. Once she was sure there were none of the serpent-wolf things following along behind – Furies, the Doctor had called them – she turned her attention to the pair in the back of the car. It was quite uncanny. Jo had encountered shape-changers in her time and the Doctor had told her about android replicas, but this was altogether different. The unconscious man on the back seat was the man she had met in the hospital but now his appearance was changed, just as the Doctor had changed his appearance on at least two occasions. If she understood correctly, the man was another Time

Lord and his new appearance was permanent, or at any rate long term.

'He's even got your nose exactly right,' Jo remarked.

'Go now, Jo!' the Doctor insisted in such a peremptory tone that Jo jumped. 'If it's flashing amber and there are no pedestrians you have right of way.'

She drove on. Roche briefly awoke, as he had done three or four times since they had left the scene of the accident, and muttered something incoherent. The Doctor told him, 'You're going to have to stay awake, old chap. We're nearly there.' To Jo he said, 'Turn in at this pub on the right. There's a sizeable car park that backs onto a field.'

Jo obeyed. She parked next to the sign that said 'For Patrons Only'. She helped the Doctor support Roche as they walked him through a gate into the field, Troy Game following close behind. It was a meadow rather than a field, with grasses and wild flowers as high as Jo's waist. There was a sewage works in the distance and a caravan site to the right, but Jo's attention was drawn directly to the welcome sight of a blue police box a dozen paces away.

Inside the familiar surroundings of the white control room the TARDIS engines hummed reassuringly. Jo stepped on a piece of broken crockery; she felt it crunch under her foot. Roche became markedly more alert than before; he gazed hopefully – hungrily even – at the console and tried to break free of Jo and the Doctor's support. Then his look gave way to an expression of dismay as if he'd just realised that this TARDIS was inadequate for whatever it was he had planned.

'Come on,' the Doctor barked. 'We've a way to go yet.'

'Where?' asked Jo.

'The zero room.'

He led them down corridors that had been inaccessible until recently. Jo was inclined to think of them as hallways rather than corridors, because they rarely ran straight for very long and tended to be features in their own right. Their angles were usually punctuated with fluted half-columns, and their walls were often adorned with mirrors and landscape paintings, and niches and alcoves with statuettes of people and gods and monsters in them, and cupboards with vases of flowers on them, as well as the ubiquitous (and usually featureless) roundels. There were doors and archways which led to rooms and other hallways. They stopped briefly at one doorway which the Doctor told Jo led to the TARDIS sickbay. He opened the door and she looked in at the dirty and unconscious youth on the couch. Then he closed the door and they went on.

'Did you recognise him?' the Doctor asked.

'No. Who is he?'

'His name is Ezekiel Child.'

Jo frowned. 'I know that name.' She shifted uncomfortably. Lord Roche was tiring, and as a result he was becoming more of a burden. 'Oh! Didn't we meet a Professor Child in Israel?'

'One and the same.'

'But it can't be! He can't be more than… Ah, is he another time traveller?'

'Not exactly Jo. He's suffering from a particularly nasty form of Jeapes' Syndrome.'

'What on Earth is that?'

'It's a little difficult to explain. Imagine if all the days in your life were pages in a book. Whenever you go to sleep a page of the book is turned over and you wake up to a fresh page. With Jeapes' Syndrome you are still effectively reading through each page in the correct manner, but the pages themselves are out of order. In the case of Ezekiel Child, the pages have gone into *reverse* order. When he wakes up it will be to the start of yesterday's page, and then the day before yesterday after that, and so on for the next twenty-seven years.'

'That's horrible,' said Jo. A thought struck her. 'Is that the cause of the time fracture or a consequence of it?'

'It might be a contributing factor, one way or another, but it's difficult to draw a distinction where time anomalies are concerned. What worries me is that there's usually a knock-on effect that has no apparent connection to the fracture event itself.'

They had reached the antechamber of the zero room. At the far end a sloping walled structure housed a column which partly concealed a pair of roundelled doors.

'In here,' the Doctor said, leading the way through the doors.

They found themselves in a large, almost featureless room with much bigger roundels than the ones in the rest of the Ship. The walls were a grey shade of blue, reminiscent of the glacier-blue interior of Lord Roche's own TARDIS. The Doctor was surprised by this. 'It's normally rose pink,' he explained. 'It seems the old girl has adapted herself to accommodate our guest. I don't suppose for a moment that his Ship would do the same for me.'

'Now what?' Jo asked.

'We leave him here for now. He has everything he needs. I'll look in on him in an hour or so.' In a more sympathetic tone he added, 'After the ordeal he's been through he'll need the time to recover.'

They left the zero room, closing the doors behind them. On their way back to the control room Jo gave the Doctor a succinct account of her last few hours. The Doctor, for his part, was unusually attentive. Several points gave him pause for thought.

'The newspaper – you're quite sure it was a different one the second time around?'

'Quite sure, Doctor.'

'Hmm. A discrepancy like that could be an effect of the fracture. The universe is struggling to maintain consistency, and on the whole it's succeeding where the broader picture is concerned. The devil is in the details.' He paused, frowning. 'Yet I can't see how that *particular* detail relates to Ezekiel Child. It's too random. It's as if there's a blurring of the boundaries between quantum universes.' He paused again, but this time he smiled. 'Hark at me, Jo – theorising without data.' He frowned once more. 'Nevertheless it is worrying.'

'Do you mean it's more complicated than you thought?'

'On the contrary, Jo, things are falling into place. You see, I too found a TARDIS today. A dead TARDIS. It had been resting in an ancient lake for many centuries. I'm quite positive now that it was Roche's TARDIS.'

'But I thought the one I found in the hotel room belonged to him.'

'And so it did.'

'But how?' said Jo, confused. Then realisation dawned. 'Oh, I get it. You mean the TARDIS you found was the same as the one in the hotel room, only... older?'

'I do indeed. And I didn't just find the same TARDIS. I also encountered an older version of one of the Furies. At first I thought it must have forced its way on board but now I'm not so sure.' The Doctor was silent for a time as he put his thoughts in order. They were passing the door to the sickbay once more but Jo did not look in this time. She was afraid to open the door in case she awakened the patient.

'That hotel room you investigated was a part of Roche's TARDIS,' the Doctor continued. 'A construct of its atrium circuit. You and the Sentry Fury were allowed inside the construct but not the TARDIS proper. Roche must have set the HADS to relocate his TARDIS if it thought it was being attacked by the Furies. The question is, why let them inside the construct in the first place? It makes no sense.'

'Maybe it was to trap them.'

'Hmm. Not bad, Jo. Not bad at all. It would have cost him his TARDIS, but in the circumstances it was a price he was willing to pay. All he had to do was seal them inside and send them into the distant past. Cut off from the vortex they would eventually starve to death. Unfortunately he didn't send them back far enough.'

'But it didn't trap them. Did it?'

'Not that time, no. The presence of the ancient Fury in the stone TARDIS suggests he made a second attempt – or at least he did originally, before we came along. So why didn't it work the first time?'

'Maybe he needed something from the landing site to complete the trap,' Jo suggested. 'But he landed in the wrong place.'

'I suppose it's possible,' the Doctor conceded. 'The question remains, where and when was he heading?' Then he shook his head decisively. 'It's academic now. Whatever he was planning, we've got to prevent him from making that second attempt. That shouldn't be too difficult so long as we have him safely on board.'

Jo frowned. 'Let me get this straight. If he doesn't make that second attempt the stone TARDIS will never have collapsed. So the time fracture will never have happened.'

'Top of the class, Jo.'

'But what about the Furies?'

'Well, unless I'm very much mistaken it was the fracture that drew them here in the first place.'

'I see,' said Jo after a time. 'It's one of those self-fulfilling paradoxes, isn't it?'

'I'll make a temporal physicist of you yet.' They had arrived at the door to the control room. 'There's just one remaining question,' the Doctor said, going through the door. Inside the control room, Troy Game was standing with her back to the console.

'What's that?'

'The question of *what* we are going to do with *this* young lady.'

'Jo Grant told me you would take me back to my world,' Troy Game said.

The Doctor raised an eyebrow. 'Did she indeed? I must say, that was very good of her.' In a low voice he added, 'Jo, you can't just go round promising lifts to all and sundry. This isn't a taxi service, you know!'

'She's not "all and sundry", Doctor,' Jo replied, also in a low voice. 'She's from the planet Caresh, I think she said, and she's stranded on Earth and she's been looking for Lord Roche because she needs to get home because her world is in danger. But Lord Roche is in no state to help her so I told her you could help.' A thought struck her. 'You said there were normally knock-on effects from a fracture. Do you suppose that's why her planet is in danger?'

The Doctor tapped his chin. 'Did you say Caresh?'

'Yes, Doctor. Do you know it?'

'No. I know *of* it though. It's one of the landmark worlds.'

'So you could take her home?'

'In theory, yes.'

'Does that mean you're going to help her?'

'Jo, in case you haven't noticed I have a lot on my plate right now.'

'But you just told me you'd averted the fracture!'

'It's not quite as simple as that. First of all, I still have to persuade Roche to abandon his attempt to trap the Furies. I can't very well move on until I'm sure I've convinced him. Secondly…'

All this time Troy Game had been listening politely, aware that they were talking about her as if she was not present. At last she spoke up. 'Excuse me.'

'Secondly,' continued the Doctor, 'assuming the danger to Caresh *is* a knock-on effect of the time fracture, it will probably sort itself out as the fracture heals.'

'Excuse me,' said Troy Game again, a little less timidly this time.

'And thirdly, I have just spent a number of years in exile on your decidedly primitive little world on account of my previous interventions. Some were of the opinion that I was treated with too much leniency. So if you think I'm about to go risking my freedom by provoking the Time Lords with further acts of…'

'Excuse me!' Troy Game was decidedly forceful this time.

'Yes what?'

'I wish to say, if you are unable to help me please do not worry. I will await Lord Roche's recovery and rely on him instead.'

Jo bit the inside of her cheeks in an effort not to smile. The Careshi woman had inadvertently said exactly the right thing.

'I did not say I would not help!' the Doctor declared indignantly.

'Does that mean you will?' Jo pressed.

'Yes. No. Maybe. It depends!' The Doctor pressed his palms to his temples in exasperation. 'Very well, I promise I'll look into it, just as soon as I have confirmation that the time fracture has healed.' His expression brightened. 'And I think I know how I can do that.'

'How?'

'By using Solenti's tracking device. If there are any Furies within a fifty-mile radius the device will detect them. If the Furies are gone we can be sure that the fracture is healed.'

The Doctor switched on the scanner. The view outside panned through 360 degrees. They saw the field, the pub, the caravan site, the sewage works and a cluster of houses. There was no sign of any of the creatures.

'No immediate danger,' the Doctor said. He took Solenti's device from his pocket. He was about to put it into its slot on the console but thought better of it. He pushed the red lever instead. 'This works best outside. I'll just be a minute.'

But as the main doors began to swing open the interior door to the control room was flung open behind them. The Doctor, Jo and Troy Game turned to see a young man striding through it.

He had cleaned himself up since Jo had seen him through the door of the sickbay, and he had found himself some clothes. He was wearing one of the Doctor's frilly shirts and a pair of baggy trousers. His hair was clean but uncombed, and he was growing a very patchy beard. When he turned Jo saw that he hadn't quite managed to get all of the mud out of his hair; a thin streak of it ran behind his left ear and onto his shirt collar.

In a calm, restrained voice Ezekiel Child said, 'Would someone mind telling me what the *hell* is going on?'

Chapter Ten
Artist's Impression

'What's the last thing you remember?' the Doctor asked Child as they passed through the gate into the pub car park.

'It's difficult to say,' Child replied. 'So much of it is confused, I can't even say what order anything happened in. I remember running down endless corridors thinking something was after me. I remember thinking I was going to drown in mud. And I remember...' He broke off with a frown. 'Did we really come out of that blue box just now?'

'Appearances can be deceptive, Ezekiel. Here's my... er, the car.'

They got in and the Doctor started the engine. 'You're quite sure you want to go straight home? I could take you to a hospital in case you're suffering from shock. You have been through a great deal, you know, probably more than you realise.'

'I'll be fine, Doctor. My house is only a short drive from here.'

In the TARDIS control room Jo and Troy Game watched an animated sequence on the scanner showing the orbit of Caresh around its two suns. It was essentially similar to the computer program Troy Game had watched at Cloud Base, but with a higher degree of precision so that even after several hundred speeded-up orbits the planet continued to switch between the suns in an unpredictable manner.

'It seems to account for the "8", but not the "1",' she mused.

It took Jo a moment to realise she was referring to the number on the hotel room key. 'I think that's just coincidence,' she said. 'I wonder what it looks like closer in?'

The view zoomed in and the point that was Caresh became a

disc about the size of a coaster. To Jo's surprise it appeared as a pencil drawing rather than a photograph. Both the north and south poles had ice caps of roughly equal size, which was unusual; on most planets summer at one pole was winter at the other. Between the poles the sea was dotted with perhaps 150 islands, most of them clustered into one of five groups. Some of the larger islands had been roughly shaded in.

'The Doctor told me it was a landmark world,' Jo said. 'Yet all it seems to warrant is an artist's impression. Perhaps nobody has ever seen it from orbit. Troy Game, can you see your home?'

Troy Game looked uncertain. 'I think that one is Dassar,' she said, pointing at a medium-sized island midway between the equator and the south pole. 'But we rarely use maps. You have great faith in the Doctor. Do you believe he can take me home?'

'He promised he'll do his best. It might turn out to be a bit of a roundabout route, but I'm sure we'll get there in the end.'

'That is reassuring. But I am afraid of what I will find there. Caresh has endured a long succession of cold years. I think the ice has spread much further than this picture shows.'

Jo felt uncomfortable; there was nothing she could say to that. If the coming ice age was going to bring about the extinction of the people of Caresh, what could the Doctor do about it? Could he help evacuate them to an uninhabited world? It seemed unlikely. According to the database entry there was only one other planet in the Careshi solar system and it was not capable of supporting life; besides, the Careshi had not developed space travel.

The Doctor had his TARDIS, of course, but Jo could not see him transporting a planet's population across space. It was not practical, for one thing, and for another it was not the sort of interference that the Time Lords were likely to tolerate.

Sometimes there was no alternative but to let nature take its course.

Jo glanced at her watch. 'I don't suppose he'll be much longer,' she said vaguely. 'I think I'll go and check on Roche.'

* * *

'Take the next right after the cricket ground,' Ezekiel Child said, his voice quavering slightly. 'Carry on to the end of the road.'

The Doctor complied. They were heading back into the town, towards the seafront. Child had been quite calm when they left Nyetimber but now he was increasingly on edge; he glanced nervously down every side road they passed, and once the sudden appearance of a man in a shop doorway made him jump out of his skin.

'We'll soon have you home,' the Doctor said sympathetically. 'Make sure you get plenty of rest. I can assure you everything will be back to normal before you even know it.'

'I'm fine, Doctor, really,' Child said through chattering teeth.

A thought struck the Doctor. 'Weren't you wearing glasses?'

'What?' Child put a hand to his face. 'You're right, I must have left them in the TARDIS. It doesn't matter, I only wear them for reading. Turn left here.'

The Doctor pulled out onto the main road – Aldwick Road, the route the bus had taken earlier. It occurred to him that something was very wrong. He turned to Child and said, '*What* did you just say?'

Jo was not sure that she could remember the way to the zero room. The hallways did tend to branch. But she had not gone wrong yet for here was the door to the sickbay. Ezekiel Child had left it ajar.

Jo was about to walk on when something made her look inside. She was sure she had heard a sound from within. The sound of someone *breathing*.

They were approaching the park near the place where the bus had hit Lord Roche. There was a boarded-up ice cream kiosk in the park, intermittently visible through gaps in the bushes.

'I'm sorry Doctor. I meant "turn left here *please*".'

The Doctor ignored this. 'I never once used the word "TARDIS" within your hearing. I made a point of it! Now who are you really, and what do you want?' He was looking at Child as he spoke, but a movement – no, two movements – near the ice cream kiosk had caught his eye. In utter disbelief he turned to look at them. 'Good grief,' he said.

'Keep your eyes on the road, Doctor,' his passenger said. 'Unless you want to leave the steering to me.' With that he grabbed the wheel and made the car swerve across the road.

The heavy breathing was coming from the person lying on the middle couch. Cautiously Jo walked over to see who he was.

She told herself she would not scream, but she could not prevent herself from uttering a shocked gasp. For the man lying on the couch was the Doctor. She could recognise his features despite the fact that he was caked in mud.

But how could that be? She had entered the TARDIS with him. He had not been out of her sight until the moment he left with Ezekiel Child.

So the man on the couch could not be the Doctor. He merely *looked* like him. In which case he had to be Lord Roche.

That still didn't make sense, though. Or did it? Roche had been installed in the zero room. He might have recovered more quickly than expected and come out again. Or, more likely, he *thought* he had recovered and had come out too soon. He had headed for the control room, but by the time he reached the sickbay, he knew he needed to lie down so he lay on the couch Ezekiel Child had recently vacated. There was still mud from Child's clothes all over the couch, which was why Roche was so dirty now.

But why would he have lain on the one dirty couch when there were two clean ones available? And how had he got the mud all over his front?

As Jo considered this the man's breathing began to change. He was waking up.

And then something very strange happened. Roche's features changed. For a split second Jo thought he was going to revert to the form she had seen in the hospital, but no – this was something else. The man on the couch was – *had always been* – Ezekiel Child.

Ezekiel Child woke up. And vanished.

The Doctor struggled to regain control of the car.

The other man in the car was Lord Roche.

The two Furies were still on Earth, and they were guarding the ice cream kiosk.

The time fracture had not healed.

'This isn't the way!' the Doctor shouted, but to no avail. The Peugeot was on the wrong side of the road and oncoming traffic swerved to dodge it. It mounted the kerb, passed within a yard of the nearer Fury and almost hit a pedestrian. The Doctor pushed his foot down hard on the brake as they ploughed into the bushes.

'We seem to have attracted their attention,' Roche was saying, his voice wholly lacking any urgency or sense that he was aware of the danger they were in. 'That's good. It's useful to remember that although they can outrace a TARDIS in the vortex once they've got up to speed, they are really quite sluggish on Earth. They don't really live up to their name then.'

The Doctor, shaken by the impact, recovered his senses. He attempted to put the car into reverse. But the Fury was closing in on them. The two identical Time Lords climbed out of the car and broke into a run.

'They home in mainly on mindscent,' Roche continued in conversational tones. 'You probably knew that. They can distinguish between human and Time Lord easily enough. But they are not good at telling one Time Lord's mindscent from another. Especially two Time Lords who are as alike as we are now.'

'We are not alike,' the Doctor retorted coldly.

They ran across the park. Roche made a dash for the ice cream kiosk. The second Fury blocked his route. But Roche was expecting this; he withdrew, with the second Fury in pursuit.

185

'This way!' Roche yelled.

He ran down an alleyway which opened onto a broad tarmacked walkway. On the far side of the walkway was a low sandstone wall and, beyond this, a secluded beach sectioned off by groynes. A man and woman were catching the last rays of the sun as late afternoon turned to evening. The woman glanced up as one man leapt over the wall, immediately followed by another, identical man.

The Doctor caught up with Roche. He grabbed him by one shoulder and spun him around. He grabbed both his shoulders and held tightly. 'You're deliberately bringing them after us!' he said. 'You're going to get us both killed.'

'No, Doctor,' Roche said, panting from his exertions. 'Not... both of us. That is not the... plan.'

'Plan?' The Doctor shook his head. 'You're fulfilling what you're seeking to prevent. Believe me, Roche, I've seen it!'

Roche tried to break free but his recent ordeal had weakened him. The Doctor was by far the stronger of the two. But Roche was the more savage. He brought his head down heavily onto the bridge of the Doctor's nose. Dizzy with pain, his grip broken, the Doctor staggered backwards and fell.

Seconds passed. The woman screamed. The Doctor raised his head to see the Furies slithering over the wall and onto the beach. Roche was now sitting cross-legged close to the wall, his eyes closed as if in a trance. The vortex creatures were passing within a few feet of him, completely oblivious to his presence. They were interested only in the Doctor. With two of them and only one target their comparative sluggishness was less of a disadvantage. The Doctor leapt to his feet and tried to dart around the one on his left but it changed direction to block him. He tried to dart between them, but they anticipated his intentions and closed up again. They continued to advance and the Doctor continued to back away.

Whether or not it was their intention, they were driving him into the sea. It occurred to the Doctor that that might be for the best – perhaps they were allergic to salt, or perhaps the water would slow them down further, allowing him to swim away from them. He turned and ran into the waves – the tide was some way in so he did not have far to run – and did not stop until the water had covered the tops of his trousers. He looked back. To his horror the Furies were still after him. The sea had not slowed them down; indeed, the waves did not break against their snake-like bodies but passed through them instead.

There was no question about it, they were going to kill him. An unnatural coldness had started to spread through the skin of his chest and upper arms. Not just a coldness, a *hardness* too as if his flesh was already beginning to crystallise. His blood felt viscous, his hearts less and less capable of pumping it around his body.

Roche's voice seemed to come from the end of a very long tunnel. 'Not him you fools, *me*! Over here! Come on, come and get me!'

The Furies hesitated. They turned to look at Roche who was standing a safe distance away at the water's edge, a triumphant smile on his face. 'I must thank you, Doctor, you make a fine decoy. It was never my intention to let them kill you. But I needed to get them away from my TARDIS. As long as I was on my own one of them would always stand guard, but with two of us to chase…'

As one, the Furies lost interest in Roche and turned back to the Doctor. Roche's smile vanished. 'No!' he shouted frantically, 'He's not the one – it's *me* you want! Come *on*!' When it was clear they were not to be called off so easily he ran into the sea until he was dangerously close to the creatures. To the Doctor he shouted, 'Try to reduce your mental activity so you'll give off less mindscent. Then they'll come after me.'

'I know what you're planning, Roche,' the Doctor called back, barely able to make himself heard above the crashing of the waves. 'It won't work that way. The only way to stop them is to heal the fracture.'

'It's too late for that, Doctor. You can't heal the effect unless you go after the cause.' Roche was starting to back away but the Furies

187

were not following him. 'Damn it, Doctor, can't you just let it go?'

The Doctor's head was pounding and his skin felt like porcelain. His vision was starting to fade but he would not give in, not yet. 'What is the cause, Roche? Tell me that!'

'Caresh. Caresh is the cause. But it's better this way, believe me. Caresh is already lost.'

He might have said more but the Doctor's consciousness was slipping away. The world had gone dark, and the only sound was the sea. The last thing he was aware of was the touch of cold fingers on his arms and neck, pulling him backwards into the water. Resigned, he let himself go.

Chapter Eleven
The Darkening of the Sun

The chase was a great deal shorter than before. Then, it had been over a distance of more than fifty thousand light years. This time it was less than two hundred miles through space, and a few weeks through time.

The quarry would try to evade them. It would suppress its mindscent. But they were prepared for that this time. They had learnt much since their first attempt; they had developed. No longer creatures of pure instinct, they would bring their new skills to bear.

They knew how to increase their sensitivity to mindscent. The quarry would not be able to evade them this time.

Some time later, as he began the three-mile walk back to Nyetimber, the Doctor considered the latest state of affairs.

He had not drowned, of course. The couple on the beach dragged him out of the sea in the nick of time.

Roche was gone and so were the Furies. And so was the ice cream kiosk.

The car was too caught up on the bushes to move easily. Given time, and help, the Doctor might have got it back on the road. But it was not his car, and chances were another interfering busybody with a mobile phone had reported the 'accident' by now. Best to avoid the awkward questions. And best to avoid public transport while he was in his present state. He was soaked from head to foot, his forehead had been bleeding and his shirt was as rigid as if it had been heavily starched.

He took the tracking device out of his jacket pocket. It was unharmed by its immersion in the sea. He checked it for Furies: there were none. As far as his own personal safety was concerned, that was good news. But in every other regard everything had gone wrong.

'That's the last time I ever do Solenti a favour,' he declared. He had said this many times before but this time he really meant it. Then again, he had meant it all the other times as well.

If all went to plan, Roche thought, he was making his last ever journey in this particular TARDIS. He felt a pang of regret. His Ship, as he had come to think of it, was almost a part of himself.

He was especially fond of the floor scanner. When the Ship hovered (and it often did) it was like looking through a viewing window onto the drifting landscape or seascape below. Right now he was passing over the fields of Cornwall. Externally his Ship had taken the form of a light aircraft. It was not a model anyone on Earth would recognise, for he kept no terrestrial aeroplanes in his TARDIS-shell room and he did not have time to design one. But the basic outline was more or less correct, and in any case he was too high up for anyone to notice.

The date was 11 August 1999. Almost the entire sky over the south-west of England was free of cloud, as it had been for several weeks. Crowds of people were gathered in the fields below to watch the total eclipse of the sun. Roche could see a sea of faces wearing eye-protectors and looking up into the sky. He switched on the wall scanner. The sun was a fat crescent, perhaps twenty minutes from totality. Earth was, if not unique, at least very rare in having a moon that exactly covered its sun. But it did not happen very often, especially in this part of the world.

The Furies were either clinging to the outside of the aircraft or else following a short distance behind in the vortex. It made little difference; he was leaving nothing to chance. The HADS would operate only if the Furies attacked the Ship while he was not within sensor range. The chameleon circuit would select an exterior resembling a shepherd's bothy – again he had none of terrestrial design in his shell room, but they tended to look the same the universe over. Admittedly the one he intended to use was a little larger than usual, but nobody was likely to investigate it closely.

He had found a suitable landing spot. Close to the crowds, but cut off by a barbed wire fence and some bushes. There was little risk of anyone stumbling into the atrium region at the critical moment. He checked the Ship's settings once more. Spatial displacement was unimportant, though a certain amount of drift was inevitable. Temporally, the Ship could go back 1,382 years without an operator present. Further than that and there was a risk to its integrity. He settled for a nice round figure of 1,300 years. The Furies couldn't possibly survive that long without receiving energy from the vortex, surely?

'Last time, old chap,' he said, patting the console. Even if everything went according to plan he was still faced with the prospect of being stranded on Earth, perhaps indefinitely. There was always a chance that the Lady Solenti would turn up to photograph the eclipse – gathering yet more material to look at if and when she got her sight back – but he was not pinning his hopes on that faint possibility. She was more likely to be as far away from the action as possible. Probably in her beach house on Lanare, sitting out the crisis by immersing herself in her studies. She did not like to get involved.

Few in the crowd paid much heed to the presence of a twenty-foot-high mud-brown shepherd's bothy in the next field. Those who noticed it at all wondered why they had not seen it before, but obviously it *had* been there because that sort of thing couldn't just appear out of thin air.

Beyond the fence the Furies stood by the bothy's single door, waiting for their quarry to emerge. But the vehicle did not open in the way they expected. A vertical crack appeared in the wall on the other side of the building. It widened to a gap. Roche emerged from the gap at a run.

Wrong-footed, the Sentry Fury made to take its place by the new entrance while the Hunter Fury went in pursuit of the quarry. But they had scarcely moved when the sunlight, which had been gradually dimming, went out altogether. There was darkness in the middle of the day; only the light from the sun's corona remained, a ring around the silhouette moon. Tens of thousands of awed spectators were watching the eclipse.

This was no ordinary crowd with conflicting emotions that cancelled each other out. Here, the response was *unanimous*. The solid tidal wave of mindscent hit; the Furies screamed, immobilised by the pain of sensory overload.

Roche stopped running. He turned back to look at his Ship.

The atrium field folded back on itself. The margin of projected field which had overlain the real field was gone, returned to its host TARDIS. It took the Furies with it.

The bothy, no longer mud brown, was now the colour of the surrounding fields. Bulges appeared randomly in its walls, as if the building was made of rubber and a cartoon fight was going on inside. Roche's TARDIS changed into a grass-green ice cream kiosk, a grass-green shower cubicle, a grass-green computer bank and an eight-foot globe of a grass-green planet before it finally stabilised, the bulges no longer appearing. It dematerialised, not with the usual sound of the time rotor but with a scream like the tearing of metal, as if it could not bear to be parted from its operator.

Roche exhaled; he was free at last. His TARDIS would die, he knew that; it would appear 1,300 years in the past, inert, but with the Furies entombed inside it. It was not a small price to pay but it was a necessary one. And despite what the Doctor seemed to think, it had *worked*.

And here he was, looking just like the Doctor during his exile on this world. Could he make something out of that? Perhaps he could pass himself off as the Doctor, pretend he was suffering from amnesia and take it from there. Would anyone remember the Doctor? Had he made any lasting friendships here? Maybe. But if the rumours were anything to go by, he had probably made more enemies than friends. In which case, Roche thought, it might be advisable to change his appearance again.

He considered the idea, then shook his head. It was not the sort of decision one should hurry. For now, he simply sat cross-legged on the grass and waited for the sun to return.

Chapter Twelve
A Careshi Perspective

Whatever her instincts told her, Jo realised that the most sensible course of action was simply to wait. She had no idea where the Doctor had gone, so she could not very well rush off after him in order to warn him that Child was really Roche and the real Child had disappeared because his life had gone into reverse because the time fracture had not healed after all, and...

He probably knew already.

She returned to the control room where Troy Game stood watching the scanner. It was showing the view outside once more. The bad news was that there was no sign of the Doctor; the good news was that there was no sign of the Furies either.

'Jo Grant,' the Careshi woman began.

'Just Jo will do,' said Jo wearily.

'Jo. May I talk to you?'

Jo mustered her strength to be supportive. 'Yes, of course you can. What do you want to talk about?'

Troy Game was silent for a moment. 'May I talk to you where there are people?' She indicated the scanner. At the edge of the field was the pub. 'If we sit outside we will see the Doctor when he returns. Or you could leave him a written message.'

Jo was not altogether happy about leaving the safety of the TARDIS. The time fracture had not healed so the Furies were probably still at large. On the other hand, despite the brief misunderstanding in Room 18, she and Troy Game were not their intended prey; it was unlikely that the creatures would have followed them this far.

'Well, we did use their car park,' she said. 'I suppose it's only fair that we give them our custom. Besides, I could do with a drink.'

They took their drinks into the pub garden where they found a table for two. All the other tables were occupied: an elderly couple, a young couple, another young couple with three children, a gathering of thirteen or fourteen people of all ages, and others.

'I'm beginning to remember what happened before I left Caresh,' Troy Game said. 'I'd forgotten more than I realised, but it's all coming back. The trouble is, it's very slow. It's trickling back, one random detail after another. But the details are starting to form a picture. It's sketchy, and there are more gaps than details, but when I try to guess what is in the gaps, I tend to know if my guess is right or not.'

She sipped her pure orange juice and continued. 'I only remember some of what happened, and I only understand some of what I remember. But I do know I have to get back to Caresh soon, or it will be too late. Perhaps I will know what to do when I get there, but without the Doctor's help I have no hope at all. Not now that Roche is gone. Jo, do you think the Doctor really will take me home?'

Jo nodded. 'I'm sure of it, Troy Game. I can't say how long it will take, or what might happen along the way, or what the eventual outcome will be. But I can promise you one thing, he will do what he can. He will do his best and, believe me, that's the best "best" you're ever going to get.'

Troy Game smiled. 'I knew you would say that.' Seeing the change in Jo's expression Troy Game quickly added, 'I don't mean I got it from your mind. Not just then.'

'When did you?' Jo asked, a little coldly.

'When you and the Doctor were talking in the TARDIS before he left with Lord Roche. I sensed your absolute faith in him then. I wasn't prying. It's just that it was... impossible to miss.'

Jo sipped her Cinzano and lemonade. There was a short, not quite uncomfortable silence. Making conversation, Jo said, 'I expect you'll be relieved to leave Earth.'

'I thought I would be. My ability to sense people's thoughts was useful to begin with, but I came to hate it because I didn't like what people were thinking. There was too much bitterness and spite and unseasonal lust and loneliness. It was worst at the hospital where we found Roche. I just wanted to get away from Earth as soon as possible.'

She took off her sunglasses, rubbed her eyes. Jo saw her irises for the third time. 'Today may be the last time I see Earth,' Troy Game continued. 'Now I realise I had a unique perspective on the world. Nobody else can sense the thoughts of others, and not all the thoughts I sense are bad ones, and some of them only seem bad because I am judging them from a Careshi perspective. If fertile time was permanent for us I would have been flattered by the attention.'

'It's not always flattering or welcome, believe me,' Jo said with feeling.

'Maybe not, but I would at least have understood what was going on. I would have realised how Sai-mahn felt.'

She played with her sunglasses. 'It's fading,' she said at last. 'My ability to sense what people are thinking is diminishing much more rapidly than my memory is returning. The world is falling silent around me. When I sang in the subway I knew how people were responding to my singing, and I could respond to them in turn. It was wonderful. I never sang that way before, and I never will again. All I can sense now is a background murmur, like the sound of the sea. Even that is dying. Your faith in the Doctor was the last thing I was able to understand.'

Jo was conscious of the chatter and laughter of the other patrons in the pub garden. She imagined going deaf. Would it be like that? Would it be so bad, given that Troy Game had only had the ability for a fortnight or so?

A minute passed without either of them speaking, then another. Troy Game finished her drink. 'It's gone.' She put her glass on the table next to the sunglasses and rose. 'Can we go back to the TARDIS now?'

They left the pub and went through the field to the battered police box. Jo was aware of some curious glances directed at them. Troy Game hesitated at the doorway, taking in her last view of Earth.

'It's so terribly *quiet*,' she said.

The Doctor eventually returned, looking somewhat the worse for wear.

After he had cleaned himself up he told them about his tussle with Lord Roche and the Furies, and how he had failed to avert the time fracture after all.

'An unsuccessful conclusion, then,' Jo mused.

'Conclusion? On the contrary, Jo. We haven't even started yet.' The Doctor pressed buttons on one of the console panels, took readings from another. He frowned in concentration, then looked up at the two women and grinned. 'I was afraid the fiasco with Solenti's device might have undone our good work. But I needn't have worried. The updated information in the navigation system is still intact.'

Completely at a loss, Jo said, 'Where are we going?'

The Doctor looked at her in amazement. 'I do wish you'd pay attention, Jo. Where do you think we're going?'

A smile broke out on Troy Game's face. 'You're taking me home,' she said.

The Doctor winked at her and pulled a lever. The glass column in the centre of the console rose and fell, rose and fell.

The blue police box became transparent then faded completely away. The TARDIS had departed from Nyetimber, and the Earth.

It skimmed the vortex like a flat stone thrown obliquely across a lake. It reappeared in an empty part of space several light years from the nearest star, but a thousand light years closer to the Careshi system. The navigation computer performed its second calculation which took into account the TARDIS's new location, and executed its second dive into the vortex.

It would continue like this until the TARDIS ultimately arrived at its destination. The duration of such a journey depended on a number of major factors, including the level of activity within the vortex and the TARDIS' ability to assess this accurately, in addition to several minor factors including one which the Doctor liked to think of as the old girl's 'mood'.

Inside the TARDIS the three travellers discussed matters arising, the Doctor breaking off occasionally to make a minor adjustment to their course. It was evident that Roche had been in the Citadel on Dassar Island when the Furies had attacked and that he had fled in his TARDIS, though not before Troy Game had followed him on board. What he was doing on Caresh in the first place was still unclear, but Troy Game believed he was engaged in the final stage of a project which had been going on for centuries. This project was supposedly going to save Caresh from some unspecified threat but she believed it would do nothing of the sort. Unfortunately, her recollection was still far from complete.

'You're quite sure he was talking about an immediate threat?' the Doctor pressed. 'Something quite distinct from an impending ice age?'

'We have not used the warm year calendar since my childhood, Doctor,' she told him. 'This urgency is a recent development.'

'Is there anything you can think of, anything at all, that might have prompted it?'

Troy Game thought hard. 'Yes,' she said at last. 'Lord Roche asked the chancellor of Dassar College to chart the movements of a neutron star. As a sun watcher the task was assigned to me. From its increase in brightness I calculated that it was drawing closer to the Careshi solar system at a rate of one-tenth of the speed of light. I was in the Citadel making my report when the Furies attacked.'

'That's it then!' cried Jo. 'The neutron star must be on a collision course with Caresh!'

'It's not very likely,' the Doctor said irritably.

'But if it's moving closer...'

'Just because the distance between two objects is decreasing, it doesn't necessarily follow that one is heading directly towards the other.'

'But surely it's possible?'

'It's perfectly possible, Jo. But I don't think that's what's happening here. You see, if the neutron star *was* going to collide with Caresh there is absolutely nothing Lord Roche could do about it.'

'Couldn't he sort of nudge it out of the way?'

The Doctor gave her a look. 'Jo, sometimes I despair. A neutron star is several times the mass of the sun, and several million times the mass of the Earth. It would require an immense amount of power to deflect it, far beyond anything you could possibly imagine.'

'But he's a Time Lord,' protested Jo. 'I thought you Time Lords *had* unimaginable powers.'

'He is one Time Lord working on his own. In theory it could be done, but he'd need the backing of the High Council to pull off anything like that.'

'How do you know he doesn't have their backing?'

'If he did, he would hardly have asked me to take over from him, would he?'

'It was just a thought,' Jo said, deflated.

'Roche seemed to think the neutron star was important,' Troy Game pointed out.

'I don't doubt it,' said the Doctor. 'Listen to me, Troy Game. Is there anything else you can think of that might give us some kind of clue as to what we might be up against?'

The Careshi woman's big eyes looked sorrowful as she shook her head. 'I can't remember,' she said.

'Pity,' the Doctor mused. 'Because if he *is* manipulating that neutron star, I'd very much like to know what he's doing, how he's doing it and above all, *why*.'

Troy Game's partial amnesia was the source of much frustration, but the Doctor at least had some idea of how it had come about. When she boarded Roche's TARDIS it had attempted to bestow the gift of language-telepathy upon the new traveller, not 'realising' that this was an innate skill among the Islanders. So rather than give her a skill which she already possessed it had awakened other telepathic faculties which had hitherto lain dormant, but in doing so it had closed off access to her recent memories. The Doctor's TARDIS, on the other hand, was generally more accommodating than Roche's; if anything it was helping to reverse these unfortunate effects.

'If we are going to find any answers, the best place to start looking is in the Citadel,' the Doctor eventually concluded. 'I'll materialise the TARDIS inside the main chamber.' But when Jo raised an eyebrow, he added, 'Well, I'll try and get as close as possible.'

In the event there was no sign of the Citadel when the TARDIS materialised and the scanner completed its 360 degree pan. By Troy Game's reckoning they had missed Dassar Island altogether. But they had not missed Caresh, of that she was certain; there was no mistaking the two suns, the black flowers and that wonderful, wonderful sea.

'Not a bad landing, all in all,' the Doctor said. 'Now, if we can work out our bearings...' He reached for the lever that operated the main doors while Jo kept an eye on Troy Game, curious to see how this long awaited homecoming would affect her. Jo envisaged her either throwing her arms around the Doctor or else rushing out through the doors onto her native soil where she would laugh or weep or both...

Troy Game caught the Doctor's hand before he could pull the lever. 'Whatever are you thinking of?' she demanded. 'You can't possibly go out looking like that!'

'I have never heard anything so ridiculous in all my life!' the Doctor exploded when Troy Game had explained herself. 'Have you the slightest idea how many worlds I've visited, or how many life forms I've encountered?'

'Come on, Doctor,' Jo said. 'I'm not thrilled about it either, but you know, "when in Rome" and all that. And it *will* grow back. Eventually.'

'You can keep your ear lobes,' Troy Game told them brightly.

'Thank you very much indeed!' the Doctor replied. There was the beginning of a smile on Troy Game's face which vanished as soon as the sarcasm registered. 'In any case it's academic,' he continued. I can assure you I do not keep hairdressing accessories in the TARDIS...'

'I've got some clippers in my room,' said Jo. 'And remember those eye-protectors we wore on Erekan because of the high levels of ultraviolet light?'

'Jo!' the Doctor barked. 'I am not doing it and that's final.'

It was not final, of course. They argued some more and the Doctor eventually conceded, with rather poor grace. Jo fetched the battery-powered clippers and a cloth to put over the Doctor's shoulders. She switched the clippers on. The Doctor sat stiffly on a UNIT crate as she began to shear away his shock of white hair. There was complete silence except for the combined hum of the clippers and the control room. Jo eventually broke the silence.

She said, 'Are you going anywhere special on your holidays this year, sir?'

Hidden behind a rock in the forest above the fiord, where the trees were too weary to shake the snow from their branches, two Islanders kept watch over the blue box on the ledge below them. Nothing had happened since it appeared out of nowhere, but they maintained their vigil nonetheless and in time their patience was rewarded.

The box opened inwards. Three figures, one of whom was unusually tall, emerged. The younger of the two watchers – the woman, whose name was Rak Shal – raised the brass telescope to her eye. She exhaled through her teeth and passed the instrument to her kinsman, Rak Irik. 'I think it's Roche,' she hissed, a hint of fear in her voice. 'Look!'

Rak Irik looked through the telescope. He said nothing for a long time. Rak Shal clicked her teeth together. Still he did not speak. Eventually her impatience overcame her.

'Well? Am I right? Is it him or not?'

He kept her waiting a little longer. 'He is very tall,' he said at last. 'His skin is pale. He does not look like the pictures, but they are old and he might have changed. Also, consider the manner of his travel.'

'It has to be him. We should kill him now. They would thank us for it!' She stood up, her crossbow raised.

'Don't be stupid, Rak Shal!' hissed the other. He grabbed her by the collar and pulled her back down behind the rock. 'If he is Roche, do you really think he can be killed that easily? Do you think you would get a second shot if you missed with the first?'

She glared at him, saying nothing.

Rak Irik relaxed his grip, his anger giving way to curiosity. 'He's got some nerve coming here at this time. But why so far from Dassar? And why accompanied? Why make himself vulnerable?' He looked at his kinswoman and saw cunning in her eyes, reflecting his own.

She said, 'Are we thinking alike, Rak Irik?'

Interlude
The Tides of Lanare

Lanare was two-thirds ocean and one-third land. It had three major moons. Its tides were complex and difficult to predict, even for the merfolk who lived in the ocean. It was not unknown for one of their number to lose her bearings and find herself washed up on a beach, bewildered and unable to find her way back to her clan.

When Jess began her frantic barking outside the beach house, Solenti supposed that this was what had happened. She was more than a little interested; she had been spending a lot of time in the library listening to recordings of merfolk song, and following transcripts of the music's intricate patterns on a tactile computer display. The merfolk were not generally regarded as intelligent, but Solenti believed she had detected the rudiments of abstract language in their singing. She relished the opportunity of meeting one of the creatures.

But the barking continued, and Solenti was shocked by the realisation that Jess was frightened. Very frightened. Solenti hesitated at the exterior archway. Jess did not scare easily; a beached creatures would have aroused her curiosity but not her fear. There had to be something else out there.

'Jess!' Solenti said, her voice firm and commanding. She had not spoken loudly enough for Jess to hear her but the dog was within telepathic range; after several moments the barking stopped and Jess finally responded, her thoughts rendered incoherent by fear:

'He can't, it isn't, he's here but he can't.'

'Jess, get a hold of yourself,' Solenti demanded. 'What do you mean? What can't he do?'

'He's here but he...' Unable to control herself any longer the dog began barking again.

Solenti walked through the archway onto a flight of steps that led down to the beach. She felt for the handrail. There might be danger outside, but if so the house was unlikely to afford her much protection; on the other hand, Jess was more likely to come to her senses if her mistress was close by.

'Jess!' she demanded again as she descended the steps and walked onto the beach. 'Tell me what is going on.'

The sand was warm beneath her bare feet. She was aware of the Labrador hurrying towards her, pressing herself against her legs. Solenti reached down and caught hold of her collar. Then, almost as an afterthought, she patted the dog's side and spoke gently to her.

'Who is here, Jess? Is it the Doctor?'

Jess shook. 'No.'

'Roche?'

'No, Lady.'

'Someone to see me?'

'Yes.' Jess sounded pathetically eager to give a positive response at last.

Solenti frowned. 'Well who, then?' she said, and she felt the twist of fear in Jess' answer.

'I don't know, Lady. I cannot know. He has no scent. I cannot smell him at all.'

The man without a scent regarded his surroundings.

There were local heat gradients in the temporal axis caused by the movement of a slow-to-change-temperature fluid over a quick-to-change-temperature solid. The solid was fragmented but firm enough to support him; the movement of the fluid was apparently random, but there was a pattern to the randomness.

The important factors were the heat gradients in the spatial axis. They occupied two bodies which stood together on the fragmented solid. Two life forms, two mindscents, one of them the right species.

The same species as Lord Roche. An individual *known* to Lord Roche.

The individuals were aware of his presence. He turned to address the taller of the two, then hesitated. This time he was not acting with the authority of the Curia of Nineteen. This time he was prepared to reveal secrets of the Realm, and for that there could be no forgiveness.

The man without a scent spoke. He said, 'Roche.'

His voice was a roar, glacial-slow and heavy. It was difficult to locate his position by it, but Solenti supposed he was a few metres further down the beach, with the waves breaking around his legs. If he had legs.

'I am not Roche,' Solenti replied evenly. 'Who are you?'

'Magus Amathon. Get me Roche.'

'He is not here.'

'Roche needs to be here.'

'Roche is *not* here.'

The voice was more than just slow, it was impersonal, and the words did not linger in the mind after they had been spoken. Solenti had to repeat Amathon's words back to herself for fear of forgetting them. Now that Jess had calmed down the only sound was the advance and retreat of the waves, and Solenti found it hard to shake off the impression that she had been facing out to sea holding a one-sided conversation with an imaginary correspondent. Eventually, though, Amathon spoke again.

'Find Roche. Tell Roche he must not continue.'

'Why? What is he doing? And who has he upset this time?'

'Tell Roche.'

'Now just you listen to me, Magus Amathon. If you want me to tell Roche I demand that you first tell me what is going on.'

Amathon seemed to consider this. 'You shall know,' he declared at last. He then proceeded to tell Solenti what she wished to know.

Or rather he showed her.

* * *

Solenti saw for the first time in ninety-one years. It was… disorientating.

He showed her the Realm. A pocket civilisation, tier upon tier of architecture, landscape and nature, a delicate yet enduring structure in the midst of chaos. In engineering terms alone it was a marvel, but it was much more than that, and much more than a mere dwelling place, though it was that too. It spoke beauty, and told of the character of the dwellers. It hinted at layers of meaning that could be apprehended without being understood.

He showed her the region of space-time onto which the Realm was mapped. Its position was midway between two suns, one somewhat brighter than the other.

'Ember and Beacon,' said Solenti, surprised to find she recognised them. 'The suns of Caresh. Why map the region there of all places? Don't you realise a planet passes through it every year?'

Amathon did not answer. There was no need; of course he knew.

Solenti found herself standing on the flagstones of a plaza between a fountain and the portico of an elegant and imposing building. This, she was informed, was the Palace of Equilibrium where the Curia of Nineteen gathered. Her point of view rose above the surrounding buildings so that the city unfolded below her. She rose higher still until the entire mathematical construct that comprised the Realm was visible as a jewel-like world of tiered discs floating serenely in the red-brown swirl of the vortex.

As she watched a black, spherical object appeared in the swirl, speeding onward in the general direction of the Realm. It was not quite a collision course; at its closest approach it was fully three Realm diameters from the Realm itself. But it set up ripples in the vortex, and they broke against the shore that was the Realm's perimeter. Soon after the black sphere had passed, the largest wave of all struck the rim wall. A sliver of Realm broke from the main body and floated away into the vortex, where it fragmented and then dissolved.

'When did *that* happen?' Solenti asked, surprised to find herself dismayed by the vision.

'This is a mathematical simulation of a future event,' Amathon told her.

'Based on what, may I ask?'

'A ballistic projection. An object in space-time will pass through the mapped region.'

'An object in space-time?' Solenti echoed. What could Amathon possibly mean? He clearly wasn't referring to Caresh – a planetary mass would have no effect on the vortex. It had to be something more massive than a planet – or something with a more *concentrated* mass, such as a black hole or a neutron star. A body with a steep gravitational gradient. Perhaps *that* was what interacted with the vortex, rather than the object itself.

'You've got a problem on your hands,' Solenti said at last. 'But I don't see what it has to do with me. It's hardly my fault if a rogue star happens to pass through your world.'

'Not your fault. The fault of Roche. He redirected the object.'

'Redirected?' she said, completely taken aback. 'You mean, Roche is responsible for *that*?'

'Yes.'

'Well, I hope you're not expecting me to sort it all out.'

'No.'

'Then what...'

'Watch.'

Time reversed and the Realm was whole once more. The second simulation began.

The moving black sphere appeared in the swirl, setting up ripples in the vortex again. This time it *was* on a collision course; it passed obliquely through the transparent dome that marked the artificial sky of the Realm, continuing on through a plateau on the uppermost (and smallest) of the seven tiers, leaving a deceptively small hole in its wake. Nothing happened for several tense moments. Then the hole began to expand, slowly at first but picking up speed at an exponential rate until the Realm was devoured leaving nothing apart from a ring, slightly thicker on one side than the other. Because of a peculiarity of vortex physics, the ring persisted for many seconds before it finally fragmented.

'It is *this* that you must prevent,' Amathon told her. 'We know that Roche intends to make one last alteration to the object's trajectory. We know that this will be the result. Your intervention is therefore required.'

Again the process reversed and the Realm was restored. Solenti found herself descending, not to the plaza this time but to a formal garden with box hedges and an armillary sundial. She supposed the sundial was an affectation, for Beacon and Ember were not visible in the Realm's artificial sky. Her descent continued until she found herself underground inside a circular room. It was hot inside, incubator hot, with a distinctly reptile smell in the air. There were three alcoves in the wall; two were empty but the third contained a leathery, semi-transparent dark-brown egg sac. Solenti recoiled as she made out the indistinct form of a snake-like embryo.

'Furies!' she spat. 'You *cultivate* them?'

'The Realm is not without its defences,' Amathon informed her.

'Indeed not! I had no idea they could be bred in captivity. If the Time Lords ever found out...' She broke off, and considered the significance of what the magus had shown her. Two empty alcoves, which suggested two Furies had been dispatched, undoubtedly in pursuit of Lord Roche. By rights they should have killed him by now, but he must have evaded them somehow or else Amathon would have no need to involve her. But he had involved her, and he'd let her see that he was keeping one Fury in reserve.

Solenti nodded, acknowledging the implied threat. 'If the Time Lords *do* find out,' she said, 'it will not be through any fault of mine.'

The vision passed. Solenti found herself in darkness once more, and ankle-deep in sea water. But she had seen. She had *seen*. The neural pathways that dealt with vision were intact; there was no longer any real doubt that her sight would return the moment she regenerated. She could do it right now if she wanted to, right here on the Lanare shore.

No. Not yet.

She had seen... and *what* she had seen! Yet on an instinctive level she knew that Amathon had tarnished the beauty of the Realm by the very act of revealing it to her. The Vortex Dwellers would know at once what he had done and they would punish him for it, for all that his actions had probably saved the Realm.

Solenti shrugged. So much for Amathon; he'd made his decision. She called to Jess and waded up the beach. Something didn't quite fit, however, and she found herself going over everything Magus Amathon had shown her. When she arrived back in her study she realised that it was Lord Roche himself who did not quite fit. Because if she knew Roche as well as she thought she did, he was behaving totally out of character.

Roche had been through a lot lately. Solenti did not know how the business with the time fracture had resolved itself – if indeed it had – but that paled into insignificance compared with these latest developments. On the one hand he had escaped from the Furies. On the other hand he was wise enough to realise that would not be the end of it. Roche was no coward, but he knew when he was outmanoeuvred and outclassed, as he was now. With the wrath of the Vortex Dwellers hanging over him there was absolutely no way he would take any action that might further antagonise them.

Yet Amathon still seemed certain that the Realm was doomed if Solenti did not intervene. What was she to make of that? Did he know more than he was saying? Did he have some direct means of viewing the near future? Solenti supposed that was possible. The Vortex Dwellers had a lot in common with the Time Lords – perhaps more than either realised. But even if Amathon had looked into the future and seen that the final change had been made to the object's trajectory, it didn't necessarily follow that Roche was responsible. Did it?

Then the solution came to her. She buried her face in her hands and cried out, 'Oh no! I don't believe it!'

Jess had been dozing in her basket. She was jolted awake by the outburst. 'Lady?' she thought. 'Are you threatened?'

'Only by my own stupidity, Jess. I *knew* I shouldn't have involved the Doctor. But I didn't trust my instincts, and now it's too late. It seems, Jess, that the Doctor is going to finish what Roche started.'

Chapter Thirteen
Fell

The suns were low on the distant horizon where the fiord met the open sea. Beacon rivalled Ember for brightness despite being further away, and the three travellers cast long double shadows on the snow-covered ground. Troy Game clambered over the rocks below the ledge where the TARDIS had landed. She was fairly sure-footed but her sense of balance was affected by the return to full Careshi gravity.

She stepped onto a large rock that was half in, half out of the water. She crouched and touched the water's surface. It was cold but not quite freezing. She pushed back her sleeve and thrust in her whole hand, her wrist, her elbow. Her skin responded in a manner that told her, beyond a shadow of a doubt, that this was *right*. She had found her sea once more.

Only then did she allow herself to weep.

After a time she made her way back up to the ledge where her two companions waited. They looked very different now. Jo, wrapped in furs which largely concealed her figure, could just about pass as a native Careshi, despite her pale skin. The Doctor, on the other hand, could not help but draw attention to himself, but that could not be helped; more importantly, his new appearance was unlikely to arouse revulsion or hostility.

'Not Dassar,' Troy Game confirmed when she'd rejoined them. 'I don't know where, but we must be closer to the equator. The sea here is not yet ice.'

The Doctor slowly nodded his maneless head in acknowledgement and said, 'I could try a short hop in the TARDIS. The trouble is,' he rubbed the back of his neck, 'the old girl's database is far from complete for this particular planet.'

'I thought you said Caresh was a landmark world,' Jo said.

'In theory it is, but in practice it's rarely used by the...' He broke off, looking up the mountain slope. After a few seconds' scrutiny he said, 'I could have sworn I saw a movement just then.'

Jo and Troy Game followed his gaze. There was no movement now, but there was something else which both women saw at the same time: the glint of sunlight reflecting off metal. Now that they were aware of it, it was possible to discern the outline of a structure, a low tower or pylon on a higher ledge.

'Curious,' the Doctor said. 'The ledge seems to continue along the mountainside. There's another tower, look, and another one there. You know, I'm inclined to get a closer look at one of those things.' He turned to Troy Game. 'I doubt it's a particularly difficult climb, and it might give you a better idea where we are, don't you think?'

Troy Game nodded. 'I will come with you.'

'Good! Jo?'

'If it's all the same to you, Doctor, I think I'll stay here. I'd rather acclimatise myself to the local gravity before I start climbing.'

'That's probably wise,' the Doctor agreed. 'We shouldn't be more than half an hour all told.'

The Doctor's estimate was typically over-optimistic and it was more than half an hour before they had even reached the ledge. This was hardly surprising; there was no path to speak of, the slope was very steep in places and the snow-covered rocks were treacherous. In the last few minutes of the climb both the Doctor and Troy Game were aware of a rumble like distant thunder, although there were few clouds in the sky.

'The acoustics of a dense atmosphere and mountains on three sides,' the Doctor announced airily. Troy Game, some distance ahead of him, wondered if this was supposed to be an explanation – and if so, was it for her benefit or his own? Giving it no more thought, she climbed onto the ledge.

It extended in either direction as far as she could see, curving around the mountains but maintaining a more or less constant height above sea level. It was between two and three metres wide. There was a horizontal cable suspended above it throughout its length at roughly twice her height – this, evidently, was the purpose of the towers or pylons. On the floor of the ledge ran a pair of parallel rails, the distance between them maintained by a series of wooden planks.

Troy Game knew at once what it was, having seen something very like it running through the outskirts of town near Cloud Base, though that one had lacked the overhead cable. It was a railway track. Recognising it was one thing; finding it on Caresh was as surprising as anything she had recently experienced. For several moments she stood transfixed as the train itself – the source of the rumbling – snaked around a mountain spur. In its own way it was as impressive as the metal-and-glass building that had been her first memory of Earth, though it was nowhere near as tall and seemed to be made mostly of timber. It consisted of six essentially featureless blocky carriages, the first of which had a window at the front, and a metal arm on top which maintained contact with the overhead cable.

She had no idea how fast it was moving, but she had ample time to step aside and watch from the refuge of the gantry tower as it rattled past her.

The Doctor was beside her. 'How fascinating,' he declared. 'You know, I've always wanted to drive one of them.'

'I think I know where we are, Doctor.'

'You do? Well that's the best news I've heard all day.'

'No Doctor, you don't understand. The places I know do not have such things.' She indicated the train which was now heading away from them. 'Lord Roche does not allow it. But here... Here they do not respect Lord Roche, and we will not be welcome.'

Before the Doctor had a chance to comment Troy Game was making her way down the mountainside. She looked back once to urge him to hurry.

Well before they had reached the lower ledge it was obvious that Jo was gone. The Doctor made a perfunctory search of the TARDIS but he did not expect to find her there. The presence of two extra sets of footprints in the snow made it all too clear that she had been taken away.

The island was not Fell, as Troy Game had feared, but Stakisha. This information gave her scant comfort, for they were both part of the same island chain; indeed, Stakisha was connected to Fell via a part-natural, part-artificial causeway.

They had followed the footprints for a short distance into the forest. They found themselves in a clearing, where they were quickly surrounded by a group of Islanders dressed in leathers and furs and armed with swords and crossbows. Their leader, who was armed with an unwieldy looking rifle, addressed the Doctor.

'Lord Roche,' he said with a degree of deference. 'My name is Rak Toos. I must ask you to accompany us. Your companion will not be harmed so long as you co-operate.'

'I am not Lord Roche. I am the Doctor.'

Rak Toos did not look impressed. 'That will be determined.' To two of his subordinates he said, 'Disarm him.'

'My dear fellow, you really have got the wrong end of the stick. I am not Roche and I am certainly not armed.'

The two subordinates – both women – shouldered their crossbows and searched the Doctor, then Troy Game. They placed the contents of the travellers' pockets on a large rock in the middle of the clearing. Rak Toos patiently sorted through the items: Simon Haldane's sketch of Roche, the key to the flat in Chichester on a torch key-ring, the TARDIS key, some money, a pair of wire-clippers, some mints, some throat sweets, a flashlight, two front row tickets for the first performance of Peter Shaffer's *The Royal Hunt of the Sun*, a squashed flower from Erekan, an egg timer and the two items of obvious importance.

'What's this?' Rak Toos demanded, holding up the first of these: Solenti's tracking device.

'Something I should have thrown away a long time ago,' the Doctor replied. 'It's a means of finding one's way if you must know.'

'Is that all it does? Can it be set to explode, for instance?'

'Not that I'm aware of, but be my guest if you want to give it a try.'

Rak Toos examined it curiously, then abruptly lost interest and threw it back onto the pile. He seized the other object with a gleam in his eye and said, 'What have we here?'

'It's a sonic screwdriver.'

Rak Toos glared. 'I was speaking rhetorically, Doctor. I know perfectly well what it is. It is well known that Lord Roche carries a sonic screwdriver.'

'Is it also well known that a sonic screwdriver is not a weapon?'

Rak Toos frowned, bemused. To Troy Game he said, 'What is your name?'

Troy Game told him.

'Ah! Of House Dassar, am I right?'

Troy Game conceded that this was the case.

'Dassar Island, Lord Roche's base of operations. Your clan have been his curators for centuries, am I not right?' Without waiting for an answer Rak Toos turned back to the Doctor. 'Yet you carry no weapon. Not even a mercy gun.'

'A mercy gun?' There was venom in the Doctor's voice. 'I would not even countenance that name for such a device, let alone carry one.'

'He is telling the truth,' Troy Game said. 'He is not Lord Roche. He is the Doctor and he's here to help us. Caresh is in great danger and we need him.'

'Is this what you claim?' Rak Toos demanded.

The Doctor nodded slowly. 'It's true enough. I'm not altogether sure what it is that Roche has been up to, but I rather get the impression he has left your planet in the lurch.'

'And you're going to Dassar to complete his work, is that it?'

'Complete it or put a stop to it. Whichever proves to be the more beneficial course of action.'

'Beneficial for who?'

'For *whom*.'

'Beneficial for whom, Doctor?'

The Doctor gave him a long look. 'For everyone.'

Rak Toos was about to make a scathing remark when a shadow of doubt passed across his eyes. 'Your story takes some believing,' he said eventually.

'Come on, man!' the Doctor exploded, his patience at an end. 'Consider the manner of my arrival. Consider my appearance. What could I hope to gain if I am not who I say I am?'

'Roche made promises,' Rak Toos replied. 'He said there would be an end to the cold times.'

The Doctor raised an eyebrow. 'Did he now? Did he happen to mention how he intended to bring that about by any chance?'

'No. It was many generations ago and he did not keep his promise. Instead, he suppressed knowledge and discouraged innovation, leaving us less able to cope with the cold times when they came. And come they did. On Fell, and here on Stakisha, the cold is less severe and Dassar is far away. Consequently we have been better able to develop, and to find ways of dealing with the coming of ice if next year proves to be another cold year. If Lord Roche were to come here, however, it might be his intention to undo our work.'

'I see.' The Doctor spoke quietly, sympathetically. '*If* Lord Roche were to come here. But I don't think you really believe that's who I am, do you?'

Rak Toos was silent for a time. He looked as if he was about to speak once more when someone new hurried into the clearing. A messenger. Rak Toos turned to him and they conferred briefly. When the messenger was gone Rak Toos turned back to the Doctor.

'I'm sorry, Doctor. It's out of my hands now. You may retrieve your belongings – apart from the sonic screwdriver and the wire-cutters – and then you must come with us.'

He would say no more. The Doctor and Troy Game had no choice but to obey.

* * *

Ember had long set and Beacon was low when they arrived in the main town of Stakisha. It had been built on a gently sloping stretch of land between a mountain and another part of the fiord. Snow on the mountain peak caught the dying rays of Beacon, and a huge waterfall was visible as a jagged ribbon of white.

It was a puzzling sort of town. Most of the buildings lacked windows. Many were no higher than the Doctor's head and they resembled clusters of inverted pots. Their tops were mostly free of snow, but slush had gathered in the walkways between them making walking unpleasant. Numerous pipes protruded from the ground, some several feet wide, some ending in t-pieces and some with pitched covers perched above their openings like those above a wishing well, giving the Doctor the impression that he was walking about on top of a vast roof.

This impression proved to be accurate. A wide cylindrical structure split open to reveal a winding staircase. The Doctor and Troy Game were directed down it by two guards who continued to accompany them. As they descended into near darkness the Doctor felt Troy Game take his hand.

'This is not right,' she whispered. 'They can't do this.'

'You're afraid of the dark?' the Doctor said, unable to keep the amusement out of his voice.

'No. I am afraid of those who would deprive us of the sunlight. It is against the convention. Even on Fell the convention is respected.'

'Perhaps they thought it was too close to nightfall to matter.'

'It's a cold year, Doctor! It's *never* too close to matter.'

At the bottom of the stairs one of the guards ordered them to wait. They did so, Troy Game keeping hold of the Doctor's hand as the other guard unlocked a heavy iron door. The door swung open and Troy Game gasped in amazement.

Ordinarily the Doctor would have noted that the corridor beyond had electric lighting. He might have speculated that the electrical source was probably a hydroelectric power station at the base of the waterfall near the town, and that the Stakishans had no doubt developed large storage batteries to see them through the long cold times when the waterfall itself froze. But he did not see the corridor in those terms now. Whether it was a residual empathic link with Troy Game, maintained through physical contact, or whether it was simply imagination, the Doctor saw it as she did. Instead of merely descending a staircase, they had travelled into the past or the future of Caresh, to a time when Beacon was the dominant sun. Instead of synthetic daylight panels, it was as if the corridor walls were lined with windows looking out at a brighter sky...

'I'm increasingly of the opinion that your world was getting along fine without Lord Roche,' the Doctor whispered.

Troy Game let go of the Doctor's hand. The guards gestured them to silence and motioned them forward once more. They came to the end of the corridor, where the guards unlocked another iron door. This one was only as high as the Doctor's chest. It opened to reveal another door, no higher than the previous one, and made of timber. The Doctor and Troy Game were bundled through and the timber door slid closed behind them. A moment later the iron door clanged shut.

They were in a cell. It had a low ceiling so the Doctor could not stand up straight. There were small barred windows in the three walls, each looking out into darkness, and in the timber door that made up the fourth wall. The room was lit by a synthetic daylight panel; it was much smaller than the ones in the corridor outside and it flickered annoyingly.

On the cell's wooden floor, wrapped in a bundle of furs, lay the sleeping form of Jo Grant.

Jo eventually awoke. She felt groggy and her head ached terribly. She had been knocked out with chloroform or something very like it. Between them, the Doctor and Troy Game brought her up to date. They kept it as brief as possible.

'So what do we do now?' Jo asked.

'We need to get back to the TARDIS,' the Doctor said. He

examined the timber door. There was an opening mechanism at one end which could only be operated from outside. Beyond it, the iron door could be touched through the barred window. 'It would be a simple enough matter to get the inner door open...'

'... if only you had the sonic screwdriver,' finished Jo.

'Quite. You know, I really thought I was getting through to Rak Toos. I'm sure I was on the point of convincing him that it was in his best interest to give me as much assistance as possible.'

'What about secret passageways? There must be a hidden door somewhere.'

'Jo, much as I admire your boundless optimism, the inclusion of secret doors is not a prerequisite of cell design.'

'Well, what do you suggest?'

'We could begin by examining the floorboards, I suppose. Just in case.'

Troy Game was looking through the barred window in the opposite wall. 'Someone's coming!' she hissed.

The Doctor and Jo joined her at the window. The darkness outside was not complete; fleetingly, Jo could discern a figure moving from shadow to shadow. The figure's footsteps echoed, as if in a cavern.

The figure's face appeared at the window. It was a woman; Jo was fairly sure it was one of the people who had captured her. 'My name is Rak Shal,' the woman said in a harsh whisper. 'I don't have much time and neither do you so I will be succinct. Doctor, when I believed you were Lord Roche I wanted you dead. I listened to you speaking in the forest clearing and I now believe you are who you claim to be. Not everybody does, however. Rak Toos believes but lacks courage, therefore I must have courage in his place for the honour of our clan. Take this and use it as you will.' She passed the sonic screwdriver between the bars.

'You stole it?' the Doctor asked.

'Yes. Regrettably I was unable to obtain the wire-cutters. Make your escape before you are in Fell.'

'What makes you think we'll be taken to Fell?' the Doctor

demanded, but Rak Shal was already hurrying away into the darkness. 'No matter, we have what we want. It seems that I made the right impression after all.'

'What's at Fell?' Jo asked.

Troy Game shuddered. 'We must not go there.'

'I quite agree,' the Doctor said. 'As long as there's a chance that Rak Shal knows what she's talking about, we ought to get out of here before they come to take us.'

'Doctor,' said Jo.

'Quite apart from anything else, we don't have time for that kind of delay.' He adjusted his sonic screwdriver and turned his attention to the door's opening mechanism.

'Doctor,' Jo repeated.

'With a bit of luck the corridor won't be heavily guarded.' He activated the screwdriver and there was a satisfying click from somewhere inside the door. 'There, that's the lock taken care of. We'll make for the surface then head for the TARDIS under the cover of...'

'Doctor!'

The Doctor frowned and turned. 'What's the matter, Jo?'

'Doctor, I don't think it's a question of them coming for us.'

'You're not making any sense, Jo.'

Jo was about to explain but in the event there was no need. For just then the cell lurched to one side. By the time the three occupants had recovered their footing it was clear that the cell was moving at a steady speed.

'Of course,' the Doctor said, spelling out the situation to his companions, who had already caught on. 'This cell is a part of one of the train carriages. And the train is on its way to Fell.' He regarded the sonic screwdriver once more. 'Getting this back was quite a stroke of luck, I must say. What a pity it's too late to be of any possible use!'

Chapter Fourteen
The Wrong Kind of Snow

The cell they were in occupied the rear part of the last carriage. The front part of the carriage had been in darkness when the journey began, but now it was occupied by two guards and so its synthetic daylight panel was switched on. From time to time one or other of the guards would look in through the connecting window at the three prisoners. The Doctor attempted to engage them in banter but it was to no avail. Conversation would have been difficult anyway; the train rattled along at about forty miles per hour, making so much noise it was a wonder it did not shake itself apart.

It was clear to the Doctor that it was drawing all its electrical power from the overhead cable, and that the connection was not perfectly sustained. On half a dozen occasions in the first hour of the journey the synthetic daylight panel in the cell lost power, together with the one in the guards' section. Usually they came back on within a few seconds but twice the break was much longer, which resulted in the train gliding to a halt. When this happened the guards grumbled but took no action, which suggested it was a familiar enough occurrence. On both these occasions, three or four minutes passed before the train began moving again. It was the Doctor's guess that it took the train's crew that long to decide the problem was not going to sort itself out.

The Doctor, Jo and Troy Game watched the passing of the landscape through the three outer windows. Caresh had no moon but it was possible to discern features in the starlight, and here and there lights were visible in the windows of tiny houses dotted about remote locations on the mountainside. Seen through the left window – the one in the timber door through which they had entered the 'cell' – the mountainside dropped away, down to the fiord below. The first time they stopped the Doctor was sure they were just above the ledge where the TARDIS had landed. 'That's the very tower we investigated today!' he told Troy Game excitedly. He was on the verge of sliding the door open and risking a descent in the darkness when they started moving again.

The train climbed higher and the landscape gradually changed. The slope on the left became even steeper than before, and for the entire second hour the train ran parallel to a glacier. It topped the rise and passed through a gap in the mountain ridge. The landscape underwent a more rapid change as they emerged on the other side of Stakisha. The vegetation was more widespread and the ground sloped more gently, so the track was no longer compelled to follow the mountain contours as it lost height. Some distance in front they could make out the shape of a vast causeway extending out to sea; regularly placed lights marked its position. Not far to the right of the causeway was a harbour where several ships lay at anchor.

'We're going to have to get off this train before we reach the causeway,' the Doctor said, raising his voice to make himself heard. 'At the same time I don't relish the idea of backtracking, so to speak. We must have come about eighty or ninety miles.'

'Maybe we could get passage on a ship,' Jo suggested brightly. 'They won't be expecting us to return to the TARDIS by sea.'

The Doctor rubbed his chin. 'It's a possibility. But we've come this far. It might be better to make for Dassar by sea.'

'We haven't escaped from the train yet,' Troy Game reminded him.

'All right. This is what we'll do.' Briefly he outlined his plan. Then he glanced through the connecting window. He saw only one of the guards in the adjoining room. Earlier the man had been swigging something from a metal hip-flask; now he looked as if he was having trouble staying awake.

Now was the time, the Doctor decided, while the other one was still out of the room. He took his place by the sliding door. The two women watched through the window for the next gantry tower. As soon as it was past they slid the door open. The Doctor backed out of the opening; reaching overhead, he found a handhold on the carriage roof. Jo was beside him, her fingers meshed to provide him with a stirrup. He put one foot in it and pushed himself up. A moment later he was gone from view. Jo thought she heard the sound of him settling on the carriage roof but it was hard to tell over the noise of the train. Hurriedly she and Troy Game slid the door shut, being careful not to let the lock catch.

The Doctor was taking a huge risk and he knew it. His main worry had been that the dozing guard would notice the change in acoustics when the sliding door opened and closed. But it could not be helped, and so far there was no sign of any pursuit. If the guards were unusually complacent it might well be because they thought nobody in their right mind would consider doing what the Doctor intended to do. In which case they probably had a point.

The pick-up arm was on the foremost carriage as the Doctor had feared; it was lit by its own sparks. There were six carriages in all. Leaping from one to the other might have been an option if it hadn't been for the overhead cable which compelled him to crawl on his belly. He did this as silently as possible, then waited for a long straight stretch of track before attempting to crawl onto the next carriage. Fortunately the gap between carriages was less than two feet. He wondered briefly what the other carriages were for; was this a special prison train, or was it a goods train that occasionally diversified by carrying captives?

The Doctor's plan was to crawl to the front carriage. Once there he would wait until the train was travelling over level terrain. He was fairly certain that it was equipped with powerful headlights which would enable him to judge the optimum moment. He would then pull down the pick-up arm so that the train lost speed. Once the train had slowed to about ten miles an hour, Jo and Troy Game were to jump and make for a place of concealment. The Doctor would then relocate the pick-up and he too would jump. Once the train was out of sight the three of them would meet up on the right side of the track and head for the harbour.

He was well aware that Troy Game was very unhappy about jumping off a moving object in the dark – it was simply not something a Careshi did. The Doctor had tried to assure her that this in itself would allay suspicion, and that Jo could be relied upon to tell her when to jump. But Jo was not altogether happy either. Her spatial awareness was better than Troy Game's, but she wasn't used to the gravity and in any case the guards would see they had gone the moment they next looked in the cell. The Doctor, for his own part, was more concerned about what happened once they reached the harbour. What he wanted most was a vessel that was small, fast and didn't require a crew – in other words, one he could steal. Unfortunately, as far as Troy Game knew, the internal combustion engine did not exist on Caresh so they wouldn't be commandeering a speedboat. Their most likely option was to stow away on a ship bound for a less hostile island than the ones in the Fell group and take it from there.

As the Doctor reached the second gap between carriages he reminded himself that it didn't do to plan too far ahead. He began to wriggle across the gap. He gripped a handhold on the third carriage and pulled himself forward. His head, shoulders and upper chest were above the gap when a door below him opened and light spilled out. Someone was coming out of the second carriage; the distinctive Careshi scalp was less than a foot below the Doctor's chest.

The Doctor froze, barely daring to breathe. The Careshi stood between carriages, holding onto a vertical pole beside the door. Half a minute passed. The Doctor wondered if the Careshi was admiring the view. Then he – or she – opened the door to the third carriage and went inside. The Doctor started breathing again and resumed his crawl.

The harbour was noticeably nearer by the time he reached the fifth carriage. There were lights in the rigging of some of the ships. The causeway was also noticeably nearer, so he knew he was going to have to act soon. The ground ahead was beginning to level out but it was riddled with ravines and littered with boulders. The Doctor hoped it would be clear by the time he reached the front carriage. Trees were becoming increasingly frequent; with a bit of luck they might provide some cover.

Then something happened that the Doctor had not allowed for. Before he was even halfway along the fifth carriage a random vibration caused the pick-up arm to drift away from the overhead cable. There was a shower of sparks as the train lost power. It was slowing too early! The Doctor attempted to crawl faster but it was no good – the pick-up arm was too far away. By the time he got to it it would be too late. Jo and Troy Game would assume the slowing was the Doctor's doing and so they would jump.

In which case he still had to relocate the pick-up. If he failed to do so the train would stop, the guards would find their prisoners gone and the hunt for them would begin. The snow was patchy on this side of the mountain but there was enough of it to make it easy to track three poorly equipped fugitives.

Desperately he pulled himself forward. A branch from a tree whipped his face, then another. When he dared to raise his head again he saw a wide ravine in the near distance. The speed of the train was no more than a brisk walking pace now, but the Doctor estimated they would reach the ravine well before he could crawl to the pick-up. In the starlight he could see that the bridge supporting the track was barely wider than the track itself. The ground beyond the ravine was virtually treeless and very uneven.

Acting almost without thinking, he slid over the side of the carriage and hit the ground running. He ran alongside the train dodging barely visible rocks and roots. He was gaining on the train, but not by as much as he had hoped. When he was alongside the part of the front carriage where he judged the pick-up to be he reached for the top of the carriage, found a handhold then put one foot on the running board, simultaneously swinging himself round to get his other hand and foot in place. He clung to the side of the carriage, then reached across the roof for the pick-up. He found it. It was a bar of metal attached to the carriage roof by a springy hinge; at the other end a shallow U-shaped connector normally maintained contact with the overhead cable. The Doctor took hold of the metal bar in his gloved right hand and relocated the connector. At once the train regained power and began to speed up. Not daring to wait a second longer, the Doctor leapt backwards from his position on the carriage.

He rolled for a dozen feet. Just as he was sure he would overshoot the edge of the ravine he came to an abrupt halt against a tree trunk, which knocked the wind out of him. The tree, resenting his intrusion, shrugged him aside and sprouted thorns from its bark. The Doctor gave it a wide berth. He watched with gratification as the train rumbled away into the darkness. He hoped Jo had managed to close the door as she jumped.

The situation, then: he was badly bruised, his clothes were marked and torn, and he was alone on the wrong part of a cold (and possibly doomed) planet at night, separated from the TARDIS and his companions and surrounded by motile trees. Sooner or later the guards on the train would notice their prisoners' absence; he was going to have to listen out for the sound of the train reversing along the track and be ready to hide.

It could have been much worse. The trees were irritable rather than hostile; they didn't mind you so long as you didn't bump into them too hard. The harbour was probably no more than a couple of hours' walk away, assuming he managed to find a path in the dark. Jo and Troy Game would almost certainly have left the train well before he had. He would probably have to walk two or three miles back along the track.

It occurred to him to place obstacles on the track or detach a rail. He decided against it. It would be too time consuming, it would mark his position and, besides, a derailment might result in needless casualties. Of course, if he was the man they suspected him of being it was precisely the sort of action he might have taken anyway. If the train crew were wise they would proceed very cautiously when they came searching for him.

He switched his flashlight on and started walking along a rail, balancing tightrope-style. The railway track itself was clear of snow – presumably the front of the train was fitted with some sort of snow plough, which would account for its rapid slowing. If the women had jumped onto a bank of snow beside the rails he would be able to see their impressions. If not... Well, Jo would probably be listening out for him. In which case, the sensible thing would be for him to sing.

He sang the opening bars of 'Tharular Valdusti', a Dagusan threnody that invariably moved all but the most hard-hearted to tears. After a while it occurred to him that it would probably make more sense to sing something Jo knew, something from Earth. Preferably something catchy – and no later than 1972. One possibility presented itself – a song he had helped Gilbert and Sullivan with when they were up against a deadline. He was not one to accept money so they had expressed their gratitude by giving him a coat.

He wished he had the coat right now.

'Can you walk?' Jo asked.

Troy Game did not answer. When she did eventually speak she said, 'Your doctor friend, is he trying to kill us?'

'That's not fair! After all he's done. Would you rather he let us take our chances on Fell?'

'No,' Troy Game admitted. 'Will you help me, please?'

Jo crouched. Troy Game put one arm across her shoulders and Jo held her around the waist. They attempted to stand. Troy Game gasped in pain, then clenched her mouth shut.

'We've got to get across the track,' Jo said. 'We'll be seen here. If it comes back.'

They managed it with difficulty. Once across, Troy Game let herself fall back against a large tree. She sang quietly and rubbed one of its lower branches – no, Jo decided, the word was *caress* – and the tree shifted, as if to make its burden more comfortable.

Jo looked around her. The trees towered over her; in the starlight there was a distinctly *fleshy* quality about them. Like a guest refusing the offer of a stomach-churning delicacy, Jo found herself muttering, 'If it's all the same to you I think I'll just stand.'

Troy Game quietened. She gestured to Jo to do the same. 'Someone's coming!' she said.

Jo listened intently. She could hear nothing. She was not altogether surprised; Troy Game's hearing was much more sensitive than her own. But she continued to listen. Then Troy Game burst out laughing. It was the laugh of someone in great pain, but amused and relieved nonetheless.

'Not from Caresh!' she declared. 'Nobody on Caresh is *capable* of singing so badly.'

Jo could hear it now. It was the Doctor, singing 'Three Little Maids from School' in a falsetto. 'Not many on Earth either,' she said.

The Doctor appeared swinging his torch. Its beam swept across Jo, then across Troy Game. 'Oh dear,' the Doctor said, tutting. 'Oh dear oh dear oh dear. Don't tell me she's twisted her ankle.'

All the good humour drained out of Jo. 'No, Doctor. She's broken her leg.'

Nights were shorter on Caresh than they had been before Troy Game had gone off in Roche's TARDIS. The planet was approaching the time when it would be between suns once again. When that happened, the setting of one sun coincided with the rising of the other and night was abolished. When night returned the inhabitants knew if they were in for a warm year or a cold one: either Caresh had gone into orbit around Beacon, and the people rejoiced, or it had gone into orbit around Ember, and the people prepared themselves for hardship.

As far as Jo was concerned the night was unending. Between her and the Doctor they managed to carry Troy Game along many miles of deceptive and capricious path. Twice they had come close to falling off a precipice. Once, when they had been in sight of their goal, their way was blocked by a cluster of awkward trees and no amount of coaxing would persuade them to move. By the time they reached the harbour town the eastern sky was lightening.

They found an unoccupied works yard between two large warehouses. The gates were padlocked; almost without thinking the Doctor unlocked them with his sonic screwdriver. They went in, closing the doors behind them, and laid Troy Game on some sacking. The Doctor directed Jo to clear away the surrounding crates while he found a knife which he used to cut away the Careshi woman's clothes.

'Healing sleep,' the Doctor explained. 'She's going to need as much sunlight as she can get.'

Troy Game was barely conscious. Her leg was dreadfully swollen and her face was wracked with pain. She appeared to have aged twenty years since they had left Sussex. 'It's not going to be enough, is it, Doctor?' Jo said quietly.

The Doctor shook his head slowly. 'No Jo. After all she's been through, I don't think it is.'

'It seems so unfair!' Jo blurted. 'We got her back to her own planet but she's not going to see her home.'

'Do try and have a sense of perspective,' said Troy Game, suddenly wide awake. 'It's only a fracture.'

Jo and the Doctor looked at each other, embarrassed. 'I'm sorry, I didn't mean...' the Doctor began. He did not finish his sentence. Someone was unlocking the gates.

Instinctively the Doctor and Jo looked for somewhere to hide. There was nowhere. They turned. The gates swung open. A small, stocky woman with biceps the size of a man's thighs stood in the entrance. There was a scar under one eye and another across her scalp where the hair no longer grew. 'What do you think you're doing in my yard?' she demanded. She did not look as if she was interested in hearing their reply.

Troy Game looked at her in disbelief. 'Troy Sheltek?' she said.

The woman matched her incredulity. 'Sun watcher?'

'It is good to see you,' Troy Game said, then passed out for twenty-nine hours.

Chapter Fifteen
Across the Sea to Dassar

Troy Game could not walk, but that was all right because the Doctor and Lord Roche were supporting her between them. They carried her across the ice to where the blue box with the light on top awaited. They pulled the outer doors open, slid the lattice gate across and the three of them entered the familiar space of the Cloud Base lift. Lord Roche closed the doors and gate and the Doctor pressed the 'up' button. The lift lurched into motion.

Lord Roche smiled reassuringly at her. 'He is waiting for you. He will be pleased to see you again. He loves you, you know.'

The Doctor also smiled reassuringly at her. 'He knows you are in great pain. But don't worry, he knows what to do. Even *he* knows how to operate a mercy gun.'

Troy Game began to panic. 'No, he mustn't.' She attempted to move and in doing so put weight on her leg. She screamed, belatedly attempted to bite back the scream, then said, 'You don't understand. He mustn't use the mercy gun on me because *he's done it before!*'

'Sh sh sh,' said Roche.

The lift stopped. The Doctor slid back the lattice gate. The outer door was opened by Sai-mahn; he stood before them with the little golden gun in his hand. He was smiling, like the others.

She pushed Roche with all her might. Roche, taken by surprise, stumbled against Sai-mahn, who was trying to take aim at Troy Game. He was careful not to use the gun on Roche. She ran – or rather stumbled, each step an agony – through the hall, across the lounge, through the glass doors onto the roof patio. Most of the plants here were dead now, neglected since her departure; the remainder gestured feebly, desperate for water.

There was nowhere to go. At the end of the patio was the barrier. The street was a long way down; even in this gravity the fall would be fatal. She turned, and there was Sai-mahn with the gun. She could read his mind: he wanted to use it on her, *wanted to assert himself...*

Troy Game awoke.

It was early morning and she was in a support cradle on the deck of a ship. She had been dressed in a translucent material that kept her warm but allowed the healing rays of the suns to wash over her. Her left leg was covered in a transparent substance that hardened after application. She could hear the slow pounding of a drum and the regular rhythm of the gentle splash of many oars.

'Doctor?' she called. 'Jo? Troy Sheltek?'

A tall woman dressed in red and gold stood over her. Captain and ambassador, Troy Game surmised. And distant kin, her instincts informed her.

'I am Sha Kal,' the captain said. 'It is an honour to have you aboard *The Black Flower*, Troy Game of House Dassar.'

'The honour is mine, Sha Kal,' Troy Game responded. Less formally she added, 'And so is the luck, it seems.'

'I understand you've been through quite an ordeal?'

'I am not sure it is over yet. Where are we?'

'A day's journey from Stakisha, and so far there has been no sign of pursuit. Maybe there will be no pursuit. It was well for you that we found you when we did.'

'Where are the Doctor and Jo?'

Sha Kal smiled. 'Below.'

Below, Jo was pulling at her oar with all her might. When it had reached the end of its sweep she raised it out of the water, turned it so that the blade was parallel to the water and pushed forward. She turned it again so that the blade was perpendicular to the water and lowered it once more. She repeated the cycle, all in time to the slow pounding of the big drum. It was relentless and it was back-breaking.

The Doctor claimed he had sailed with Themistocles at Salamis in a trireme, a ship which this vessel resembled. At least he knew what to expect. All Jo had to go on was a matinee showing of *Ben Hur* at her local Empire cinema when she was fourteen. Her UNIT training had prepared her for some unlikely situations but this was not one of them. Still, it could have been worse. They could have been forced to stow away on a ship that was not even going their way.

The Doctor had impressed upon the captain that they had to get as far away from the Fell group as possible, and as quickly as possible. Fortunately Sha Kal had no difficulty accepting the Doctor's story at face value; more to the point she was prepared to give him the help he needed. She was from Dair, a neighbouring island to Dassar; in addition to being the ship's captain, she was also the Dair ambassador to Fell. She agreed to head for Dassar, although it was likely that the surrounding sea was frozen by now.

Troy Sheltek was walking along the aisle in Jo's direction. Jo tried to concentrate on the rowing, tried to ignore the stocky woman's presence, but she knew that she, and not one of the two rowers in the tiers alongside her, was being singled out.

'Jo Grant!' the woman barked. 'Take a rest, now! You're no good to us dead.'

Jo gratefully gave up her place to a newcomer. She *had* done her best; given that everyone, up to and including the captain herself, was prepared to do a session at the oars she could not have done any less. Still, it was a great relief to get back up on deck and breathe the fresh air.

Troy Game was not being a good patient. 'I do not need to use both my legs to row!' she argued, somewhat unconvincingly. But Troy Sheltek's unspoken threats compelled her to remain in her support cradle. 'It is so frustrating,' Troy Game told Jo. 'We cannot afford to lose any time. So long as the winds remain unfavourable we must rely on rowers. Each man and woman must play their part.'

'Don't be silly,' said Jo. 'I'm sure one person isn't going to make much...'

'Two.'

'Very well, two,' Jo conceded with good grace; Troy Game was in pain, after all. 'But so far there's been no sign of pursuit.'

'Jo, the people of Fell are not stupid. They know where we are headed. When they come after us, be assured it will not be in a vessel like this.'

'What do you mean? I thought you said you don't have powered boats on Caresh.'

'I said there are no internal combustion engines. But there are ships powered by steam. They are costly to run, however, and on Dassar coal is scarce and in great demand during the cold years. Matters are otherwise on Fell.'

Later that morning they were blessed with their first favourable wind. Sails were raised and the rowers were able to rest. Shortly before noon clouds gathered overhead and there was a heavy fall of snow. Troy Game was moved under a canopy.

Jo was the first to notice the dark speck on the horizon when the snow finally let up. She alerted Sha Kal who gave it her immediate attention.

'Not an island,' the captain said. 'Not in that location. Whatever it is, we will pass it close by.'

Someone handed her a brass telescope. The Doctor joined her at the rail at the ship's bow. 'Another ship?' he asked.

'No.' She continued to gaze for a full minute. 'No plume of smoke, no sail. It's ice.'

'Ice?' echoed the Doctor.

'Further south the sea is frozen. Bergs and floes drift into the currents. They are often carried onto islands.'

'Does it pose a threat?'

'Not the ice itself. We know it is there. But sometimes it carries danger.' Without turning or lowering the telescope Sha Kal addressed Troy Sheltek. 'Have the sails lowered. Prepare the arbalestiers.' Returning to her conversation with the Doctor she said, 'I am greatly afraid this is one such case.'

'What is the danger?'

She handed him the telescope. There was fear and disgust in her voice. 'Leshe!'

Four muscular men appeared on the deck dressed in thick black leather. Each carried a crossbow. Troy Sheltek handed each man a writhing dark green plant that resembled a small bald cactus; the four arbalestiers put them in their mouths and chewed them slowly. 'It heightens spatial awareness and suppresses the terror,' Sha Kal told the Doctor. 'We do not see the same as you.'

The Doctor nodded, then located the house-sized ice fragment with the telescope. Caresh was a bigger planet than Earth, with a more distant horizon. Nevertheless, it was possible to discern the creature perched on the ice. It was far too big to be an insect but the comparison was unavoidable. In appearance it resembled an aggressive locust with a crystalline body the size of a large dog, and dragonfly wings with a span of at least six feet.

'Carnivorous?' he asked.

'Omnivorous,' Sha Kal said, her voice quavering. 'At least they behave as if they were. They never learn what they cannot eat. Normally they are restricted to the polar regions but in cold years they travel with the ice. If they get a foothold on the land they are... they are not easily stopped.'

The rowmaster beat the drum at half speed. There was a profound sense of unease among the crew of *The Black Flower* as they drew closer to the ice fragment and its Leshe cargo. The creature watched them with its compound eyes. It appeared utterly relaxed. Then without any warning it leapt. The gap between the ice and the ship seemed far too great for such a leap, as indeed it was. But in the thick Careshi atmosphere the Leshe's buzzing wings provided it with powerful thrust. It headed directly for the deck.

One of the arbalestiers let off a bolt. It struck the place where the right wing joined the body. The wing went limp and the creature tumbled into the sea. At once the general sense of unease lifted.

'They cannot survive immersion,' Sha Kal said.

Under full sail *The Black Flower* proceeded on its course for Dassar throughout the afternoon. The Doctor spent some of the time repairing his clothes as nothing in the ship's stores would fit him. On five occasions large ice fragments were sighted in the distance, three with Leshe on them, but they were too far away to be a danger.

When she got the chance Troy Game brought up the subject of the mercy gun. 'You spoke of it when we were captured on Stakisha,' she told the Doctor. 'What is it?'

The Doctor seemed reluctant to answer, but eventually he told her. 'It is a hand weapon. It was created by my own people. I prefer to think of it as an arrogance gun. It endows the user with a misplaced sense of moral superiority.'

'How?'

'It remembers who it has shot. The first time it only stuns you. The second time it kills. The assumption is that, if it is necessary to use it on someone a second time, they have not learnt their lesson and so they deserve to die.'

'You disapprove?'

'Of course I disapprove!'

'Is the gun small and made of gold?'

The Doctor nodded. 'That is the usual design,' he said.

'Then it is as I thought. A hundred years ago, they say, Roche took it with him to defend himself when he journeyed to Fell. But he was overpowered and it was turned on him.'

The Doctor was immediately interested. 'He was shot with his own weapon?'

'Yes. But he recovered, and he forced them to hand it back to him. It was long ago, and he has since changed his appearance. Surely it will not recognise him now.'

The Doctor shook his head. 'Believe me, the gun does not forget. It takes more than a change of appearance to fool it.'

'Perhaps he has destroyed it?'

'They are not easy to destroy.'

'A pity,' Troy Game said very quietly.

'So he's vulnerable to his own weapon, is he?' the Doctor said, not hearing Troy Game's last remark. 'Perhaps that will make him a little less arrogant.'

Late in the afternoon the wind dropped. A thick mist settled on the horizon a few degrees south of their course. There was a cry from the lookout at the stern of the ship. Another dark shape had appeared in the distance, this time behind them. Sha Kal hurried over to investigate but even before she had raised the telescope to her eye it was clear from the pall of smoke above the shape that they were looking at another ship.

'Fell?' the Doctor inquired.

'Maybe, maybe not,' Sha Kal replied. 'But we are not taking the risk.'

The rowers took their places once more and the ship made for the protection of the mist. The drum was silenced. For several minutes the only sound was the lapping of the oars, the rowers depending on their experience to maintain synchronisation. They entered the mist without incident, and for the time being it seemed as if they had evaded their pursuer.

It was a clammy sort of cold within the mist. Visibility was down to thirty feet, then twenty, then ten. The rowers worked slowly, uncertain of the extent of the mist and wary of collisions with floating ice. According to the navigator their present course would take them close to an uninhabited islet, a place of steep basalt cliffs and an isolated beach. If necessary they could drag the ship onto the shore and defend their position. Assuming they could find their way to it.

Night fell. Below deck, lanterns were lit and the crew clustered around storage heaters. Jo listened to some of the conversations and soon discovered that they were all on the same subject: Leshe.

'They're terrified of them!' she told the Doctor in a hushed voice.

'So it would seem,' the Doctor said.

'But the one we saw didn't seem so bad. I mean, all right, it was very big and very fierce-looking, but...'

'But it was only one, Jo. And not in its own element at that. Now imagine whole swarms of them, brought over with the ice, crawling in their thousands over the land.'

Jo imagined. 'Like very big locusts,' she said, and shuddered.

'Quite. It's a safe bet that these people – or at any rate their ancestors – have had to deal with Leshe infestations on quite a number of occasions.'

'But what are they?' Jo asked. 'I mean, they can't be insects, can they?'

'Not insects exactly, no. If they were they wouldn't be able to breathe, or support their own weight, or survive in the polar climate. Their similarity to the terrestrial arthropod is simply an accident of evolution. You know, it would be fascinating to discover how their metabolism works. My guess is that it's based on the principle of cold fusion, but I wonder...'

Jo sat on a bench, listening to the Doctor at first, but gradually the sound of his voice became one with the creaking of the ship's timbers. The deck rocked gently and Jo gradually found herself drifting off to sleep.

Morning came and the mist showed no sign of lifting. They continued to make painfully slow progress. 'At least the Fell ship won't be going any faster,' Jo observed. 'They'll be too worried about colliding with icebergs.'

'Unless they've got radar,' the Doctor said.

Moments later a towering cliff of ice appeared from out of the mist directly in front of them. Orders were shouted and the rowers reversed direction. No less than eight Leshe stood poised on the ice. Close up, their faces were yellow and their bodies were dark blue, almost purple. A panicking arbalestier let off a lucky shot – the bolt smashed into the face of one of the creatures

- but his comrades were unprepared. One crossbowman's shot went wild; another was loading his bow when a Leshe swooped and caught the side of his neck with its mandibles. He fell to the deck, blood gushing from the wound. Alerted to the danger, two crew women fought the creature with iron staves, but more of the Leshe were boarding.

The Doctor scooped up the wounded man's crossbow. Loading it was slow; it had no stirrup so he had to turn the crank handle to pull back the string. He sent a bolt into the head of a flying Leshe, but by now there were three on the deck and another two preparing to leap. Jo shot one while it was in flight – an arbalestier had abandoned his crossbow in favour of a stave – and several crew, led by Sha Kal herself, arrived to deal with the others.

Somehow the Doctor found himself cut off from the rest of the crew. The remaining Leshe landed on the deck beside him; almost at once it was upon him. He grabbed it by its sticky serrated forelegs, and tried to keep it at arms' length from his face as it backed him against the rail, but it was too strong. Its mandibles opened sideways as its head pushed inexorably forward.

The Doctor's strength was failing. He did the only thing he could do. He threw himself backwards over the rail.

Jo screamed as she heard the splash above the noise of the fighting. She ran to the rail where she had seen the Doctor fall. But there was no sign of him, and the mist was closing in.

The water was terribly cold. That came as no surprise, but it was extremely unpleasant nonetheless.

The Leshe was already dead. Its inert body drifted away from the Doctor.

He had to keep moving, had to find *The Black Flower* again. He could not be much more than a few feet away from it, but which way? The rowers were backing it away from the ice cliff.

He thought he could hear the sound of the oars. He would make for the sound. It was all he had to go on; visibility was practically zero now.

His Time Lord physiology could withstand sudden changes in temperature. But there were limits. Hypothermia was not unknown, even for someone blessed with a constitution as strong as his own. This cold was altogether unconstitutional.

'Jo,' he said. 'There is a real danger that my mind will start to wander, so it's important that you listen to me before that happens. Whatever you do, do not let Roche out of the TARDIS. Not unless he is well wrapped up. He is sure to argue, but I don't want him to catch his death of cold. Or do I mean cold of death? Well, whatever it is, don't let me fall asleep.'

He waited for an answer. There was none. He briefly remembered where he was. It was stupid of him to lose the ship, but there was no point in worrying about that now. In fact, there was no point in worrying about anything at all.

Chapter Sixteen
Neutron Star

Jo watched in quiet desperation as Sha Kal and her crew lowered lanterns on poles over the side of the ship. Seven feet below deck level the waters were an inky blackness, and empty.

'Look!' cried Troy Game suddenly from the other side of the ship. 'There's something in the water.' Jo's heart leapt as she hurried across the deck, the lantern-bearers gathering nearby. But then hope died as it became clear that the thing in the water was merely the body of a Leshe.

Briefly, the Doctor awoke. He was wet but he was no longer immersed. He was lying on some sort of inflated fabric. Somewhere an engine was throbbing. He could smell damp fur.

When he awoke again he was lying diagonally on a bed that was too short for him, naked under several layers of blankets. He was in a wooden hut with three other beds, several cupboards and a large window that let in dull white daylight. A portable paraffin heater stood beside one wall. Above it, the Doctor's clothes were draped across a metal rail. They were more or less dry.

The cupboards contained dried food wrapped in greaseproof paper, bottles of water and spirits, containers of paraffin, vitamin tablets, fur coats, leather boots, flare guns, medical supplies, ice picks and the like. Evidently the place was a sanctuary hut on an island either too small or too inhospitable to be inhabited.

While he was dressing the Doctor looked out of the window. The mist was thinner than before but visibility was still less than twenty feet. The hut was perched on a shelf of black rock which was mostly free of snow. Just beyond the hut a heavy-duty tripod supported a black cylinder which pointed at the sky; the Doctor could not tell if it was a gun or a telescope or something else entirely.

He tried the door on the other side of the hut. It was not locked. Outside was another of the gun/telescope emplacements. Next to it sat a dog, a golden Labrador.

'Jess, isn't it?' the Doctor said in a formal tone. 'I must say, I'm very pleased to renew our acquaintance, though I can't say it's an altogether unexpected pleasure.'

Jess yawned and stretched. She wagged her tail briefly then loped off into the mist, looking back once to make sure the Doctor was following.

The shelf of rock overlooked a sandy beach and ended at a steep basalt cliff. At the foot of the cliff, against which a pair of upended black slabs looked suspiciously like doors, stood a wooden table. There were two chairs; a fur-clad Solenti was sitting on one. The Doctor was surprised to note that, like him, she had had her hair trimmed to within three millimetres of her scalp. She was even wearing contact lenses to make her irises look large.

'You've timed things perfectly, Doctor. I've just made a fresh pot.'

The Doctor sat down, delighted. Whatever Solenti might be planning, whatever might be at stake, a cup of tea was exactly what he needed right at that moment.

'You are aware there are monsters at large?' the Doctor asked.

Solenti waved a hand airily. 'Not on this island. I have an early warning system in place. It's simple but it's effective enough.'

'The tripods?'

The Time Lady looked momentarily puzzled. 'Oh, those. No, they're for quite a different purpose. Assuming this wretched mist clears in time – but I'm getting ahead of myself.'

She poured the tea. The Doctor took his cup and sipped. It was heavenly. 'I'm grateful to you for saving my life,' he said. 'You and Jess, I should say. It was most fortunate that you happened to be passing in your inflatable dinghy. Coincidence?'

'Hardly, Doctor. As a matter of fact that was not the plan at all. Would you believe I went to a lot of trouble to rescue you from the dungeons of Fell? Imagine my embarrassment when it transpired that you had escaped from the train long before it even reached that wretched island.'

'I'm sorry to have inconvenienced you,' the Doctor said dryly. 'Might I ask how you knew I was on the train in the first place?'

'Why, the homing beacon, of course! In the tracking device I gave you on Dagusa.' She frowned. 'I did *tell* you it housed a homing beacon, didn't I?'

'Madam, you know perfectly well you did not. Now perhaps you could get around to telling me what you want.'

'Very well, Doctor. I want to make you an offer. I am prepared to give you a lift back to your TARDIS.'

'In exchange for what?'

Solenti was genuinely indignant. 'Why should it be in exchange for anything? You simply leave Caresh and let matters take their course. Is that asking so much?'

The Doctor matched Solenti's indignation. 'That's your idea of an unconditional offer, is it? What about Caresh? What about the time fracture? What about my...?' He broke off, but it was too late.

Solenti raised an eyebrow. 'What about your *what*?' she asked. 'Or should I hazard a guess?'

The Doctor sighed. 'Very well. I was going to say, what about my companion?'

Solenti gave him a smile, rare in that it was both gentle and genuine. 'You can pick her up – I take it it's a "her"? – en route. Just as long as you give me your word that you will not go onto Dassar Island.'

The Doctor said nothing for a minute. The mist was clearing and overhead the suns were visible discs, not too bright to look at. It was early afternoon. The inflatable dingy had been dragged partway up the beach, probably above the high-water mark. It was big enough to carry a man, a woman and a large dog, therefore it should be equally capable of carrying the same man and two small women. It would be much faster than the ship; but then again it would be lower in the water. They'd been generally lucky with the weather so far; there was no guarantee it would remain as calm. Still, it was worth considering.

The Doctor shook his head. 'No, Solenti.'

'No, Doctor? You do realise I could have left you in the water. It would have saved me a lot of trouble. I doubt you would have survived for very long.'

'I will not make an uninformed decision about something of this magnitude! You're going to have to tell me all of what's going on. From the start.'

He did not really expect her to comply. But she did.

Three centuries ago Caresh entered a protracted cold period. The ice spread, and so did the Leshe. Many people died, and much knowledge was lost. But the scientists of Dassar preserved their knowledge; they recorded it onto ceramic discs which they stored in their Citadel. They planned to put it to good use when the cold time ended, assuming anybody survived till then.

Eventually the warm years did return and the scientists of Dassar concentrated all their energies into building a great machine, a machine that enabled them to see into the future. By Gallifreyan standards the techniques were primitive – the range of the machine was less than two decades and the resolution no finer than the size of a planet. On any other world it would have been of no use at all. For the people of Caresh, however, its value was beyond price. Whenever the planet passed the midway point between suns, they no longer had to depend on the sun watchers to tell them whether they were at the start of a warm year or a cold year. Now they could plan far in advance: cold periods would no longer take them by surprise, agriculture was no longer a matter of guesswork and they could deal with the spreading ice, and with the mindless armies of Leshe before they had even left their homes in the polar regions. The Dassari would not reveal their techniques to neighbouring island groups, at least not for the time being, but they would share the data they obtained. In time, even the people of Fell would be forced to acknowledge their debt of gratitude to Dassar, and in time the entire Archipelago would be united in a joint effort against the natural adversity of the Careshi climate, and against the Leshe.

For the first time in the entire history of Caresh, the ice age did not seem so much of a threat.

The Doctor poured two more cups of tea. 'It's an inspiring vision,' he said cautiously.

'Isn't it?' Solenti agreed, feeling for her cup.

'So what went wrong?'

'We did, Doctor. Roche and me. The Time Lords sent us to Caresh with precise instructions to shut down the machine.'

The machine had come to the attention of the High Council of Time Lords. On the advice of a pedantic and inflexible temporal lawyer named Remish, they ruled it in breach of their monopoly on time travel.

So Roche and Solenti were sent to Caresh to close it down, which they duly did. Afterwards Solenti returned to Gallifrey.

Roche, on the other hand, had become fascinated with Caresh. It seemed absurd, he said, that so little was known about a landmark world. He became a frequent visitor to the planet. Naturally enough the people of Dassar made him very unwelcome at first, but he overcame their hostility by promising them a more permanent solution to the problem of their unpredictable climate.

At the time it did not occur to Solenti that Roche had any intention of keeping his promise. But he did intend to. He had a plan which was simple in theory, enormously complicated in practice; a plan of such audacity that it bordered on insanity. In short, he proposed to change the orbit of the planet. Not a big change; just a slight nudge in the direction of Beacon. Caresh would then settle into a permanent circular orbit around the warmer sun. After that, whenever it passed the midway point between suns the pull of Beacon would be too strong, and the pull of Ember too weak, to allow changeover. There would be no more cold years, no more ice ages, no more incursions into the temperate lands by the Leshe.

At least that was the theory. But changing the orbit of a planet was no small matter, even for the Time Lords, and Roche was acting alone. Nevertheless, his plan was nearing fruition. As far as he was concerned it was simply an engineering problem to which he had already found a solution. A dozen light years away he had detected a neutron star that was hurtling through space at one-tenth of the speed of light. It was not perfectly placed, and it was not moving in quite the right direction, but that could be altered over time. By Roche's estimate, a series of small changes to the neutron star's trajectory over the course of two centuries would bring it close enough to Caresh to effect a slingshot – or, as he preferred to think of it, a gravitational nudge. The planet would move into its stable orbit.

The Doctor, who had listened patiently to Solenti's account up till this point, could contain himself no longer. 'It's absurd, it's utterly preposterous. It can't possibly work.'

'It's already under way and close to completion,' Solenti said. 'Don't make the mistake of underestimating Lord Roche.'

'Underestimating? Good heavens, it's not a question of underestimation, it's a question of logic! If Roche can't move a planet how can he possibly hope to move a star?'

'You're forgetting, Doctor, a star is active. That's why the neutron star is moving in the first place. It can be controlled, from a distance if need be.' She sipped her tea and grimaced. 'How much milk did you put in this?'

'I thought you liked it milky.'

'How many times, Doctor! I like just enough to wet the bottom of the cup. I bet you didn't even use the strainer.'

'I'll pour you another one.'

'It doesn't matter, I'll do it myself.' Solenti emptied the contents of the cup onto the ground. She poured herself another, but the Doctor had neglected to replace the tea cosy so it wasn't as hot as it might have been. She drank it without comment nonetheless.

'He must have used a stellar manipulator,' the Doctor said, thinking out loud. 'Don't tell me he stole one from the Time Lords.'

'Don't be ridiculous, Doctor.'

'You mean they let him borrow one?' He was indignant. 'And they don't regard that as interfering?'

'He didn't get it from Gallifrey at all.'

'Then how...' the Doctor frowned. Then realisation struck. 'Of course. The machine on Dassar. The one you were sent to shut down.'

'Precisely, Doctor. It just took a few minor modifications. That's the beauty of the scheme, you see. The neutron star is a natural phenomenon and the stellar manipulator is a product of local technology. It operates instantaneously at a distance, but it doesn't involve time travel by any stretch of the imagination, so nobody – not even Remish – can complain.'

'Well, that puts me in my place,' the Doctor muttered, remembering a recent conversation with Jo. To Solenti he said, 'I take it that's why you're here – to record the neutron star's passing?'

'I came here to warn you, Doctor. Naturally, since I'm here anyway, I took the opportunity to set up a few automatic cameras.'

'Automatic?' There was a note of suspicion in the Doctor's voice. 'You mean you're not going to stay around to watch the...' The Doctor broke off, embarrassed. 'I meant no offence, Solenti.'

Irritated by the unnecessary apology, Solenti said, 'You are quite right. I will not be staying. It is not safe here.'

'What do you mean?'

'Lord Roche did not quite finish his task. He had one last adjustment to make to the star's trajectory when he was forced to leave Caresh in a hurry.'

'So where does that leave the planet? Don't tell me the star is going to crash into it.'

'Not crash, Doctor, no. It's not a collision course. But it will make a very close approach. The tidal forces will strip off most of the atmosphere and rupture the planet's crust.'

'And your idea of an appropriate course of action is to make a home movie about it? Good grief, woman, we have to get to Dassar before it's too late!'

'*No!*' Solenti was on her feet. 'That is precisely what we must *not* do.' She bent to calm Jess, who had been resting peacefully beside her prior to her mistress' outburst. 'Listen to me, Doctor. I'm not allowed to explain, but the consequences of intervening would be far worse than letting things take their course.'

'Consequences?' The Doctor also was on his feet. 'You would condemn a whole planet and you talk about consequences?'

'It would have been so much simpler if I'd left you in the water. I could have done, you know, and with a clear conscience. But I don't like unnecessary death, and I thought you were someone I could reason with. I know the future of Caresh, Doctor, the future it would have had without Lord Roche's intervention. Next year would have been a warm year, but the following *seventy-four* years would have been cold years. Think about that! Today is positively balmy. We can drink tea out of doors as long as we're well wrapped up. But in forty years from now the entire planet will be iced over. Even the Leshe will perish. Statistically this was bound to happen sooner or later, it just so happens that it's now. There is no dilemma, Doctor. Roche and I have not doomed Caresh, we have merely failed to save it.'

Jess was growling. Neither Time Lord paid her any attention. The Doctor had begun pacing, trying to take in what Solenti had told him. 'But if there's a chance,' he said. 'Roche must have left notes. I'm sure I could complete what he started.'

'No.' Solenti spoke softly now. 'You must not.'

'Well, tell me why not. Tell me about the consequences, let me make an informed decision.'

Solenti considered. And while she considered, the Doctor noticed a movement at the top of the cliff where the last few wisps of mist lingered. He rubbed his chin. 'Lady Solenti, does your early warning system take into account attacks from the air?'

'There's no need, the Leshe can't fly far.'

'But did it occur to you that they might be able to *climb*?' As the Doctor finished speaking a shape detached itself from the cliff top. There was no question about it, it was a Leshe. It plummeted, then opened its wings and glided heavily towards them like a low-flying aircraft. It directed its attack at Solenti.

'Get down!' the Doctor yelled. The Time Lady complied, not a moment too soon. The Leshe's serrated forelegs brushed her back in its flight. It landed some twenty feet away, then turned to resume its attack. Before it could reach Solenti Jess launched herself into a counterattack. The Doctor hesitated momentarily, shocked by the sheer savagery of the Labrador. Then he found a large rock.

By the time he reached them there was a considerable amount of blood on the ground, from both the Leshe and the dog. He brought the rock down heavily on the Leshe's head, again and again. The creature stiffened, then went limp.

Solenti was screaming. Hands outstretched she was feeling the ground with her feet, making her way as quickly as she could in the circumstances. Tears were streaming down her face; she had lost one of her contact lenses. 'Jess!' she cried. 'Jess!'

The Doctor took Solenti's hand and guided her to Jess. The dog was not quite dead. The Doctor supposed there was a brief telepathic exchange between them; a moment later the Time Lady was extricating her dog from the dead Leshe.

'Maybe I can help you,' the Doctor said gently, putting a hand on her shoulder.

Solenti shrugged him off. Despite the size of the dog and the gravitational pull of Caresh she lifted Jess in her arms and carried her. She marched briskly towards the slabs at the foot of the cliff. She collided heavily with one of the chairs but paid it no heed.

The slabs were indeed doors, as the Doctor had supposed. They opened as Solenti approached them. The Doctor heard her sob one last time before the doors closed behind her and disappeared; where they had been there was only featureless rock.

The Doctor examined the Leshe. It was quite dead. There was no other sign of movement from the cliff top; nevertheless, he had no intention of staying on the island any longer than necessary. He helped himself to a few supplies from the sanctuary hut, including food, water and a flare gun, which he loaded into the dinghy.

As he set out in search of *The Black Flower* he considered what Solenti had said, and what she had failed to say. Changing the trajectory of the neutron star was hardly going to have any immediate effects aside from those intended for Caresh; there were no other inhabited planets in the Careshi solar system, and the nearest neighbouring system was several light years away. So what was she talking about when she spoke of 'far worse consequences'?

Something bureaucratic, no doubt. Remish, or one of his cousins, had probably drawn up a strict set of rules concerning non-Gallifreyan stellar manipulators and the use thereof by Gallifreyans. On the other hand, if it was something more serious than that, the Time Lords could always return the neutron star to its original trajectory. But not until after the business with the orbit of Caresh was completed.

Satisfied with that thought the Doctor rounded a floating chunk of ice, and there in front of him on the crystal-clear blue water was *The Black Flower*, her white sails billowing in the breeze.

Chapter Seventeen
Diary of a Time Lord

'Oh Doctor, I was sure you'd drowned,' Jo said, hugging him tightly and pressing her tearful face against his chest.

'We must hurry,' said Sha Kal once the Doctor's newly acquired dinghy had been hauled onto the deck. 'Our pursuers can't be far behind.'

They made good progress, despite increasing quantities of drift ice, and by mid-afternoon the volcanic peak of Dassar Island was visible on the horizon before them. At around the same time the smoke pall of a steamship appeared on the horizon behind them.

'It can't be coincidence that they're heading this way,' the Doctor said.

Sha Kal agreed. 'We'll take you as far as we can for the time being. When the ice becomes unnavigable, or the steamship gets too close, you'll be better off making your own way. I can spare you a crossbow. It will protect you against individual Leshe, but I am afraid it will not be much use against a pack of them.'

'I am very grateful to you, Captain.'

'We will need to approach the island from the north side,' Troy Game said. 'The ice will be less thick, and I know a little-used path up to the crater-lake.'

Jo looked at her, shocked. '"We"? Troy Game, you've got a broken leg. You can't possibly think of coming with us.'

Troy Game fixed Jo with a stare. 'Firstly, Jo, Dassar is my home and Caresh is my world. Secondly, we Careshi heal more quickly than you do. Thirdly, you would not be able to get into the Citadel without my help.'

'I'm inclined to think she's right, Jo,' the Doctor said. 'If Lord

Roche's reputation is anything to go by it will take more than a sonic screwdriver to breach his security.'

More gently, Troy Game added, 'I would greatly appreciate your support, Jo.'

As *The Black Flower* drew closer to Dassar, drift ice gave way to open pack ice, which in turn gave way to close pack ice.

Troy Sheltek, together with two other crew, lowered the dinghy into the water then helped her kinswoman into it. Troy Game made no attempt to conceal the pain she felt when she was moved, but once she was settled in the dinghy she sat quietly.

The Doctor guided the little vessel along a meandering lead that was far too narrow for *The Black Flower*. At times it was too narrow even for the dinghy, and he and Jo were obliged to break the surrounding ice with iron staves. On two occasions there was nothing for it but to climb onto the ice itself and drag the dinghy, along with Troy Game and their supplies. Fortunately they were not troubled by Leshe; they only saw one, in the distance, and it did not appear to notice them.

Beacon was setting by the time they arrived at the shores of Dassar. They abandoned the dinghy. By Ember's light they walked across a dozen yards of treacherous ice, Jo and the Doctor carrying packs on their backs and their companion between them. Troy Game was nearly delirious with pain but she managed to find the path for them. It led directly up the side of the extinct volcano that dominated the north part of the island.

The path was narrow and slippery. Troy Game took some dried leaves from a pouch and swallowed them before beginning the climb; Jo supposed they were painkillers. When her companions were unable to support her the Careshi woman walked with the aid of an iron stave. The party made slow progress, stopping once while she rested. Jo sat on a rock looking out to sea. *The Black Flower* was heading for the island Troy Game had called Dair, which still appeared to be free of the encroaching ice. The pursuing ship was very close now. Jo thought it resembled a

Mississippi paddle steamer. It was evidently more robust than *The Black Flower*, for it was ploughing its way through the outer margin of pack ice.

The ship had attracted the attention of a dozen or more Leshe. Jo watched with a morbid fascination as single Leshe ran then launched themselves – they were unable to fly from a standing start. The crew of the steamship repulsed individual attacks with crossbows, but more of the creatures were gathering. Then, to Jo's surprise, an explosive device was catapulted into their midst. The explosion blew a great hole in the ice and most of the creatures died in the water.

'We've got to keep moving,' the Doctor said. 'There's a chance they will send an advance party.'

Ember was touching the horizon when they reached the rim of the crater. Fortunately the lake was frozen over so it was not necessary to walk the mile or so around it to the causeway. Beyond the south rim, inland Dassar was a featureless snowscape bereft of any sign of habitation. Troy Game stopped to gaze upon her homeland for some minutes, her expression unreadable through her physical pain. Jo watched her, concerned, and conscious of movement under the ice. Unable to stop herself, she said, 'Perhaps they took refuge on Dair or somewhere like that.'

'Perhaps,' Troy Game said without apparent emotion. She started to move again, knowing the others would follow her.

The Citadel was perched on the crater's central peak. A snow-covered tiered and turreted building, on an island surrounded by snow-covered ice, it reminded Jo of Mont-Saint-Michel. The causeway added to the similarity, as did the central spire. Closer up, the high walls were a featureless yellow with no windows lower than thirty feet. The only entrance was a colossal arched double gate that opened onto the causeway. It was not open now, however.

Troy Game regarded the gate in apparent despair. She stepped forward and placed her hands on it, then pressed the side of her face against its metallic surface. She began to emit a keening noise. At first Jo thought she was crying; she had come so far, only to find the final destination closed to her. But that made no sense, for they had never expected to find the Citadel gates open. Jo then realised she was actually singing, though it was not like any song she had sung on Earth. Troy Game sustained the note for several seconds, then abruptly dropped an octave. She paused, then repeated the note, then changed to a higher pitch. And so it went on, in an increasingly complex pattern.

A small door within the gate swung open. Troy Game fell forward into the opening. The Doctor and Jo exchanged uncertain glances, then followed her in.

It was warm inside the Citadel, and the walls glowed with an orange light when the building detected their presence. Walking stiffly with the aid of the stave, Troy Game led the way along a straight corridor no wider than the still-open door. 'The appearance of the gate is deliberately deceptive,' she said by way of explanation. 'Most of the building is taken up with the machinery. My clan have maintained it since it was first built. When Lord Roche came and took it over we were relegated to the role of stewards. With each passing generation our understanding of it has diminished.'

She said no more and for a long time the only sound was the echoing of footsteps, and the thud of the stave on the smooth stone floor. But there was light at the end of the tunnel and it formed a rectangular frame around the silhouette of Troy Game. At length they emerged into a vast circular chamber.

The walls glowed blue-white and were roundelled in the manner of a TARDIS. The chamber was dominated by a horseshoe-shaped console consisting of numerous levers, switches and monitors. Within the horseshoe was a large black chair with control levers fitted at the ends of the armrests. There was one archway in the wall a third of the way around the chamber, and another on the other side.

Troy Game turned to a monitor in the wall beside the entrance to the corridor. It showed the view of the causeway as seen from above the outer door, although Jo had not noticed any cameras when they'd approached the Citadel. Troy Game pressed a button and the door slammed shut; they heard its multiple echo along the corridor.

'From here, Doctor, you have control,' Troy Game said. 'The people of Fell cannot enter.'

Without waiting for a reply she walked with difficulty towards one of the archways. Jo made to follow but the Doctor took her by the arm and shook his head. 'No, Jo. She knows what she's doing. I only hope I do.'

'Will she be all right?' Jo whispered, concerned.

'I think that's rather down to what we do next, Jo.'

The room was small, the ceiling low. A large couch almost filled the space; beside it was a bedside cabinet. A door led to a small shower room not unlike the en suite in the hotel on Earth.

Troy Game looked inside the bedside cabinet. It contained a golden pistol hardly bigger than her hand. She picked it up to examine it, careful to point the muzzle away from herself. The weapon held associations for her; it hinted at veiled memories that remained out of reach.

Those particular memories could wait, she decided; they had no bearing on the matter at hand. She put the mercy gun down on the cabinet and allowed herself to collapse on the couch. It responded to her presence, moulding itself to her size and shape.

She had been in the Citadel on several occasions in her capacity as steward. Normally Roche was not in residence and at such times the various systems, including the couch, were shut down. On one occasion, she remembered, she had been sent by the chancellor of Dassar College to deliver a message to Roche. When she arrived Roche was nowhere to be found but the systems were all up and running. There was a globe of a planet beside the archway that led to the room with the couch; she knew now that it was Roche's TARDIS, and that Roche must have been inside it. It was taller than she was and mounted on a metal base that concealed the polar regions. The planet did not appear to be Caresh, for the globe showed a single large land mass instead of the Archipelago.

Troy Game frowned at the memory, sure there was more to it than that.

The globe had also been there on her next visit, the occasion when Roche had summoned her to report her observations regarding the neutron star. When she arrived she had found Roche in the middle of a heated discussion; she was sure he was not talking to himself, but afterwards she could only recall his half of the argument.

Then the Fury eggs had appeared inside the main chamber. She remembered screaming when they hatched, and she remembered Roche, temporarily blinded and guided by her scream, grabbing hold of her and ordering her to direct him to the globe. She had no idea what was going on – she had forgotten the Furies the moment she turned her back on them (though she remembered them now) – but she obeyed him without question. The ensuing journey must have been very short or Roche had been very preoccupied, for he completely failed to realise that she had followed him on board. In time she had emerged, and after that… well, she knew the rest.

It all seemed like a dream now. Everything did. She did not doubt the importance of what she had been through, but the fate of Caresh was no longer in her hands. The Doctor would know what to do, Jo had assured her of that, and at long last she could finally rest. She could feel the pain in her leg fading. The couch was healing her. She was completely aware of her surroundings – she even had her eyes open – but the sensation was like that of the deepest sleep. A monitor screen attached to a metal arm had positioned itself at a comfortable distance from her face. It was about the size of a portable television. A picture was forming on the screen. It showed the inside of Roche's TARDIS – she recognised the oval scanner in the floor, which was acting like a window looking down on the sea. She leant forward to get a closer look and, as she did so, she realised she was actually inside his TARDIS. No, it was more than that; she was Roche himself, or rather (a distant part of her understood) she was experiencing his recorded memories.

The Ship passed over a rocky coast and headed inland, passing less than twenty feet above a writhing forest free of snow. The land rose gently, and the Ship automatically gained height until it passed over the sheer coastal cliff on the western edge of the island.

This was Uleth, the outermost island in the Archipelago. No traveller had ever found land beyond that point; few who sought it had returned.

Jo briefly looked in on Troy Game. The Careshi woman appeared to be sleeping peacefully.

The archway on the other side of the main chamber led to a series of rooms filled with ceramic discs. To Jo it looked like the largest record collection in the world. In one room nearly all the discs lay broken on the floor; it seemed that they had lain there for many years.

In the main chamber the Doctor sat in the black chair studying the controls on the horseshoe-shaped console. Most of the monitors were switched on. Some showed the Careshi solar system from a variety of angles, others showed mathematical formulae or grid diagrams of distorted space-time.

'Any luck?' asked Jo.

'I'm beginning to make sense of it if that's what you mean,' the Doctor replied. 'Our friend Roche seems to have done most of the mathematics for us, so it's simply a question of putting his plan into action.' He flicked a switch and was rewarded by a low hum which seemed to emanate from beneath the chamber floor. 'If I'm not mistaken that's the stellar manipulator warming up.'

'I know I'm going to regret this, Doctor, but what is it you're actually trying to do? I mean, I realise this equipment lets you control the neutron star, but how is that meant to help Caresh?'

'My dear Jo, I do wish you'd pay attention. As I thought I'd explained already, the plan is to use the neutron star's gravity to deflect Caresh into a permanent orbit around Beacon. It's an extremely delicate operation. If I don't get the speed and direction of the neutron star exactly right the planet will go into the wrong orbit entirely. I also have to take the rest of the Careshi solar system into account.' A change of display on one of the console monitors drew his attention away. He looked closely at it, his expression becoming very grave. 'It would seem that we don't have a great deal of time. The star's closest approach will occur tomorrow afternoon, but the deadline for the final adjustment is much sooner that that.'

'How long?'

'About sixty-three minutes at its present heading.'

'Can't you slow it down?'

'Not enough to make a difference. It seems we arrived in the very nick of time, Jo. Because if we'd missed that deadline there would have been no hope for Caresh. No hope at all.'

Jo was about to remark that they weren't out of the woods yet when she was startled by a banging noise which echoed along the entrance tunnel. She hurried over to the wall monitor. It showed at least a dozen uniformed men and women waiting on the causeway. Two of them were wielding a large rock between them; they moved in and out of view as they hammered it against the gate of the Citadel.

'They won't get in so long as the door remains closed,' the Doctor said without looking up from his work. 'But the noise is making it decidedly difficult to concentrate.'

'I hope you're right,' Jo said. 'About the door, I mean.' She eyed the crossbow which had been left leaning against the chamber wall. If it came to it, they could pick off the Fellians as they made their way along the corridor. She doubted they would be able to reload it quickly enough, but there was also the flare gun.

She shuddered. She fervently hoped it would not come to that.

* * *

Troy Game watched as the view in the floor scanner slowly changed. It was calm inside the TARDIS but there was a storm raging outside, and the sea was much more turbulent than was usual in the Archipelago. She flinched once as a white-crested wave crashed against the underside of the Ship.

Now and then the 'memory' would fade out, and fade back in again after a period of time. Troy Game realised that Roche had edited out less eventful sequences. This was his diary, she realised; somehow she was accessing it by lying on his couch. It was no wonder he didn't make a habit of leaving it switched on!

Some time had passed and Roche's TARDIS was drifting over a broad sandy beach. There were people on the beach, looking up in wonder. Because Troy Game was privy to Roche's memories of the moment she knew that this was no island. Rather, it was the continent of Fayon. She remembered seeing this land mass on Roche's TARDIS when it had taken the form of a globe. The world it portrayed had been Caresh after all; if she had taken the time to examine its other side she would have recognised the Archipelago.

So, there was an unknown civilisation on the other hemisphere of Caresh. No one on the Archipelago knew about it; presumably the Fayoni were equally unaware of the Islanders.

As Troy Game was considering this the vision abruptly ended. The sensation was akin to waking from a dream. She glared at the blank screen in frustration. She wanted to know more!

The screen remained blank, but she noticed a row of buttons below it. She touched one at random, and jumped as the image of Lord Roche appeared. It was the old Roche as he had been before his change. This diary entry was a simple sound-and-vision recording. Roche appeared to be addressing Troy Game directly; she had no access to his memories this time, and although she had no difficulty understanding the language she could make no sense of what he was saying.

'Significant viability factors must of necessity be transient. It is fortunate I arrived when I did. I envisage a technological solution, but must check legality before proceeding.'

'What do you mean, Lord Roche?' Troy Game asked, but there was no response. She remembered an expression Sai-mahn had used when he was accessing the Internet. 'Search neutron star.' Still no response. 'Search Dassar? Citadel?' Still no response. On impulse she tried, 'Search eighteen.' Again there was no response, but then she closed her eyes and tried picturing 18, the way she had the time she had drawn it on a page of Sai-mahn's sketch book.

When she opened her eyes an image resembling the figure 18 had appeared on the screen. The '8' was the orbit of Caresh around its suns, the '1' the path of the neutron star.

The image faded. Lord Roche appeared again. 'The machine on Dassar Island now operates as a primitive stellar manipulator,' he said. 'Propulsion is a simple matter of suppressing and emphasising the emissions from the neutron star, and phasing the timing to the frequency of its oscillations. This provides limited control. Already I have succeeded in altering the star's trajectory by a full two degrees. By making a series of alterations I believe I will be able to direct the star towards the Careshi solar system. Estimated time of arrival: two centuries from now.'

The image faded again. Troy Game said, 'More!'

Lord Roche reappeared. It was evidently some time later. 'Routine alteration to neutron star's orbit carried out successfully,' he said.

'More!'

There were a dozen similar entries, followed by one in which Roche looked triumphant. 'Neutron star now hurtling towards Careshi system, as predicted 209 years ago local time. It's fine-tuning from now on. I have a mathematical solution to the orbit problem which I have run through the simulator. It's looking very promising indeed.'

'More!'

In the next entry Lord Roche was looking subdued. 'In ballistic terms the solution was perfectly correct. Unfortunately, I had not accounted for the searchlight of radiation emanating from the neutron star's north pole. It will sweep across the planet's surface during closest approach. Early indications suggest this will result in total sterilisation of the Archipelago hemisphere. As yet I can find no alternative approach that will avoid this unfortunate side effect. But I have not given up yet.' The image faded.

'More!'

'Field strength measured. Worst case confirmed: radiation searchlight will eradicate hemisphere. Still seeking ballistic alternative to counter this.'

'More!' cried Troy Game.

Now Lord Roche had the look of someone who was determined to go through with a tough decision. 'I have not found an alternative solution and it no longer seems likely that I will,' he said. 'However, I am confident that the Fayon hemisphere will not be harmed by the searchlight of radiation.' His expression hardened. 'Let's not be sentimental. Saving the Archipelago was never my primary goal.'

'Just another few adjustments,' the Doctor was saying, 'and the job will be complete. With time to spare, I might add.'

'Doctor!' said Jo urgently.

'This manoeuvre does require the utmost concentration, Jo, so I would appreciate…'

'Doctor, look!'

Annoyed, the Doctor glanced up from the console, to see a determined Troy Game covering him with the crossbow. 'I must say, pleased as I am to see you walking again I'd rather you didn't point that thing at me.'

'Come away from those controls!' the Careshi woman ordered.

'Look,' said the Doctor, 'I don't know what's got into you, but it's vital I make these course changes now, otherwise…'

'I know who you are and what you are planning!'

The Doctor gave Jo a puzzled look, which she reciprocated.

Troy Game went on, 'You tricked the Doctor into leaving his TARDIS with you. You knew you could not get your own TARDIS back so you overpowered him and pretended to be him.'

'Troy Game, what are you saying?' demanded Jo.

'Your trust in the Doctor was absolute, Jo Grant. Roche knew his change of appearance would deceive you.'

'Now listen to me,' the Doctor said in a low voice. 'You are quite mistaken, I assure you. Whatever you may think I am not Lord Roche.'

'No? Then why are you proceeding with his plan?'

'Because it will work! Changing the orbit of a planet is no trivial undertaking, but believe me there's no alternative. For better or for worse, the fate of Caresh depends on me carrying out these adjustments, and that is what I intend to do. There simply isn't time to argue, Troy Game, and it's too late to back out now. If you're so sure I'm Lord Roche you're just going to have to shoot me.'

With that he lunged for the controls, and recoiled as quickly just as Troy Game pulled the trigger. The crossbow bolt glanced off the top of the console and struck the floor some distance behind the Doctor. Before she had a chance to begin reloading, Jo was on her; she knocked the weapon out of the Careshi woman's hands and caught her in an armlock.

'Now,' said the Doctor reasonably. 'Perhaps you'd care to tell me what all that was about. I can assure you I really am who I say I am. If there is something I've overlooked I would be perfectly happy to…'

Effortlessly, Troy Game broke out of the armlock and threw Jo aside. Before they had time to react she had run over to the wall monitor beside the entrance corridor. She jabbed at the button.

Outside on the causeway the soldiers from Fell watched as the door to the Citadel swung open.

Chapter Eighteen
The Suns of Caresh

In all her life Jo had never felt so betrayed. She stared at Troy Game, willing herself to speak, but all that came out was the single word: 'Why?'

'Do not be ashamed, Jo,' said Troy Game, misunderstanding completely. 'I was taken in as well.'

'You have made a very grave mistake,' the Doctor said. 'A mistake that is going to cost all of us our lives.' He might have said more but the soldiers from Fell had arrived in the chamber, armed with pistols and crossbows. Rak Toos of Stakisha was among them.

'The giant – is he Roche?' the commanding officer asked him.

'He is the man who calls himself the Doctor,' Rak Toos answered.

'That was *not* what I asked.'

'It is the only meaningful answer I can give you, Captain.'

The Fellian glared at Rak Toos, who did not flinch. 'Very well,' he said at last. 'We will take him back to Fell to stand trial.'

'What about these two?' another soldier asked, indicating Troy Game and Jo Grant.

The captain considered. 'Keep them here for the time being. That way we can ensure the prisoner's good behaviour on the way back to the ship.' To the soldier who had spoken, and one other, the captain added, 'You two. Maintain guard on them. If Roche comes back here, kill them both.'

Troy Game was outraged. 'You cannot take me hostage. I am nothing to him!'

'You are all making a very grave mistake,' the Doctor said.

'Save it for the trial, Roche,' the captain said, leading him away.

* * *

It had been snowing heavily outside the Citadel but now the wind was beginning to part the clouds. Some stars were visible, but their light was insufficient to illuminate the landscape. Some of the soldiers used electric torches.

'I beg you to reconsider,' the Doctor said to the captain. 'You must let me back in the Citadel to make the final course corrections. Once I have done so I will submit to accompanying you back to Fell.'

'Really? Would you give me your word on that?'

The Doctor allowed himself to hope. 'Yes of course I would!'

The captain smiled. 'I have no doubt of it. You have a habit of doing so. We have long since learned that it means nothing.'

Angrily, the Doctor said, 'If you don't believe me, perhaps you'd be less inclined to doubt the evidence of your eyes. Look!'

After checking there was no trickery involved the captain looked where the Doctor was pointing. His confidence wavered then, for briefly visible in the break in the clouds was an object for which there was no word in his language. It was too small and faint to be a sun, yet too bright to be a star or neighbouring planet. Its glow flickered like a strobe. Projecting from either side of the disc like a pair of handles was a long and very narrow bar of brightness – the conic searchlights of radiation.

'That thing, Captain, is heading towards the Careshi solar system at a considerable velocity. It is my intention to prevent it from passing too close to this planet. If you persist in this ridiculous business…' The Doctor broke off with a frown, adding, 'I'm not happy about the angle of that searchlight. If I'm not mistaken…'

'You seek to frighten me with things in the sky, Roche?' the captain barked, recovering his composure. 'You think I do not know what a comet is?'

'A comet? Use your eyes man!' But the bank of cloud had moved on and the neutron star was no longer visible.

In the Citadel the two soldiers – near-identical twin brother and sister – kept watch on their hostages who sat cross-legged on the chamber floor. The sister sat in the console chair, crossbow resting on her lap, while the brother stood watching the wall monitor that showed the view outside.

Troy Game had explained to Jo what she'd seen in the side room.

Jo persisted in trying to persuade Troy Game of the need for action. In a low voice she said, 'Don't you realise, the neutron star is approaching whatever we do. We *must* get the Doctor to find another way. It's what he does best.'

'Believe me, I understand how much faith you have in the Doctor,' Troy Game replied. 'But if that man was the Doctor you know, he would not sacrifice one civilisation to save another.'

'He didn't *know* about the searchlight of radiation!' Jo realised she had raised her voice but their two guards paid no attention. 'Don't you see? He didn't know because he didn't have time to check Roche's plans closely.'

'We have a chance this way,' Troy Game said flatly. 'Roche did not make the final adjustment. It is possible that the searchlight is only a problem with the final trajectory.'

'But even if that's true it won't save us. The neutron star will come too close. The tidal forces will destroy the planet, or throw it into the wrong orbit, or something. Look, I don't completely understand the physics, but the Doctor said…'

'Precisely! You have only the word of a man who claims to be the Doctor.'

Jo tried another tack. 'All right. Supposing the Doctor – or Roche, or whoever he is – was here. And suppose he made the adjustments. What would he do then? Even if he set out for the TARDIS immediately he would not get there before the neutron star's passing. The searchlight will get him along with everybody else!'

Troy Game looked uncertain. 'He will have thought of that,' she said at length. 'He has made many changes to the Citadel. It may be that it will give him shelter from the radiation.'

'But he still has to travel across the sea to get back to the TARDIS. All the ships' crews will be dead, and Solenti's dinghy doesn't have enough fuel to get to Stakisha.'

'He has ways of recalling his TARDIS. He might not be capable of swimming to it but I am. That is why he brought me here. He intended to hypnotise me and send me to it, just as he did before.'

'But it didn't work before!' Again Jo realised she had raised her voice. This time the female guard made an unmistakable gesture with her crossbow. Jo waited for a while before continuing in hushed tones. 'Think about the risk, Troy Game. Suppose you had an accident on the way to the TARDIS or you lost the key. Where would that leave *him*? Now I know the Doctor would risk his life to save a civilisation, but do you really believe Roche would?'

Troy Game bit her lower lip. 'I might have made a serious misjudgement, Jo Grant.'

'Do you mean you concede that he could be the Doctor?' Jo pressed.

'Maybe.' Troy Game considered. 'We must find out.' Before Jo had time to reply she turned to the soldiers. 'I need to go to the toilet,' she said.

Jo cringed. If this was Troy Game's idea of subterfuge they were surely doomed.

'Very well.' To Jo's surprise it was the male soldier who rose to escort her. They passed through the archway that led to the room with the couch.

Jo was unable to restrain herself. 'Is he going to… *watch* her?'

'Of course he is going to watch her!' the sister replied. 'He's a soldier! What sort of soldiers do you have on Dassar?' She peered closely at Jo, puzzled. 'But you are not from Dassar. You are a *long* way from home.'

'Further than you could possibly imagine,' Jo replied, then flinched as a blinding flash of purple lightning spilled out of the archway.

'Mercy gun!' yelled the sister as she made to dive for cover behind the console. Too late; Troy Game appeared with the golden pistol in her hand. She fired again. There was a second blinding flash and the female soldier dropped like a stone.

'Come on, Jo!' Troy Game called as she entered the chamber and made for the tunnel. 'We don't have much time!'

Partway down the volcano path the soldiers from Fell were attacked by a pair of Leshe. They dealt with them swiftly.

'I expect it's the light that attracts them,' the Doctor observed. 'You know, it would make a lot more sense to take refuge in the Citadel and wait till morning.'

The captain started to say, 'I have had just about enough of…' when the hillside was illuminated by a brilliant purple light. He was momentarily transfixed by a seemingly solid beam of darker purple. He collapsed instantly.

There was confusion among the soldiers. The Doctor heard Jo's voice calling to him. Two soldiers grabbed him by the arms. He managed to shake one off but the other clung tightly and pressed the muzzle of a gun into his back. The landscape was filled with light once more and he was free of that soldier too. He started to run up the path when the light exploded a third time. His legs gave way beneath him. He made to break his fall but his arms were not obeying him. He landed heavily on the rocky path. The light flashed again, and again, and again. Men and women were crying out in fear. Someone shouted, 'Leshe! It's bringing the Leshe!' Crossbows thunked, guns fired. Someone screamed. The Doctor willed his body to move but it was to no avail. He could hear Jo's voice: 'You've killed him!'

'No,' the Doctor willed himself to say. 'I am unharmed. The weapon has never been used on me before.' But no words came.

'He is not dead,' said Troy Game. 'I am very happy to be wrong. He cannot be Roche.'

'You have just signed your planet's death warrant,' the Doctor did not say.

'You shouldn't have done that, Troy Game,' Jo said.

'It was necessary. I had to know.'

'But not like that!'

269

On or near the path there were Fellian soldiers. Two were dead, killed by Leshe; another three were stunned. The remainder had their hands full fighting the Leshe.

'He's heavy,' Troy Game said. 'I wish I had thought of this when he was still in the Citadel.'

'Now you know what we had to cope with when we had to carry you,' Jo retorted.

'It is not the same. I did my best. Besides, I am not a giant.'

In spite of everything Jo found herself laughing. Troy Game was laughing too. Then torchlight flashed over them and a voice said, 'Be still!'

Jo turned.

Behind them was Rak Toos. He was wielding a crossbow. 'Drop him now!' he ordered.

Reluctantly, Jo and Troy Game obeyed. Rak Toos pulled the trigger and the bolt passed between the two women. It struck the Leshe that was gliding down the hillside towards them.

'I don't know if you can hear me,' Rak Toos said to the Doctor, 'but I'm sorry I doubted you before.' Despite his relatively small stature he picked up the Doctor and flung him over his right shoulder. A fireman's lift. To the two women he said, 'We've got to get indoors. Those creatures are everywhere.'

'What about the soldiers?' Jo asked.

'They'll follow,' Rak Toos said. 'They know he's not Roche now. And they cannot ignore *that*.' He gestured at the sky where a break in the clouds framed the neutron star, now visibly closer.

Rak Toos directed the last of the soldiers into the Citadel. Some were wounded and some carried unconscious comrades.

In the main chamber he found Jo and Troy Game examining the displays on the horseshoe-shaped control table. 'Can you make any sense of it?' he asked. Both women shook their heads.

The Doctor sat motionless in the command chair where he had been placed. They had tried everything they could think of to awaken him, but to no avail.

'He said the deadline was just over an hour away,' Jo said mournfully. 'That was two hours ago.' In a sudden moment of decisiveness she turned to the control table. 'I've got to do something! Maybe I'll learn as I go along.' She pressed a button. A grid pattern appeared on the adjacent monitor. 'Well, that looks promising,' she said. She pushed a lever. A red light flashed a warning and she hurriedly moved it back to its original position. 'Not that one then. Perhaps the one next to it.'

'Why not? You might as well for all the good it's going to do.'

Jo turned, hardly daring to believe her ears. It was the Doctor's voice! 'Thank goodness you're all right,' she said. 'This planet's in terrible danger and you're the only one who knows what to do, and if you don't prevent the neutron star from…'

The Doctor rose from the seat. 'Jo, stop it right now!'

Jo was stunned. She had never known such anger in the Doctor.

'Now listen to me, Jo. When I told you the deadline was sixty-three minutes away, I meant exactly that. In other words, we have *missed* the deadline.'

'But surely…' Jo began.

'No no no no *no*! Good heavens, Jo, for the past two years I have been trying to make you into a scientist. Now can't you get it into your thick little head that the moment has *passed*? Time and tide waits for no man; do you think a neutron star *cares* that it was supposed to be diverted an hour ago?' He turned to Troy Game. 'By using the mercy gun on me you have proved to your own satisfaction that I am not Roche, that I really am the person I told you I was in the first place. Well, I hope it was worth it, I really do. Because that little bit of confirmation has cost you your planet. It has also cost all of us our lives.'

'Surely it's worth trying anyway?' Jo insisted. 'Before the neutron star arrives?'

'Worth trying *what*? What do you expect me to *do*? If you have some great idea that's going to save the day then by all means share it with me, because however I look at it Caresh is finished. Finished!'

There were tears running down Jo's face. 'Maybe you're not the Doctor after all, whatever the mercy gun says. Because the Doctor I know was never this defeatist. The Doctor *I* know would have found another way.'

More gently, the Doctor said, 'There is no virtue in ignoring the facts, Jo. The deadline is passed and that's the end of it.'

'If it was Earth you would find a way.'

'Caresh is not Earth, Jo. If it was…' The Doctor hesitated, an expression of doubt on his face. He was frowning, but the frown turned into a smile. 'Jo! You're a genius!' He took her face in both hands and planted a kiss on her forehead.

Dazed, Jo said, 'What did I say?'

South of Dassar the mindless hordes of Leshe were marching across the ice. Their numbers could be counted in millions; fourteen major islands and countless smaller ones had been overrun; those who had not fled had been completely wiped out.

Snow fell, but here and there the clouds parted. The third sun of Caresh moved ever closer. Its rapidly flickering light gave the landscape an eerie quality; it made the movements of the Leshe jerky as if they were alien characters in the early days of film.

The Doctor worked feverishly at the console. 'The mathematics is far from perfect,' he explained. 'But it's the best I can do in the circumstances.' He pulled a lever, typed some numbers on a keypad, peered at a display. 'It's a redefinition of the original problem, which is always a good idea when you're overlooking the obvious. It is not the solution Roche intended, but at least it's one we can reasonably hope to survive.'

At halfdawn the Doctor's mood lightened. Jo, Troy Game and Rak Toos exchanged looks. They made for the tunnel and went out of the Citadel followed by some of the soldiers.

The sky was clear. The neutron star was brighter than the full moon on Earth. It cast a warm light. Ice was melting on the upper walls of the Citadel; Jo felt a drip run down her neck.

'I think he's done it,' she said. 'I think he's found another way.' But in her heart of hearts she knew it was too early to tell.

When Ember rose that morning there were three suns in the sky. The neutron star appeared to graze the edge of Beacon as it hurtled past, its searchlight of radiation sweeping well clear of the planet.

During the night the ice had migrated more than halfway to Dair, but it was losing its momentum now. Numerous black patches dotted it, each one representing several thousand Leshe. Most of the creatures had moved on from Dassar to follow the ice, but they would return when they discovered it had reached the limit of its spread.

Jo sat on a rock on the crater rim overlooking the sea. Troy Game, Rak Toos and the soldiers from Fell were with her, their differences long forgotten. Whether the world would be saved or destroyed, they had chosen a good vantage point from which to watch what happened.

When the Doctor came out to join them the ground was trembling and he had to pick his way carefully. He had an air of resignation as he announced, 'Well, it's out of my hands now.'

'Has it worked?' Jo asked.

'We'll know soon enough.' The ground tremor was growing increasingly loud and he had to raise his voice to be heard. 'I had to cut it somewhat finer than I would have liked. Caresh has no moon, you see – the tides here are caused by the suns, which are too far away to exert much pull. Adding a third sun to the mix was always going to be touch and go, but I think I've limited what will happen to a few minor seismic effects.'

'Minor? But Doctor, we're sitting on top of a volcano!'

'An extinct volcano, Jo. I'm quite sure of that.'

'You've said that before,' Jo retorted as she clung to her rock, but the Doctor did not hear.

Minutes passed. Gradually the tremors began to die down; eventually they stopped altogether. Jo was about to breathe a sigh of relief when her attention was caught by a massed movement out on the sea ice. The black patches had changed direction; the Leshe were heading back to Dassar.

'Doctor, look!' Jo cried.

The Doctor looked. 'Yes, I see,' he said, apparently unperturbed. 'But it's not quite over yet. Watch!'

As if on cue a ripple extending to the east and west as far as the eye could see sped towards them. It passed under the sea ice, shattering it as it went. The sound was deafening. The minor tidal wave had expended itself before it reached the shore, but by then the black patches had slid into the sea. After a time the shattered fragments of ice settled again, free for the most part of their deadly cargo.

The Doctor regarded the sight for several minutes without speaking. Jo wondered if he was regretting the deaths of the creatures, mindless and voracious though they were. 'Come on, Jo,' he said at last. 'We've got some important equipment to shut down before we go.' With that he led the way back to the Citadel. This time they walked around the rim and along the causeway for there was no guarantee that the ice on the lake would still support them.

'I had given up hope,' the Doctor admitted as they entered the chamber. 'But you reminded me that Caresh is not Earth. That was when I realised there was an alternative, one I had completely overlooked – and so had Roche.' He called up a schematic of the Careshi solar system on one of the display panels on the console. It still showed the old figure-eight orbit. 'Lord Roche was determined to move the planet into a circular orbit around Beacon. He persisted with this, even when he realised he couldn't do it without wiping out the Islanders.' The Doctor rubbed the back of his neck. 'If only he'd thought that it didn't have to be the more luminous sun – that a *closer* orbit around the *less* luminous sun would have done just as well. He'd have had time then to work out the mathematics properly instead of leaving me to do a last-minute bodge job.'

'But you managed it,' Jo said. 'You did it without the searchlight thingy sweeping across the planet. It might not be perfect, but at least we're alive.'

'Not perfect? It's far from being perfect. But the planet has a stable climate now. They no longer have to live in fear of prolonged cold periods.'

'Or Leshe,' added Jo.

'What I don't understand is why he went to such lengths to save the people of Fayon. You know, I think it's time we found out how the other half of the planet lives. Once we've got back to Stakisha...'

The Doctor was interrupted by a familiar sound like the whirring of a giant cooling-fan. A cylindrical structure about eight feet high appeared beside the archway. It was white and roundelled so that it had the appearance of an inside-out TARDIS.

'Jo, get out of here now,' the Doctor said. 'Hurry!' But it was too late. Solenti had emerged holding the harness of her dog – an Alsatian this time. 'Doctor,' she said, her voice almost a purr. 'And... did you say Jo?'

'Jo, meet Solenti,' the Doctor said resignedly. Solenti held out her hand and Jo took it. 'And...?'

'Jess,' said Solenti.

'Jess?' echoed the Doctor. 'Are we talking about the same...' He looked at the dog more closely. 'Yes, I do believe I understand. Hello, Jess.'

Unsure, Jo bent to stroke the Alsatian. The guide dog wagged her tail.

'So, have you come to offer to help with the washing up?' the Doctor asked Solenti. 'What a pity it's already been done.'

'You didn't keep your word, Doctor.'

'I never *gave* you my word, Solenti. You left before I had a chance. You also left a good deal unexplained, as usual.'

'Well, it doesn't matter now. I don't know how you do it, Doctor, but everything seems to have worked out for the best.'

'I'd hardly call it the best. Quite apart from anything else there's an unresolved time anomaly that needs dealing with.'

'I wouldn't worry about that any more. Not that I can give you the details, you understand, but suffice to say…'

'The ones who sent out the Furies no longer felt threatened?' the Doctor hazarded.

'Not any more,' Solenti confirmed, then bit her tongue. 'I shouldn't have said that, should I? You know, I do believe that's the first time you've ever caught me out like that. I'm going to have to be on my guard from now on. Anyway, I thought you'd be pleased to know how it all turned out. Come along now, Jess.' With that she went back into her TARDIS and vanished.

'She might have offered us a lift,' the Doctor muttered.

Once the Doctor was sure everything was shut down they left the main chamber. As they walked along the entrance tunnel Jo said, 'What did you mean about the ones who sent out the Furies?'

'I'm not entirely sure, Jo,' the Doctor admitted. 'But my guess is that Roche upset someone or something in the vortex. They reacted by sending the Furies to try and kill him, which in turn caused the event that ultimately resulted in the fracture.'

'How did he upset them? Do you suppose it was something to do with the neutron star?'

'I wouldn't doubt it for a minute. But whatever it was, our own actions must have made them happy again.'

They emerged onto the causeway. Outside the sky was blue, the suns dazzling and the ice in the lake was creaking loudly. Jo was still pondering. 'If Earth is free of the time fracture now, Professor Child's life won't have gone into reverse after all. So he won't have been there in 1972.'

'That is perfectly true.'

'So did we meet him or not?'

'That's a little difficult to answer. The best I can do is say we did from our point of view, but we didn't from his. Does that help?'

Jo thought for a minute. She smiled. 'Not really, no. To be honest I didn't expect it to. But what will happen about 1999? Was it the real 1999 we saw, or will it have changed too?'

'As to that,' said the Doctor, 'you'll just have to wait and see.' Then his eyes widened. 'Good grief! Look at that!'

The departing neutron star was almost lost in the glare of Beacon. But in the place midway between the suns of Caresh, where its original path would have taken it, was a floating jewel: seven tiered concentric discs of blue and green, fleetingly seen like an invisible object in rain. The disturbed vortex washed over it briefly, then subsided, leaving it intact.

Epilogue

In the Palace of Equilibrium eighteen members of the Curia of Nineteen gathered. They sat in three concentric rings, a prime number in each despite the vacant seat in the innermost ring.

The first item on the agenda concerned the sentencing of their colleague Amathon. He had acted against consensus and he had compromised the Realm. On the other hand his intentions had been good and the outcome exceeded all expectations.

They agreed on a commuted sentence.

The second item concerned the small matter of two Furies at large on the planet Earth. But it *was* a small matter, and it would be dealt with in due course.

Amathon found himself on a bleak mountainside on a world with three moons and a harsh blue sun.

This was an unexpected development. He had expected nothing less than death, and he had no concept of – let alone a belief in – an afterlife. Instead he had been exiled to a world of matter. Perhaps there was a reason why he had been sent to this particular world, or perhaps the dwellers merely regarded it as a suitable punishment for his offence. Either way, it opened up new possibilities.

He still bore the chains they had put on him for his arraignment, but they had no substance here; he shrugged them off and they dissolved as soon as they touched the ground. Unencumbered, he made his way down the mountainside to see what the new possibilities were.

Zeke Child and the Keller brothers leant their bikes against the fence that marked the border of the nature reserve. They did not bother to padlock them.

'Is this a wind-up?' Ben Keller asked Child. 'Because if it is, it's got to be the most tedious, obvious and unimaginative wind-up of all time. Even by your standards. You might not have much of a life, Zeke, but I for one can think of a better way of spending my Sunday.'

Child shook his head, unperturbed by Ben Keller's tone. 'This isn't right. Not what I expected at all.' He climbed over the fence and made his way to the lake's edge. He stood staring into the waters for a long time. The level was the same as it had always been.

'If you want to cycle back with us, you'd better get a move on.' That was Patric Keller's voice.

They stopped off at a pub. Child bought the drinks by way of apology for wasting his friends' time. When Ben left the table to go to the toilet, Patric Keller asked Child if he'd found what he was looking for.

'In a way yes,' Child said. 'I don't mind telling you I felt pretty stupid just now. But then I had this premonition – a vision, rather, or a memory of my own future, if that makes any sense. The business with the lake was just the first in a long line of embarrassing failures. I was headed for a lifetime of them, plans that never reach fruition, a failed marriage – all that sort of thing.'

'I thought you didn't believe in that sort of crap.'

Child smiled. 'I don't. That's the whole point. The vision just reminded me that my future is in my own hands. That might sound obvious, but I've never properly considered what it really meant before.'

Some weeks later a shepherd's bothy, fully twenty feet in height, materialised in a field in Cornwall. A vertical crack appeared in the back wall. It widened to a gap. The Time Lord Roche came out running.

Darkness fell. Roche stopped running and turned to look back at the building. It was supposed to be responding to the presence of a threat, but it was not doing anything of the sort. Had he shaken off the Furies after all? Or were they seeking to outwit him?

It seemed unlikely. They had not shown much sign of intelligence thus far.

The sky was overcast. Thousands of people watched for a break in the clouds, to see the corona of the eclipsed sun. They watched in vain; minutes passed and the dull daylight returned. The time of totality had passed unseen. The long-anticipated event had proved to be a washout.

Roche's curiosity eventually overcame his natural caution. He walked around his TARDIS and found the two Furies waiting beside the doorway to the bothy. The Furies had turned themselves (or possibly each other) to stone.

It took Roche a very long time to decide that this was not a ruse; they really were finally and utterly dead. He'd escaped them and it hadn't even cost him his TARDIS.

Back in the control room he checked the temporal-gradient detector on the console. It confirmed what he already suspected: the time fracture had healed.

It was the Doctor's doing, he was certain of it. Roche had no idea how he'd managed it, but somehow he had intervened.

Did that mean Caresh had been saved too? He wasn't sure. He began setting a course for the planet, then hesitated. Perhaps that was not such a good idea. Even if their world had survived its encounter with the neutron star, Roche doubted the Careshi would be very pleased to see him right now.

He entered a new set of coordinates. He flipped a switch and the dematerialisation process began. One day he would return to Caresh – even if he had to pass himself off as the Doctor – but not yet.

Outside, the bothy faded into nonexistence. Where it had been, there was nothing but the petrified forms of the Furies.

And there they remain to this day. Many have seen them, but no one ever remembers them.

* * *

On a shelf of rock on the north shore of Dassar, Troy Game watched as the steamship sailed away. The captain had offered her a lift to Dair but she had declined, saying she would make her own way in due course. The Doctor and Jo stood on deck, waving to her from the railings. She turned away pretending not to notice them; she did not like prolonged goodbyes.

The afternoon was giving way to evening. The neutron star was out of sight, heading away from the altered solar system. Already the effects were being noticed; never had Ember felt so warm. Ice still floated on the sea but its days were numbered.

Dassar was one of the fourteen major islands that had been overrun by Leshe. Troy Game was in no immediate danger from them on her shelf of rock, but the fact remained that her homeland was gone. One day her people – the ones who had escaped to Dair – might return to claim the land. But that was one day.

The steamship changed course and headed in the general direction of Stakisha. Soon it was lost in Ember's glare. Troy Game watched it go, then made her decision. She discarded her clothes and dived off the shelf of rock. She seemed to fall for a long time before she finally broke the surface. The water was icily cold but that was all right; her metabolism was designed to cope with this. It was the right sea; it was *her* sea.

She swam deeper until her skin took on a scaly appearance and webs formed between her fingers and her finger-length toes. Her lungs were close to bursting for she was still an air-breather, but she made no effort to make for the surface.

She thought, *This is the place where I want to be.*

About the Author

PAUL SAINT was born in the year that *An Unearthly Child* was first broadcast. He didn't watch *Doctor Who* properly until he was ten, but was often in the room playing with his Lego while it was on. He remembers being terrified by the metal probe-thing that came out of the machines in *The Krotons*. He owns a telescope, and enjoys looking at other worlds and clusters of galaxies from his back garden.

ESCAPE VELOCITY by Colin Brake ISBN 0 563 53825 2
EARTHWORLD by Jacqueline Rayner ISBN 0 563 53827 9
VANISHING POINT by Stephen Cole ISBN 0 563 53829 5
EATER OF WASPS by Trevor Baxendale ISBN 0 563 53832 5
THE YEAR OF INTELLIGENT TIGERS by Kate Orman ISBN 0 563 53831 7
THE SLOW EMPIRE by Dave Stone 0 563 53835 X
DARK PROGENY by Steve Emmerson 0 563 53837 6
THE CITY OF THE DEAD by Lloyd Rose ISBN 0 563 53839 2
GRIMM REALITY by Simon Bucher-Jones and Kelly Hale ISBN 0 563 53841 4
THE ADVENTURESS OF HENRIETTA STREET by Lawrence Miles ISBN 0 563 53842 2
MAD DOGS AND ENGLISHMEN by Paul Magrs ISBN 0 563 53845 7
HOPE by Mark Clapham ISBN 0 563 53846 5
ANACHROPHOBIA by Jonathan Morris ISBN 0 563 53847 3
TRADING FUTURES by Lance Parkin ISBN 0 563 53848 1
THE BOOK OF THE STILL by Paul Ebbs ISBN 0 563 53851 1
THE CROOKED WORLD by Steve Lyons ISBN 0 563 53856 2
LAST MAN RUNNING by Chris Boucher ISBN 0 563 40594 5
MATRIX by Robert Perry and Mike Tucker ISBN 0 563 40596 1
THE INFINITY DOCTORS by Lance Parkin ISBN 0 563 40591 0
SALVATION by Steve Lyons ISBN 0 563 55566 1
THE WAGES OF SIN by David A. McIntee ISBN 0 563 55567 X
DEEP BLUE by Mark Morris ISBN 0 563 55571 8
PLAYERS by Terrance Dicks ISBN 0 563 55573 4
MILLENNIUM SHOCK by Justin Richards ISBN 0 563 55586 6
STORM HARVEST by Robert Perry and Mike Tucker ISBN 0 563 55577 7
THE FINAL SANCTION by Steve Lyons ISBN 0 563 55584 X
CITY AT WORLD'S END by Christopher Bulis ISBN 0 563 55579 3
DIVIDED LOYALTIES by Gary Russell ISBN 0 563 55578 5
CORPSE MARKER by Chris Boucher ISBN 0 563 55575 0
LAST OF THE GADERENE by Mark Gatiss ISBN 0 563 55587 4

TOMB OF VALDEMAR by Simon Messingham ISBN 0 563 55591 2
VERDIGRIS by Paul Magrs ISBN 0 563 55592 0
GRAVE MATTER by Justin Richards ISBN 0 563 55598 X
HEART OF TARDIS by Dave Stone ISBN 0 563 55596 3
PRIME TIME by Mike Tucker ISBN 0 563 55597 1
IMPERIAL MOON by Christopher Bulis ISBN 0 563 53801 5
FESTIVAL OF DEATH by Jonathan Morris ISBN 0 563 53803 1
INDEPENDENCE DAY by Peter Darvill-Evans ISBN 0 563 53804 X
THE KING OF TERROR by Keith Topping ISBN 0 563 53802 3
QUANTUM ARCHANGEL by Craig Hinton ISBN 0 563 53824 4
BUNKER SOLDIERS by Martin Day ISBN 0 563 53819 8
RAGS by Mick Lewis ISBN 0 563 53826 0
THE SHADOW IN THE GLASS by Justin Richards and Stephen
Cole ISBN 0 563 53838 4
ASYLUM by Peter Darvill-Evans ISBN 0 563 53833 3
SUPERIOR BEINGS by Nick Walters ISBN 0 563 53830 9
BYZANTIUM! by Keith Topping ISBN 0 563 53836 8
BULLET TIME by David A. McIntee 0 563 53834 1
PSI-ENCE FICTION by Chris Boucher ISBN 0 563 53814 7
DYING IN THE SUN by Jon de Burgh Miller ISBN 0 563 53840 6
INSTRUMENTS OF DARKNESS by Gary Russell ISBN 0 563
53828 7
RELATIVE DEMENTIAS by Mark Michalowski 0 563 53844 9
DRIFT by Simon A. Forward ISBN 0 563 53843 0
PALACE OF THE RED SUN by Christopher Bulis ISBN 0 563 53849 X
AMORALITY TALE by David Bishop ISBN 0 563 53850 3
WARMONGER by Terrance Dicks ISBN 0 563 53852 X
TEN LITTLE ALIENS by Stephen Cole ISBN 0 563 53853 8
COMBAT ROCK by Mick Lewis ISBN 0 563 53855 4
SHORT TRIPS ed. Stephen Cole ISBN 0 563 40560 0
MORE SHORT TRIPS ed. Stephen Cole ISBN 0 563 55565 3
SHORT TRIPS AND SIDE STEPS ed. Stephen Cole and Jacqueline
Rayner ISBN 0 563 55599 8